THE
AGE OF
REINVENTION

KARINE TUIL

Translated from French by Sam Taylor

SCRIBNER

LONDON NEW YORK TORONTO SYDNEY NEW DELHI

Originally published with the title *L'Invention de nos vies* in
France in 2013 by Editions Grasset & Fasquelle
First published in Great Britain by Scribner, an imprint of Simon & Schuster UK Ltd, 2015
This paperback edition published by Scribner, 2016
A CBS COMPANY

Simon & Schuster UK Ltd
1st Floor
222 Gray's Inn Road
London WC1X 8HB

www.simonandschuster.co.uk

Simon & Schuster Australia, Sydney
Simon & Schuster India, New Delhi

A CIP catalogue record for this book
is available from the British Library

Paperback ISBN: 978-1-4711-5396-9
eBook ISBN: 978-1-4711-5397-6

Printed and bound by CPI Group (UK) Ltd, Croydon CR0 4YY

Simon & Schuster UK Ltd are committed to sourcing paper that is made
from wood grown in sustainable forests and support the Forest Stewardship
Council, the leading international forest certification organisation. Our
books displaying the FSC logo are printed on FSC certified paper.

For Ariel

Love is not that sweet thing everyone talks about. Maybe people are tortured in order to make them say that? Whatever, everyone is lying.

ORHAN PAMUK, interview, April 2011

All success cloaks a surrender.

SIMONE DE BEAUVOIR,
Memoirs of a Dutiful Daughter

Literary success represents only a small part of what I think about. Success slips through your fingers, it escapes you whichever way you turn [. . .] and it is my own life that is, ultimately, the most important thing.

MARGUERITE YOURCENAR,
interview with Bernard Pivot, 1979

PART ONE

Let's begin with his wound. Yes, let's begin there. The last of the stigmata inflicted during a brutal upbringing that Samir Tahar spent his whole life escaping, it was an inch-long gash on his neck. He'd gone to a plastic surgeon in Times Square who attempted to sand it off with a grinding wheel, but it was too late: he would keep the scar forever as a souvenir, would look at it every morning and remember where he came from, from what place/what violence. *Look at it! Touch it!* They looked, they touched. The first time was always a shock: the sight of/the contact with that whitish scar which betrayed the fury of its creator, signaled the taste for a power struggle, for contradiction—a form of social brutality that, brought to incandescence, presaged eroticism—a wound that he could hide beneath a scarf, a foulard, or a turtleneck sweater, so that nothing could be seen of it. That day, he was concealing it behind the starched collar of a $300 shirt—purchased in one of those luxury clothing stores that Samuel Baron only ever entered now with the vague hope of stealing from the cash register—and everything about him breathed opulence, complacency, consumerism, a zero-defect design. Everything about him denied what he had been: even his manners were affected, his voice tinged with an aristocratic accent, this man who, in law school, had been one of the most vocal supporters of the proletarian left! One of those radicals who had used their original mortification as a social weapon. Now, newly rich, an A-list lawyer, a big spender, a thunderous orator, a *lex machina*, everything about him spoke of identity change, vaulting ambition, social redemption—the exact counterpoint of what Samuel had become. Was he hallucinating? Maybe. This isn't *real*, thinks/prays/screams Samuel; that can't be *him*—Samir—that brand-new, famous, deified man, a personal and original creation, a prince surrounded by his camarilla, with his slick, specious rhetoric. On TV, he is primped and sexy, appealing to men and women, worshipped by all; an object of jealousy, perhaps, but also of respect; a virtuoso of the bar, fearless and shameless, smashing the prosecution's argument to pieces with the jackhammer of his wit . . . That can't be him, that artificial courtroom wolf, *there*, in New York, on CNN, his first name Americanized in capital letters—SAM TAHAR—and beneath it, his occupation: *lawyer*, while *he*, Samuel, was wasting away in a dingy apartment in Clichy-sous-Bois, rented for €700 per month, was slaving eight hours a day as a social worker for a charity, helping troubled youths who always seemed to ask: *Baron—is that Jewish?*, and would spend his evenings reading/posting on literary blogs (with the username Witold92)/writing pseudonymous books that were systematically rejected—*His great social novel? We're still waiting for it*—that can't be him, Samir Tahar, transformed beyond recognition, his face covered with a layer of beige foundation, eyes turned to the camera with the perfect command of an elite actor/lion tamer/marksman, his dark eyebrows waxed and shaped, his body corseted in a bespoke designer suit that was possibly even bought for the occasion, chosen specifically in order to seduce/persuade/attract attention, the holy trinity of political communication, the lessons that had been rammed down their throats at law school and which Samir was now putting into practice with the arrogant self-assurance of a campaigning politician. Samir, a guest on American television, representing the families of two U.S. soldiers killed in Afghanistan,[1] intoning a paean to

---

1 Santiago Pereira, twenty-two, and Dennis Walter, twenty-five. The former dreamed of becoming an artist but was pressured into enlisting by his high-ranking father. The latter stated: "Success, to me, means fighting for my country."

interventionism, glorifying moral fiber, trying his hand at senti-
mentalism! Samir, being questioned by the journalist[2]—who
treats him with deference, as if he's the conscience of the free
world!—and remaining calm and confident, apparently having
muzzled the beast within him, controlled the violence that for so
long contaminated his every gesture. And yet, when you first met
him, that was all you saw: the surreptitious wound, the tragic
echoes of the horror of his formative years, spent inside the grimy
walls of a twenty-floor tower block, fifteen or twenty of them
(maybe even more) crammed on a stairwell that stank of dog/
human piss; all those years spent pent-up there, on the eighteenth
floor, with a view of the balconies of the tower block opposite,
sweat suits swaying in the wind—fake Adidas, Nike, Puma bought
for nothing in Taiwan/Ventimiglia/Marrakesh/the local Goodwill
store, sweat-stained grayish undershirts, frayed underpants,
rough toilet paper, plastic tablecloths, panties misshapen by too
many washes/pounds lost or gained, hung out to dry in front of
the satellite dishes that swarmed over the roofs/façades like rats
in darkened basements where nobody ever went anymore out of
fear of theft/rape/violence, where nobody ever went unless threatened with a pistol/knife/box cutter/knuckle-duster/billy club/
bottle of sulfuric acid/pump-action shotgun/pepper spray/rifle/
nunchuks (this was before the unrest in the East and the arrival in
bulk of weapons of war from the ex-Yugoslavia—what a godsend!
Just take a family vacation and—bingo!—load the good stuff in the
trunk among all the kids' toys: assault rifles, automatic weapons,
Uzis, Kalashnikovs, explosives with electronic detonators . . . even
[whatever floats your boat] rocket launchers, if you buy them

---

2 Kathleen Weiner. Born in 1939 in New Jersey to a shoemaking father and a
housewife mother, Kathleen graduated from Harvard. But her greatest claim to
fame remained her supposed liaison, at the age of sixteen, with Norman Mailer.

cash-only. So you go off to a forest where you can practice alone, no witnesses, and then you wage war in underground parking garages sticky with puddles of engine oil and urine where nobody ever went anymore unless accompanied by a cop—and cops never went down there anymore. You wage ideological warfare in squats where twenty-five-/thirty-year-old lepers rejected/remade the world, or sexual warfare in basements stinking of damp and dope smoke where fourteen-/fifteen-year-olds roasted NONCON-SENTING minors, ten or twenty of them taking it in turns, 'cause they had to prove they were men, 'cause the violence inside them had to force its way out somehow—they told the judge this in their defense—'cause they needed some kind of outlet for it. Or gang warfare carried out on wasteland turned into a battleground, night and day, by dozens of people crowding around to watch rheumy-eyed pit bulls fighting, each of them named after some fallen dictator—Hitler being the most popular—betting heavily on the biggest, the most rabid, the most deadly, yelling at the beast to tear its opponent to shreds, to bite its fucking eyeballs, turned on by the blood/the ripped flesh/the groans of pain and dying), while Samir stayed upstairs, studying like a freak, refusing to accept a life with no future, no money, having to choose between a job as a cleaner/warehouseman/delivery driver/caretaker/security guard, or dealer, if you aim really high, if you're ambitious; wanting to impress his mother, Nawel Tahar, a cleaning lady for the Brunet family.[3] Nawel, a petite, black-eyed brunette and model employee, knows all about them: she cleans their laundry, their dishes, their floors, their children, scouring, scrubbing, pol-

---

3 Her employer, François Brunet, is a French politician, born September 3, 1945, in Lyon, Socialist Party member and parliamentary deputy, the author of several books, the latest of which, *Toward a Just World*, had been a best seller (source: Wikipedia).

ishing and vacuuming, declaring only half her earnings, working Saturdays and public holidays, sometimes evenings in order to wait on them/their friends, politically committed men, feverishly scanning the papers for their name, googling themselves whenever they hear that someone has written an article on them—good or bad, who cares, as long as people are talking about them— happy to fuck women under thirty in rooms rented by the year, preoccupied by their weight, the ups and downs of the stock market, their wrinkles, obsessed by the loss of their youth, their savings, their hair; people who sleep together, work together, swap jobs, wives, mistresses, take it in turns to big each other up, lick ass, and get their cocks sucked by Albanian whores—the best in the world, apparently—whom they will attempt to liberate from detention centers where they were kept by ambitious administrators, whom they will try to save by using their connections— vainly, alas—sickened by immigration policies that tear away their objects of desire, their cleaning ladies, their kids' favorite babysitters, the construction workers paid cash-in-hand who transform industrial wastelands into luxury lofts where they continue the revolution until the Assemblée Nationale Métro station because beyond that it's not really their area anymore, *Nawel, you can have the leftovers it's a shame to waste them and we don't have a dog*, yes, the tragic shards of fate and hate that twenty years spent swallowing the choke pear have burned into their gaze—a hardened, shadowy gaze, sharp as a carbide knife that will scalp you and yet you'll like it all the same. But all that was before Samir's social success as a TV puppet, animated for your pleasure: Bravo, you've done it! *She* was conquered. Because there were two of them in front of the screen, two of them suppressing their hysterical aggression, two accomplices in failure: Nina was there too, Nina who had loved him, at twenty years old, when everything was still to play for, when everything was still possible. What ambitions does she have now? (1) Obtaining a raise of €100 per month. (2) Having a child before it's too late—but what kind of future would the kid have? (3) Moving to a two-bed apartment with a view over a soccer field/trash cans/a muddy lakeside area where two ivory-colored swans flap their wings/die—the lost territories of the French Republic. (4) Paying off their debts—but how? Short-term solution: a government debt forgiveness commission. Long-term solution: God only knows. (5) Take a vacation, one week in Tunisia maybe, at an all-inclusive beach club on Djerba . . . well, they could dream.

"Look at him!" Nina shouted, eyes riveted to the screen, hypnotized by the image, drawn to it like a moth to a halogen lamp—a moth that will burn alive—and, watching him too, Samuel felt certain that Sam Tahar had long ago put behind him what had happened in 1987 at the University of L.—the incident that had destroyed Samuel forever. Twenty years spent trying to forget the tragedy of which he himself had been the unconscious orchestrator and the expiatory victim, and all for what? For it to be broadcast on CNN, at prime time.

They had met in the mid-eighties, at law school in Paris. Nina and Samuel had been together for a year when, on their first day back at school, they made the acquaintance of Samir Tahar. Like them, he was nineteen years old, but he seemed slightly older: a muscular man of medium height, with a nervous walk, whose beauty was not instantly obvious but who had you spellbound as soon as he opened his mouth. You saw him and you thought: *Yes, that manly authority, that animal magnetism—fuel for sex*. Everything about him promised pleasure; everything about him betrayed his desire—an aggressive, corrupting desire. That was the most disturbing thing about him, this guy they knew nothing about: his sincerity in conquest. It was the first thing you noticed: his taste for women—for sex, his weakness even then—perceptible in his ability to seduce them instantly, almost automatically, his sexual voracity, which he didn't even try to control, which he was able to express in a single gaze (a fixed, piercing, pornographic gaze that unveiled his thoughts and was constantly on the lookout for the slightest hint of reciprocation) and which he had to sate—quickly, urgently; his self-proclaimed and unabashed hedonism, his absolute coolness in conversation, as if every friendly or social relationship with a woman or a girl could only be justified by the possibility of its being transformed into a different kind of relationship.

But there was something else too . . . You could sense the predatory nature of this son of Tunisian immigrants; you could sense the belligerence, fed on a feeling of humiliation so powerful that it was impossible to work out who, in his personal history of relationships marked by mistrust, could have had such an enduring and forceful effect upon him. He had his mother's ambitions for himself: he wanted to succeed, to break the cycle of failure and poverty, of surrender and defeat; the family cycle, in short, which had already cost the life of his father, destroyed the dreams of his mother, and caused the breakup of a family. He was going to cut through the bars of his social jail cell, even if he had to do it with his teeth. A social climber? Sure, if you like . . . He was an immigrants' son who refuted social mimicry—one of those who had assimilated the republican message: study hard, work hard. A role model. People envied his provocative, transgressive boldness, his aggressive way of thinking, which was not without charm. How could you not be won over by this slightly mocking student who could tell you about his childhood in the poorest part of London or in a dilapidated ghetto, then his adolescence in a tiny attic room and his return to a seedy public housing project, with a flair for the sordid details that could move you to tears and, five minutes later, talk about a meeting between Gorbachev and Mitterrand as if he had been there? His strength was his taste for politics and for stories. He could spend whole evenings reading autobiographies and speeches by Nobel Prize winners; he liked learning about these people who had achieved greatness, because that was what he wanted for himself: greatness. The aura, the charisma . . . he already had those.

For a man like Samuel, for whom the whole of existence was nothing but a mass of neuroses and whose only ambition was to use this mental suffering as material for a great book, it was a providential friendship. Because when he first met Samir, he was in pieces. Out of nowhere, he had just learned the truth about his origins—and it was chaos. His parents had waited until his eighteenth birthday to inform him that he was actually born in Poland as Krzysztof Antkowiak. There you go, son, your innocent childhood is over— welcome to the adult world! An open world of perfect transparency is opening its doors to you! Samuel would have preferred to remain in ignorance. He didn't know what shocked him most: learning that his parents were not really his parents or discovering that his true first name was a derivative of Christ's: Samuel had been raised, after all, by a couple who were first secular (a pure, hard, uncompromising secularism, loudly and proudly proclaimed, according to those who knew them at the time) and then Jewish Orthodox—a spectacular turnaround with no rational explanation. That story alone could fill a book. A few hours after his birth, Samuel was abandoned by his mother, Sofia Antkowiak,[4] placed in

---

4 The daughter of Polish farmers, Sofia Antkowiak dreamed of becoming a famous dancer but became pregnant after a one-night stand with a soldier. Two months after giving birth, she threw herself under the wheels of the Warsaw-Lodz train.

an orphanage, and then adopted by a French couple of Jewish origin, Jacques and Martine Baron. Their names no longer provoke even the tiniest spark of recognition, and yet they were among the most active agitators on the French political and intellectual scene in the sixties and seventies. Members of the Union of Communist Students and the French Communist Party, friends with Alain Krivine and Henri Weber, Jacques and Martine Baron—both of them from the same middle-class assimilated Jewish background—had long ago given up any desire for recognition. Rejecting determinism and gregariousness, they decided to reinvent themselves, transforming their identity in a sort of magic trick. Both of them gravitated toward the major intellectual figures of the time. Together, they had attended a prestigious École Normale Supérieure and had passed the philosophy exam. They taught literature and they were young, beautiful, feverishly committed; they had everything, except "what mattered most"—a child. Jacques was sterile, and for a man like him, who had based his whole life around transmission, this was an unbearable situation. They applied for adoption and, after two years of waiting, were finally approved. That night, they celebrated the imminent arrival of their child, along with about thirty of their closest friends. After several glasses of wine, someone asked what name they were planning to give the child. To their shock, they realized they had never even thought about it. Martine replied first: They could name the child Jacques, like her husband. Or Paul, perhaps, or Pierre. Everyone nodded their agreement and they drank to the future PierrePaulJacques. For Jacques and Martine, that night would be remembered as one of the happiest of their lives. Two weeks later, however, Jacques surprised all his friends by deciding to have his son circumcised, even though he wasn't circumcised himself. He named the boy Samuel—which, in Hebrew, meant literally: *His name is God*—and organized a huge party to which all his friends were invited. And then, just as the rabbi pronounced the child's name out loud, something completely unexpected occurred: Jacques told the rabbi that he wanted to revert to his real surname, Bembaron, and to change his first name: from now on, he would be Jacob. He wished to follow his son into the bosom of the church. The partygoers—consisting essentially of journalists, writers, professors, activists from the extreme left, and atheist intellectuals—were dumbfounded. Their eyes showed incomprehension, even consternation. *So he's returning to the ghetto?*—that was what they were thinking. Jacques/Jacob appeared a man transfigured: his face was hot and red and he looked exultant, and yet he had not touched a drop of alcohol. But he saw the rabbi, he saw the golden embroideries that decorated the Torah scrolls, he heard the heartrending notes of an organ hidden in the attic, and he had a flash of illumination: there was no other explanation for this sudden turn toward the sacred. Later, he would refer to this event as his "return"—not a return to the ghetto, but a return to himself, to the sacred text. They left the center of Paris behind—the Latin Quarter, the Café de Flore—and they left behind their friends, who no longer understood them, who said, *They're crazy, it's so sad, it's a tragedy, they're going through some sort of crisis, they'll come back.* They never went back. They moved to a two-bedroom apartment on Rue du Plateau, in Paris's nineteenth arrondissement, and enrolled their son in an ultra-Orthodox Jewish school where teachers with beards and black hats taught prayers and sacred texts. There, in the presence of his own teacher—a man in his seventies with a magnetic charisma—Jacob felt good. He had never been as happy as he was with this man who taught him Hebrew and initiated him into the mysteries of the Torah, the Talmud, the Kabbalah. He felt reborn. No longer was he political, rebellious, angry. And if he did, ultimately, keep his surname—Baron—it was only because he was forced to by French law. Samuel knew nothing of his origins. Jacob waited until he was eighteen before revealing the truth. When this finally happened, Samuel at first did not react at all. Then, after a few minutes, he left the room without a word, and then the house. No more than an hour had passed. In a public bathroom, he shaved his beard, cut off his payot, and threw away his black robes. Lies. Bullshit. Betrayal. It was over. His parents had anticipated some anger, but not this brutal rejection, this sudden and absolute rupture. Samuel squatted in various places, and met Nina in college. So she wasn't Jewish? Good! That was what he wanted—to provoke his parents. Because for practicing Jews, worried about the perpetuation of their race, this was a serious issue. They told him: Either you come home or you stay with her and you will never see us again. Nothing could have been better calculated to dissuade him from returning than this unequivocal ultimatum, this aggressive demand. He stayed with an aunt. She kept his parents informed. They colluded with her, the hypocrites, but for them it was better to know that he was safe, was not living on the street. He was deeply in love with Nina at this point, dependent on her to a frightening extent. But Nina, raised in a rather strict military family, was extremely moral: faithfulness mattered to her. Her mother had gone to live with another man when she was seven years old. She woke up one morning and found a card on the living room table— one of those brightly colored postcards that people generally send to thank someone who has invited them to a party. On the front, it said, "THANK YOU." On the back, a few words in a shaky handwriting. Thank you for the years we spent together. Thank you for not judging me. Thank you for forgiving me. Nina's father burned the card with a cigarette lighter, in front of her. Neither of them ever recovered from this incident. He started drinking, and she filled the vacuum where her confidence had been with morality and rules. Samuel nicknamed her "French Justice."

Samir's sudden appearance in their lives caused the first cracks in their suffocating union: from now on, there were three of them, joined at the hip, moving as one, like a wave. You could see them from afar: the gang, friendly and complicit, without even a hint of jealousy or deceit; the loving couple and the free electron. Everyone in college gossiped about them: look at them, always together, showing off their intimacy, their collusion. And, deep down, they were excited by this: it was their own private game. But then, out of nowhere, tragedy hit. A few days before the oral exams, not having heard from his parents since the ignored ultimatum, Samuel learned that they had died in a car accident. A policeman told him at dawn, having first asked if he was the son of Jacques and Martine Baron. *Yes, that's me.* And he truly was his father's son in that moment when the policeman told him that their car had veered off the road and fallen into a ravine. Samuel does not remember how he reacted—the aftermath of the announcement is a black hole. Perhaps he collapsed, cried, yelled out, *It can't be true I don't believe you Tell me it's not true!* And the policeman: *I'm sorry, but it is.* But he remembers the wake, the vision of the two corpses covered in a shroud, with those men in black praying around them and him standing there with his prayer book in his hands, saying Kaddish for the peace of their souls. Samir was there, in the background, wearing a skullcap, hands crossed over his stomach. He too was thinking of his father: there had been no one at his funeral, no one to cry for him. That same day, Samuel, accompanied by his aunt, repatriated his parents' bodies to Israel, in line with their last will and testament. But before leaving the morgue, he took Samir to a quiet corner and solemnly told him: "Look after Nina for me. Don't leave her on her own. I'm counting on you." And that was exactly what he did. He took her out to eat, to watch movies, he gave her books, he went with her to bookstores and museums, he helped her revise, and barely a week after Samuel's departure, when she returned from an oral exam in tears, Samir led her to a room that a friend had lent him, took her in his arms to calm her down, and there, within a few minutes, was on top of her (she was still crying) and removing her clothes (she was wearing a skirt, luckily) and pacifying her the only way he knew. Sex was his form of consolation, his way of making things better; it was his reply to the brutality of life—the purest reply possible, he had never found a better one. That might have been the end of it, but no, it was impossible. Whatever there was between them was too strong, too powerful. It overwhelmed them. They were suddenly defenseless, interdependent—they had never expected *this*. And while he should have told her that it was a mistake, while he should have walked away—this was how he normally acted, in all sincerity, because he got bored quickly; he didn't like to repeat his conquests—instead he fell in love. Not only did they see each other again, they never left each other's sides. For several days, they were inseparable. He loved her, desired her, wanted to live with her, and he told her this. It was the most terrible betrayal: Samuel would return; he'd just lost his parents in tragic circumstances; Samuel was his friend. In a fair, just, moral world, his behavior was outrageous, but, *We do not live in a fair, just, moral world*. That was what Samir thought. *I know what I'm talking about, because I know where I'm from. The world is violent. Violence is everywhere.* This was all he could find to tell her. *Love is violent too. You must choose.*

Samuel returned, but they did not confess their affair. Samuel thanked Samir—*a true friend, someone you can rely on when things get tough, a brother you can trust.* It went on like that for nine months, maybe more. Nina did not want to tell Samuel anything. He was living alone in the apartment his parents had been renting, surrounded by their furniture, their belongings—a death chamber. She never went to see him and he never went to see her. It was over between them. They never made love anymore. And when the school year ended, Samir gave her an ultimatum: *It's him or me.*

Samuel had no trouble remembering those years, and soon he would no longer be able to hold back the tide of images of Samir the Star that flooded his mind, the waves of Samir crashing through the barriers that had been repaired, smashing down the fragile interior edifice he had spent years reconstructing and which now exploded and was drowned and dispersed by Samir Samir Samir.

You're impressed, aren't you? By his success. Admit it!

Nina looked at him with a mixture of pity and anger.

Yes

It's true

You're right

So here we are . . .

For a brief moment, she had imagined what her life might be now had she gone with Samir twenty years ago, had she made a different decision when he commanded her to *choose*: irresistible Samir, so confident, so self-assured, versus Samuel, weak in love, cowardly in adversity, devastated by the violence of the break that Nina had provoked and who could find no better way of keeping her than slicing open his veins with a box cutter in the college auditorium, one of those small knives with a retractable blade, made of blue plastic—you just push the safety catch, once, twice, you have to do it in a single movement, press down hard, even if it hurts, then let the blood pour out and the sadness with it—Samuel who had found no better way than this of proving that he loved her, that he was ready to die for her, to put an end to this unbearable pain, to cure all his ills with the stroke of a blade.

When he awoke, he understood that she had chosen him. Putting her love to the test. The risks and dangers of this. And yet, it *had* to be done. And there she was, hair messed up, face pale, almost corpselike—*he is suffering, so I suffer too*—sitting on the edge of the bed, practically at his feet, *like a dog*, he thinks. There she was: Nina, fully present, plumping his pillow, holding his glass as he drank, helping him to eat—time to atone, to set in motion the mechanism of expiation—Nina, surrendering to the heroic romanticism of suicide *for love*. How beautiful it was, how powerful, how great. Nina never leaving the room except when the nurses asked her to. As for Samir, the case was closed. Neither of them ever attempted to see him again. His name was taboo. They pretended to forget him.

Upon his release from the hospital, Samuel quit his parents' apartment (too expensive), donated their furniture to charity, rented an efficiency, and gave up pursuing his law degree. (He even wondered why he had begun it: to piss off his father, he supposed, but he was no longer very sure. His suicide attempt and the spell in the hospital that followed it seemed to have annihilated all his determination and willpower; from now on, his vision of life was blurred and murky, everything ambiguous.) He took a literature degree by correspondence and began a job teaching foreigners to read and write. Nina too gave up her studies—she had never liked law—and became first a sales assistant, then a waitress, then a receptionist. Nowadays she worked as a model for a few major store catalogues—Carrefour and C&A, mostly.

Look at him! My God, look at him!

There was something masochistic in the way they kept watching Samir's media consecration. They could have changed channels, but no—their suffering fed their rage, their fury. (Finally fuel for a book, thought Samuel. Finally a chance to write a novel that might actually be published!) Samuel and Nina sat petrified in front of their Firstline TV set, bought at Carrefour for €545, payable in three installments, interest-free—an object whose acquisition had caused so much tension and discord between them, with Nina pleading for its purchase for years while Samuel argued against, seeing it as a threat, before finally yielding—realizing that nothing would ever be the same again, that something had been corrupted/destroyed/soiled forever, something like innocence, like the artificial bliss that ignorance provides.

Moving closer to the screen, Samuel examined Samir, wondering if he'd had a nose job, scrutinizing his tumid lips, his amazingly smooth forehead, the way he shone and swaggered on the screen, and seeing his own reflection superimposed on Samir's image, in a cruel comparison. "Get out of the way!" Nina shouted. "I can't see!" Samuel moved aside, then walked behind Nina, watching her as she knelt in front of the TV, in a sacrificial posture, intoning something—but what?

Samir smiled mechanically at the journalist, proud and happy to be where he was, where he belonged—you could see it in his puffed-out chest, the quiver in his upper lip. He lit up the screen. Nothing they had been through seemed to have affected him in the slightest. He was like a man who escapes from a crashed and burning car without a scratch, while the vehicle's other occupant is dead at the wheel.

2

His mother[1] hadn't called (five times—Samir had counted—it was becoming obsessive) to wish him a happy birthday, nor to ask how he was. He knew this because she had left a disturbing message. In a voice that sounded distraught, she had asked him to call her back—it was "important," it was "urgent"—in spite of the fact that he had long ago made clear to her that he did not want any contact with her. It wasn't that he didn't love her—he did, as he had emphasized—or had anything against her. And it certainly wasn't due to a lack of respect—he held his mother in high regard—that he never returned her calls, but simply a desire for consistency: the need to act in accordance with the life he had chosen. You are forty years old; you have made a brilliant career in the United States; you have married the daughter of one of the richest businessmen in the country. Never mind what you did to get here: this is what you wanted, and you have worked hard to arrive at this point. You have had to fight—it wasn't easy; no one helped you or recommended you to someone more influential. You have built your own life, and you have acted alone, determined to be number one, to be the best, obsessed by the goal of becoming rich (and what's wrong with that?), of owning a beautiful house (the most beautiful you can find) and a luxury car (the most powerful you can find). Yes, you have a rich man's tastes—so what? Why should you care if they call you nouveau riche? That's what you are, what you wanted to be. You almost gave up, more than once, because the odds were

---

1 Nawel Tahar, née Yahyaoui, the daughter of Ismail Yahyaoui, a metalworker. Born in Tunisia, she was forced to give up school and find a job after her father died in an accident at work.

so stacked against you, everything was so difficult: taking a degree in another country/creating an American branch of one of the most prestigious law firms in France, and making a name for yourself there. Sometimes you would worry that you made the wrong choice in leaving France, in severing all connection with your family, with your mother—yes, you have to plead guilty to that private corruption—but what does she want from him now? he wondered. Why had she called? It couldn't be money: he sent her that regularly, he never forgot: the bank transfers appeased his sense of shame, absolved his sin. He helped his mother. He was a sort of social worker. *You're a good son*, his mother had written to thank him, *and, I hope, A GOOD MUSLIM*. The issue of his racial identity: the very thing he hated

the very thing he had escaped from

and silenced the truth of

and betrayed.

He had burned that letter.

And while he wondered if his mother had suddenly become irresponsible, reckless, insane, he felt his wife's hand in his: her perfectly manicured hand, guiding him through the darkness. Blindfolded, he let her lead him. He could see and guess nothing at all as he was taken to a secret place—nothing had filtered through to him, no one had talked—feeling a little confined in his new Dior suit, purchased especially for his CNN appearance. *And I was good*, he thought: relaxed, eloquent, lucid, "a natural-born TV star," as the presenter had told him in a complicit voice that suggested she wanted to see him again, wanted to chat, to share a drink/maybe more *if we hit it off* (that's what he thought) and, inside his head, he had replied, *A natural-born sex star too . . . but you don't know that yet* (that way he had of bringing everything back to sexual performance, as if the bedroom were the sole arena where he could fully express his abilities, measure himself against others, and dominate them . . . that absolute confidence in his own erotic appeal . . .). In those moments, his mother ceased to exist. Hearing suppressed laughter and giggling in the darkness, he knew he had won, that he had rid himself of his past like a murderer dissolving his victim's corpse in an acid bath. Now there was only him, Samir, surrounded by a huge crowd of people who had assembled purely to wait for him, to acclaim him. With a nimble movement, her fine hand undid the blindfold like a kidnapper releasing a hostage, and Samir saw the hundreds of guests singing, "Happy birthday to you, Sami!," he saw the lynx, the two wolves of the East, the golden tigers and the white tigers, the Saharan leopard, the Asian lion—caged, tamed by the whips of panther-women in tight-fitting bodysuits that left nothing to the imagination, an elephant[2] striding, magnificent, on a foam-covered carpet, an aging gorilla with glassy eyes that might have been stuffed were it not for the fact that it extended its massive, hairy paw toward anyone who dared to caress it through the bars of its prison. This strange menagerie was offered for the enjoyment of men in ties and women in masks—rhinestone-encrusted masks overstitched with gold thread, lace masks (made on bobbins, by hand, with needles), cloth masks, leather masks (natural, pitted, studded, or dotted with long metal spikes in the shapes of reamers), peacock-feather masks, latex masks, raw silk masks, masks in black felt or velvet, masks in transparent net, blindfold-style masks, pirate masks, Zorro and Fantômette masks, oxygen masks, African and Venetian masks, scary masks, and sexy masks—all worn to attract the lens of the photographer who was there to immortalize Samir Tahar's fortieth birthday party in one of the most exclusive/exces-

---

2 The star of Blake Edwards's 1968 movie *The Party*, this elephant now plays cameo roles in private parties.

sive clubs in New York, filled with the cream of American intelligentsia: politicians, lawyers, publishers, and economists who had come en masse, alone or accompanied, invited here by *Rahm Berg's daughter*, Ruth. Sami Tahar's wife was one of those women with a perfect résumé: a pampered childhood in the bosom of an upper-class Jewish-American family; studied law at Harvard; brilliant at public relations, brilliant at math, brilliant at everything . . . and altruistic too, a humanist who, several times a year, gave out food to the needy; a rich girl, immensely rich, who never forgot to donate 10 percent of her earnings to charity as required by Jewish law; respectful of traditions, naturally; she studied literature and poetry with Joseph Brodsky, who described her as one of his most gifted and subtle students; she studied Latin and Greek, she studied law, but she also studied the Torah with her maternal grandfather, Rav Shalom Levine,[3] a rabbi with beard and sidelocks who looked like he had stepped out of a novel by Isaac Bashevis Singer.[4] So, she was an impressive girl. And yet Tahar had not noticed her when she first appeared at his law firm, having been invited to work as an intern by his partner, who had not bothered to inform him. How had he failed to notice her? Because she was too sober, too modest, with that look of extreme classicism that young women often adopt when they begin their first job, hiding their inexperience behind long skirts, ruffle blouses, even foulards, clothes borrowed from their mother or their grandmother, silk

---

3 Born in Poland in 1890, Rav Shalom Levine was for forty years in charge of burying sacred texts with the dead. According to Jewish tradition, the texts must not be burned or torn. A longtime member of the Jewish Writers' Club in Warsaw, he habitually quoted this line from the Pirkei Avot: "Who is rich? He who is satisfied with his lot in life."

4 Despite winning the Nobel Prize for Literature in 1978, Isaac Bashevis Singer stated: "I consider the fact of being vegetarian to be the greatest success of my life."

scarves in richly brocaded colors that age them ten years, because they are ashamed of their youth. They believe that they will win favor by appearing older, that their skills will be more easily recognized . . . Yeah, right! What they have yet to understand is that they would gain ten years in their professional ascendancy by wearing split skirts, short skirts, low necklines. They have not yet understood the power they possess. Youth is their power. They are twenty-five/thirty years old. They are highly educated, hardworking, ambitious. They have all the advantages won by feminism without having to demand anything themselves, without having to fight, but they lower their eyes under the gazes of male, sixty-something, unhappily married executives. It's unbelievable! They lower their eyes when these men compliment them on the color of their hair. Watched by these old predators, they pretend to be frightened deer, pure angels, feeble maidens; they act like women from another era; they fall to pieces and shame their mothers. But look at those men, those apostles of performance, cocks hardened by Viagra, with their flat stomachs and their dyed hair, eyes riveted on their prey, ready to pounce. The attempts at flattery, the first phase of seduction, and then maybe, to round it all off, possession. The young women notice none of this, or pretend not to. The chauvinistic remarks, the double entendres—they are disregarded. The women think this is just part of the game: a hand nonchalantly draped on a shoulder (a sign of friendliness); an invitation to dinner (a work meeting); personal and intimate remarks (at least they're showing an interest). Their youth weakens them, the women think, so they dress up to hide it. Some of them wear men's clothing: suits in dark colors, Derby shoes, sometimes even a tie— *it's all the rage apparently*. Ruth Berg was one of these women, an androgynous girl who, for her eighteenth birthday, asked for (and received) a breast reduction operation. Oh, yes, it's true. She got her boobs from her great-grandmother Judith, a cold, brusque woman whose only feminine attribute was that enormous chest, a chest which (according to family legend) nursed practically half of the newborns in Warsaw.[5] While most women dreamed of having breast implants, Ruth Berg went to the surgeon carrying a photograph of Diane Keaton in *Annie Hall*, dressed in pants with darts and a man's waistcoat, hat glued to her head—a chic little New York intellectual. How could Samir possibly have noticed her? His fantasies revolved mainly around femmes fatales, with opulent chests and voluptuous asses. When it came to boobs and butts, a little excess did not bother him—in fact, it turned him on: it was the first thing he saw. Only afterward did he notice fine features or intellectual curiosity. Ruth Berg was too petite for him, too discreet, flat as a pancake, tits like fried eggs, not even a handful, nothing but skin and bone. She, on the other hand, noticed him right away: that enigmatic man with the strong French accent. She noticed him the moment he emerged from his office, carrying a stack of folders, illuminating the room with his million-dollar smile; the smile told all in an instant about his social position, his desire to be relaxed, cheerful, happy. Ruth wasted no time hunting down her colleagues' opinions about his life story, but the same words were constantly repeated: brilliant, boastful, secretive, hardworking . . . and a womanizer. Watch out, girl: He's dangerous. With a magnetism like that, no one can resist him. See her, over there? And her? They've both been to bed with him. But it never lasts. As soon as a girl tries to tame him, he bridles and flees— you'll never break him. "He's a Frenchman," they all say, with a sneer. Don't you understand? *That* is all he thinks about.

God knows why he has such an effect on her. He's older than her, indifferent to her charms. But she goes for it anyway, asking an-

---

5   One of whom, Yonathan Strauss, later became a famous harpist.

other woman[6] from the law firm out for a coffee, one day after work. She wants to know more about him, to discover details, anything that might increase her chances. Six months after her fling with Tahar, the girl is still bitter. She is practically in tears as she tells Ruth how their relationship "destroyed" her. "Keep away from that man—he's an opportunist, a manipulator." Watch out! Danger! He attracts her, and she doesn't know why. It's as if he's a vacuum cleaner and she's a dust bunny. She swears that Tahar is not her type and her colleague laughs. "Tahar is everyone's type." There's a silence. Ruth watches her intensely as the other woman goes on: "He's everyone's type, men and women, because he's not like the others. He's shadowy, secretive, dominant . . . it's exciting." Suddenly her tone softens and she leans closer to Ruth: she is going to tell her a secret. The woman smiles, flicks her hair away from her right eye, and, in a tone of false complicity, says: "He is—" But she doesn't have time to finish her sentence. Ruth Berg stops her with a movement of her hand. All she needs to know is his social image.

So how did Ruth grab Tahar's attention? How did she manage to tame him? Not through sex, of course—she was too disciplined, too predictable for him. There was nothing surprising about her. She was a virgin when they met, incredible as that may seem. She must have kissed three or four boys in college, but even then she hesitated to use her tongue the way she'd been told to, the way she'd practiced, alone, licking the palm of her hand like a cat (it tickled, nothing more), and even when she had tried to submit to the desires of the computer studies undergraduate who had taken

---

6 Sofia Werther (but is that her real name?). Believed to be born in 1979. Though known for her depressive tendencies, she did manage to wangle a date with Woody Allen after one of his clarinet concerts at Carnegie Hall by pretending to be a Czech movie producer.

her somewhat roughly in his arms, due to his inexperience (Adam Konigsberg, the son of a surgeon from Mount Sinai Hospital; highly eligible),[7] the only thing she felt was disgust, the sensation of having something gluey and viscous in her mouth, like an inedible oyster. Was *this* what all the fuss was about? She had let a boy fondle her once (Ethan Weinstein, the son of a Republican senator),[8] but he had grabbed her tit like his hand was a mechanical shovel, as if he were trying to crush it. She had developed a genuine aversion to human contact after this, and when Michael Abramovich (the son of a New York banker)[9] had tried to slide his hand into her panties (somewhat clumsily, as he was right-handed but was having to use his left hand) in the movie theater, while watching *A Clockwork Orange*, she had lost all self-control: she had slapped him and screamed at him and, on her way out of the theater, had hidden herself in a darkened corner to throw up the popcorn he had been generous enough to buy her before feeling her up. "What did you expect?" said her college roommate.[10] "Any guy who takes you to see *A Clockwork Orange* on a first date is either a movie buff or a psychopath." She suspected the latter was more likely. The boys she met—all upper-class Jewish-Americans, either spoiled,

---

7 Adam Konigsberg announced to his parents, at a very young age: "I'm going to be rich when I grow up." Today, he is the proprietor of several sex shops.

8 After studying political science, Ethan Weinstein became a Democratic senator to "piss off" his father.

9 Long considered a "failure" by his father, Michael Abramovich—who had dreamed of becoming an actor—committed suicide at the age of twenty-seven by throwing himself out of a window.

10 Deborah Levy. A brilliant child, raised by parents obsessed with the idea of scholarly success, she gave up her studies to pursue an American man of Indian origin. Having converted to Hinduism, she was now living in Mumbai with her eight children.

very spoiled, or completely spoiled, whose ambitions extended no further than blowing Daddy's money on the beaches of Goa or Cancún—were not the types to inspire a girl like her: a Jewish princess raised on milk and honey. She had grown up with them, she'd studied with them, and on religious holidays she had prayed with them in the same synagogue, surrounded by worshippers who lived in the same neighborhood, frequented the same clubs . . . and now she was expected to marry one of them? The horror! Social horror/community horror. "You will marry a Jew"—the eleventh commandment, imposed by the father. You will not marry the son of a gentile, you will not share his bed, you will not bear him children. A dilemma. She had seen Sam Tahar. A Jew, she thought, but also a Frenchman. A Sephardic Jew—not the same thing. She'd heard that Tahar's father was a Jew of Tunisian origin who had moved to France in the fifties. She'd heard that his mother was a Jew born in France whose parents, Polish Jews, had fled their country during the First World War. She'd heard that his parents had died in a car accident when Sam was twenty. That he was an only child. That he had no family. She'd heard he was a nonpracticing Jew, an assimilated Jew ("ashamed," some said), anticlerical and pro-Palestinian. And provocative too. Capable of reciting a poem by Mahmoud Darwish[11] at the table of honor during the annual meeting of the National Jewish Committee. Don't mention religion. Don't mention Israel. Don't ask him to be the tenth man to make up a minyan (not back then anyway; once he came into contact with Ruth and her family, he quickly fell into line with their religious habits and adapted to their ways of thinking). Avoid foreign politics. Talk to him about women instead—that's what everyone

---

11 Palestinian poet. In December 2005, he told the Arab newspaper *Al-Hayat* (London): "I don't believe in applause. I know it is insincere, deceitful, and that it can turn a poet away from poetry."

told her. And in that domain, the only person who could exert any influence over him was his American partner, Dylan Berman,[12] the only person able to tell him: "This is ridiculous—you've gone too far now and you need to stop." He was also the first person to warn Tahar, when he realized that Berg's daughter was fixated on him: "Leave her alone—she's not meant for you." Tahar replied with a smile, as Berman argued: "Go out with your secretary, call your ex, you can even screw one of the firm's clients if you want, but stay away from this girl!" "Why? She's an intern. She's not a minor. And she likes me—it's obvious that she likes me." But Berman was not the kind of man to mess around with influence, power, and money: those things enabled him and his family to live, they kept his firm going, provided him with a very healthy income and a spotless reputation; Berman did not mix up the bedroom and the office, love and finance: "No sex in business! She's Rahm Berg's daughter. Berg—one of the richest men in the U.S.! This firm's most important client! If we lose him, we're fucked—do you understand? Hurt his little girl and, believe me, he will make you pay. Listen, if you need to make photocopies, ask your assistant or do it yourself. Don't ask her anything, not even the time." "You think your threats are going to stop me? The more forbidden this girl is, the more she excites me." "Then why don't you screw the prosecutor's assistant, Nabila Farès?" "Nabila? Are you kidding? That'd be like screwing my sister!" "What do you mean? She's an Arab!" He often made this kind of mistake, forgetting the man he had become: a Jew among Jews. "Look, Sam, just forget Ruth Berg! If you touch a hair on her head, her father will kill you." But Berman was not counting on his associate's stubbornness—Tahar's obstinacy was that of a working-

---

12 Dylan Berman, born in 1965 in New York. Son of a Brooklyn tailor, he decided at a very young age that he wanted to become a lawyer. He has boasted of being one of the best-paid members of his profession in the United States.

man's son, a boy who had suffered humiliation; it was a kind of revenge—nor on his charisma, his powers of invention, and his attractiveness. Women liked him, and so did men. Even children adored him. And as for the clients . . . even at $1,000 per hour, he was the one they all wanted, demanded—no one else.

In his office, there were articles about him strewn all over the coffee tables. He also collected them in a large black leather folder on which his initials were embroidered in gold thread, and he kept this folder on a shelf filled with law books that hung on the wall behind his glass desk. There were articles in which he was only quoted, and some short pieces, but also major spreads, some laudatory, others damning. He cut them carefully from papers and magazines himself and placed them inside transparent sheet protectors with the meticulousness of a lepidopterist. Ruth Berg read them all, didn't miss a single one—not even that sex test in a men's magazine that he'd taken the time to fill out. That was how she knew, from the very beginning, that he would *never be faithful*, that he thought about sex *all the time*, and that he had *tried everything*. She sought out information on the Internet, then used it to compliment him. She was sweet and perspicacious. Any man would soon notice a girl as powerful and self-assured as her, and Tahar more quickly than most. Another man might keep his distance, thinking she was too difficult to seduce, too intimidating. But not Tahar. He had far too much confidence in his ability to make women love him. He knew all about sexual dependence and how to arouse it: in that field of inquiry, there was nothing that *anyone* could teach him. He had drawn a line under his love affair with Nina—too much suffering. Even now, thinking about it was still painful. When he met Ruth, he already knew what he didn't want: to be in love, to feel tied to someone, attached. It was not through her freedom or her sexual curiosity that this intern in Prada boots would seduce him,

but through her social invulnerability—because that was truly rare.
That in itself was enough to justify him giving up on other women
and centering his life around her. This was a woman who never
feared other people's looks, who never felt offended or humiliated,
who had nothing to gain or to prove. She had never had to fight for
anything. Politics, for her, was a game; money, a resource; social
position, a question of relationships and opportunities: it was all
there, revealing the world to which she belonged and making clear
her success. Her class reflex was, *spontaneously*, to think in terms
of her clan. It was to travel in a private jet and consider it normal;
to sit between Bill Clinton and Shimon Peres at dinner and think it
dull. Her idea of a moral dilemma was to hesitate between donating
to a foundation that battled poverty in Israel and a foundation that
battled hunger in the Sahel region. But this was not a girl who had
been corrupted by money. She was not one of those spoiled, arrogant, superficial girls—she knew she was privileged, she was aware
of how lucky she was, but she belonged to the heirs' club. She was
above it all. There was an aura about her, a halo floating over her
head. No one had ever made her feel out of place, because she was
precisely the kind of girl who knew her place. Up on the rostrum.
In the first row. In the foreground of a photograph. And, quite naturally, without posing or making any special effort, she was in all
those places. When she spoke to you, you felt elect. As soon as she
entered a room, you knew she was important. How? Because she
knew it herself. Her father had told her she was, repeatedly. Her
friends and family had made it clear to her. Salespeople in the stores
where she shopped made her feel it. When she called someone, they
always called her back the same day. When she suggested lunch,
she was the one who chose the day, the place, the time. No one
would dream of canceling on her. And no one EVER made her wait.
She knew all about the advantages bestowed by an enviable social
position, but there was nothing arrogant or contemptuous about

her. She always greeted her father's employees—hello, goodbye, how are you, how's the family?—and she did it sincerely. She made it a point of honor not to lose the sense of human contact. And yet, at the same time, she did all of this with a distance that marked her out as *different*. They were nice people, she respected them, but they did not belong to her world. Her world was a quarter-mile radius around Fifth Avenue and the presidential suites of the most prestigious hotels; her world was an oasis of comfort and frivolity, concealing an empire of darkness. Her world was that of the Reconstruction or the Renaissance: the façade was golden but the foundations were built on ashes. The company was run by her father on behalf of her grandfather—an Auschwitz survivor who was happy to talk politics and ecology, who didn't mind teaching you to play bridge, who (grudgingly) gave out his recipe for chopped liver, who could spend hours telling you the story of Job and the creation of the world, could explain why Isaac preferred Esau to Jacob. This was a man who helped organize the Bible Quiz every year and who would explain the meaning of a word to you, but would never tell you why there was a number tattooed on his forearm. This was why, when she talked about herself to Tahar, she mentioned the books she'd been reading recently, her vacation in Italy with her daddy on Steven Spielberg's yacht, the beauty of the beach at Martha's Vineyard where she once met John Kennedy, Jr., and nothing more. She was the daughter of a man who had built an amusement park over the cemetery of his heart. A girl like that had everything it took to impress Tahar: one of the best address books in New York; social respectability; the esteem of powerful men. For Tahar, this was what counted. For a man like him who had never been esteemed or famous, such assets were important.

Not only did Rahm Berg not kill him, but he gave him and his daughter a three-hundred-square-meter penthouse with a view over Central Park, an apartment valued by one of the most prestigious real estate agencies on the East Coast at more than $17 million. He could have said no, but he wasn't that proud. This gift consolidated his uniqueness, he thought. In essence, it was a dowry. And what a dowry! Five bedrooms, six bathrooms, and a seventy-square-meter terrace, including a private area with a Jacuzzi. Rahm Berg wanted his daughter to feel good. He wanted her to be happy—and happiness was waking up in a spacious bedroom, eating breakfast with a view of New York, flicking through the *New York Times* and seeing her name in print. Berg said it jokingly but he said it all the same: "My daughter is a princess." That was also Samir's pet name for her—"My Jewish princess." Ruth's father, accompanied by her grandfather, wearing a yarmulke and a large black hat on his head, had attached a glass mezuzah to the frame of the front door and of every other door in the apartment—twenty of them in total. Twenty little glass cases containing a Hebrew prayer beseeching the Lord to protect the household. This was an important ritual. He had not forgotten any of the doors, but in fact it was on his daughter's head that he really wanted to attach a mezuzah, to protect *her*. A daughter, a home, and a Jewish life—that was what Rahm Berg had given him. It hadn't been easy, of course. He'd had to assert himself, to plead his cause with the patriarch, but persuading people was his special talent, after all. It was his job. He'd had to win over the mother, an extremely verbose blond woman, the perfect mother, a dermatologist capable of detecting a malignant melanoma at first sight, a peerless cook who would make up to 120 sufganiyot for Hanukkah, an accomplished sportswoman—it was no mystery where Ruth got her many virtues from.

You're a good son and, I hope, A GOOD MUSLIM.

Why did he think about that phrase as he entered the club where the party was being held? Why now? It was his birthday they were celebrating, not a Jewish festival. They weren't going to play klezmer music or carry him in on a chair, then throw him in the air and shout, "Mazel tov!" It was not even something he had to think about: *Judaism is just a minor detail in my life*. So why was it all he could think about right now? Why did he suddenly feel hot? He was sweating—his shirt was damp. (And it was not just any old shirt: it was a shirt that cost more than $300, made of the finest and most loose-woven fabric, now so soaked with perspiration that it was sticking to his skin, and an image of his father filled his mind, haunted him: his father coming home from work, his cheap shirt stained with yellow halos in the armpits, stinking up every room he entered with the acrid stench of sweat—an odor he associated inextricably with poverty.) He was sweating like a pig! It was anxiety. Because, deep down, he knew—he had always known, from the very first day—that Judaism was not just a minor detail in his life: it *was* his life. Everyone looked at him and saw a Jew. His partners were Jews, his wife was a Jew, his children would be Jews. Most of his friends were Jews. His parents-in-law were not only Jews but practicing Jews, Orthodox Jews. They stopped work at dusk every Friday until nightfall on Saturday. They consulted rabbis the way some people consult fortune-tellers, to find out what decision to take, what attitude to adopt. They obeyed at least 400 of the 613 commandments. They often went to Israel, to Jerusalem, to pray before the Wailing Wall, to pray and write down their wishes on a piece of paper that they slipped into one of the wall's burning cracks. The only time he went to Jerusalem with his father-in-law (one year after he met Ruth: they were not yet married, or even engaged) was his first family trip. It was also an ordeal: he lost a liter of water, waiting in line at customs in Israel, literally liquefied by the fear of being unmasked in front of Ruth and her father. On that occasion by the Wailing Wall, he managed to pilfer the little piece of paper that Berg had slipped into a crack and, after waiting until he was alone, read these words: "Oh Lord, my God, King of the Universe, I ask of you:

"Wish number 1: To protect my family and ensure them good health.

"Wish number 2: To help me keep what I have acquired.

"Wish number 3: That my daughter breaks up with Sam TAHAR."

Berg had three wishes—three wishes that he could be fairly certain would be granted if he had faith (that was what he believed); he had only a tiny piece of paper and a few minutes to write those wishes; he had to be brief, concise. And yet somehow he felt it necessary to ask God that his daughter should break up with "Sam Tahar." He didn't write: *Lord, cure my mother* (who, at the time, had metastatic liver cancer), or *Lord, give my little sister a healthy baby* (she was three months pregnant, and one of her blood tests had required an amniocentesis) . . . No, kneeling before the wall of stones baked white-hot by the sun, amid one of the most dazzling landscapes in the world, one of those places that are so stunningly beautiful that it is impossible to witness them without being moved to tears, without being assailed by questions of existence, all he could think to wish for was the disappearance of his daughter's boyfriend from her life. What did he even know about that man? Nothing, or very little anyway. Don't imagine that Rahm Berg agreed to give his daughter's hand in marriage without proof. Tahar claimed he didn't have his parents' religious marriage certificate: "They must have lost it, and the consistory archives were destroyed in a fire." He had no family. How could he be believed? Berg didn't like this: either you were a Jew or you weren't. Why should he take this man's word? It was worthless. His first name was in his favor, admittedly: Sam was the diminutive of

Samuel, wasn't it? As for "Sami," as most of his friends called him, it meant: "His name is God." So, yeah, there was nothing wrong with his first name. But his surname was a little suspect, wasn't it? Tahar . . . Rahm Berg hired a student specialized in genealogy to investigate, and these were his findings: "Arab family name *sometimes* belonging to Sephardic Jews. Corresponds to the Arabic word (but also the Hebrew word, which is identical) *Tahir*, he who is pure, upstanding, virtuous, honest." "That's me!" said Sam. Tahar the Pure—Berman had to laugh at that. It was a prophet's name, biblically inspired. And it was true that he looked honest, with his beautiful North African Jewish face, his black and shining hair, which he often wore slicked back like a Camorra godfather, his olive skin, his slightly hooked nose, and his piercing soot-black eyes, heavy-lidded and long-lashed—a dark and handsome man, nothing at all like the Bergs, who were Ashkenazi Jews, pale-skinned, blond, or redheaded, having to wear SPF 60 sunscreen protection every day, and a baseball cap, and sunglasses. *That Arab!* The idea that he was Sephardic bothered them, he knew; perhaps it even disgusted them. *Come on, let's be honest—he's not like Us.* (He's less virtuous than Us, less civilized, less upright, less astute than Us.) All they saw when they looked at him was an *Arab* Jew—and for the Bergs, for the snobbiest branch of the family, who aspired to pure aristocratic status, this was horrifying. While it was true that he was refined, educated, cultivated, he was also too exuberant, too solar, too tanned. Where they whispered, he brayed; where they frowned, he laughed; where they were deep, he was shallow. He wasn't like them. And that foreign-sounding surname, "Tahar," offended their ears. "Tahar" was a downgrade, a stain. And, in fact, one of the first things Ruth's father ever told him was: "My grandchildren will be Bergs." He had said it somewhat abruptly, to make it clear how matters stood right from the start, to assert his authority. His roof, his rules. Tahar had frozen. How could he justify such a humiliation, such a rout? What class reflex made him believe he could get away with this, without provoking anger, a backlash? "It's all right, take it easy . . . Come over here." His gestures were paternal; he looked as if he were about to take Tahar in his arms. He had something to tell him, something he had never told anyone before. Rahm Berg knew the power of emotion. He knew how to make people bend to his will. He didn't say: I don't want my descendants to have a North African surname. He didn't say: It would be more advantageous, given my reputation and status and political and economic influence, for my lineage to have the same name as me. He didn't say: It's a useful, socially powerful, door-opening name that could advance your career by ten to fifteen years. He didn't talk about himself at all. On the contrary, he was self-effacing. Looking sincere (and he probably was), he said, in a voice strangled not by tears but by a sort of suppressed rage, that almost all of his family had been exterminated during the war: "The name of Berg is becoming extinct. The Nazis exterminated my name. And my daughter is the last Berg, for I have no sons." That day, Tahar felt profoundly moved. So that was why he agreed to let his children be named Berg and to renounce forever the name of his own father. But still, whenever he read his children's names on their schoolbooks—LUCAS BERG, 5, and LISA BERG, 3—he felt his heart contract. Even physically, he had passed on nothing to them: with their pale skin and chestnut hair, both children resembled their mother.

His father-in-law had also tested his knowledge of Judaism—but he could have no complaints there: Tahar knew the essentials. He'd been well educated by Samuel, and simply from spending so much time with his partners, he was able to give the approximate Shabbat hours. He was a very clever parrot. He also knew how to ask the right questions. They gave him the honor of leading the Passover Seder. True, he didn't speak Hebrew, so his reading was phonetic, and with a strong French accent, which made everyone laugh. But one evening, when the whole family was gathered together and Ruth's mother coldly asked Samir to laugh less loudly, Ruth whispered, half joking and half serious: "Don't be mad, Sami. To them, you're an Arab." He glared at her. He would have liked to tell her, there and then, in front of her entire family: That's what I am. An Arab—a real Arab. The son of Abdelkader Tahar, who was the son of Mohammed Tahar, blacksmith, and Fatima Ouali, seamstress. So go fuck yourselves!

His father was another wound. A deep and throbbing wound, one that cut to the bone. Abdelkader Tahar was thirty years old when he met the woman who would become his wife—Nawel Yahyaoui, from Oulad el Houra, in the center of the Kef Governorate in Tunisia. His father, Mohammed Tahar, arranged the meeting. He liked her: virtuous/upstanding/pure; two long braids encircling a soft-featured face; skin the color of sand and downy like an apricot . . . he had never seen anything like her. She was the one for him, he sensed it, knew it, and—without asking her opinion (why bother?)—he married her. Together, they migrated to France in the early sixties: they'd heard there was work there. Ten years employed at the saltworks in Varangéville, working like crazy . . . it wore him out. And then some luck. A friend who worked as a chauffeur for a businessman was off for a month, and Abdelkader replaced him. It was a dream: a door opened, he entered. Day and night he had to schlep around the spoiled kids of a Saudi family, from Place Vendôme to the most notorious quarter in Paris, where they would find girls and drugs; Abdelkader waited for them, loaded the car for them, and the tips they left him were huge. It didn't last, though: they went back to Dubai, and Abdelkader got a job working for a rich and powerful boss.[13] Nawel Tahar worked in a school cafeteria—the children loved that. In 1967, Samir was born: a little dark-haired baby with shining eyes like black diamonds—and what a personality! "He used to kick me like he was trying to get out." But, although no one could pinpoint why, Nawel was unable to become pregnant again. Three years later, Abdelkader's employer moved to London and asked his chauffeur to follow him. They stayed there for five years. They moved to a little two-room apartment on the third floor of a pebble-dashed house in Edgware Road, London's Arab quarter. How they loved those noisy streets, crowded with a colorful array of people: lost tourists, maps in hand; kebab vendors, their hot wares served in newspaper pages; seamstresses in traditional dress who sold embroidered headscarves for next to nothing; restaurant owners from Lebanon, Syria, Iran, Morocco, Tunisia, Algeria, all offering hookahs along with their hot food; stall owners selling low-priced food imported from the East: huge cans of tuna in oil, crushed olives, candied lemons, sesame seeds/paste/bars, halal meat, halvah imported from Syria, couscous, jars of saffron threads, multicolored spices whose pungent fragrance filled the air, saturating the clothes and skin of everyone around, exotic fruit juices, dates as fat as a child's hand (the most expensive kind, sweet and tender, purchased only for special occasions), dried apricots and pitted prunes (bought by the customers in bulk and used to stuff meat), pistachios, almonds (fresh or salted), and even black rocks from the Atlas Mountains that, when burned, protected you from the evil eye and lifted your spirits. Nawel never tired of going out to

---

13 Erwan Leconte, Franco-British businessman born in London in 1930, whose mother said of him: "When you have a son like Erwan, you can call your life a success."

buy these products, which reminded her of her childhood, or simply to chat with other customers—immigrants like her, homesick and impervious to nonsegregation. They learned English in a few months, thanks to evening classes provided for free by activists from a left-wing charity. Their integration was a success. But when the boss returned to France, Abdelkader decided to follow him again. He felt he owed him everything. *I need you, Abdelkader*—it was the first time anyone had valued him or been grateful to him, and it moved him to tears. They went to live in Grigny in a social housing project that was still relatively clean and safe (it wouldn't last), but, at sixty-four years old, just as Abdelkader was preparing to retire, he was stopped by the police on his way out of the Strasbourg–Saint-Denis Métro station. They asked to see his ID papers. But you didn't say please . . . Oh, we didn't say please! He wants us to say please! Yes, I don't see why you shouldn't call me sir or say please, I haven't done anything/I haven't stolen anything/I haven't killed anyone . . . So you say. Show us your papers! Say please . . . etc. He was taken into custody . . . questioned . . . etc.

"Death by natural causes" was the verdict of the judicial police's report. Attached to it were photographs of his smashed skull. "Before us, XYZ Public Prosecutor of the French Republic at the High Court of ABC, is remanded the person who, upon questioning, provided us with the following personal information:

"Mr. TAHAR Abdelkader

"Born: January 15, 1915

"In: Oulad el Houra (Tunisia)

"Father: Mohammed Tahar

"Mother: Fatima Ouali

"Occupation: manual worker

"Marital status: M

"Children: 1

"We informed him of the charge against him, namely that:

       "On April 4, 1979, in Paris, he did deliberately insult a judicial police officer during an identity check.

       "And, upon his request, we recorded his statement:

> "I contest the charge. I wasn't carrying my papers, the policeman was rude to me he didn't say please etc. so I replied to him but I never insulted him I swear and that's all."

And what followed . . . Abdelkader Tahar yelled, he banged his head against the wall, and went crazy (they say)—case closed.

So there was no doubt about it: Samir could not say "my father" and hope for social advancement; he couldn't say "my father" and expect respect. He couldn't say, "I am the son of Abdelkader Tahar," and be given a better table at a restaurant, or a bank loan, or have people bowing and scraping before him. Ruth could. She entered a room, she said, I am the daughter of Rahm Berg, and they served her, treating her like a princess, finding her charming, finding her a room, a table, a chauffeur, a taxi, finding her an opportunity, a good deal, a cushy job, a plum position, a sinecure, inviting her to lunch, wanting to see her, to see her again, telling her: it would be a pleasure, a privilege, an honor. And, at her side, he too had become a man treated like a god—particularly now, on his birthday . . .

Tahar had not suspected a thing during all those months when Ruth was organizing this surprise party. He watched her now as she welcomed their guests, makeup and hair in perfect order, her body sheathed in a $10,000 dress inlaid with pearls, and thought that he owed her everything. That night, in his thank-you speech, he made public the love and admiration he felt for her—the type of exhibition that he had long considered ridiculous and embarrassing, but whose virtues he had come to appreciate from living in the United States. The guests clapped and cheered; his wife shed tears of emotion; his children rushed up to hug and kiss him. The photographer immortalized this moment. The perfect Jewish family. Snap!

3

Twenty years later, the bomb explodes, causing internal carnage and mortification. It happens just when Samuel least expects it: at forty years old, as he is mourning the man he *should* have been; it comes when he no longer possesses anything, when he has already deliberately trashed every chance he's been given, every ability he had—it's incredible how much determination someone can put into their self-destruction—and here he is now, staggering to his feet in the middle of the night (he looks like he has a limp), heading straight toward the wall, he's going to crash into it, but no, he steadies himself, holds his course, rises to the challenge. And here he is now, frozen before Nina, watching her statuesque body lying on the mattress on the floor, stretched out on her back in a mortuary pose; he examines her closed eyes, the purplish eyelids, dark rings from sleepless nights spent watching him get shitfaced, the mass of black hair that she trims herself with little beveled nail scissors, and her opulent white breasts that he can see through the oversized T-shirt—that obsession she has with always wearing clothes a size too large . . . to hide what? She is *objectively* the most beautiful woman he's ever seen, and every time he looks at her, overtly or surreptitiously, he feels the same shock. He should be used to it by now, after all the time they have been together. You get used to everything, they say—but not that. She is a tall brunette with black-edged eyes, fine features and a stunning, voluptuous body. She has high, rounded buttocks, wide hips, and a narrow waist, legs that are long and amazingly muscled for someone whose main form of exercise is running through the corridors of the RER train station or after her bus. A woman whose every gesture electrifies the most mundane activity. Look at her reading, look at her working. Watching as she enters a room or crosses a street is, in itself, an erotic experience, not because Nina tries to attract the male gaze or wants to be the center of attention—she is too discreet for that, too natural and unambiguous—but because she seems hampered by her perfect physique. There is nothing free about her movements; she can't let her hair down, put on a pair of shorts and a low-cut tank top, and go out for a walk because, if she does, if she acts spontaneously, lets loose her sensuality, she will be whistled at, checked out, heckled, and hit on. And for a girl like her, so detached from the iniquitous laws of attraction, so indifferent to the artificial physics of seduction that rule social life, this is unbearable. It is clear, watching her, that she has no idea what to do with that hypersexualized body of hers, which magnetizes everyone around her, no matter what she does, filling the mind of every passing male with just one desire: to possess her. God should have provided a user manual with a body like that. Such beauty is a prison. Faced with her, no one thinks they are in the same league—and it's true: no one is. She is not the kind of girl to fuck on the first date, or even the second. Not that she's especially prudish—her moral compass does not always point north—but she is all too aware of the devastating effects of her impressive, alienating beauty. And the truth is that she is the one who is most impressed, most alienated by her beauty. So she ties her long, smooth, dark hair in a ponytail, and that is the best thing to do. True, she has just turned forty; she is now entering the climacteric phase; she knows that soon, in a few months or a few years—within a very short, and rapidly shortening, period of time (a time she does not fear the passing of, because age, she thinks, will calm the agitation that her presence always creates whenever she enters a room)—men will no longer turn around and stare. Samuel is watching out for that moment. With a woman like her, you live with the permanent fear of losing her. You see and you understand that a man can take her from you at *any* time; many men have the desire to do it, and perhaps the means too: charm, humor, wealth, whatever . . . The fact is, he *can* take your place. In a matter of months, weeks, hours, he can steal the place you have managed to keep through pity, intimidation, and blackmail, the place that is constantly under threat due to your repeated failures. You are sitting on an ejector seat, and you must use all your charm/cunning/negotiating skills to stay there. You walk, always, on the edge of an abyss. You never feel secure. Even in bed with her, you worry you are not up to the task. You go to bed in a state of anxiety, you sleep uneasily, and you wake up with your stomach in knots. Being married to a woman like this is like driving an armored truck containing millions of dollars in cash while running a high fever: Concentrate! There are bank robbers lurking in the shadows, everywhere, waiting to shoot you in the head so they can make off with the loot. What you have, they want—and more intensely, more powerfully than you do, because as yet they have never touched it, never possessed it; they don't know what it is to have a woman as beautiful as that. If she were a spy, she could obtain state secrets simply by laying her head on a pillow. But she is not aware of her power. Whenever she enters a room, she slouches slightly, lowers her eyes . . . and yet it makes no difference: she still lights up every corner, hardens every prick, and this is what terrifies Samuel: losing her . . . (And he *is* losing her, he can feel it, so why does he suggest to her, as soon as they have switched off the television, that they do some research on Samir?) *Get the laptop—let's see what we can find on him.* And now here they are, sitting next to each other, eyes fixed on the screen like two students cramming for an exam. Samuel googles the words "Samir Tahar" and reads the following question: *Did you mean: Sam Tahar?* Within seconds, dozens of links appear on the screen—professional contact details, interviews, references to current legal cases. No Facebook or Twitter profiles.

He clicks on each link, prints each document. He discovers

that Samir got his master's in criminal law from the University of Montpellier and joined the firm Lévy et Queffélec, where he worked for two years before taking over the branch they opened in New York. Samuel googles *Levy, Berman and Associates.* Having passed the bar exams in Paris and New York, Samir made his name representing an American firefighter who was seriously burned while rescuing victims of the Twin Towers attack, and two families of soldiers killed in Afghanistan. His name is also often mentioned in relation to lawsuits brought by feminist groups; in fact, he has represented several gang-rape victims. He also learns that Samir is married to Ruth Berg, the daughter of Rahm Berg.

On Wikipedia, he finds this article:

Born in Jerusalem on May 4, 1945, Rahm Berg is an American businessman, former president of the RBA Group, listed on the Fortune Global 100. He is also one of the world's biggest collectors of modern and contemporary art.

His first name, Rahm, means "high" or "lofty" in Hebrew. His mother, Rebecca Weiss, is descended from a long line of ultra-Orthodox rabbis. His father, Abraham Berg, born in Jerusalem, is a former member of Irgun, a paramilitary Zionist group active in Palestine and then in Israel between 1931 and 1948. He emigrated to the United States with his family in the late 1950s.

Rahm Berg is a fervent supporter of the "Jewish cause" and of Israel. He has financed several artistic projects and, in particular, one major exhibition entitled "Guilty Silence" at the Somerset House gallery in London.

When he types "Sam Tahar" into Google, he notices something he missed the first time around. The search engine provides the most-searched-for combinations involving his name. Samuel reads:

sam tahar lawyer

sam tahar new york

sam tahar jew

They are dubious to begin with—they know that the description "Jew" is often attached to famous people on Internet search engines—but as they open the links, they realize there can be no doubt. "So Samir's either pretending to be a Jew or he's become a Jew—that's pretty clear, don't you think?" "Yes," says Samuel coldly, apparently troubled by this revelation. "You think he converted?" Nina asks. "It's possible . . . *Anything's* possible where he's concerned." The two of them are suddenly struck silent by a large portrait of Samir in an American magazine. Caught by the lens of a famous photographer, he is posing in a black suit and white shirt, his face aggressively lit from below, as if to underline his importance and his duality, suggested by the article's subtitle: *God or the Devil?* Above the full-page article runs the headline *WHAT MAKES SAMI RUN?*, while the piece itself, written by a young American novelist,[1] is part of a series of profiles entitled *Rising Stars*, highlighting the upward trajectories of leaders in various professional fields. Samuel's English is not good, but Nina's is. "Give me that," she says, grabbing the laptop and placing it (underside hot and motor whirring) on her knees. As she reads, she translates for Samuel. But after only a few seconds, her face tightens and she goes silent. "What is it? What does it say?" Samuel

---

1 Samantha David, twenty-eight, author of the political novel *The Reconciliation*. Has also written works of erotica under the pseudonym Lola Monroe.

asks. Nina does not reply. She reads on, incapable of dragging her eyes away from the screen. "Tell me what it says!" Samuel shouts. He's losing control now, this is torture, he's about to crack. "Tell me what it says in the article! Why have you stopped translating?" Nina remains silent. She has to read the piece three or four times so she can fully understand what's at stake and decide her strategy. He grabs her shoulders and gently shakes her: "Tell me! Tell me! What does it say?" But she only looks at him, her mouth half open, without making the slightest sound.

4

Here they are now, the Tahars, walking hand in hand through the main entrance with a complacent, seen-it-all look on their faces while the night watchman[1] assigned to guard their building checks them out with a mix of fascination and contempt. Later, he will describe them to his wife as "those rich bastards," but for now he's all smiles—good evening, ma'am, good evening, sir, laying it on thick in search of a tip. It's an importunate sort of obsequiousness, and Tahar will end up slipping him a few bills, but not now because—tough luck—Ruth's cell phone starts ringing: it's her father, wanting to congratulate her again, tell her how proud of her he is, etc. They take the elevator—Ruth's father still talking—and enter their apartment, and finally she is able to hang up, after thanking her father ten times over. (And Samir finds himself wondering just how much input this man had in the organization of his party, hoping the answer is not too much because he can't stand the idea of being indebted to his father-in-law again.) *One last drink before bedtime?* he asks his wife. But no, she's had too much to drink already and she's tired. "I can't believe you still have so much energy. I feel like I've kissed so many people tonight that I must have caught every germ in Manhattan!" But there's no way he can sleep now—it must be the excitement, the emotion. Before going to bed, she hands him the large white envelope

---

1 Marc Costanza, the security guard for building number 23 on Fifth Avenue, is forty-five years old, the son of an Italian immigrant. Born in Little Italy, in New York, he quit school very early to work in the family shoe repair store. Now he works as a night watchman and is taking acting classes. His ambition? "To be the next Al Pacino."

containing the list that she left at Ralph Lauren. He can't resist opening it in front of her and remarking on the amount of money each guest paid. "Stan, that son of a bitch—I made him who he is and all he gets me is a hundred-and-fifty-dollar scarf. Dylan gave fifteen hundred euros—I hope he didn't hand it over in cash," he jokes. "You have enough clothes to last you until you're fifty," Ruth says. And then, after kissing her husband, she moves off toward the bedroom. Samir watches her slim figure vanish down the hallway, holding her precious high heels by their straps in one slender hand, her bare feet gliding delicately over the carpet like the ballet dancer she must once have been, back in her childhood when, idolized by a father who saw her as a creature of earthly perfection, she had tried out every single activity a wellborn girl ought to try: ballet, music, and foreign languages, essentially. The results had been beyond even her father's expectations: just look at the way she walks, stately and supple; admire her posture, her virtuosity at the piano; the ease with which she expresses herself in German, Hebrew, even Japanese, which she learned quite late, purely for the pleasure of being able to read haikus untranslated.

Samir watches her and instantly feels regret for having bedded so many other women, for having cheated on her whenever the opportunity has arisen, a slave to the irresistible urges of his nature, a hostage to his obsessions, to his own body which freely possesses/enjoys/desires whatever it wishes, sating his fantasies with a liberty that both distresses and impresses him. It is stronger than he is. The way he behaves toward women is offensive, he knows: ready to *do it* at the drop of a pair of panties, incapable of self-control; in public, in private, always on the alert, checking out every woman who enters a room, searching for that spark in their eyes. Sometimes he even spots them in a newspaper, on TV, and writes to them, inviting them to lunch—*I love your work*—novelists especially, looking at their photographs in the literary pages of *Vanity Fair*. "Doesn't it scare you?" Berman would ask, each time he discovered some compromising liaison. "Sure, of course it does. I'm scared all the time. Scared of losing my wife, my family. Scared of falling in love. Scared that one of these girls will pester me afterward, cry rape because I didn't call her back. I'm scared of catching a disease—I know, I know, you've told me before, it's crazy not to take precautions: it's irresponsible, inexcusable, I'm endangering my wife, my life . . . I might lose everything for ten minutes of pleasure. Ha, are you shocked? Well, let me shock you even more . . . sometimes it doesn't even last ten minutes. And I hate myself afterward. I'm filled with regret, with guilt. I'm terrified of what might happen. But don't you see? Desire is so much stronger than fear, so much bigger: fear just shrinks to nothing beside it. Every time, I tell myself not to do it again, to control myself, but it's stronger than me. As soon as I see a girl I like, a girl who excites me—and she doesn't have to be beautiful: she can be plain, common, coarse; sexual attraction has nothing to do with beauty— anyway, as soon as I see someone I desire, I dive right in. You think I'm addicted? Yeah, you're probably right. But what am I supposed to do about it? Suppress what I feel? It'll happen naturally as I get older, won't it?" Berman has already warned him about this several times: "In the U.S., you have to control yourself, you have to restrain yourself. Don't you understand that? You will, believe me. This isn't advice—it's an order. Do not covet your neighbor's wife. Don't even look at her. Avoid being alone with her. I don't care if she's sexy or if she comes on to you, you have to say no. Talk to a shrink. Talk to a friend. Talk to me. Take deep breaths. Take a tranquilizer. Take a cold shower. Whatever it takes. Never let desire get the better of your conscience, your morality, because in this country, morality rules everything. Your morality is what will determine your future in American society. Lose your morality and you'll lose your job, your wife, your kids' respect, everything. Does that shock you? Then live somewhere else. Go back to France, where people's private lives are private. François Mitterrand managed to lead a double life—two women, two families. You could do the same." But this is impossible. Unthinkable. Tahar wants to stay in New York. His life is here, his career and family are here. He loves the life he leads here. He loves his job. And, in his own way, he loves his wife. But married life—with its strictly fenced-off codes and rules, its well-worn and signposted paths—is not for him. Life with Ruth is so calm and tranquil, but Samir needs adrenaline, danger, in order to feel alive. And this means limitless sex. Even age is not really a limit. Hearing this, his partner loses it. This is Samir's weakness: seventeen-year-old girls who look like they might be twenty-two, made up like inflatable dolls, teetering on five-inch heels borrowed from their mothers or bought cheap online, the girls saying they'll probably never wear them, and then, next day, wearing them out to a club. They want men to find them attractive. They want men to look at them and think: *Whoa! She's the sexiest girl I've ever seen!* Samir thinks this, and says it too. And generally it works. They have two or three drinks and a conversation that invariably revolves around what kind of music they like or which TV shows they've seen recently, and then they do whatever he wants. Tahar has a theory about this: a girl of fifteen or sixteen is just as mature as a girl of eighteen. Sometimes he even goes further: "No one wants to talk about this, but I'm going to tell you the truth," he told Berman. "I'm in favor of lowering the age of consent." "Thank God you're not running for office!" his partner replied. Tahar doesn't try to hide it: he likes ogling girls as they come out of high school, especially the French High School of New York. "I sit in a café and I watch them. I pick out the most sensual and mature ones—you can spot them right away—and I shoot an imaginary movie. I'm behind the camera and in front of

it too. I see myself in action, seducing them, kissing them, fu—"
"Tahar, shut your mouth! I don't want to listen to this shit! Even
hearing it is a crime. So shut the fuck up or I'm out of here!" Berman yelled. But Tahar went on: "What's the big deal? How does it
harm anyone, as long as they're consenting? That's all that matters:
they *want* to do it! I'm not talking about raping them . . . They're
not exactly shrinking violets, believe me! In fact, they're a lot more
forward than most women my age. And yeah, I do sometimes fuck
older women—but not often, because they're so damn complicated. Age makes them fragile: they want reassurance all the time,
and I can't stand that. That's not why I'm there, you know? When
I'm with a really young girl, I feel totally desired. They go over-
board to prove they're women and they love it. I'm always quite
moved by their little excesses. They don't understand that this is
not how it's done, you see: they don't see anything artificial about
framing their ass in a garter belt, for example—they don't even
know how to wear it properly; they probably bought it on sale at
Victoria's Secret with gift vouchers they got from their grandpar-
ents for their birthday. They're not embarrassed to wear glitzy ac-
cessories in flashy colors, and that's what I like about them: they
haven't yet been perverted by the mechanics of sex, with all its
codes and rules, its obsession with performance. They're separate
from all that; they're like kids with their noses pressed to the store
window, and I find that touching." Hearing him talk like this, Berman called him a pedophile. "Do you really not understand what
I'm saying, or are you just pretending not to understand? It's not a
question of age—it's a question of sexual maturity." He couldn't
give up sex. He had tried suppressing his urges; he'd seen a shrink,
who'd prescribed tranquilizers; he'd even seen a rabbi—yes,
seriously—who had recommended that he be discreet, choose
times and places that made it less likely he'd be caught, places far
from home. Never in public. Never in daylight. One thing he never

told Berman: once a month he dressed entirely in black and went to a cheap hotel full of whores, where he had sex with girls who called him Samir. He was not the kind of guy to pay a call girl a thousand bucks an hour—"Are you kidding? They're charging the same rate as me, and I did eight years of study!" He promised to be careful. In the United States, his partner had repeatedly warned him, you get a trace of your semen on a woman's dress, blouse, underwear, or T-shirt and you are socially dead. "In some ways, Bill Clinton paid for everyone's sins!" Tahar knows all this. But nothing can hold him back completely, and when, that night, he receives a text from Elisa Hanks[2]—a tall, voluptuous blonde who works for the New York prosecutor's office and whom he met during a trial—he can't resist. Now, having just taken off his pants, shirt, and shoes, he is standing on his vast terrace overlooking Central Park, a glass of vodka in his hand, a cold wind whipping his face. Leaning on the railing, he admires the skyscrapers rising into obscurity like control towers. The Hanks girl has sent him a text wishing him happy birthday; he thanks her and asks what she's up to—no woman sends a text as bland as that in the middle of the night unless she has something in mind—and, bingo, she replies immediately with a sexually loaded message that he has no trouble decoding. Then she asks if he's near his laptop because she wants to chat with him on Skype. He knows what she means, but he daren't go back to his office to switch on his computer so he can check out this girl as she undresses for him on-screen. What does she have to offer him, after all? Big tits—he's already noticed them.

---

2 Elisa Hanks had not always wanted to be a lawyer. Until the age of seventeen, she had been destined for a career as a ballet dancer, but a car accident left her paralyzed for two years. So she gave up her dream and enrolled in a law degree program, on the advice of her father, the lawyer John Hanks, who was hoping she would take over his firm—which she did, without much enthusiasm, ten years later.

But what else? Long blond hair that she always wears in a bun . . . God, he'd like to see it let down. The vision of that girl naked, hair falling down over her breasts, excites him so much that he unties the belt of his monogrammed bathrobe, pulls it off his shoulders, and lets it fall to the floor. He has a sculpted body, ripped from all his athletic activity (he's proud to say he has the same private trainer as Al Gore), and his tanned skin contrasts with the whiteness of his expensive boxer shorts. Slowly he aims the camera on his cell phone at his boxer shorts, which are bulging with the proof of his excitement, then takes a picture. He sends it as an attachment, making certain that the addressee really is Elisa Hanks. Then he waits. His phone vibrates again. He waits for a moment, letting his excitement rise. Finally he reads the message he has just received. But, this time, the name on his screen is not the one he expected.

The message is from his mother.

5

Article published in the *New York Times Magazine,* February 22, 2007:

Above the desk, on the wall of his sober, elegant office, are two Robert Mapplethorpe photographs: in the first, a naked woman in black leather gloves is aiming a revolver; in the second, a man shot in profile, tattooed and muscular, is wielding a knife. A taste for provocation? In the straight-and-narrow world of the law, Sam Tahar cuts a mysterious and slightly sulfurous figure. This olive-skinned man, who looks like he's just walked off a set of *The Godfather*, has a secretive nature bordering on paranoia. The first thing he says to me, with an enigmatic smile, is: "You won't find out anything about me."

And yet, the story of his rise—from his birth in 1967 to parents who were literature professors—is undoubtedly intriguing. Arriving in the U.S. in the early 1990s, he has become, in less than fifteen years, one of the most high-profile lawyers on the East Coast. His critics would argue that his marriage in 2000 to Ruth Berg—daughter of Rahm Berg, one of the richest men in the country—is not unconnected to this fact . . . But after two hours of conversation during which he reveals himself to be, by turns, irresistibly seductive, brilliantly manipulative and thoroughly professional, it becomes clear that his rise cannot be reduced to that.

"My life has been marked by tragedy," he admits in a rather grave voice. "I've had to fight to get where I am today." Then he adds: "You won't make me say more than that." His biography is revealed succinctly and somewhat reluctantly. In the course of the interview, he lets slip the fact that his parents died in a car accident when he was twenty. That he left for the U.S. shortly afterward to rebuild his life. That his real first name is Samuel. That his parents were North African Jews, secular and politicized, friends with the philosophers Benny Lévy and Emmanuel Levinas.

But the man himself, though perfectly polite and affable, clams up as soon as his personal life is mentioned: "I am my work," he says. Then: "I like people for what they do, not what they are." There are no personal photographs on his impeccably tidy desk, no objects that might betray a private life he is determined to keep private: "I don't like talking about myself, I don't like having my picture taken." And you will find no trace of Sam Tahar on any social network: "I don't have time for that," he says. "I prefer to read books. I love literature, politics. I love words generally." Immediately he quotes a few lines from Martin Luther King's famous "I have a dream" speech: "'No, we are not satisfied, and we will not be satisfied until justice rolls down like waters and righteousness like a mighty stream.'Damn, now I've said too much," he jokes.

But is Sam Tahar really as discreet as he makes out? He did agree to appear on CNN, after all. "That was strictly professional," he objects. "I didn't want to put myself forward, but my client refused to appear." And who are his latest clients? The families of two young soldiers killed in Afghanistan, soldiers who have in a few days become symbols of heroism: "I don't know if I would have the courage to do what they did," says Sam Tahar. To hear his version, his life has been completely unremarkable. His childhood was "uneventful" (meaning: a normal, middle-class upbringing), and he spent several years in London (which explains his almost perfect English—although he does have a slight, and very cute, French accent, a fact that only adds to his *je ne sais quoi*): "There's really not much to say about me," he concludes, inscrutably. And yet, when you look into his dark eyes, flickering with intelligence and humor, that seems very hard to believe.

Despite his deliberate elusiveness, Sam Tahar is nonetheless a brilliant communicator, a subtle diplomat who has built his career with a determination that is somewhat awe-inspiring. Having studied law in Montpellier, in the south of France, he joined the firm of Pierre Lévy, a famous French criminal defense lawyer. He stayed there for two years. Lévy says of his protégé that he is "intellectually peerless. A very gifted and great lawyer," before adding with a laugh: "And he could seduce a chair leg!"

Yes, Sam Tahar is famously charming—a little too charming, according to some of his critics, who prefer to remain anonymous: "It's simple: whenever he talks to anyone important, Tahar immediately goes into full-on seduction mode." Another detail: all his friends and protectors are thirty or forty years older than him. "He seems to have a thing about gray hair," smirks one of his competitors. "Age is not important to me," Sam Tahar explains solemnly. "I choose my friends based on our affinities, and it's true that I have always had more in common with people older than me. They are more interesting, more amusing than people of my own generation, who are obsessed by one thing only: success."

Pierre Lévy, certain of his protégé's potential, sent

him to the United States, where he passed the bar exam in New York before being appointed head of the firm's newly opened branch in Manhattan. This was where he met his future wife. Ruth Berg opened the doors of American high society to him, but he seems to be more attracted to the ghettos. For, while he may hang out with elderly aristocrats, it's in the Bronx that he finds his clients. He made his name defending a young, illegally employed Mexican waitress who was raped by her employer; two members of the Jewish Orthodox community accused of dealing Ecstasy; a black store owner who robbed a jewelry store, leading to the deaths of two people . . . but his most famous cases are those made in conjunction with feminist groups, representing teenage gang-rape victims. "Being a lawyer does not mean proving your client's innocence. It means taking apart your opponent's arguments," he explains. To his critics, who accuse him of opportunism and always going for high-profile cases, he replies with a quote from Sun Tzu's *The Art of War*: "If you wait by the river long enough, the bodies of your enemies will float by." When you mention his success, however, he quotes a line that he attributes to JFK (though I can find no evidence that Kennedy ever said it): "The art of success consists in surrounding yourself with the best." I say he seems to love political speeches, and he admits: "If I hadn't been a lawyer, I would have loved to be a speechwriter for a great statesman." In his office library, there are autobiographies, interviews and documentaries retracing the key moments of French and American political life. I ask him which of these great men he would like to have met, and he instantly replies, "René Cassin," the man who wrote the Universal Declaration of Human

Rights in 1948: "In his acceptance speech for the Nobel Peace Prize, he said that people should recognize that they cannot work efficiently on their own, that they must feel supported by the understanding and determination of everyone else. That's an important idea for me, as I've really built myself through encounters with other people." So is he really such a shadowy figure? I doubt it. Watching him disappear quickly when our interview is finished, I think of the title of a book by Budd Schulberg: *What Makes Sammy Run?*

6

Nina translates the article for Samuel, without dwelling on the details. He isn't fooled, however: "All right, I get it . . . You think I didn't understand that he remade his own life by pillaging mine? He calls himself Samuel and claims he lost his parents at twenty in a car accident . . . that's *my* story. I left the two of you together and went off to bury my parents in Israel, and you and he leapt straight into bed! I should have dumped you when I had the chance. I should never have stayed with you after what you did to me. Hang on, I'm not finished . . . He says he loves literature, but how many books is he claiming to have read, that son of a bitch? I bet he never got past page fifteen of *War and Peace*! And the worst of it is, he's making himself out to be a Jew—a Sephardic Jew like my father! You think I'm just going to let him get away with this? Fuck that! I'll tear his bullshit story to pieces!" Nina tries to calm him down: "Does it really matter? It's all in the past. He doesn't live in France anymore. What difference does this make to our lives? What does it change? We've lived together for twenty years without giving him a moment's thought . . ." "What does it change? It changes everything!" "He took two or three bits from your life story, but that's all. He finished his law degree, and you didn't. The career is all his too, so what's your problem?" What's his problem? Oh, he sees where she's headed with this. He is the failure, no doubt about it. What exactly is at stake, right now, in the privacy of their conversation? What challenge? What test? What corruption? Why does he turn toward her and say, in a peremptory, almost cutting tone: "You're going to get in touch with him and see him again"? "What? Are you crazy?" No—the answer is no. She has no intention of calling him, or seeing him again. It's over.

Water under the bridge. She's turned the page. Now they need to move forward together, get on with their lives, but he interrupts: "Listen to me, now. We are going to get in touch with him, both of us [she shouts: "Never!"] and this time I'll see if you really want to stay with me . . ." "What is wrong with you? You're completely crazy!" Nina loses her temper: "Never, do you hear me? I will never see Samir again!" and it's clear what she means: never again, after what happened between them. Neither of them has forgotten the past: it is between them, it is in them, and that threat of his, that blackmail—the only way he found to keep her because he knows (and what is he trying to prove by putting her to the test?) that she would have stayed with Samir if he hadn't attempted suicide: she would have made her life with him, perhaps they would even have had a child—or two, or three—and this idea makes him sick at heart. Twenty years later, nothing has changed. "He's pillaged my life and you don't even care? He has built his life on the ashes of mine and I'm supposed to just lie back and take it?" "I don't understand what you're talking about—what exactly are you planning to do? Meet him? Threaten him?" Yes, he can see himself now, gun in hand, the chamber loaded, finger tensed on the trigger. "This is insane. What's wrong with you, Samuel? Call him if you want and tell him what you think. Or go see a shrink. But don't ask me to see him again." "You're scared of seeing him again, aren't you? Admit it! Are you scared, Nina?" "No." She wishes she could find the words to reassure this broken man, but she can't.

There is something deeply tragic—something that speaks of human fragility—in living with a person whose extreme sensitivity informs every aspect of his relationship with the world, his social place; a vulnerable, unprotected soul, his resistance to brutality being tested in the laboratory of society. "I want us to see him again. Together." And finally she surrenders: she agrees to do what he wants even though, deep down, she knows she will be the one caught in this trap. Twenty years on, she thinks again about Samir. She could have loved him—this is a plausible hypothesis, nothing more. But for a woman like her, so strict in her morals, it is a form of torture. The volcano may have been dormant for twenty years, but all it takes is a single shudder of the earth and lava will spurt from its mouth; get too close and the burning discharge will cover everything.

"What exactly are you trying to do? Test me? It's pathetic, ridiculous . . . You want to know if I still have feelings for him? If I might fall back in love with him? Or are you just trying to get your revenge on him for what he did to you? Yes, maybe that's all it is, after all—bitterness." She's right: he has become a bitter man. He thinks: *Why him? Why him and not me?* He compares himself to Samir, counting up the points that society has awarded them for success. And he loses.

One hour later, the discussion is over. She says, I'm sleeping on the couch. A temporary retreat before her definitive withdrawal. She is moving up the gears—toward a breakup, toward the future. Not him, though. He is sunk in the past, thinking about the evidence he keeps in a folder, hidden at the back of the storage room off the hallway. He waits until she falls asleep and, when the coast is clear, he goes into the hallway. Yes, the moment has come. He pushes open the storage room door with his knee. It gives way. He can enter now, but he remains in the doorway, then takes a step back, repelled by the lingering stench of mildew that impregnates his clothes. So he wraps a scarf around his mouth like a gag and enters the storage room carefully, presses the light switch—but it's broken (as he should have expected), and he remains in murky dimness, tempered only by a ray of light that filters through the window above the door. The light illuminates an army of roaches climbing up the wall in procession, entering the cracks, resistant even to insecticide. He is filled with disgust, but he moves forward anyway, groping with his hands to right and left. He bangs his head into a wooden peg, then ducks down. His hand touches something fleshy, he scratches himself on sandpaper, keeps searching, and finally, under a ladder, sees the pocket folder with the word "PERSONAL" written on it. Rushing, he shoves aside the ladder so roughly that it almost hits him in the temple—but he catches it just in time and finally manages to grab the folder and get out of the storage room. His T-shirt is covered with dust and whitish threads; he rubs off this detritus with the back of his hand, like a lizard shedding its skin. In the living room, he approaches Nina: *Are you asleep?* She doesn't reply. He gently shakes her: *You're not asleep—I know you're not.* She's as tortured as he is, lying on her back like a patient on an operating table, body open to the surgeon's sharpened scalpel. Samuel sits close to her, tries to kiss her, holds her and presses himself against her, but she refuses, holds him back, then opens her eyes, stares at him without tenderness, and pushes him away so violently that it shocks him. This is dangerous—she has woken the beast inside him—but she knows how to handle it. She has learned how over the years: never full-on, never during an attack; you have to know how to get past the beast, to the man behind it. So she tries to bring him closer to her . . . but it's no good. He is beyond psychology, beyond reality, he is desperate, and all she can do is look into his eyes as he takes off his nightshirt, mounts his assault. Again Nina refuses and, as he begs her, she slips away, jumps off her improvised bed, and runs toward the bathroom. Locking the door behind her, she tries to forget that he exists. Ten minutes later, dressed in a gray sweat suit, she goes outside, calling to him: *I need to get some fresh air.*

The door bangs as if blown shut by a gale. The crack is so loud, Samuel wonders briefly if it's broken, but he doesn't get up to check: he is obsessed by the past, by Samir, and Nina is now nothing more than a shadow in the background. Anyway, who cares if it's broken? he thinks, sitting on the threadbare couch and opening the folder. Inside is a pile of documents. He glances at the first few: his baccalaureate diploma (passed with flying colors); a philosophy essay with the title *Is a Sudden Awareness of the Truth Always Liberating?*; and three school reports from his final year. On the last of these, he reads the principal's evaluation: "An intelligent, sensitive student," and then, beneath this, his abrupt conclusion: "SUCCESS AWAITS." Samuel wonders whether he should laugh or go out and find this principal—who may well be dead, of course, after all these years—and say to him: Look at me, look what I have become. He might even threaten the old fool—some prophet he turned out to be! He puts the report on the pile to the side and continues his search. He discovers several letters that he sent to his parents, the postmark indicating that he was in Meaux at the time, at a summer camp organized by a Jewish scout movement for boys, the Eclaireurs Israélites de France. To his parents, he wrote: "I love you" and "I miss you"—he doesn't remember ever having been capable of saying those words. There are also some old Métro tickets; a torn copy of Kafka's *Letter to His Father*; a booklet containing the principal Jewish prayers in Hebrew; a broken cassette tape and a pair of damaged earphones; school photographs, family photographs. Samuel goes through the folder methodically. At the bottom, inside a black cardboard envelope, he finds them: five newspaper cuttings. A couple have been glued to a sheet of A4, the others are loose. All have the same headline:

Law student attempts suicide in class

What happens after this? He has no memory. Maybe he drank, fell asleep, but in any case when he wakes up, Nina is in their bed and the documents have vanished. She smiles at him, asks if he's slept well. Something has changed, he can tell: she is no longer against his idea; in fact, she seems amused by it. Does she want to test out her powers of erotic attraction, twenty years later? Is it the danger that excites her? The possibility of love? Of history repeating? She borrows some clothes from a stylist who works at one of the catalogues she models for: the designs are simple, the materials cheap (rayon, acrylic), but she likes them. All she has to do is find the right size and pick out her favorites—the ones that have been withdrawn from sale by management because they weren't popular enough. Nina buys a large plastic bag with a zip and arranges her chosen clothes inside it. When she gets home, she places her things on the living room table and puts on an old Otis Redding song. "Are you ready?" Amazement in his eyes: "They lent you all those?" She tries on a black dress in fake lace, a red ruffle dress, a green dress with a fitted waist . . . it goes on for a long time, this fashion parade. Samuel undresses in turn and she passes him a suit. "Look at me!" She changes again, slipping on an ultra-tight black number that she wears like a second skin. The two of them are transformed as they admire themselves in the mirror. They look so elegant, parading and strutting around the apartment, like movie stars. They take selfies together. Dressed up/in swimwear. Indifferent/in love. Then they store the images of their fake success on their laptop in a folder entitled *Us*.

The lure of exhibitionism. On the Internet, they seek out elements of their mystification and create accounts on various social networks in case Samir googles them.

Lie.

Write that you work for a bank, a publishing house, a television channel.

You love traveling, movies, books.

You have ambition, friends, contacts. Show your influence. It's a game. Nina scrolls through a series of photographs displaying all her artificial glory; she rereads each piece of information, polishes, cuts. Finally, she chooses her profile picture. Her eyes edged with kohl, complexion illuminated. It excites her to play at transformers, and to find she is so good at this new game. The genie is out of the bottle now—Samir is no longer the only one with the power of reinvention.

7

He's too excited, so Samir first opens the message sent to him by Elisa Hanks. "Hugely promising!" she has written. "Let's meet somewhere." He hesitates before replying. He is desperate to get together with this girl in the efficiency he rents on the top floor of a building located a few blocks away from his office, a minimalist fuckpad that he found about one year after his wedding, when he realized that he would *never* be faithful and that he ought to organize his sex life within parameters that he himself had defined, in a place chosen for its discretion, rather than running the risk of being caught *in flagrante delicto* coming out of a hotel room or kissing on the street, with witnesses everywhere, perhaps even private detectives, hired by his rivals. He thinks of all the things he could do to this girl if he could find the strength to leave his apartment: it is nearly two a.m. and he is tired and a little drunk. But Elisa Hanks is insistent. She sends him another text: "Damn Sam, you are full-on sexy!" She is one of the most influential women in New York and she is creaming her panties for him—it's maddeningly sexy to a guy like him, someone whose biggest turn-on is overturning the balance of power. *And* she's hot! That severe look, with her hair always up in a bun or in braids, dressed in perfectly tailored clothes, always in dark colors (black or navy blue); a well-bred American girl who never forgets to take the day off work so she can prepare the Thanksgiving turkey herself, never wears lipstick, allows herself only one brand of cologne (made by Amish women), would never miss church on a religious holiday, but who has no objection to being fucked by the young wolves of the New York bar—Jews by preference, with unpronounceable names, the kind of men her father always warned her about. Samir waits a few minutes before sending her this message: "Keep your pussy warm for me—I'm on my way!" He goes back into the apartment, puts on pants, a shirt, and shoes, and exits noiselessly. Ruth is asleep. She must have taken a sleeping pill, so there's no chance she'll be waking anytime soon. By the time he picks up his car keys from the valet,[1] he has completely forgotten the message from his mother.

Ten minutes later, he is standing in front of the door to his efficiency. He sent the girl his address by text, and she is waiting for him there, dressed in a little cotton spaghetti-strap dress. He pushes her inside, kisses her, unties her hair, slides the straps off her shoulders, and takes her—all of this lasts no more than a few minutes. They lie on the couch for a moment afterward. Elisa Hanks smokes a cigarette. Damp blond hairs stick to her face. Tahar turns toward her, borrows her cigarette, and takes a few drags before returning it. And it is then, as he turns, that she sees the scar on his neck. She hadn't noticed it before. But just as she is about to touch her fingers to the wound, Samir grabs her hand rather roughly: *Don't touch me!* He gets up from the couch and quickly dresses, his expression strangely blank. She doesn't give up: she asks where he got the scar, but his only response is to order her to leave *right now*. "Already? But I just got here . . . I thought we could hang out for a while." "I'm tired and I have an early start tomorrow," he says, starting to pick up the room. The girl sits up, covering her breasts with her hands. He can see that she's upset, can sense she's on the verge of tears. She puts on her dress and gets to her feet. For a moment, she stands there, motionless, in the middle of the room, as if waiting for something, while he continues to tidy the room with fanatical care, placing the cushions in a perfectly symmetrical

---

1 James Liver, forty-three, a poker player who dreams of winning the big prize that would "change my life."

arrangement, scrubbing at a stain on the coffee table, picking up a fallen hair clip and handing it to Elisa: *Here, this is yours.* But he's wrong—it's not hers. She doesn't wear hair clips. It must belong to another girl, the one before her. When was that? A few hours ago? Yesterday? A display of jealousy—exactly what Tahar hates most. He can accept such fits from his wife, but from this girl he barely knows, to whom he owes nothing? No chance. He moves toward her, brushes a lock of hair behind her ear, kisses her on the cheek rather coolly—a stranger to her body, to her odor, to everything that, a few minutes earlier, had driven him to a rage of desire. Why bring emotions into something that lasted only a few minutes and that neither of them will even remember a year from now? At the door, though, she still has to ask: "Will you call me?" "Sure, sure," he says distantly, secretly furious. Anyone who makes demands on him, who questions him, he automatically eliminates from his life. As soon as she's gone, he airs the room and finishes tidying it. Then he leaves. A police siren screams through the night. He smokes a cigarette as he walks to his car, and it is only behind the wheel of his Aston Martin, driving at eighty miles per hour, that he remembers the message his mother sent him a few hours earlier. At a stoplight, he grabs his phone and finally reads her text: "Samir, call me back, I beg you. It's about your brother."

8

How his mother can write "your brother," Samir has no idea. He knows nothing about this person, doesn't want to know anything. He is not his "brother" but his "half brother"—they do not have the same father, or the same identity. For him, this man is nothing, he is a stranger. He is twenty-four years old and looks/acts about eighteen. He still lives with their mother. A tall, thin man with reddish blond hair and blue eyes: a European type, nothing like Samir at all. Whenever she was with him, his mother (dark hair, black eyes) would always be asked: "Are you the babysitter?" "No, I'm his mother." And Samir had to reply: "He's my *brother*—François."

Three years after the death of his father, in the first months of 1982, his mother discovered she was pregnant. By whom? How? She didn't say anything to begin with: she hid her pregnancy, vomited secretly at night or out in the street, cried alone and in silence. She bought baggy clothes, size XL—ponchos, lots of black—and claimed she was getting fat: it was stress-related, hormonal. She covered the dark rings around her eyes with thick layers of foundation, but it did no good: they stayed purplish, like bruises, while her legs became heavy and swollen, in spite of the support stockings that her pharmacist recommended. She was on her feet all day long. Her employers noticed nothing, or pretended to notice nothing: they didn't want to have to give her a day off, an hour of rest. As she came toward the end of her pregnancy, however, it finally became impossible to hide. She might give birth any day—on the sidewalk, in the bus, in the dirt, like a dog . . . Samir had seen that happen once: a little, short-haired, blood-smeared mongrel, hiding behind the trash cans, three or four damp puppies curled up beneath her. He must have been eight years old at the time. He had wept with rage. Later that day, he saw the bitch wandering the streets alone. Apparently the garbage collectors had thrown the puppies into the dumpster, laughing as they did so, all of them crushed together in a little mass of flesh, and the same thing might happen to her if she didn't say something. It could happen at any moment—and then what? Samir found some papers in her underwear drawer: her maternity folder, containing ultrasound images, blood tests, etc. He was so shocked, he made her confess, holding the pictures up to her, and she whispered (tearfully): "Yes, I'm pregnant." Then, a few seconds later, in a solemn voice: "That's all I can tell you for now." "That's all you can tell me?" A single mother, in the ghetto . . . he feels ashamed. They'll be a target for the prudes now, the religious freaks, the Islamists— there are more and more of them around these days, watching over those they consider too modern, too free, those who expose too much bare skin. Opprobrium is guaranteed. They have to get out of here, and fast. They steal away one night, like thieves. Not a word of goodbye. The neighbors will be gossiping about this for months. Samir has no idea where they're going: his mother won't tell him until they get there. All she says is that they will live in Paris "from now on"—that phrase speaks of change, a break from the old, a promise of the new. Pumped with excitement, they carry their suitcases and Tati bags onto the Métro. The bags are worn and frayed. People stare at them as if they're gypsies. In silence, they eat the tuna and candied lemon sandwiches that Nawel made, checking every ten minutes that they are still on Line 10. They get off at the Porte d'Auteuil station, as the woman from the RATP explained to them: she took pity on them when she saw them standing in front of the map on the wall, their faces showing panic like children lost in the woods. *We're almost there.* They bump shoulders as they heave the bags—no wheels, loaded with their poverty—along the sidewalk. Samir takes the heaviest ones:

Nawel is weak now, her belly huge. "This is it." She points to a tall building in cut stone, decorated with marble statues. The place is luxurious! Samir's never seen anything like it. *This is where we're going to live?* There are no names on the intercom, only initials. Samir is impressed. They enter the lobby and he goes into raptures—have they won the lottery or what? But disenchantment sets in quickly. There is an elevator, but it's private: you can only enter it with a key. Samir is leaning on the call button as hard as he can when a man in his sixties appears and explains that he can't use it: "You have to be an owner, and you have to have paid for the elevator's installation. Anyone who didn't vote for it at the last general assembly has to take the stairs." With these words, he enters the elevator and the door slides shut in front of their eyes. Nawel motions with her hand: *Don't get mad, son. Don't react.* At every landing they reach, Nawel says: "It's a bit higher." By the time they make the sixth floor, they are panting, soaked with sweat, dry-mouthed and damp-palmed: they don't have enough strength even to complain when they discover the place where they're going to live *from now on*: a tiny attic room, ten square meters, the only light source a window in the roof. The ceiling is low, the space divided by exposed beams. They have to lower their heads like penitents as they walk—but what sin are they expiating? Samir says nothing. He looks for the bathroom. *What century is this?* He finally finds it out on the landing, at the end of a dark, narrow hallway: it's a Turkish toilet, the enamel filthy and the stink pestilential. The door has no lock. Samir goes inside, pulls down his pants, and, standing there—legs parted, gaze fixed on the jet of urine to make sure he doesn't get splashback on his shoes—he begins to cry. When he has finished—pissing and weeping—he goes back to the room and helps his mother rearrange things. The advantage of living in such a tiny space is that this does not take long. His mother manages to cook a chicken with olives to celebrate their new home. Ten minutes after she switches off the camping stove, there's a knock at the door. They open it to two students who live in neighboring rooms.[1] In a panic, Nawel apologizes to them for the noise, the smells—*we didn't mean to disturb you*; she spends her whole damn life apologizing—but in fact, they have not come to complain. They were attracted by the aroma, they'd never smelled anything like it, and she invites them in to share the meal. After that, the four of them will often eat dinner together. The students bring drinks and cakes. The food is wonderful, the air warm, and everyone laughs.

Samir has figured it out. The attic room belongs to his mother's boss, François Brunet. He must have bought it to accommodate a young au pair who would give English or German lessons to his sons. He must have bought it to "invest in real estate because it's the only sure bet," or maybe to fuck his parliamentary assistant.[2] Whatever he bought it for, it was not to provide accommodation for his cleaning lady, her son from a first marriage, and his child with her. Samir doesn't ask questions—he is happy to have escaped the ghetto—and enrolls in the Janson-de-Sailly high school, where he is surrounded by spoiled rich kids, Catholics with double-barreled surnames, and bling-ridden Jews. It's like a foreign country and he loves it. He fits in from the first day, as if he's always belonged to this world. He tells the others he's the son of a Saudi business-man, that he has come from Dubai and will be staying in Paris

---

1 David Sellam, twenty-three, and Paul Delatour, twenty-four, fifth-year students at the Université Pierre-et-Marie-Curie. The former dreamed of working in a hospital; the latter intended to take over his cardiologist father's office in the eighth arrondissement of Paris.

2 Linda Delon, twenty-eight, real name Linda Lamort. She changed it because her original name means "Linda Death" in French.

for only two or three years before returning to his palatial home life, his megabucks allowance, his thousand-square-meter house, his servants and sports cars, *Living the dream, man!* He reinvents himself and they believe him. He buys his clothes for peanuts from other kids who are slaves to fashion: they get bored of their latest acquisitions, he takes them off their hands, and in two months he's better-dressed than an American movie star. *Where do you live?* Samir struts across this minefield: things were too tense in the palace—his father has three wives. This explanation goes down very well in the right-wing circles he now frequents. Life is good here in the land of things left unsaid: no one asks him who his father is. Lying is good: what prospects for integration and personal evolution it offers! Life is a fiction, each day a new chapter. And he is the hero of this story. All those possessions he's invented for himself—and his ability to evade blows, no matter how violent the attack. Even he is amazed by this capacity to bounce back. With an imagination like his, he could be a writer, but even now, at fifteen, he is too fascinated by money and the freedom it brings to commit himself to an artistic career, which he feels sure would end up a cage. *I want to succeed/I am going to succeed,* he thinks, *even if I have to invent an entire life to do it.* As he watches his mother struggling under the weight of her baby, slaving away in the tiny attic room, he vows that, one day, he will give her everything.

The night her contractions begin, he is hugging her in front of the TV. It is nearly midnight. She tells him it's time. Unfortunately, the medical students are on duty—no way to contact them—so Samir and his mother put on coats and rush out to the street, where they walk, keeping close to the walls like gangsters. It's dark and his mother is breathing more and more heavily, practically panting. They head to the Métro and then suddenly, halfway down the steps, she collapses. Samir thinks about that dog again—he is afraid she is going to die, afraid he will be left alone, placed in a home—and rage rises suddenly inside him like bile. "Help!" he yells, and people do. Five minutes later, the ambulance arrives. His mother is put on a stretcher. The contractions become more violent: she had forgotten how terrible the pain was—as if she were fighting to the death against a huge, heavy object inside her. A few minutes after that, sirens drowning out her screams, she gives birth in the ambulance, between two firefighters.[3] She weeps with shame. They tell her: it's a boy. She hadn't known; she hadn't wanted to know; she had hoped it would be a boy. The firefighters ask if there is someone they should call—"like the father"—but she shakes her head and says she will do it herself, a little later, *when I feel better, when I have enough strength*, adding inwardly: *to bear his coldness*.

Her boss, François Brunet: a tall, thin, straight-backed man; blond hair and diaphanous skin; always dressed in a black suit and a white shirt with pearl cuff links; and a navy blue (or sometimes burgundy) tie, the only eccentricity he allows himself. Refined, rather foppish manners. With his excellent knowledge of art, music, and literature, he is intellectually commanding, but he is also politically committed, testifying to his highly developed moral conscience. You look at him and you trust him. You meet him and you give him your credit card number. You find yourself alone with him, in a dark alley, and you feel completely safe. You do not detect the predator inside him. You do not perceive the violence, the erotic charge hidden by his straitlaced appearance. He lives with his wife—a tall redhead from the Bordeaux aristocracy—and their three children in a handsome apartment in Place Vauban, surrounded by books and classical music CDs (Bach is his favorite),

---

3 Frédéric Dupont and Louis Minard, both thirty-five, were years later registered with dating sites under the names John Lewis and Ben Cooper.

by cats and contemporary art (his great passion). He addresses everyone as *vous*, even his parents. He has a horror of familiarity, but he doesn't mind being verbally abused during sex.

The day, in the late 1970s, when Nawel turns up for her job interview with this man, he notices her immediately, sitting among the four other applicants. She has the purebred beauty typical of Orientals and he is excited by the voluptuous figure that she hides beneath an overlarge polyester dress she sewed herself. In reply to all of his questions, she replies, *Yes, sir*, or *Very good, sir*. He gives her a permanent contract, secretly hoping she will be his. The very moment she entered his apartment, he thought about having her. His wife, upon seeing Nawel and the other applicants, said: "I would rather hire a Romanian or a Pole: they're cleaner and more discreet than Arabs. But do as you want." And she is the one he *wants*. He questions her, feigns an interest in her, her feelings and opinions, and one night, he asks her to join him in his office. Nawel wants to refuse. She is frightened. But she goes in anyway.

The obscenity of desire. The pornography of origins. What gives him the right to invite her in his office, after her working day is over, and then to lead her into the private salon he has had installed there, this private salon where he meets with journalists, with colleagues, and with women? What gives him the right to talk to her as if they were already intimate, to pace around her like a wild beast sniffing its prey? *I like you, Nawel*, he keeps saying. *I like you a lot.* What gives him the right to kneel before her, to slip his hands under her little black dress and pull down her panties while asking her *not to tell anyone about this*? He tells her to relax and she lies still. He tells her do this to me, do that to me, and she does. But the situation is more ambiguous than it appears. She does these things because she wants to. With him, she feels free. For the first time in her life, she surrenders to the desire of a man who really looks at her. She loves it. She submits. Such docility: it is astounding to a man like him, used to working with strong, politicized women, feminists who never let down their guard and repel all of his attacks. He sees himself, a man of power, kneeling at the feet of this Arab cleaning lady, and he feels humiliated. And he loves that. He is the prisoner of his urges. This dusky maiden drives him mad with desire. She makes him lose his head, his dignity, his sense of calm, and he knows it: there is something orgasmic in this loss of control, this letting-go, for a man like him, raised on the precepts of a strict Catholicism, brainwashed with a bourgeois morality that allows nothing and condemns everything. So she is his flower of the East. What a cliché! Aversion as a sexual stimulant. But it is stronger than him: it crushes him, takes him over, and he can think of nothing else. For five minutes of pleasure with his cleaning lady, he is ready to do anything, even if it means losing his job. *Oh, it's really not such a big deal*, he tells himself: *Just a little servant-screwing, happens all the time*. He hates her for having turned him into this limp and wimpish creature, this underling. That little brunette has overturned the balance of his well-ordered existence, and now he's in a panic.

The only thing that truly calms him is hunting. Three years before he met her, he joined a shooting club in the sixteenth arrondissement of Paris. There, earplugs muffling the noises of the world, his mind concentrated solely on the target, he is able to relax. Around that time, he began traveling in Africa, hunting wild beasts. He loves the color of blood, the smell of it. He has spent his career battling against the death penalty, but he accepts the ambiguity. He loves the contrast between the purity of nature—wide-open sky, rich landscape painted in blues and greens—and the deathly vision of sacrificial corpses, ripped apart, entrails cooling, fur stained red. He enjoys the spectacle of death—a death he caused—and, most of all, he enjoys making love after hunting, feeling the touch of a warm body, just like the warm body of the dying animal on the sun-scorched earth. The body that says nothing. That lets him do what he wants. Once he even fucked a woman with his hands still stained by blood. The remembered afterglow of that mad, primitive act still fills him with pleasure even now. When he travels in Africa, alone or with a friend, he generally has no trouble getting a woman to come to his hotel room; he has his networks there, of simple folks who respect his position, his discretion.

But when he is with Nawel, obsession grips him once again. The more he sees her, the more he wants her. And she's in love with him—you can see it a mile off. Soon he becomes convinced that he must break it off with her, but he doesn't know exactly *how* to do it. When she told him that she was pregnant, he asked her to have an abortion—nicely to begin with, because he didn't want to rush her—and then more firmly, in the hope of intimidating her. He undertook to pay all her expenses and even to compensate her—those were his words—for the injury she suffered. But she could not keep it: one must be responsible, one must act like an adult. She refused. For her, being responsible, acting like an adult, meant keeping the child, whose father she loved. For years, she had believed herself sterile, and now "God" had "given" her a child. Realizing that he was not going to be able to change her mind, Brunet helped her find another job—in a dry cleaner's on Rue Montorgueil—because it was impossible to keep her on under his roof and risk the possibility of his wife asking questions, becoming suspicious. Nawel agreed. She signed the "resignation letter" he wrote for her. She imagined him installing her in a beautiful apartment where they would begin their life together again . . . instead of which she found herself scrubbing at oil stains, coffee stains, bloodstains, semen stains, grease stains, stains that can be

removed and stains that remain, all those dirty things, those stinking things, those revealed intimacies. This was the very opposite
of her dream. This was reality. She worked ten hours a day in a dry
cleaner's: taking delivery of the laundry/noting each item/identify-
ing each stain/sorting the colors/sorting the materials/brushing
the fabric/preparing for stain removal/scraping off dirt/filling
the machines with perchloroethylene/loading and unloading the
machine/checking the fabric/rubbing and rubbing/steam-ironing
with an inflatable mannequin/rechecking the fabric/putting it in
a slipcover—that was her day. Every time she closed up the shop,
she had to fight against the desire to shove her head inside the
dry-cleaning machine and inhale the toxic vapors of trichloroeth-
ylene. The only thing that held her back was the child growing in
her womb. She hardly ever saw Brunet anymore. Until the day the
child was born.

After several hours spent staring at her child, after counting his fingers, checking that he had all his limbs, she called Brunet from the
hospital. "Your son has been born," she told him in a voice no louder
than a murmur, a voice that expressed fragility, fatigue, struggle,
and solitude. He did not reply at first—he let the silence float up
between them—then announced calmly that he would be around
to see them before lunch. At two p.m. he entered the room, holding
a stuffed animal—a blue dog of breathtaking softness, purchased in
the most expensive toy store on Boulevard Malesherbes. He showed
her no tenderness at all, but he took the child gently in his arms, his
hand under the baby's neck, as if this were something he had done
thousands of times before. And then he got a shock. Because the
baby was a tiny version of himself, a perfect replica: white skin, eyes
that would soon turn pale, that little tuft of strawberry-blond hair.
He had imagined the child would be swarthy like its mother, with
shining black eyes (*an Arab face*, he had thought), but seeing that it

was white, and blond, like him, he suddenly relaxed. He could love his son now. "What are you going to call him?" he asked. She looked at him somewhat fearfully, then replied: "François." "Ah," he said, and that was all. He didn't protest. He knew he would not raise this child who bore his name, that he should remove himself from its life, not rename it as he wished. That she could name him whatever she wanted, do whatever she liked . . . He would not acknowledge the child. The next morning, he came one last time to tell Nawel that he would pay her hospital bills and give her two years' salary to "help with the costs of bringing up the baby," as he put it. She could have asked for three or four years' salary and the payment of her rent on the attic room, and he would have agreed: he didn't want a scandal. But she didn't ask for anything. He looked into her eyes for several breaths. There was emotion on his face. He still loved her, he knew. But he told her coldly that he did not wish to see them again—neither her nor the child. He had too much to lose: his peaceful marriage, his children, his political career, everything he had acquired through years of sacrifice.

He was still in her hospital room when Samir arrived, accompanied by the two students, arms filled with presents. Brunet nodded to them, said goodbye to Nawel, and left. In fact, he would go to see them a few more times, in the attic room, but his visits would end after he met a young right-wing activist with whom he fell instantly in love.[4] Two years later, he would ask Nawel to leave the attic room. He did not admit the truth to her: that he wanted a place to meet his mistress, who was also married. He told Nawel that he had to sell it, but that he would continue to pay her child support. Nawel refused—she had nowhere to go, she had no money—and

---

4 Manon Perdrix, twenty-eight, a mother of two who dreamed of a "strong France" and a "big family."

it was him, "once again," who found her a two-bedroom apartment in Sevran belonging to a friend of his. It was all settled in a matter of weeks. François Brunet hired a firm to renovate the attic room and, two months later, not a trace remained to show that Nawel and her children had ever been there.

Samir had never been close to this brother, who did not look like him and whom he had always regarded with a measure of mistrust. He himself was the child of an arranged marriage, maybe even a forced marriage, while the other son was a love child—a child of corrupt desire, transgressive passion. The other son was Western while he remained Eastern—he knew this, it was undeniable, and it drove him mad with rage, with jealousy. So, no, he couldn't stand her writing "your brother." Blood kin? Bullshit. He had chosen his family. His kin was made up of friendships, intellectual and sexual affinities, not the fantasy of a perfect genealogy.

He does call her in the end, though. *She's my mother*, he thinks. And he feels a little ashamed: he has just celebrated his birthday and it never even crossed his mind to invite her. It's impossible: she knows nothing of his life in New York. He decided very early on—even before he was trapped by the lie of his Judaism; yes, even before he started studying law, maybe even while he was still living in the sixteenth arrondissement—that his mother would be an obstacle to his success. The shame of his origins: he did all he could to elude them. He never invited anyone to their apartment and told his mother in no uncertain terms that she must never pick him up from school.

Dialing her number, he feels guilty again. She picks up on the first ring and he imagines her waiting next to the phone for her exiled son's call. "Ah, Samir, my son—at last!" Hearing her voice, her Arab accent, wrenches his heart. "What's wrong, Maman?" he asks. His voice is despondent. You can sense his vexation, his irritation: he would prefer not to talk to her anymore, to sever the cord definitively, but he has never been able to. It is stronger than him. He loves his mother; he feels admiration for her courage, esteem for her resilience; and he feels pain. A life of lies—and for what? "It's your brother . . . I'm worried that he's going off the rails . . ." Hearing this, Samir orders her to be quiet: he knows the line might be tapped. As a lawyer, he deals with sensitive cases; he is careful. Then he changes his mind, reassures his mother: "Don't worry, it'll be okay. I'll try to talk to him." Instantly she is calm. She imagines herself with her two sons—a good place to be—and her tone suddenly becomes lyrical: "I am waiting for you, my son. I want to see you. You are so far away and I miss you so much. So . . . still no girlfriend?" "No, Maman, I don't have a girlfriend. I'm busy with work." "It will happen Insha'Allah. Oh, I almost forgot—happy birthday!" "Thank you, Maman. Goodbye." He hangs up and rushes back to his apartment. He hands the car keys to the valet and, in the lobby, suddenly feels sick. He remembers the evening, his wife, Elisa Hanks's sweaty body. He remembers his brother, whom he hasn't seen for two years, with whom he never speaks, and he feels bile rising up inside him. His body shakes violently and he vomits on the carpet, observed by the night watchman, who asks him if he's okay. No, he's not okay: he's suffocating, bent double, one hand on his belly, breathing hard, in, out, in, out, the stench of the soiled carpet. Then he stands up, takes a deep breath of fresh air, says he'll be fine, and walks quickly toward the elevator—without even glancing back at the employee—thinking how lucky he is that he doesn't have to clean up that shit.

9

The day he asks Nina to get in touch with Samir, Samuel turns up for work as if it is just another day. In truth, though, he knows what he is risking; he knows what he has to lose. But for the past twenty years, not a day has passed without him thinking, *She only chose me because I forced/blackmailed/threatened her, and I need to know if she will stay with me again, now, of her own free will*. This is what is running through his head as he enters his office, where a woman is waiting for him, curled up in a chair and crying her eyes out. This is his life: violence. This is his life: a ten-square-meter office filled with people who come with or without an appointment, who enter and say hello my husband beats me my son beats me I'm here illegally my daughter is pregnant my son is in prison, who say they insulted me they raped me robbed me I'm living on the street, who say I'm on a credit blacklist I can't afford to feed my children I only eat every other day, who say I'm alone I'm a widow(er) I'm old, who say I don't have any children I have ten children I'm dying help me help us, who cry for help, and every time he knows what to do, he finds a solution. He likes being with these people, listening to them, talking to them, calming them down, explaining things to them, going out of his way for them, making phone calls to find them money or a place to live. His life is other people. He likes being useful—it gives his life meaning, it lifts him up—but not this morning, because his mind is full of Tahar, overflowing with Tahar, just thinking about it gives him a headache. So, no, today he doesn't work—he just sits at his desk, head in his hands, and waits for Nina's call. When the day is over, he still hasn't heard from her. It's five p.m. He goes home and finds her lying on the couch, reading a magazine. He walks up to her, kisses her, and asks if she's called Samir. Yes, she did, but he wasn't there—"His secretary said he'd call me back." "That's all?" "Yep, that's all." "So what else did you do today?" "Oh, I never stopped." But he can see, in her worried look, that she spent the whole day waiting for that call.

10

Nina Roche called. Samir pinches himself. He has to read the words three times over to convince himself that he's not dreaming—it really is her name written on this Post-it note. Could it be a coincidence? Someone else with the same name? He leaps to his feet and runs out of his office, charging into his secretary and demanding: "What time did she call? Did she say anything in particular?" "No, nothing." He is trembling. He feels like he's going to faint, to collapse in a rush of emotions.

It must be a joke. It can't really be her. Impossible. Twenty years without a word, and now this? He goes back into his office, sits down, cradles his head in his hands, and laughs quietly to himself. *I can't believe it.* Then he convinces himself that it really is her, that she wants to see him again, twenty years on and she's filled with regret, he feels sure of it now. But how does he feel about it? *Do I really want to see her again after all these years? To see her twenty years older? Has she changed? Why now?* He's trembling, confused. He wants to talk to her right now, out of curiosity, to hear her voice, and suddenly he remembers that he has lied—that he's no longer Samir Tahar, that she must know nothing of his life here, he must never see her again, it's too risky. How would he react if he saw her now, twenty years after she left him? He doesn't call her, but he's dying to. He can think of nothing but her, and then—realizing that it's nearly one a.m. in Paris—decides that he has to call her now or never. It's too strong—he can't bear it anymore—he has to get back in touch with her. He can feel, he knows: *You're going to destroy your own life, your calm, ordered, perfectly structured life*. And yet he says to his secretary, in a voice that barely masks his excitement: "Get Nina Roche on the line. I'll take the call in my office."

He sits in his large black leather chair, one hand resting on the phone, ready to pick up. His heart is banging against his rib cage. The phone rings and he hears his secretary's voice—"Miss Roche for you"—and the next voice he hears is hers: he recognizes it instantly, warm, husky, deep, the voice that used to drive him crazy. All he wants is to hear it. "I'm sorry to call so late," he says in French. "I hope you weren't asleep?" "No, not at all. Happy birthday—I remembered." "After all this time?" "I saw you on TV yesterday, by chance, and I . . ."

You remembered me.

They talk for a long time. On the other end of the line, Samuel listens in, wild-eyed with anxiety, and realizes: this is suicidal, it's madness. He listens to them chat, exchange promises to meet again. She plays the game perfectly—puts her heart into it, and quickly he is thrown off balance. Fear grips him, and he signals with his hand: *Cut it short*. She squints in concentration, holds up a hand—*Hang on*—and laughs again, that openhearted laugh that expresses their complicity, her happiness at having found him again—the horror—and, a few seconds later, she finally hangs up. *You got what you wanted*. He pretends to be pleased: Go and get something to drink, we should celebrate. But when Nina stands up and he sees her from below, standing tall and statuesque, when he sees that heavenly body, the emotion suddenly grips him—and he grabs her by the arm, pulls her brutally toward him, and kisses her, to possess her, to tell her: You're mine. You belong to me. Samuel believes that conflicts are resolved by sexual dominance. Aggression as erotic power. Hostility as fuel for desire. This is the only means he has found to go on. And she lets him do it, although she shouldn't. But it proves nothing, this sudden docility, this unexpected obedience, because on her face is the most awful expression of detachment.

11

He had never expected to see her again. The call was a shock, and now it's all he can think about: the phantasmagoria of love and eroticism conjured by the mere sound of her name. He wishes he could tell her now: I missed you so much, I thought of you often, you still mean so much to me, I loved you, I adored making love with you, and all I want now is to be with you. Suddenly, hearing her voice, he misses her again, feels the ache of her absence with a new intensity. This natural kind of sexual attraction—without the effort required by seduction, without any lines or moves—this raw, brutal passion, is something he has only ever experienced with her. It is unique; he knows that now. And that is enough to make him hound her, to insist: *I want to see you again.* Because he wants her, and can think of nothing else. Maybe he can slowly wear her down, maybe she will eventually give in to him through weariness—it doesn't matter how it happens. *I really want to see you again.* This thought obsesses him, crowds out his mental space to the point where he is caught in a whirlwind of fantasies and erotic images and he finds it almost impossible to concentrate on anything else—work, family life, politics.

Everything else leaves me cold.

Ruth's bourgeois morality. Her concern with convention. Her almost boring constancy; the way she is always where he expects her to be. With her, he has never felt fully himself. He has been merely a perfect simulacrum of masculine archetypes—skillful lawyer, good father, conscientious Jew, loving husband, attentive son-in-law—roles he has always fulfilled with a little too much eagerness, as if he found a subconscious satisfaction in being this man of whom people said, *He has everything*, of whom even his wife could say, *He's the perfect man*. But no matter how brilliantly he invents a new life for himself, it will never truly be his. He has constructed a character the way a novelist does. But with Nina, he feels he could return to the source of himself, to the original version, the essential, Eastern him—to that spontaneity he misses so much and that he rediscovers only during his brief visits to his mother.

Starting the next day, he sends her suggestive messages. He is open about his desire for her: she is all he ever wanted and he will prove it to her: he'll arrive in Paris next Monday at 8:10 a.m. Nina does not show Samir's texts to Samuel; she erases them. This troubles her, and she knows it. He is forward, insistent . . . what can she do? Nina is one of those passive, reserved girls who find in their with-drawal an intensifier to their desires; if he wants her, let him find her, let him take her. But then he asks the question that obsesses him: *Is there someone in your life?*

When he sees the name "Samuel," he feels as if everything disintegrates around him. He feels suddenly fragile, and for a man like him—a strong, virile, self-controlled man—this is a source of suffering; it is proof that he has not paid his debts to the past. He is losing, he can feel it. He is sinking. He had forgotten this awful feeling of uncertainty, the inability to control his emotions, these futile, desperate attempts to reason with himself. Quickly he real-izes that it's too late: he's fallen for her again, head over heels. He calls her. "You stayed with him?" He asks this lightly, ironically, but in truth it is tearing him apart. "Yeah," she replies, "are you surprised?" He hesitates: "No, not really. You should be a saint by now." He hears her laughter at the end of the line and it drives him crazy. "Any children?" "No." He feels relief. If she had children, perhaps he wouldn't be able to insist on seeing her again. On a general basis, he prefers to avoid having affairs with women who've had children: maternity makes them less available, and they never give themselves fully, as if part of their souls remains tied to the child. (Some even go so far as to wear their child's scent—those insipid kids' perfumes that instantly desexualize them.) And he couldn't have stood the idea that one day he would meet the children Nina had with Samuel, and think: She should have had them with me instead.

He wants to know if Samuel is aware that she has called him. *Oh, yes, he was sitting next to me when I saw you on TV.* (And he thinks contentedly: *So he* saw *me.*)

This is the moment she chooses to tell him that she read the interview with him in the *Times*. At the other end of the line, there is silence. So she knows. He tells her he would prefer to talk to her about this face-to-face. "You think I want to see you again?" she asks. He waits a few seconds before replying, then says in a controlled voice: "Of course you want to see me again. And I want it too."

12

In the airplane, Samir puts on his earphones and chooses *No Country for Old Men*, a Coen Brothers movie starring Josh Brolin.[1] But it makes no difference: all he can think about is her, and the moment they will meet again. He would prefer not to have to talk to her—he wants her to be there, waiting for him by the arrivals board, and he wants to take her in his arms, kiss her, and go with her to the nearest hotel so they can make love. Why complicate things? But when he gets to the airport, the only person he finds is the seedy-looking chauffeur sent by the hotel, a little bald guy[2] holding up a sign that reads SAM TAHAR.

---

1 The American actor Josh Brolin has played in over thirty movies. A French journalist asked him if he had ever considered quitting Hollywood and he replied: "People used to say to me: *You're about to make it big!* After ten years, I started replying: *Shut up, man!*"

2 Alfredo Dos Santos, forty-five, has been a chauffeur for ten years. He leads two very separate lives—one in France, the other in Portugal.

PART TWO

PART TWO

1

She is his success. Look at her: so entrancing in her black lace dress, her long hair falling loose over half-bared shoulders. She is the best thing in his life and it's good that Samir knows this, sees it for himself: twenty years on, she is still with him, still just as beautiful . . . Quite a sight, isn't she? Feast your eyes. Even without money, she has been able to preserve her beauty, thanks to her ingenuity. Every day, when the department stores open or at lunch when they are packed with tourists, when overscented salesgirls flit through the aisles waving thin strips of white perfumed paper, Nina goes to one of the big-brand perfume sections and uses all the samplers she can find: anti-wrinkle creams, foundation, eye shadow, serums, and colognes—she chooses the most expensive products and asks for samples, saying that she wants to try them before buying. In this way, she has managed, through all these years, to look after her skin and wear the best fragrances without ever spending a centime. For her hair, she would go regularly to a hairdressing college where the students tested out the latest styles on her. Sometimes she would patronize the African hairdressers near Porte de la Chapelle and have her hair braided for a few euros—into a long, glistening plait that she wore on her head like a crown and that made her look like a princess.

Samir had booked a table for them at the Bristol. He called Nina as soon as he arrived, and she warned him: she was coming, yes, but with Samuel. *Sure, no problem.*

They take the bus, then the suburban train. People stare and whistle at them—*Are you going to the Cannes Festival?* Samuel and Nina laugh. She struggles to walk on her four-inch stilettos, gripping tightly to Samuel's arm and holding herself upright. *We want people to notice us. You should wear your hair like that all the time.* It took her over an hour to straighten it. After that, she went to the manicurist—her nails are blood-red. She did the makeup herself—not too much. She wants to look her age: not older, not like a whore. He holds her close to him and thinks: *This is my wife.* Pathologically possessive? Oh, yeah. There is something puerile and pathetic in the way he boosts his own confidence by parading Nina like a trophy, but he has found no better way of resisting decline. His place in society is down to her; he owes her everything. He is nothing without her—he has persuaded himself of this through the years they have spent together: *If she leaves, I die. If she leaves, I'll kill myself.* He knows this, says it, and yet here he is, running the risk of losing her, testing her in the flame, playing with fire, on a suicide mission.

It is still early when they reach Rue du Faubourg Saint-Honoré, so Nina suggests they walk for a while. He prefers taking her into boutiques—just to look around, not to buy anything—for the pleasure of being welcomed, respected, seen at her side. He asks her to try on a dress with a plunging neckline; under the complicit gaze of the sales assistant,[1] he takes the dress over to the changing room himself. It'll be fine, he tells her, and when she goes inside, he follows her. You're crazy, she says, someone might see us. But this is exactly what he wants: to be seen. He draws the curtain and kisses her. "You're crazy." "Yes, I'm crazy about you."

---

1 Kadi Diallo, thirty-four. The daughter of an African diplomat, she worked as a model for Dior before taking part in a humanitarian mission in Sudan. After three years, she returned to France, where she found this part-time job as a sales assistant. Her ambition is to be manager of the boutique.

2

Samir never feels fear—not on television, not in court, not with beautiful women or powerful men or judges. He is cool, unemotional, and years of speech-making and negotiating have toughened him up even further. But the mere idea of seeing Nina sends him into a panic. All the signs are there: accelerated heartbeat, trembling hands, practically stuttering. This isn't like him at all. What has happened to that self-confident swagger, that winning arrogance? Gone. He is shaking—really shaking. He feels his wrist: pulse throbbing, out of control. Even the blue vein that snakes down his forearm is quivering, for God's sake! He checks himself in the mirror, as if making an inventory. He changes his clothes three or four times—his shirt's too fitted, his collar badly ironed, the color too dark—then orders a whiskey and waits in his hotel room, switches on/off the TV, sits down/stands up, and finally grabs his laptop and googles Samuel and Nina. Nothing but a few profiles on social networks—this reassures him. He checks out their photographs. There are only a dozen of them, but he sees love/harmony/contentment and it revolts him. Nina's still as beautiful as ever, almost unchanged, while Samuel stands alongside her, outshone, a mere shadow. Angrily he shuts his laptop. Seeing them together is unbearable and he no longer feels sure he wants to go down to the hotel bar. He makes a few phone calls, hoping they will clear his mind, and then—five minutes before they are due to meet—finally decides to go downstairs. Time for the confrontation. He exits the room, banging the door behind him. *Calm down*. Walks quickly. But in the hallway that leads to the elevator, he sees a woman[1] from behind who looks like Nina, and emotion pours through him once again.

---

1 This woman's name is Maria Milosz, and her life merits more than a mere footnote.

3

They see him right away. *It's him. Look over there, at the back*—suntanned skin, impeccably styled hair, sitting on the velvet couch, phone in hand, a newspaper open on the coffee table in front of him. They're late, but they don't rush—better to take their time. As they close in on him, they sense his disarray. Samir looks at them too, and judges them instantly (Nina, even more beautiful than her photographs, even more breathtaking than she was twenty years ago—incredible; Samuel has changed, aged, and he thinks: *I'm better than him*). They're standing up and he's sunk in this stupid sofa. The position humbles him, reducing him to nothing, the lowest of the low. He wasn't able to keep her—that woman is the one great failure of his life—and in Samuel's eyes he reads the message: *Look at us. She left you for me. Look at us and suffer.* And boy, is he suffering. His heart's doing somersaults inside his chest and he's walking like a robot remotely controlled by a child or a sadist. He looks like he's going to crash into something. He feels like he's going to collapse. Time has not faded his desire. His whole body is reeling, exuding what he feels. And yet he loved her/had her. And there, the earth trembles, cracks open. He had imagined a gesture of affection, some humor/emotion, good evening, you've changed/haven't changed a bit, a sip of wine, a smile, a fluttering of eyelashes, nothing too disturbing, nothing to shake his cool self-confidence/arrogance. He had imagined a breezy, peaceful reunion, no conflicts or torments, just happiness at seeing each other after all these years, a little nostalgia, for old times' sake. He did not envisage the panic and dread that is rising within him now. He should never have exposed himself to this—should have remained mistrustful, protected himself—but now it's too late: he's exploding inside, he's in pieces, breathing too hard. He's a wreck. He holds out a damp, trembling hand—a hand that expresses his anguish better than any words could—and when Samuel ignores it and hugs him instead, taking him affectionately in his arms (when he hates him), smiling at him complicitly (when they are enemies, and have been ever since Nina first yielded to him), a childish idea fills his head: *One day, I'll take her back.*

They sit down. The ordeal of seeing them together, in love, all smiles. The ordeal of sitting opposite them, seeing them caress each other, limbs intertwined. The ordeal of listening to them recount their personal and social success. The ordeal of feeling close to her and not being able to touch her. The ordeal of being in the middle of a crowd of strangers, in a hotel bar, sitting down, dressed up, respectable, when he wants to be alone with her in his room. The ordeal of thinking about the chaos of his own private life when their happiness is exhibited before his eyes like a whore he can't afford.

Samir examines/scrutinizes/sniffs out the lack of taste, and then, suddenly, he understands. He is the Sherlock Holmes of social codes. He *sees* and he *knows*. What is that oversized, badly tailored suit that Samuel wears like a scarecrow? What are those fake leather shoes? And the plastic sole with the price sticker still glued to it? Maybe Samuel has money, maybe he's a success, but he's a rube. He's dressed up all shiny and tawdry, without any finesse or refinement. He looks him up and down now—*Compare the two of us.* This is the true confrontation, the duel: two gunslingers whipping out their social indicators, two poker players bluffing about what they have in their hands; two men who want the same woman, their eyes meeting, judging, measuring, and analyzing . . . it's a battle, a form of combat. You could cut the tension with a knife! And, in the middle of it all, the woman whose mere presence is the cause of all this sexual tension, this weird electricity. Such creatures are rare. It is not simply a question of beauty: there are plenty of beautiful girls in this hotel bar, perfect bodies perfectly fitted into four-thousand-dollar dresses, girls with sculpted features whose coruscating beauty sweeps all before them. But a woman who captures the light with such intensity, a woman whose erotic power you can sense even at a distance, across a crowded room, a wide radius around her that should be sticker-taped WARNING: YOU ARE NOW ENTERING THE DANGER ZONE . . . you can search for a long time and never find such a woman. Not that she is particularly secretive or reserved, but she seems to be holding something back, as if she is cordoned off, and the man who sees her has only one desire: to uncover what is hidden. What is it like to go to bed with a girl like that? Does she close up even more? Does she let loose what's within her? Samir knows—it's explosive. You go in like a bomb disposal expert, every part of you protected, your features tensed and concentrated, uncertain whether you will get out alive. You go in and you discover that, with a girl like that, you will never really be able to possess her, to make her love you.

He wasn't expecting this—Samuel's offensive presence, his possessive control-freakery, his sickening exhibitionism, *Look at us, we're together*, rubbing it in—and for a man like Samir, used to being the center of attention, it is unbearable. It's unbearable to think that she chose to stay with this loser: a man who can't dress, who talks too loud, a man with dirty fingernails, callused hands, a man who doesn't even wear cologne. So he makes conversation, and Nina starts talking, ordering a glass of wine with a hand signal. She doesn't say she works as a model for Carrefour, but simply that she works "in fashion." No, they still don't have children, but yes, of course they want them. Samir tells them about his life in the U.S., embellishing as he goes along, his success/career/money. It gets to Samuel: his money, the money he wears on every inch of his body. The priceless watch, the leather shoes, the hand-tailored suit, even the corruptive way he hails the waiter with the back of his hand, the way he keeps making more and more demands: to move somewhere else ("It's too noisy here"), to try a different wine ("I don't like this one"), to get a clean glass ("Look closely—you see that stain?"). "You're never satisfied, are you?" Samuel jokes. "I can be—I'm just demanding." Samir tastes the wine the waiter hands him: "This one is perfect—thank you." Nina takes a sip of her own wine.

"Tell us about your life in New York . . ."

"It's exciting. Exhausting."

Samuel stares at him and says: "Paul Morand said: *New York shatters your nerves. No European can live there more than a few months.*"

"He wasn't wrong!"

They lift their glasses and toast their reunion.

"So?" Samir says, looking at Samuel. "Did you ever become a writer? I googled you, but I didn't find anything."

He has good technique, of course. Aggressive questioning is his area of expertise. Samuel replies that he "got into business." Business? Yeah, right. Social work, more like—solving local problems does not make him a successful businessman. He knows this, and tries to stay vague, but Samir won't let go.

"You gave up writing?"

"No, I still write."

"But you haven't been published?"

"No."

"And yet there are so many books published each year. It's incredible. You'd think everyone in France had become a writer, that it's . . ."

"Easy? No, it's not easy. Not for me, anyway."

Nina interjects: "He still writes, but he doesn't send his books to publishers anymore."

"Well, that would certainly reduce your chances of getting published!"

"I googled you too, you know. There's nothing under the name Samir Tahar . . ."

Samir laughs: "It was a mistake. They misspelled my name once, and after that it was reproduced everywhere. Everyone calls me Sam . . ."

"Or Samuel."

"Yeah, sometimes."

Tension crackles between the two of them. You can feel it.

Finally Samuel asks: "So you converted to Judaism?"

"No, no, that was just a misunderstanding because my wife is Jewish."

"You could have. I don't see a problem with you converting . . ."

"My wife is Jewish—that's all."

"I read a big interview with you in the *Times*, you know."

Nina sighs. Samir looks at her, embarrassed. *What is he up to? Is he trying to unnerve me?*

"I need to explain that . . ."

"There's nothing to explain. You used bits and pieces of my life to concoct your own biography! You pillaged my private history and used it to create your own! It's completely insane. How could you do such a thing?"

"What was I supposed to do? Ask your permission? You don't know what it's like with journalists—they want to know everything. I told them what they wanted to hear. Is this why you wanted to see me?"

"Ha, that's very Jewish—answering a question with another question."

"What do you want me to say? That I did it deliberately? Well, I didn't. I just didn't feel like talking about my life."

"And twenty years later, the first thing that comes to mind is *my* life?"

"Well, it did have an effect on me, I guess . . ."

Nina finally intervenes: "That's enough, now. This is getting ridiculous. Samir already told you he didn't mean to hurt you. You just have to take his word for it."

The next moment, Samuel gets to his feet, claiming he has an urgent call to make, and vanishes. Time to put his plan into action. So now they're alone. They don't speak. They look at one another. Language has lost its power. Samir can't take his eyes off her face, her body. He wants to say: *I want you I love you it's so hard to look at you without being able to touch you I have to touch you let me caress you I want to make love to you come with me now*. Instead of which, he says: "It's good to see you again."

"Kind of strange after all these years, isn't it?"

"I wouldn't call it strange. I'd say it was powerful, overwhelming."

She smiles and he feels the desire, once again, to touch her face with his fingers, to stroke her legs. That dress with the low neckline—she wore it to tempt him, didn't she? But he does nothing. Again, he manages to control himself. Keeps his feelings bottled up. A tight lid on the bottle.

"Samuel hasn't changed. He's still kind of neurotic . . ."

"I think he's nervous, seeing you again."

"I'm nervous too. Seeing you."

To conceal her embarrassment, Nina takes another sip of wine.

"How did you decide to move there? You changed your life so completely . . ."

"You should know! I was running away, wasn't I?"

She looks at him, feeling uneasy.

"If you hadn't left me, I'd probably still be here, in Paris."

She laughs: "When I see what you've become, I'd say it was the right decision . . ."

A grin/grimace deforms Samir's face. Suddenly he cracks.

"What the hell would you know? What are you even talking about? You have no idea! I almost went crazy!"

He pronounces these words with such fury that she recoils.

"I can talk about it now with a little detachment, but believe me, at the time, it was the end of the world. Looking back now, I'd say it was the worst ordeal I've ever been through. It took me years to get over it. A simple breakup . . . incredible, isn't it? But nothing bothers you."

She doesn't reply. She looks away, sees Samuel in the distance. He is pretending to make a phone call, overacting a little in his desire to be noticed: he puts his hand through his hair, blinks furiously.

"How is he now?"

He is taking her back to the suicide, to Samuel's fragile mentality. He is making her face her choices, her mistakes. She replies simply, "He's fine," when the truth is he has never been so unfine, so bitter, so desperate, when the truth is he wakes up every morning telling himself he's a failure and goes to bed every night yelling that he can't take it anymore. Oh, yes, he's fine, absolutely fine, he'll probably collapse one day under the weight of all his self-reproach, he hates what he's become, this spineless man with no ambitions, this mediocre husband, oh, yes, he's fine, he wakes up with back pain and falls asleep with stomach pain, he's fine, he never gave her a child, what does he have to offer her, he's fine, he's been seeing a psychiatrist for two years, but he's fine, he feels old, like he's aging too fast, he's fragile and somewhat ashamed of acknowledging the fact, because what difference does it make really, whether he's healthy or not, and none of this matters to her anymore, now she's face-to-face with Samir, who won't stop staring at her, does it deliberately, making her blush/her heart beat faster. He senses her unease, but won't let go: "You're as beautiful as ever." And he sees it—they both see it—the way she crosses and uncrosses her legs, holds her hands in fists against her stomach. And this is the moment Samir chooses to tell her: "I missed you so much." Nervously, she grabs her glass. Looks away. He keeps talking, his voice hypnotic: "I never got over you." She doesn't reply. Still staring at her, he goes on: "No other woman ever made me feel the way I felt with you. I want you to know that: I've never felt that close to anyone else." And for a long moment they are motionless, only their eyes speaking.

By the time Samuel returns, the check has been paid. Samir suggests they dine with him. He took the liberty of booking a table for three in the hotel restaurant. On me, he insists. "I have to go," Samuel replies. "I need to deal with a problem at work." Then, turning toward Nina, he says: "But you can stay, darling. I'll join you later." This is better than Samir could have dared to dream. He had thought Samuel wouldn't let her out of his sight for a second, like a father afraid of losing his child. "Do stay, Nina—it would make me very happy." Nina feels abandoned. Samuel is exposing her, offering her as bait; it disgusts her. In that moment, she tears up the plans they made together and replies that she is going home: "I'm tired, sorry. Another time, perhaps." Samuel looks at her. He is angry, she can feel it. By acting in this way, by withdrawing from the game before it even starts, she is also evading the challenge he set her, the test of her resistance. She says no, and that's final. He has no doubt that this rejection will only serve to kindle Samir's desire. The next morning, he will call her: *I want to see you again. I can't stop thinking about you. I couldn't sleep last night. I miss you, Nina—I miss you so much.*

On the way home, Samuel walks quickly through the long corridors of the RER suburban train station, Nina struggling to keep up.

He talks loudly and she starts to cry. *That's it—cry! Cry for what you've lost!* But he's wrong: she is crying for them, for what she is losing, here, now. Her mascara runs in charcoal lines over her pale skin. She tastes her own tears. *You're crying for him, aren't you? It affected you, seeing him again, didn't it? Admit it. You're trembling! It did something to you—you can't deny that. It was obvious you wanted to stay with him.* She doesn't reply. Is this really her, this limp and lifeless thing? *Look at the state you're in!* They board the first train, and sit on separate seats. The carriage is almost empty. Nina watches her reflection in the train's window. She doesn't recognize herself. *This is what he's done to me*, she thinks. This is the result of her sacrifice. Is it the fear of aging that tortures her so? No, it's the disappointment. All these years, she was waiting for someone, for something, but no one ever came to rescue her and nothing ever happened. A girl like her could have lived a thousand lives. She makes a mental list of her gifts and talents—those she was born with and those she acquired through education, hard work, perseverance, charm—and she comes to this conclusion: *I blew my chance.*

They do not exchange a single word during the trip, and even afterward, in the street, they walk without talking, without touching. Samuel is ten feet ahead of her and suddenly she feels afraid that he's going to leave her behind. She's wearing a dress and stiletto heels. She yells at him to wait but he only speeds up. So she takes off her heels and walks barefoot on the filthy ground. She might cut herself, but what does it matter? She runs behind him like a little dog, crying/yapping, and he feels strong and powerful, striding in front of her, and even when they get home and go to bed, he shows her who's boss by rejecting her, scorning her warmth and love, refusing to listen to her words. He's tired, weary. *Leave me in*

peace! You don't get it, do you? It was so easy! All you had to do was
talk to him, seduce him—no one was asking you to marry him! No
one was asking you to do it with him! He doesn't use the word "I."
No one was asking you to sell yourself! You just had to manipulate
him—women know how to do that, don't they? Especially you . . .

4

All that Samir remembers of his meeting with Nina is her refusal to stay and dine with him—that unbearable public humiliation. He had been waiting for that moment, but it had given him nothing but the confirmation of his fears: that she was no more free now than she had been twenty years ago. Why had she called him? What had been the point? What game do women play when they dominate men? He is struggling to breathe, as if still in the grip of his old pain, and he's angry with himself for having insisted on seeing her again, for having believed even for a moment that he could try to start things up with her again without suffering as he had before. He remembers this vividly now: how atrociously he had suffered. And he sees himself again now in the college restroom, bent double over the toilet bowl, spitting up greenish bile. *My whole body is infected*, he had thought then—*infected by this love*. He sees himself again in his tiny bedroom with all those girls he would seduce, wherever and whenever he could, purely for the pleasure of the conquest, hoping he might forget her for a few minutes in this way. And finally he sees himself again in his mother's apartment with the young Muslim woman, a student at the university, whom his mother had asked him to meet. "Do this for me," she had pleaded, "and Insha'Allah, you might like her." He sees himself again, looking at this girl, trying vainly to find her charming. He tried so hard in his quest to forget Nina: talked to the girl for a long time, invited her—on his mother's insistence— to a restaurant, but only once. Once was enough. There had been no spark at all.

———

In his hotel room, Samir tries to calm down. He undresses, takes a shower, drinks a glass of wine, and decides to turn up to his meeting. He wears a black suit, a white shirt with tiny iridescent buttons, and a pair of new shoes. With his slicked-back hair and the gold chain that his mother gave him for his thirteenth birthday—which he always keeps around his neck like a talisman—he looks like a dandyish pimp, wearing too much cologne. Samir is convinced that women love this look, this heady perfume. The flashy machismo is instantly erotic—check it out, babe—promising power and debauchery, brutality and tenderness. He even leaves the top two buttons of his shirt undone to reveal his bronzed chest sprinkled with brown hair. He is showing off, parading himself. He did not come to Paris just to see Nina or his mother. He didn't come here to meet Pierre Lévy either. No, he's in Paris for a special evening that has a peculiar fascination for him. About once a year—or every other year if he has no excuse to make the trip—he takes part in a very private evening organized by the famous shoemaker Berluti. Ever since he married Ruth, when a friend of the family nominated him, he has been a member of the Swann Club—named after Marcel Proust's character, Charles Swann. Thirty or forty privileged clients like him—men who systematically buy the twenty unique models of shoes produced by the brand each year—meet in an extraordinary venue: in Venice, for example, on a specially converted gondola, or in Paris, in one of the city's most luxurious hotels. In the taxi on the way to the hotel where tonight's gathering will take place, Samir buttons his shirt to the top and adjusts his bow tie. When he gets out of the vehicle, a beggar calls out to him. Samir makes a hand movement that says: *No cash on me, in a rush, sorry.* He walks to the hotel. The others are already there: men of all ages, dressed in tailored suits or tuxedos, all wearing Berluti shoes. The very best models, naturally. Huge silver candelabra sit atop a large table, the flames flickering in the cool night air, with a bouquet of white roses in the center. At each place there is a can of shoe polish and a perfectly folded gray linen cloth. Bottles of Dom Pérignon stand in ice buckets positioned at regular intervals on the table. And then, at last, the moon appears, round and full, in the dark sky above: *It's time!* Champagne corks pop and fly. The evening's hostess announces that the ceremony can now begin. Excitement ripples through the assembled guests. They clink their crystal glasses, take brief sips of champagne, then put their glasses down and remove their shoes. Placing the shoes on the table in front of them, they pick up the cans of polish in various colors, then they pick up their squares of Venetian linen—a material so soft and fine that Samir can't help caressing it between his fingers before, with slow, careful, precise movements, he uses it to massage the leather. At last comes the moment they are all awaiting: glazing the shoes with Dom Pérignon. "This is the true act of impertinence," the hostess says, and they laugh complicitly. The burnished leather shines like a blade. "The champagne sets the polish," a guest explains to Samir, who shines his shoes for a long time, as if for him it were a pleasure to be prolonged, while another guest reminds the gathering that this tradition was begun by Russian czars and high military officers. When the ritual is over, they exchange a few words and their business cards, compare their shoes, and promise to see one another—*Next year!* It is almost one a.m. when Samir leaves the hotel with the feeling of, once again, having experienced something exceptional. He rushes through the dark night in search of a taxi. He is meeting two old friends from the ghetto in a nightclub near the Champs-Élysées: guys who have made a killing in the textile industry and are now awash in money. They don't know that he lives in New York. He told them he works in finance in London. They meet at a black Plexiglas table placed next to the dance floor, with a champagne bucket to attract blond/

brunette/redheaded sluts. Naked girls[1] coil themselves around luminescent handrails that light up their slim bodies, their muscles toned by making the same mechanical movements every night—the same pelvic thrusts and rolls, the same contortions designed to excite the customers. It's management policy: the customers must be hot, they must be thirsty, they must consume. Strobes sweep the vast room in rhythm with the electronic music that pounds ever louder. It's exhilarating. Samir feels good here, a stranger surrounded by other strangers, nameless and anonymous, just a face in the crowd. He can seduce a girl here and tell her his name is Samir. He can kiss her/caress her/pour her champagne/offer her coke and take her to the toilets to fuck her. Which is, in fact, just what he does, one hour later, with a girl whose name he doesn't remember (let's call her X):[2] the act lasts no longer than a few minutes and costs him €300 (three €100 bills slipped into her H&M bra as he leaves the cubicle), but afterward he feels good—relaxed, at peace—and he can return to his hotel and call his wife in the taxi on the way back. It's eight p.m. in New York and the children are getting ready for bed. *I miss you . . . Have you eaten dinner? Did you do all your homework? How are you, sweetie? Yes, Daddy loves you—big kiss, mwah!*

---

1 Charlène, twenty-three, and Nadia, twenty-five. The former dreamed of becoming a ballet dancer. The latter had been an aerobics instructor for several years before being hired by this club on the insistence of her boyfriend, Bruno "B.B." Benchimol. She has told her parents that she is working "in events."

2 X's real name is Mouna Cesar. Though her parents are metalworkers, she pretends to come from the aristocracy.

5

The failure of that first meeting, the disappointment—*We ideal-ized him, didn't we?* was Nina's conclusion—is, for Samuel, a victory. It is a victory to be able to say that, even with "all his money, his confidence, his condescension," Samir wasn't able to impress them—or seduce her. It is a victory to discover that she is still so attached to Samuel, and this revelation leads him gradually to the realization of the goal that is already, consciously or subconsciously, in his mind: to find out whether, given the same dilemma she faced twenty years ago, she will remain with him by choice rather than through coercion. She lists Samir's faults—but who is she trying to convince? "He's arrogant, pretentious, narcissistic, superficial. He wants everyone to worship at the altar of his success. He's everything I hate." They both say repeatedly how much they despise Samir for showing off his wealth: it's disgusting, they say, it's vulgar, ostentatious. How pure they are, how incorruptible . . . how frustrated. And what liars! Their integrity is invented. An illusion.

Nina does not tell Samuel that she has received several messages from Samir. They come in bursts. He wants to get her back, to win her heart. All she admits to is one message stating that he wants to see her again—alone this time. Samuel understands, but says: "Go ahead. I have no problem with that, if it's what you want."

"It's not, really. I don't have anything to say to him."

"Go and see him."

"Are you asking me to meet him on my own?"

"Yeah. So? I don't have anything to fear, do I?"

"You're not going to bother asking me if I want to see him?"

"You want to. It's written all over your face."

"I'm honestly not that interested."

"Are you sure?"

"Does it matter?"

"No."

Does he really trust her? Is he testing her? He says: *Go ahead*. So she does.

6

Since arriving in Paris, Samir has already received several calls from Pierre Lévy. His former boss is very keen to see him, asks him to drop by the office in the morning. Do you have time for lunch? Or dinner? No, not really. He can't say: I have to see my mother, I want to spend time with her. He doesn't know if he can talk to him about Nina, not yet, so he invents excuses: business meetings, a cardio exam, a visit to a sick friend, and Pierre finally interrupts to say he understands, though the truth is that he's hurt. He's hurt that Samir doesn't have time to see him. It saddens him to realize there is such a wide gap between his own feelings—and his attempts to express them—and Samir's icy indifference. "Did I do something to upset you? I get the feeling you're trying to avoid me . . ." For a long time, he has treated Samir like a son, though he has learned, over time, to make their relationship more equal, without losing his initial affection—a demonstrative affection that made Samir feel suffocated to begin with. He wasn't looking for a father. He'd had one that he loved—a weak but noble father, a poor but honorable man. This time, he didn't call Pierre to give him his flight details. Usually, Pierre is the one who meets him at the airport, and often Samir stays with him when he's in Paris, in the large apartment on Place de Mexico in the sixteenth arrondissement. Pierre lives alone: he has never married, never lived with a woman. The only women Samir has seen him with are a few Eastern European models he's encountered in nightclubs: he has a taste for icy blondes, and this has become a running joke between them: "Why don't you open a branch in Minsk?" "Because I don't want to have to fall asleep with a picture of Lukashenko above my bed." So, no, he doesn't understand why, this time, his protégé didn't tell him what time he was landing, nor why he booked a room at the Bristol: "What's wrong with my place?" He is saddened by this new distance, though he doesn't say anything. "Come around in the morning if you like—I'll be in the office." And Samir goes, thinking that he ought to tell him about Nina. On the way, he stops to buy boxes of chocolates and macaroons for Pierre's employees. He arrives about ten a.m. and Pierre greets him warmly, exuberantly, holding him tight and kissing him on both cheeks. "You came! Just because I asked you to! Shall we go out for a coffee?" "No, let's stay here, it's fine." They sit in Pierre's large, light-filled office, the very place where, seventeen years before, he had been interviewed for his first job. He feels uneasy in this room. He has the impression that everything went wrong here, between the desk and the chair, that everything went wrong in a few minutes of conversation: a misunderstanding that committed him for life.

"So what can be so urgent and so time-consuming that you fly all the way to Paris and are too busy to have lunch with me?"

Samir smiles silently—a grin of complicity.

"Ah, I see . . . And what is she like?"

"Brunette. Very beautiful."

"She must be, for you to fly for eight hours and not even be able to spare an hour or two for your best friend. How long have you been together?"

"Nothing's happened yet . . ."

"So you're flying the flag for platonic love now? You really have changed, Sami! You're crossing the Atlantic just to fuck a woman?"

Samir laughs. "Not just any woman."

"Given how much it costs to fly business class from New York to Paris, I would tend to believe you. Tell me about her . . ."

"She's a girl I loved when I was twenty years old."

Pierre starts to laugh. "Well, she might have changed a bit in twenty years. You might not even recognize her . . ."

"No, I saw her yesterday. She's even more beautiful than she was twenty years ago."

"Married?"

"She lives with an old friend of mine."

"What a fine and faithful friend you are!"

"I'm crazy about her."

"Well, enjoy it while it lasts."

"You're a cynical man."

"Not at all! Just realistic . . . Which explains why I never got married."

Pierre stands up and angles the blinds to let in less sunlight. Now it enters the office in thin shafts that fragment into bursts of iridescence.

"Actually, I meant to say . . . thank you for the birthday present," Samir says.

"You liked it? Your wife suggested we put the money toward a list she'd given to Ralph Lauren. Are you sure your wife knows you, Sami? I've never seen you wearing Ralph Lauren! Your children, maybe, but you . . . ? Doesn't she know you have the same tailor as the President of the United States? Jesus, Sami—twenty thousand dollars on a suit!"

"Thirty-five thousand."

"For one suit!"

"Yes, but what a suit! Hand-tailored in the most supple fabric I've ever touched. You know the joke, don't you? The only thing Democrats share with Republicans is their tailor."

"I can still see you now, in your little gray pin-striped suit, the day of your job interview . . ."

And it starts again, this psychotic reliving of the morning when he became *someone else*. And so the expiatory process begins again too: Why did he lie? Precisely because of that adjective that he hated so vehemently: "little." He lived in a *little* apartment, with his *little* mother, who dreamed he would marry a "nice *little* woman," he had *little* money, he wore a *little* suit . . . but his dreams were BIG.

"You've come a long way, that's for sure. But the apotheosis was your birthday party. I've never been to anything like that in my life, and as you know, I'm not the sort of man who's ever been short of invitations. Your wife really impressed us. Where did she get all those ideas?"

"She hired the biggest events firm in America."

"There were wild animals there, for God's sake! Did she steal them from the zoo in New York?"

"The elephant was an old movie star, and it was on its last legs. I thought it was a bit pathetic, to be honest!"

"And I turned up carrying a book! Still, I bet you can't imagine what I had to do to find it . . ."

"I know—it's a rare edition. I loved it. Did you bribe someone at Christie's?"

"I seduced the head of the precious books department. What I don't understand is how a man who loves political books as much as you do has never run for office himself."

"In the U.S.? I think that would be tricky . . ."

"Surely you'd have more chance there, as a Jew, than you would in France."

And there it is: the stab of the knife blade into the crack in his identity. Each time this happens, he has the impression they are talking about another person.

"Yeah, you're right. I should give it some thought . . ."

"Your father-in-law would certainly have the means to help you."

"Berg? Nah, he's got more than enough on his plate with his own affairs . . ."

They laugh. A moment later, there is a knock at the door. "Come in." A man appears—a fairly short man in his early thirties, running slightly to fat, and, as Samir notices immediately, a North African. He has dusky skin and thick, curly, jet-black hair that covers his skull like a helmet. His face is round and adolescent-looking. He is wearing a conventional gray suit, a white shirt, and a burgundy tie that is knotted so tightly it looks as if he's being throttled. "Oh, I'm sorry—I didn't realize you were in a meeting." "That's all right, Sofiane—come in, I'd like to introduce you to Sami, our American partner." The man walks up with a friendly smile and offers Samir a firm handshake. "Sami, this is Sofiane Boubekri, our newest employee. He's been with us for three months now." "Pleased to meet you." (We should really have a close-up on Samir's face when this man first enters his field of vision. There is surprise and curiosity in his expression, but also a sort of disdain—a disdain that does not betray any feelings of superiority but, on the contrary, Samir's jealousy and envy, without any nuance or detachment.) Samir feels hot; he is sweating. He would like to find out what this guy is doing here, in the place that should have been his, in the office that was given to him, under his real identity. He hates him at first sight, and Sofiane Boubekri probably senses this because he says right away that he should leave them in peace. "I'll come back later. Great to meet you." As soon as he has turned on his feet and closed the door, Pierre asks Samir what he thinks of him.

"Dull."

"Dull? I don't know what you mean."

"What made you hire that guy? He's nothing special."

"Nothing special? He came from Braun and Vidal! He studied at Paris II and spent a year at Cambridge. He's funny, very lucid. Where do you get the idea that he's nothing special?"

"I don't know . . . It's just an impression he gave me."

Pierre laughs. "You think he's dull . . . Guess who he's married to!"

Suddenly Samir seems infuriated. "How the hell should I know? I don't know the guy from Adam . . ."

"You remember Gaelle, that gorgeous lawyer we hired three years ago?"

Samir shrugs.

"Yes, you do—you remember her. You even invited her to dinner, and she rejected you. She's a redhead, quite small, very pretty ..."

"All right. So what's your point?"

"Well, he's married to her and they've just had a son who they named Djibril."

"Wow, good luck to the kid—trying to make his way in France with a name like that!"

"What is up with you, Sami? Do you have a problem with Sofiane?"

"No ... It would have been nice if you'd told me, that's all ..."

"But you work in New York! You come here once a year at most! I'm hardly going to send you his CV. Besides, you trust me, don't you? If I tell you he's a good guy, an excellent lawyer ... In fact, let me be honest: I think, in pure procedural terms, he's better than either of us."

"He might be better than you. I kind of doubt he's better than me. Where's he from, anyway?"

"What do you mean, where's he from? I already told you: he studied at Paris II ..."

"Really? I bet he got beaten up a few times by those morons from the GUD."[1]

"Finish your thought. You mean because he's an Arab? I don't know—I never asked him about it. But I can tell you that when I was there, I got my skull cracked a few times, and I never just lay down and took it. I was president of the local branch of Jewish

---

1 Group Union Défense is the name of a succession of violent French far-right student political groups, founded in 1968 at Panthéon-Assas University (otherwise known as Paris II) by Gérard Longuet.

Students in France. I don't know how many fights I got into with those fascists . . . Weren't you ever politically active?"

"Yes, I was in the UNEF-ID,[2] but I gave it up pretty quickly. I was never really a joiner."

"Me neither. You can't hold it against me."

"Hold what against you—hiring an Arab?"

"Clearly, you have a real problem with that . . ."

"I have no problem at all."

"Oh, come on! You turn up all smiles, everything great, then you see Sofiane, I tell you he works here, and suddenly you're angry and irritated . . ."

"I'm not angry or irritated. I was just surprised, that's all, and I have another meeting."

"Listen, I can see where you're going with this, and I'm not sure I want to get into it with you. He's an Arab—so what? He speaks fluent Arabic, he has clients in Dubai, in London, he—"

"So you hired him because he's useful to the firm . . ."

"What the hell are you getting at? Yes, of course, I hire all my employees because they bring added value to the firm. All employers do that, don't they?"

Losing his temper, Pierre knocks over his cup, spilling coffee on the papers arranged on his desk. *Shit!* Samir gets up and helps him clean the fast-spreading brown stains from his desk. "It's fine, I can do it . . . I think you'd better go to your meeting." Hearing these words, Samir grabs his coat and stands immobile for a few seconds, watching Pierre, not knowing what he should do. Then, finally, he mutters that he's sorry—*really* sorry—and walks away.

---

2 The Union Nationale des Étudiants de France—Indépendante et Démocratique was a far-left French student union that existed between 1980 and 2001.

7

That evening, Samir arranged to meet Nina in a large Parisian restaurant situated under the alcove of an elegant townhouse with a view over a verdant garden. It's beautiful and chic, he thinks, the kind of thing that might impress her: that bourgeois minimalism, that well-ordered sobriety, that quietude provided by the feeling of being among your own kind—something he discovered quite late, mainly through his wife, who had never known any other world. Having asked the hotel concierge to reserve a small table set aside from the others, he arrived early. Even so, he has trouble concealing his excitement when he sees Nina enter the restaurant, shoulders slightly hunched in a defensive posture, wearing a little low-cut red dress that gives a glimpse of her opulent breasts. When she walks into the room, she is all that he—and every other man in the room—sees. He stands up to kiss her cheek, letting his lips linger on that soft square inch of skin close to the corner of her mouth, while his hands touch her arm, feeling her shape and warmth through the fabric. She turns him on—everything about her turns him on, even her perfume, a mix of mandarin, incense, and cedarwood—and he finds it hard to move away from her. It's physical: even if he takes a step back, lets go of her arm, looks away from her face, it is obvious that he wants her, that his body and mind are in turmoil; it is obvious that he wants to touch her, to keep her next to him, to take her. They sit side by side, their bodies close, looking out across the room, waiters scurrying past in both directions. Nina has never been taken anywhere so elegant before, she has never tasted such fine food. She is excited, nervous; he sees this and is pleased. He pretends to be surprised by her reaction. This is all perfectly normal for him. It is normal to be

served, pampered, flattered. He enters the room and they give him
the best table. Before he has even ordered anything, the waitress
brings him a glass of his favorite champagne. He asks a question
about the menu and the chef himself comes out to greet him. His
aura of power is natural now. And he has acquired something else,
through imitation, through contact with his wealthy wife whose
every wish is granted: the false simplicity of people who have everything. We are together, we are having a conversation; I am a
normal man, an accessible man; this surprises you, delights you;
but look more closely, look at how I hold myself, listen to the way
I articulate my words . . . can't you perceive the distance between
us now? The extraordinary self-importance conferred by a privileged social position. Samir is there, at the center of everything,
in complete control. And suddenly Nina feels pathetic in her little
red dress that she borrowed and showed to Samuel with genuine
excitement. She has the impression that her perfume—a copy of
a Prada eau de toilette that she bought at the flea market in Saint-
Ouen, not in a perfumery, because she couldn't afford to—is a
little *too* intoxicating. Under the table, she hides the high heels she
bought in a secondhand store, for fear that he will see them. Who
are you kidding with your cheap fancy-dress outfit? Nobody. And
certainly not a man like him, capable of spotting a designer brand
at fifty feet. Leather? Nope, plastic. Satin? Nope, polyester—you
sweat inside it, it's allergenic, it makes you itch like crazy. Cashmere? Nope, just acrylic—a fabric that pills, that soaks up body
odors. It's obvious, embarrassing, your lack of money, of taste, and
it makes him even happier: this social gap shifts the balance of
power in his favor—it's erotic. Here in this restaurant, he is the
dominant force—you sense that he has power, has money—but in
a room, in bed, she will be the one with power over him, an authority that society denies her, a control beyond her capabilities in this
place where she is afforded no influence, where she can only claim

to belong at all because of her proximity to Samir. She feels unwell, ill at ease, and a confession bubbles to her lips: "Samir, I lied to you. I'm not what you think I am. I don't really work in fashion and Samuel isn't a company director . . . I'd prefer you to find out now, rather than later." "I already knew." He says it arrogantly, but does not reveal how he knew. He can't say to her: It's because of the way you both look, your clothes, the way you enter a hotel, the way you avoid the waiters' eyes, and above all—the most telling detail— because of your shoes: you, Nina, perched on worn-out high heels that make you wobble as you walk, heels with square tips when the fashion is for pointed tips; and him in his cheap leather, too-big shoes, with soles that squeak when he walks—*And for fuck's sake*, he thinks, *if you're going to buy a pair of shoes in a bargain store, the first thing you do is remove the damn price sticker!* He doesn't dare ask her what they really do/are, but she tells him anyway: "Samuel is a social worker in Clichy-sous-Bois. As for me, well, I do work in fashion—I really am a model—but only for department store catalogues. When the marketing team at Carrefour are pre- paring their summer or winter promotions, they call me. I always play the perfect mother in those pages devoted to barbecues or Beaujolais Nouveau or pork products or school supplies! And I don't even have kids!" She says this ironically, self-deprecatingly, and he is touched by it. "I really need to get hold of that catalogue. I can imagine how sexy you must look holding a pig's head in your hand." And she laughs.

When dinner is over, he asks her to come for one last drink at his hotel bar. He has hopes of getting her up to his room. He is desper- ate for her now. They sit opposite each other this time and drink tequila. He looks at her and finally says what he feels. *God, you turn me on, Nina. You're incredible.* But she immediately changes the subject, asks him to tell her about his wife. All right, he gets the idea. He shuts up. He doesn't feel like bringing Ruth into it, or his kids: he's alone and free in Paris, and he wants Nina: *Come upstairs with me.* This is not a suggestion or a request, it's an order. He wants her to obey—*Come*—to let herself be led, *Come!* but she rears up at this, digs her heels in: No means no, don't ask me again or I'll leave and you'll never see me again. *Tell me you don't want me, then. Tell me that and I'll stop.* They look at each other for a long moment with an intensity that rekindles old memories. *Tell me, and I'll stop.*

Can't you understand? I'm scared.

8

It is nearly eleven p.m. when she comes home, slightly tipsy, hair mussed. Samuel is awake: he is waiting for her, his face closed like a fist, standing in front of the bookcase. He looks like he's about to fall over. A cigarette trembles in his hand. The ashtray is heaped with butts and a smell of nicotine pervades the room. Nina does not say a word. She walks over to the window and opens it. A cold wind stirs the wreaths of smoke, clears the air. "So, did he fuck you?" Samuel asks while Nina closes the window. He is brutal with her, excessive in his black/white vision of the world. For Samuel, everything has to be true/false, good/evil, right/wrong; he has never been able to hold a more sophisticated view of things. His lack of ambiguity makes her despair; it's ridiculous, the idea that she should obey this desire for moral probity. *You're going to leave me aren't you tell me you're going to leave me and go back to him it's true isn't it admit it.* Look at him: cigarette trembling between his lips, bottle of beer in his hand, his body braced for the crushing blow.

I'm a loser.

I'm a failure.

I never even gave you a child.

The fatal trilogy.

So it happened . . . you saw him again, you were impressed, you were turned on, all the old feelings came back, I get it. You know what? I arranged this because I wanted to test you, and you failed! You're just like him—an opportunist! A social climber! The two of you are pure products of a society that's rotten to the core. Succeed, succeed—that monstrous social ideal, that grotesque ambition. You gave in to it just like all the others! Not me . . . I've never been like you. I was raised by people for whom success meant nothing; people who placed faith, study, and neighborly love above all; people who were never obsessed by material objects. So what did you want me to do? Go over to the other side, with nothing but my own virtues, with the education that my parents gave me? But if you want to go over to the other side, you have to prove you are capable. It's a rite of initiation. You have to bite back if you're bitten, betray others if you're betrayed, be brutal if you've been brutalized—it's social, it's political—don't look so surprised—it's a struggle, a combat. To go over to the other side, you need luck, power, money, or all three. You can't wait for it to be given to you—you have to take it by force, with your head, your hands, your ass—am I shocking you? Yes, if you really want to succeed, you have to be ready to offer your ass up on a plate . . . The place you want, you have to take it from someone else. And who cares if they feel robbed, betrayed, hurt? Who cares, because you can be sure they'll do the same thing to someone else in turn, and that someone else—you can be certain of this—will take someone else's place through their greed for success, for power, for money. I thought I could, that I might be able to win without cheating, without lying. But that's as unrealistic, as absurd as thinking you can butcher a man without getting your hands bloody. It's as Utopian as thinking you can wage war without killing civilians. If you want to wage war, you have to kill . . . and you have to like it. If you want a foreign land, you have to conquer it, kill whoever it belongs to, have no qualms about wiping them out, one by one, bang bang bang! You have to eliminate them, see? But I'm one of those soldiers who never had the courage to desert nor the strength to shoot. I was never anything more than a lookout, sitting safely in the rear base, expressing my indignation at the horrors of war, whining from the comfort of my armchair. And you want me to feel proud of myself? Yeah, right—all I feel is shame. Shame! Resentment! Jealousy!

Bitterness! Yes, I've become a jealous man, a bad man, a failure. I am the shit of society! A parasite! I'm telling you—I'm nothing!

He is lying. He does feel proud of himself. Being a loser, being perceived in that way by society, is a victory over the system, over compromised principles, over corruption. It is the proof that he has not given in to ambition and money, the assurance that he has remained a good man, a true man, faithful to the people and to social concerns—finding decent housing, a job, feeding the kids, paying your debts—not one of those champagne socialists who write newspaper columns defending the rights of illegal immigrants but send their children to the kind of exclusive private schools where you have to be nominated by someone more powerful than yourself, select establishments where, thank God, their progeny will not have to fraternize with *sons of immigrants* or *sons of concierges* who *bring down the level* and damage the schooling of their precocious, spoiled brats. He wants to be a magnificent loser, an obscure writer, a social failure—a pure concentrate of violence, he thinks. Contrary to what he tells Nina, he is hugely proud (arrogant, even—a feeling of superiority) of having *resisted*—this is the word he uses, this man who never even participated in a social struggle—whereas (so he says) Tahar has become the symbol of the worst of society's excesses: a smooth, aseptic lawyer; while he wants to be a writer of harsh truths, even if it means never being published, never being read.

He has never obeyed social codes. Showing his disgust, he was always *against*. He imagined himself a free man, but in truth there was never anyone so attached to company and comfort; he imagined himself a rebel, spitting on the class system and on capitalism, whereas he was actually spitting on himself. He disqualified himself, gave himself a red card. All of his pain is self-inflicted. In which case, he has no right to cry about it, but all the same he can feel the tears now, welling up inside like a river overflowing its banks, pearling on his lower eyelids, pouring down his cheeks. *Look at you, blubbering like a little kid! You're pathetic. Let's not forget that this was all your idea—you wanted me to call him!* Nina speaks but does not move, offers no consolation, and he sinks, slowly, like a body dragged down to the depths of a murky river by the lead weights tied to his ankles.

Samir's return has contaminated their life. They are sick now, and beginning to regret (without daring to admit it) ever having gotten in touch with him, ever having seen him again. He is so successful, so rich, and they have nothing.

"I don't want to see him anymore. Let's stop this now."

"Out of the question."

"Why are you doing this? You'll destroy everything."

"Maybe."

Finally, it is stronger than her, and she throws herself at him, kisses him, weeps, shaking, but he pushes her away.

"I want a child."

"No."

"I want to stay here with you!"

"No."

"I love you. I'm forty. I want a child—it's now or never."

"Never."

When she hears these words, she walks to the bathroom and does not come out again until an hour later. By then, a metamorphosis has taken place: she is wearing so much makeup, she looks like a geisha—or a whore.

I'm going out.

He's been drinking—drinking a lot—and his eyes are filled with hatred and violence as he asks Nina if she's going back to meet

Samir at his hotel. *Where are you going dolled up like that, you slut? Back to see him? Not had enough, eh?* He is sitting on the couch in the living room—an IKEA sofa in faded colors that he found in the business section—and he's smoking: the ash falls onto the stained cloth and burns a hole in it. *Be careful.* No—he takes another drag on his cigarette. *I don't give a fuck.* Bluish clouds of smoke veil his darkly lined face. Nina no longer recognizes him: Is this really the man whose child she wanted to bear only an hour earlier? She says she doesn't need him, that she's not afraid anymore, and as she is about to leave the apartment, she hears him shout: *Going back to see your rich boyfriend? Go ahead, get the hell out of here.* And that is just what she does: she gets the hell out of there.

In the suburban train, some kids[1] are talking loudly. She wears headphones so she doesn't have to hear them. Samuel calls her cell phone three or four times to find out where she is, where she's going, *Why are you doing this to me?* She doesn't answer.

She arrives at Rue du Faubourg Saint-Honoré, enters the hotel lobby—hello, madame—not feeling very sure of herself. In the bathroom, she stands in front of a large mirror and reapplies her makeup: gray eye shadow, crimson lips, hair loose, a little perfume, and she leaves. The scent radiates from her, impregnating the atmosphere. All eyes converge on her, as usual: men, women, children, everyone is attracted to her. Finally, she goes up to reception and asks to speak to Mr. Tahar. *Just one moment, please.* And the

---

1 Kamel, Léon, and Dylan, sixth-graders from the *collège* in Sevran. On the first day of school, in response to the question, "What job would you like to do when you are older?" Kamel replied: "President of the Republic"; Léon said: "Video game designer"; and Dylan announced that he wanted to be "the most famous armed robber of all time." Everybody laughed.

receptionist moves away from the desk, whispers a few words to a man who appears to be his boss.

He thinks I'm a whore.

He thinks I'm a whore.

He thinks I'm a whore.

She smiles. *Stay calm. Wait.* At last, the man comes back to the desk, dials Samir's room number, informs him that there is a young lady downstairs wishing to speak to Mr. Tahar. Then he hands her the receiver. At the other end of the line, she hears Samir's voice: *Who's this?* (even though he knows it's her: he was expecting her) and she says simply: "I'm here." She hears him breathe into her ear. Finally his voice orders her: "Come up. Suite 503."[2]

---

2 Suite 503 has been the venue for many adulterous liaisons—in particular an affair, which remained secret, between a famous French actress and a male French politician (whose only personal ambition was to have an affair with this actress in Suite 503).

9

Samuel calls her ten, twenty times, but she doesn't pick up. *What is she doing? What have I done?* And then it comes, rising up inside him: he was mad to let her go, he's filled with regret, calls her again, screams, MADNESS, what got into me, how could I think that I (the master of SELF-DESTRUCTION) could ever hope to hold her back, I could never keep her, I am a FUCKHEAD, an IDIOT, a piece of SHIT, that's what I am, I deserve to DIE, I don't deserve a girl like that, she left me, that BITCH, that WHORE, and I did everything for her, I was always there to listen, always there when she was SICK, with her all I did was SUFFER, with her I could never feel confident, could never EVOLVE, she RUINED my life, and all for what? So she can go back to HIM, that JERK

that MAGGOT

it's too late

it's too late

TOO LATE

you've lost her

How could I ever believe I could KEEP her? The only way I was ever able to POSSESS her was through threats, through CO-ERCION, no surprise, a girl as BEAUTIFUL as that, she's TOO good for you, TOO beautiful for you, you never did anything to HELP her, put her FIRST, help her SUCCEED.

SUCCEED

SUCCEED

What was IMPORTANT for her (you think): being known/recognized/loved/valued/seen in the papers/loved for what she represented, for her BEAUTY, you never did anything to make her HAPPY, and look at her now:

DULL
SAD
UPSET
BITTER
Wait
Hang on a minute
she
is
going
to
BETRAY YOU
    She's probably betraying you right now in fact, she's with him, in his bed, he's fucking her while you mope about, she is NOT coming back, she will NEVER come back because you were never in her league, you only managed to keep her because she PITIED you, because you have nothing to offer her, it's over, it's OVER, you've
    LOST HER

10

"Come in." Nina stands in front of Samir. She occupies the space and she is all he can see. Her beauty is shocking. He pulls her toward him, kisses her without a word, his eyes closed. He moves closer and breathes in her perfume, the smell of her skin, touches his face to her neck, breathing in/out, intoxicated by her, suddenly feverish, burning with the desire to undress her and see her flesh again at last, that perfect body, designed to make you gape, make you yearn, designed for love, and Samir senses that he will not be able to take the time to seduce her, to coax her from her shell, slowly soften her up, because she is here for *that*. There's no need to go through that bland, pointless social phase—asking her to sit down for a chat, ordering something to drink, questioning her, asking her why and how she came. No, he has no intention of listening to her—not now anyway, there'll be time for that later—because right now he wants to touch her, feel her, take her. This is all that matters, all that means anything to him, this intimacy that the years have kept from them, this bodily familiarity. But she's about to say something, and he puts a finger to her lips. *Shh, quiet. Come.* She lets his fingers stroke her chin, her neck, the top of her breasts. "Samir, I . . ." She says his name, and it's a liberation for him, a man living under another identity for so long. It's a recognition. What does it awaken in him? What desire? "Say it again. Say my name. Say it." *Samir, Samir.* Holding her face in his hands, smoothing her hair, he kisses her, his tongue in her mouth, and once again the feeling takes hold of him: he is filled with her, crazy for her. Slowly, he leads her toward the bed. *Say my name.* He undresses her and stops for a moment to look at her. He is in her thrall, and he knows it. He could try to be cunning, to not focus on her appearance, but such ruses would be in vain. Her beauty is central to everything: he can't simply bypass it, evade it. He knows he must come to terms with this feeling of vertiginous panic that grips him when he sees her naked, and he calms down, or pretends to, watching/breathing her in until he is sure he can take her without losing control. The intensity of the instant: he is inside her, with her—it's overwhelming—and when she lies back, her hair stuck to her face by sweat, eyes closed, half drifting into sleep, he finally gets up and orders champagne, wine, and food.

We are together.

The questions and the revelations come later—after dinner. They are lying next to each other on the bed. *I want you to tell me the truth.* It's a command, not a request, and something inside him clicks. He is going to speak. She wants to know why he stole Samuel's identity and elements of his biography in order to construct his new life. If his friends and family know the truth. If he has thought about the consequences. "I guess you never imagined there'd be an article about you in the *Times* . . ." Exactly—she's right. Never once did he imagine having such a meteoric rise. "Where I come from, people hardly ever move or change. They end up dying in the same hole they grew up in." He has seen his old friends a few times: most are unemployed or stagnating in menial positions. They have kids, money problems, tiny apartments, secondhand clothes. They never go on vacation, they wait for the end of the month the way some people wait for the Second Coming, dream of changing their car/television/life. Some ended up in jail. He doesn't regret what he did. Sure, he lied. Yes, it was a kind of betrayal. But only in the final and glorious aim of achieving something with his life, when society offered/promised him nothing. "You want to know why I reinvented myself? Shall I tell you?" She doesn't reply. She looks at him. *What does it matter?*—in a shock of bliss—*What does it matter, when I love you?* He sits up and grabs her shoulders. "Nina, my entire life is built on a lie."

11

"After Samuel's suicide attempt, and after we broke up—and let's not forget that you were the one who gave in to his blackmail; I loved you!—after I lost everything that mattered to me, I left Paris. You never knew that, did you? I never told anyone about it, apart from my mother. I got a scholarship at the university in Montpellier to study law. I didn't want to see you and Samuel anymore. I didn't want to run the risk of passing you in the street. I didn't even want to hear your names mentioned! I distanced myself from all our mutual friends and acquaintances. I erased their numbers from my address book. I had decided to forget about you completely. And I never tried to see you again . . . I . . . no, actually, that's not true. I'm lying. Once, just once, I took a train to Paris. I'd just moved to Montpellier and I felt terrible: I wanted to see you. I spent the whole day standing in front of your apartment building, hidden behind a car, just waiting for you to appear. But when you did finally emerge—I remember you were wearing a denim skirt and a white top—I didn't dare speak to you; I was paralyzed by the fear that you would reject me again. That hurt so much; I was in pieces by the time I got home. After that, all I did was work. Whenever I think back to that period, I see myself locked in my room, poring over my law books. I see myself learning dozens of books by heart, telling myself: *She'll regret this*. So, deep down, you played a part in my success. Subconsciously, I was trying to prove to you that you'd made the wrong choice. I wanted to amaze you . . . Ridiculous, isn't it? Anyway, I got my master's and was admitted to the bar—I was in the top ten, in fact. Then I got my MAS. That summer, I worked as a waiter in London. And when I came back to France, I started looking for a job . . . This is where things became more complicated . . .

I had a fantastic CV, believe me—I'd spent hours perfecting it. And every diploma, every line on that résumé was a victory over adversity, over the contagion of failure and resignation. That résumé was my life's work. So I had no doubt about my abilities, and I sent it to the best law firms in France. That evening, I took my mother and my brother to a restaurant to celebrate. I felt happy and proud . . . this was the culmination of twelve years of work and self-sacrifice! Nobody helped me! No one! And within ten days, I was utterly disillusioned. I started collecting rejection slips. Three in one day . . . then six, then eight, then ten. It was a slap in the face. I couldn't believe it. I would wait for the mailman in the lobby every morning . . . I'd sent my CV to a bunch of law firms, having gotten their addresses from the phone book. They all said no. No, but good luck. No, but we'll call you if anything comes up. I didn't even get an interview! They had all decided I was unsuitable without even bothering to meet me! That was a bad time. I felt very low. I started boxing, as a way of preventing myself from going under, but it did no good. I could feel myself sinking. I tried to analyze where it had gone wrong. What mistake had I made? But I thought: *Look at you—you are faultless. You were efficient/convincing/dynamic. You're exactly the profile of applicant they're looking for. Not only do you have the necessary diplomas, but you passed them with spectacular scores. You even won the speech-making prize at the law conference! And you won it easily! They applauded/praised/were jealous of you. Everyone said: He's one of the most brilliant students of his generation/he'll go far/give it five years and he'll be one of the most famous lawyers in Paris. And now they are all rejecting you! They send you long letters full of excuses to justify those rejections. Because, of course, they are terrified. They don't want to be accused of discrimination in their recruitment procedures. So they abide by the rules: they give you lots of valid reasons why you don't correspond to their needs for that particular position.* Put yourself in my place: I was angry! Filled with hatred! I hadn't dared tell my mother the truth: I let her believe I'd been hired by a big firm. Every morning I would get up early, about six a.m., dress in a suit, and leave the apartment with the words, 'See you this evening!' It was my first acting gig! I would take the bus, then the RER, to the business district. And you want to know the truth? It was a nightmare. Seeing all those clean-shaven executives bustling past, stinking of colognes that their wives bought for them at a hundred euros per bottle from a special perfume store in Florence . . . I wanted to kill them. My life might easily have tipped over to the other side in the space of a few seconds. I could feel that violence welling up inside me. I wasn't scared. Quite the opposite: that violence made me feel strong. It was with me all the time: as I looked through the windows of luxury boutiques, telling myself I couldn't afford to buy any of their wares, that I didn't even dare go in; as I watched those beautiful and very young women parading around on the arms of doddery old men . . . hatred! I felt like everything was out of my reach—but why? I would sit in seedy cafés and read. My existence was making me sick. I'd lost over twenty pounds in two months. Back then, I was boxing three times a week with a guy I'd met in law school, and one evening, we decided to go for a drink afterward. I'd just had another rejection letter. I was desolate. My friend kept telling me that things would work out, that I'd get a job, but the more he repeated this, the more I felt the violence rising up within me—like when you keep releasing the safety catch on a box cutter, so that, in the end, all you're holding is the blade itself and you are bound to cut yourself, to make yourself bleed. He kept saying: You have to stay positive, it'll come! But I couldn't stay positive. Optimism was something reserved for the privileged few—those people with life insurance policies and positive bank balances. Optimism was a luxury I couldn't afford anymore. I knew I had very little chance of being hired by a good firm, of succeeding in a world whose doors opened only to those who knew the secret codes; I knew my way would always be blocked by someone else, someone with more influence, better recommendations, and I wanted to know why. Oh, I had my own ideas about it, but all the same I asked him: 'Is the fact that I have an Arab-sounding name the reason for all these rejections?' My friend started to laugh. He said I was paranoid, that the idea was ludicrous. But I wasn't paranoid. I had sent my résumé to a dozen firms and had received only rejection letters—some of them hadn't replied at all—whereas another guy from our law school, a guy with no personality, no sense of judgment, no ability—this guy who had failed the final exam twice and who everyone said would end up dropping law as a profession and taking over his father's business—this guy wound up being hired by Bertrand and Vilar, one of the biggest firms in Paris . . . And you know what my friend said to me? He said: 'You're looking at this the wrong way. You're making yourself the victim, accusing other people . . . it's counter-productive.' He didn't completely deny the persistence of discriminatory practices, but he refused to believe that racism was a systematic and organized part of society. I, on the other hand, felt certain that I had not found a job simply because I was an Arab. The human resources guys, the employers, would see my name and immediately think: *Cross that one off the list. Leave that one in the ghetto where he belongs!* And it was at that moment, as I explained to him that my name and my identity were the problem, that he told me to change my first name. He was completely serious. He thought it was possible that success was more likely in modern-day France for someone named Louis, Hugo, or Lucas than for someone named Mohammed. He was just describing a social and political reality. And he was right. He told me: 'Write Sam Tahar instead of Samir. Maybe that'll make a difference.' So, one evening, I tried something. I felt I had been a victim of discrimination, you see, but I wanted to be certain of it, so I sent my CV to a dozen law firms with this name typed at the top left-hand side of the first page: SAM TAHAR. All I had done was remove two little letters—it was hardly a betrayal. I just wanted to see what would happen. And guess what? Within a week, I had been invited to three job interviews. The first two went well; the senior partner even assured me that I would have a response very soon. The third interview took place at a large firm on Avenue George-V that specialized mainly in criminal law. On my way in, I noticed a little clear plastic box stuck to the pediment of the door—you know, one of those objects containing a parchment that Jews put there to protect their houses? The man who was interviewing me was named Pierre Lévy—a Mediterranean Jew, in his forties, who immediately made me feel at ease. An intelligent, perceptive guy. I don't know exactly how it happened, but in the middle of the interview, he said, in a buddy-buddy tone of voice, 'Sam's short for Samuel, I take it?' Without thinking, I nodded. It was completely spontaneous. I wanted that job. And I didn't really understand the implications . . . Well, okay, I understood that the guy was a Jew, but I didn't see any harm in it, I didn't see the danger. Sam, Samuel, Samir—did it really matter? Then, when he told me that he'd once been engaged to a 'North African Jew'—Claire Tahar—whose brother was named Samuel, I realized that he assumed I was a Jew, and in that moment I must admit that I wavered, I got a little scared. I thought: *Maybe he's going to hire me because he thinks I'm one of them.* I had in mind the cliché of Jews helping each other out. Later I realized how false this was, because—once they reach a certain social level, Jews don't want to stay with their own kind anymore. The ghetto mentality is something that bothers them greatly. I hadn't said much during the interview: I didn't feel I'd really shone. In fact, I remember thinking that I'd been less convincing in that interview than in the previous two—I'd slept badly the night before, I was stressed—and yet, as he walked me to the door, this man told me that I was now part of the law firm Lévy and Queffélec. Unbelievable, isn't it? The next morning, he introduced me to the firm's other two partners; he showed me my office—a nice one with a street view—and he took me out to lunch at a restaurant. As we were looking at the menus, he asked me if I was religious and I replied that I didn't eat pork. That was all. I didn't lie. He laughed and said, 'Oh, I see. So you're just a Yom Kippur Jew!' I could have denied it then, but I didn't say anything.

"During lunch, he told me how happy he was to have appointed such a highly qualified lawyer to his firm, and I began to feel scared. I wondered what would happen if I admitted that I'd been hired on a misunderstanding; that I was actually Muslim, not Jewish, as he believed—and, perhaps, as he wanted. But I needed that job, so I persuaded myself I would tell him the truth later, after a few months of experience, or I would leave his firm one day without ever having had to confess. You can imagine what happened next: I never managed to tell him. And I have stayed with that firm for my entire career. Working with a man like that—a man as experienced and cultivated as that—was everything a young lawyer like me could hope for. Not only was Pierre a good lawyer, he was also a generous man, an attentive friend, the kind of guy who comes to pick you up from the airport in the middle of the night just for the pleasure of seeing you again, without even having to ask him, the kind of guy who would never leave you the check in a restaurant—he never even lets you see it—who will transfer you money immediately if you show even the slightest need of it, without demanding to know what you need it for or why you can't cover the sum yourself, without ever suggesting to you that you owe him, the kind of guy who will stand surety for you if you ask him and, most importantly, if he likes you, because that's just how he is: a kindhearted, sincere person. If he likes you, he'll give you everything he has—and if he doesn't have it, he'll arrange for you to get it. You think I'm joking? What I'm trying to say is that there aren't many guys like him in the world. I couldn't take the risk of damaging a friendship like that. I felt worse and worse about it, and I decided I would tell him everything when I set up on my own. In the meantime, I thought about legally changing my first name. I made inquiries. I started thinking about it, and that was when Samuel came to mind. I never expected to see Baron again. 'Samuel?' It was a good choice. Everyone would call me 'Sam.' I would have preferred a more elegant name, like Edouard or Paul or Adrien, but I figured that would sound ridiculous: a French first name next to my Arab-sounding surname. It would attract attention, people would ask questions—and that was the last thing I wanted. Sam was good; it was neutral. In fact, most people call me Sami. A few months later, I officially changed my name to Samuel Tahar. Lévy wanted to create a branch of the firm in New York, so he asked me to go there for three years, on behalf of the firm. I passed the bar exam and moved there permanently. When I say it like that, it sounds very simple, but it was actually one of the most difficult periods of my life. I was on my own, I wasn't earning much money yet, I didn't feel I belonged anywhere, I didn't know anyone, and even the people and places that fascinated me—all those groups where the most influential New York intellectuals gather, not only lawyers but journalists and writers—I didn't dare approach them for fear of being rejected. You can imagine how I felt on my graduation day, all alone. I hadn't told my mother about it, of course, because I didn't want her to turn up: I had drawn a line under my past. So while all the other students were accompanied by their parents, I received my diploma in the most absolute solitude. I had to give some reason for this, so that's when I thought about using Samuel's personal history—his parents' death. When I heard my name announced that day and walked, alone, toward the stage, I had to fight hard not to collapse. That day, I realized the true consequences of my lie: the knowledge that I would never share my life with anyone. In sadness and in happiness, in sickness and in health, I would always be alone.

"As for what happened after that, it was a simple exercise in mimicry. I began to hang around with a new group of friends—mostly bourgeois Jews who welcomed me like a brother. I had a good instinct, a sort of talent for socializing. And I think I made them laugh. For five years, I had read every political biography that had been published, every major interview. I used all this—and my imagination—to tell stories. Everyone would invite me to their dinner parties: I knew how to be scathing when the situation merited it; I could be cruel too, and they loved that. My transgressive tastes, the freedom with which I spoke my mind—that was a source of fascination in those corseted circles. I knew all the codes: I'd assimilated them, just by watching other people and learning. I was like a chameleon—I adapted to whatever background you set me against. I could even get into people's heads when I talked to them: I would mimic their tics, adopt their systems of thought. When I began getting invited to a higher social sphere, I took classes with a maître d' who I'd met during a business trip in Paris. I thought: *Why not? No one knows me. I want to learn.* So he taught me how to hold my silverware, how to sit at a table—all those social proprieties I had never properly learned before. On my thirtieth birthday, I spent a week in Burgundy studying oenology, after which I was capable of distinguishing between wines and evaluating which was better. Later still, I learned about music. I had felt humiliated one evening when, having been invited to the opera by a few colleagues, I'd spent the whole night with my mouth shut—I wasn't even capable of bluffing my way through, because I knew absolutely nothing about classical music. It was not the kind of thing you learned about in the ghetto. The day after this debacle, I went to a record store. It was perfect—they had Bach, Chopin, Mozart, Dvorak—and I told the sales assistant not to leave out anyone important. On my way out, I bought a season ticket for the New York Opera, and that was a revelation. I never managed to enjoy the theater in the same way, though—I would always get bored. I gave up after falling asleep while watching a play by a Polish author in the original language, with subtitles. I would just confess to everyone: 'You know, I've never really liked the theater.' So, you see, I was a self-made man. Through sheer force of will and hard work, I invented myself. It may have been built on a lie, but the success I built is still all my own. *I* made those life choices, *I* made those career plans, *I* made those decisions! I never wanted to suffer again, in any way. Which explains why I was never able to really connect with many people. Complicity, friendship—sooner or later, it always involves revealing things, confiding secrets, and that was something I could not allow myself. I always keep people at a distance. You know something strange? I almost called you *vous* when you phoned me! Easy familiarity is something that immediately places people at the bottom of the social ladder. But in the U.S., there is no *tu* and *vous*, so you have to create distance in a different way: a cold look, a strong handshake, a scowl instead of a smile . . . these things create a balance of power, a tension—and I liked that. The only people I ever trusted enough to confide in were my partners at the firm. But even with them, I never dared tell the truth. Do you understand what I'm saying, Nina? I'm trapped."

There is a question she's dying to ask him. But she hesitates, out of fear she will hurt him, before finally phrasing it: "Didn't people ever think you were an Arab? I mean, I look at you and I can tell right away that you're North African . . ."

"Of course they did, yeah. I had to justify myself. But I didn't have that problem with Jews because they just saw me as a French Sephardic Jew. My skin is dark, I've got a hooked nose—I fit the type, basically. But yeah, non-Jews thought I was an Arab all the time."

"Did that cause you problems?"

"Not until September eleventh, not really. In the U.S., there's the whole melting-pot thing where people don't really look at each other that way. But after the Twin Towers attack, yeah. It was terrible . . . Even that day, while I was still traumatized—I had several friends who worked in the World Trade Center, at Cantor Fitzgerald—anyway, I was walking the streets of New York, in shock . . . I felt like screaming but I couldn't even speak. And yet I really wanted to call my mother to let her know I was okay—I'd told her I was living in New York, although that's pretty much all I'd told her about my life. All the lines were busy that day—it was hard for people to contact their loved ones, which only added to the anxiety. It was so terrible. You can't imagine, really. I'm trembling now, just remembering it. But anyhow, I was lucky: I got through to my mother right away. And I was so emotional, hearing her voice, that without even realizing it, I started speaking to her in Arabic . . . I probably only spoke for a few seconds before I looked up and saw the looks of hatred on the faces of people around me. Suddenly I had become an enemy, a pariah. After that, I went through a very tough time: I was constantly stopped by police, especially in airports, and asked if I was a Muslim, if I was an Arab. And, each time, I would lie, and I would hate myself for it: I'd say I wasn't an Arab Muslim, and sometimes I would even go further, like on one trip to Israel, by saying, *No, I'm a Jew*. Everywhere I went, I heard awful things: that the Muslims could never be assimilated, that sooner or later they would all become dangerous Islamists. That they could only live in dictatorships because they needed to be dominated. That they all looked the same. That they should be sent away, cleansed from American society. That they should never be trusted. I heard some incredibly violent and racist things. And what was worst was that, quite often, I found myself nodding in agreement! One day, when we were dealing with a case involving a Turkish doctor, my partner said something about how you could never trust an Arab, and I smiled. I smiled! Was I ashamed? Of course I was. But what else could I do? I was like one of those guys who pretend to be homophobic to cover up the fact that they're actually gay! But at the same time, my opinions were not too different from all those people expressing their anger and their fear. I felt sickened by what had happened. What common destiny could I possibly share with the bastards who had done that? Their version of Islam was nothing like mine. But I also heard terrible things from the other side. Once or twice, for instance, I found myself near a group of Arab Muslims who didn't know I could understand what they were saying, and they all seemed to believe that the September eleventh attacks were incited by Israeli secret services with the aim of justifying an American attack, that the Jews knew about it beforehand, that none of the victims in the Twin Towers had been Jewish . . . there were conspiracy theories everywhere! And, hearing that kind of disgusting anti-Semitism, I wanted to smash their lying faces . . . but I didn't, of course. I listened impassively as they spewed forth their hatred, revealing the horrors of their obscene imaginations as if they were just passing the time of day . . . So, yeah, let's say that I never really felt like I belonged to either side. I was alone."

Nina sits up. Suddenly feeling emotional, she decides that she wants him to know about the sadness in her and Samuel's life together: the genesis of their failure, their disillusionment. "I told you that Samuel was a social worker in a troubled area. A little while ago—three or four years—he began hearing anti-Semitic remarks. It began subtly, quietly, then it became more openly threatening. One morning he arrived and saw graffiti on the wall of the charity where he works: 'filthy Jew' and that kind of thing. He asked to be transferred to another city and they advised him not to admit that he was Jewish. Can you believe it? They told him to change his first name or to go by 'Sam.' In the end, he chose his father's name, Jacques. He's afraid of reprisals, so he doesn't dare say anything." "I don't like it when you're so serious," Samir says abruptly. He doesn't want to admit it, but he is moved, and in such moments of emotion, the only language he knows is sex. *Come here—you talk too much.* And he pulls her to him and takes her. She stops talking; closes her eyes and moans softly. The truth? What truth? Sex is all he has ever known. He is brutal, fiery, sensual, but also affection-ate, demonstrative, passionate. Everything about him betrays his urgency, and no sooner have they finished making love than he is telling her it is time to go. He wants to be alone now. *It's late—I'll call you a cab.* For a moment, she had imagined she would spend the night with him, maybe even three or four days; that he would take her far away from the dreary pathos of her life . . . but no, he's tired, jet-lagged, he has calls to make. She is still half naked, her body wrapped in a too-small towel, her skin afire. He says: *Get dressed*, and she gets dressed. She doesn't feel angry or an-noyed; she is not aggressively demanding with him. There is an attraction between them, maybe even a complicity, but beyond that their relationship is so complex that she doesn't understand it, and she is not the kind of woman to analyze such things, to dissect his words and behavior in the hope of understanding his feelings for her. For a man like Samir, used to having to explain himself to his wife, to other women, this is perfect. He doesn't want to be possessed. Watching her walk toward the door without making any gestures of affection or displaying any signs of discontent—her face as smooth and blank as a robot's—he thinks: *You behave like a man.* He says he would like to see her again, touching her cheek, stroking her thighs through the soft fabric of her dress, and she doesn't reply. This drives him crazy. *Tell me you want to see me again—tell me!* She laughs, and leaves without a word. When he's

alone again, he walks to the bed and grabs his phone: his wife has
left him several messages; she wants to know how he is, to find
out if he's lonely without her. Yes, she misses him. She says this
twice, then adds: "I wish I was in Paris with you now. If I could, I'd
take the first plane out there." Her obsessive, unconditional love
for Samir. The way she still looks at him, ten years after they first
met, as if she has just fallen in love with him for the first time—and
there is nothing fake or calculated about it. She is not one of those
women who like to appear passionately in love when people are
watching, simpering in their beloved's arms, their lips bubbling
with sweet nothings and ridiculous nicknames. No, she is like that
all the time. With him, she loses all the strength and haughtiness
that characterizes her presence in society. With him, she feels vulnerable. Does she know that he cheats on her? Does she suspect?
There is a kind of neurotic resistance in this love-blinded woman's
refusal to see the truth, given up completely to the desires of her
chosen man; this woman who rules the social world like a queen,
but who in private disappears into the shadows. She knows she is
important to him, though, and this ambiguous relationship—so
puzzling even to their closest friends—is the only way they can
function together. She questions him, practically interrogates him,
and Samir offers no reassurance at all. Because the truth is that
this little game excites them both: she is completely dependent on
him and, deep down, she likes it.

They speak for a long time. When they finally hang up, Samir
checks the messages on his cell phone. Nothing from Nina. It
drives him wild, this indifference of hers, and he can't restrain
himself from dialing her number. He wants to hear her voice. But
she doesn't answer. He tries three or four times—in vain. Then,
suddenly, her voice at the other end of the line, a chilling and
barely audible whisper: "I can't talk to you."

12

Back at the apartment, she discovers Samuel, face reddened by alcohol, slumped asleep in front of his computer screen. Nina moves closer and sees a news page; she clicks on "History" and finds out that he has been researching Samir—his law firm, his wife, his children. It is obsessive, and she feels suddenly terrified as she realizes what is happening: history repeating. She could never have imagined that, twenty years later, all the old emotions would remain intact, that nothing would have changed—the desires and enmities unaltered by time, absence, distance. She gets into bed and is falling asleep when Samuel gently shakes her. He is above her, trapping her on the bed, his pupils dilated, something strange in his expression as if he is about to do something unusual. She pushes him away—it's late, she's tired—but he shakes her again, gently at first, *You're hiding something from me, come on, tell me, I want to know, tell me what happened*, and then with increasing force. *What is wrong with you?* Tearful, she refuses, *Leave me alone, I'm sleepy*, but he insists, hammering away at her, haranguing her with questions, and delivering his unequivocal conclusion: *You have to tell me everything. I know it's a risk, but I'll take it.*

And then something surprising happens. Even though she knows she should just go back to sleep—because how could he really want to know what happened between Samir and her? How could she believe he would be able to hear about her betrayal without suffering?—she sits on the edge of the bed and answers his questions.

"We had a drink at the hotel bar."

"And then?"

"We went out for a walk near the Tuileries Garden."

"And then?"

"He suggested we have one last drink at his hotel."

"And then?"

"I agreed."

"Did he ask you up to his room?"

"Yes."

"And did you agree?"

"Yes."

"Did you show any reluctance?"

"No."

"So you followed him up to his room . . ."

"Yes."

"But were you expecting anything to happen?"

"Maybe. I don't know."

"Explain. I don't understand."

"I don't know. I didn't really think about it. He asked me to go up to his room for a drink, and I agreed. I didn't think about what might happen."

"You go into a hotel room with a man—a man you once loved, a man you had a relationship with—you go into a hotel room with him and you don't imagine what might happen. (I say 'might'; I still don't know what actually happened.) I find it hard to believe you . . ."

"Well, I thought about it, but . . ."

"Oh, so you did think about it."

"Yes, I thought about it."

"And what exactly did you think?"

"About what might happen if he was . . . *forward*, let's say."

"But you still went up with him?"

"Yes, I wanted to take the risk."

"What did you do in his room?"

"We talked."

"You talked. Is that all?"

"We talked. We had a drink."

"What did you talk about?"

"About him, mostly. About his life in New York. And then . . . I wanted to find out how and why he built his new life on a lie by stealing your history."

"And what did he reply?"

"Are you sure you want to talk about all this now?"

"Are you tired?"

"Yes. I'm tired and sleepy."

With these words, Nina lies down, pulls the sheet up to her chest, and turns onto her left side, her back to Samuel.

"Did you fuck him?"

He asks the question in a harsh, icy voice. Nina doesn't reply. She doesn't move.

"Answer me. Did you fuck him?"

And so, without turning around, she replies in a monotone: "Yes."

13

Every time he sees his mother, Samir pulls out all the stops. The presents that he brings clink and rattle as she opens them, a symphony of heavy metal: ostentatious bracelets and silver clasps on purses. Nothing is too good for her. He brings her wads of dollar bills, euros too, gifts purchased in the best stores—costume/gold jewelry, black/white diamond pendants, silk foulards and scarves bought from Hermès or Dior, sometimes even dresses, when he has time: baggy, colorful smocks (always famous brands, because he knows that impresses her, that it reflects his success, makes her feel like she belongs), duty-free souvenirs (milk chocolates, mostly, but also perfumes, hand luggage, leather key fobs) . . . This is how he expiates his guilt, how he eases his conscience. So, this morning, as soon as he wakes up, he calls the concierge,[1] asks for a car with a chauffeur, a bouquet of roses (the freshest, rarest, most fragrant they can find), and a Chanel handbag—a classic model, in quilted black leather with gold chains—money is no object, oh, and he'd like it all by noon, thank you. *Certainly, sir.* Always obsequious, always available: Samir enjoys these manifestations of subjugation provoked by his enviable social position; he revels in these flowerings of excessive politeness, interpreting them as a form of respect, the sycophancy demanded by his status as a customer—in a hotel, he is the king, and he wields power as he pleases: do this, do that, a bill subtly palmed, perfect, thank you. He had called his mother the day before, from the phone in his hotel room, to tell her he was in Paris: *I'll come and see you for lunch tomorrow.* He never warns

---

1 Jacques Duval, fifty-four, has been working at the hotel for thirty years. His father was concierge at the Ritz. He has become "exactly" what he wanted to be.

her in advance that he's flying to France: he likes to surprise her, to hear his mother's natural, spontaneous emotion on the other end of the phone line. Never—in any of the women he has hit on/ loved/met—has he encountered that candor, which owes less to simplicity of character than simply to love, he thinks, to the purity of maternal feeling. And yet, she is the one he's betraying. He is sitting on his bed now, in his underwear, the breakfast tray on his knees, the television showing CNN, and he is thinking about Nina. For a moment, he thinks about calling her again, but decides against the idea. Attachment—it's a mental illness.

He has not seen his mother for two years. The last time he came to Paris, in the winter of 2005, he thought she looked older. She complained of chest and leg pains, so—suddenly afraid he might lose her—he took her to the American Hospital for three days of tests. Her hair was whiter, her body shrunken, and he noticed that, whenever she spoke, she seemed to be fighting against some invisible force that held back her thoughts. And yet she was a strong woman, in the prime of life. She was barely even sixty.

He always dreads these meetings, but he has never stopped visiting her. He could have. It was a possibility he considered when he first met Ruth and, in particular, Ruth's father, and realized that there was no chance of him confessing the truth to these people; he had to make the resolution to live forever under the new identity he had inadvertently created. In fact, it would have been more opportune to stop visiting her. But he had not been brave enough to break off their relationship definitively—not because he wanted to protect her, but because he wanted to protect himself. He couldn't live without her. Something powerful still connected him to her, even if he was incapable of saying exactly what it was. Filial duty? Neurotic love? Yes, probably: as for all sons raised on the milk of the purest human tenderness, his mother remained the most important woman in his life. But there was another reason for the survival of these ties that bound them: the fear of casting her aside too brutally; the dread of hurting a woman who had endured a hard life, a life full of humiliations, one of those miserable existences that makes you seek out, in vain, the person or persons responsible, makes you search for the root causes: a penniless childhood, a forced marriage, exile and poverty, manipulation—a shitty life. He could never think of his mother without feeling outraged and angry. Ultimately, even in New York, in the richest and most bourgeois surroundings—where people are only allowed to enter after proving the prestige of their genealogy—he had never ceased to be Nawel Tahar's glorious vengeance on the world, the son who would avenge his mother's suffering. And every time he saw her, he was reminded of his broken promise: to keep her close by him in his hour of victory. He had won, of course, but elsewhere, without her. Each time he saw her now, she seemed slightly duller, as if another layer of dust had obscured the image of her he kept in his mind. But this impression was always tempered instantly by the affection she lavished on him; awakened by love, she was transformed—strength and color returned—and each time they were together after a long separation, she reacted the same way, with the same effusions of joy. She could spend hours in her kitchen, making the meals he loved, tidying her house, dressing in nice clothes, choosing the right perfume, for *him*. He had never told her that he'd had children, and she had never asked. Occasionally she would ask if he ever thought about settling down and starting a family, but that was all. He told her he'd met a few women, but had not loved any of them enough to marry. And generally, she did not press the point. Once—and once only—she told him how much she would love to have grandchildren, and he quietly, solemnly replied, "Insha'Allah, it will happen."

As soon as he gets there, he feels uneasy. The place is a vision of horror—his childhood home befouled. He feels as if he is entering a zone of absolute ruin. How is it even possible to find such poverty, one hour from Paris? All he sees is the degradation of the place, the walls covered with obscene graffiti and misogynistic insults, the trees engraved with penknife lettering, the disemboweled carcasses of cars, surrounded by wastelands invaded by scalpel-sharp brambles and greenish black stinging nettles. Everywhere he looks, there are spare parts, scraps of metal, and fragments of wood sharpened into stakes, and kids of ten or twelve roaming the sidewalks, patrolling, on the alert, swear words filling their mouths, lips set in scowls, ready to rip into anyone who goes near. The vandalization/bastardization of language. The drug-dealing and poverty. He saved his descendants from this, at least, took them away from the determinism, the fatalism. He got what he wanted. He needed to know that his children would be protected, sheltered from want, benefiting from the very best that the world has to offer. That they would not be exposed to the violence of society. And what's wrong with that? He doesn't believe in the virtues of suffering, the advantages of being tested. He doesn't believe that you are made tougher by enduring life's slings and arrows, overcoming difficulties in order to succeed, experiencing poverty and humiliation and abuse. On the contrary, he feels certain that poverty makes you fragile. Deprivation weakens you, physically and morally. At best, it makes you resentful—and anger can be an energy, of course. Sometimes it can help smash down doors. But if you go through those doorways, you'll soon see how your rage stigmatizes you. Go through those doorways and you will immediately become a mimic, you will choose a form of conformism that does not exclude originality but gives you a chance to belong. Because, for the social elite, it is not rage that rules but self-control.

Here is the true capacity for resistance. This is how you *really* stand out. And this self-control—Samir understood this when he met Ruth—although perhaps connected to mental strength, is essentially a question of education. Learning to keep your emotions in check—everywhere, all the time. Never complaining in public.

He thinks of his children. The advanced training they are receiving. Their delicate manners. Their extraordinary intellectual aptitudes maintained by the hours of weekly classes given to them by handpicked emeritus professors—retirees from Harvard or Stanford, concert musicians from the finest orchestras. They have everything. And on Sunday mornings, it's Samir himself who gets up at dawn and, even before he does his daily hour of exercise, makes them recite their lessons, checks their knowledge. He overdoes it, of course, and not only with his children. His friends and colleagues gently mock him for his obsession with performance, which he doesn't even try to conceal. He knows how to produce members of the elite. He succeeded with himself, didn't he? And in these moments of satisfaction, of personal glory, he is able to persuade himself that he made the right choices; he is able to feel strong and proud. But quickly this feeling is followed by shame . . . shame and humiliation . . . the shame of having betrayed the memory of his father, ignored his family's history, rid himself of their suffering . . . the shame of not having admitted what he is . . . the shame of having built his success upon a lie . . . the shame of having capitulated . . . the shame of having abandoned his mother . . . the shame of never having found her a better place to live . . . That is her choice: she never wanted to leave her apartment, despite his repeated proposals. Her life is this ghetto. Her life is this pile of shit. But it's a pile of shit swarming with life, and her neighbors are close by if there's ever a problem, and the local kids do her shopping for her. She's not alone here, whereas if she lived *among rich people*, they'd let her die. *They wouldn't even know I exist.* It's different here. *Yeah, sure*, he thinks. *The truth is it's dog-eat-dog wherever you live.*

The chauffeur dropped him off a few hundred yards from the ghetto: he didn't want to go any nearer, said it was too dangerous. Didn't want to have stones thrown at his car. Samir walks quickly across the wasteland, feeling conspicuous in his gangster's clothes, his arms laden with white roses, carrying a Chanel bag. People call out to him, then yield when they see who it is—*Oh, it's the big boss*. He still has connections here: he's untouchable and he knows it. People touch knuckles with him, kiss his cheek—*Welcome, my brother—let him pass, he's one of ours*. He takes the stairs—the elevator's broken—and passes a woman of African origin, in her thirties, a child tied to her back with multicolored cloth, a bottle of water in her left hand, a bottle of milk in her right. She lives on the fifteenth floor. *It's like this all the time.* Samir offers to help her, just avoiding a puddle of urine. He carries the bottles to the door of her apartment and then, breathing hard, goes back down to the eighth floor, wondering how she survives. He arrives at the door of her apartment and breathes in for courage, breathes out to loose his anxiety. He feels emotional. He rings the doorbell once. She must have been waiting just behind the door, because she opens it immediately—and as soon as she sees him, the floodgates open and she starts to weep (and she's not pretending: these are *real* tears) and kisses him as if he is more than a mere mortal. *My son . . . my son . . .* "Okay, Mom, take it easy! You're suffocating me!" He feels oppressed by displays of affection. *Come in, come in, yaouldi.* And he follows her and—wham, there it is! Childhood, like a boomerang, hits him in the face, memories hurtling past him as he walks. He hands her the flowers, the bag. She cries even harder: "Oh, it's too much, you shouldn't have, it's so beautiful, too expensive [and what she means is: too expensive for a woman like me], why did you spend so much money? You're too generous, such a good son"—and now she says, as if echoing what she had written to him: "And a good Muslim too, I know." Here it is, oozing from him once again, the panic whenever she pronounces those words. His heart pounds, he can hear it: boom boom, boom boom. What if he died right now? Who would explain to his wife, to his children, what he was doing in this woman's apartment? If he died now, here, what would happen? His mother wouldn't tell anyone. She would have him buried in the closest cemetery, in the middle of the Muslim section. Ruth would find out a week later, from Pierre Lévy, perhaps. *This is where he's buried.* The shock. The anguish. Quick, a chair. He sits down. On the table are dozens of salads and some bread that she made herself that morning: a sort of thick, crumbly corn pancake that he adores. But now, suddenly, he has no appetite. His stomach is in knots—the emotion, perhaps. She bombards him with questions about his work, his life in New York, and reproaches him for the fact that he has never invited her there, not even once—*Just so I can see where you live, a mother has the right to know that, doesn't she?*—that he has never told her about his life, his house, his girlfriend, that she knows nothing about him. All he ever tells her are the superficial things, but she wants to know EVERYTHING about him—*You're not ashamed of me, are you?*—how and where he lives, what he eats, what he does, who his friends are, his partners . . . But today, Samir answers quickly because he can guess, from the distracted way she asks him all this, that she really only has one subject on her mind: the reason why she wanted to see him—François.

"So tell me about him: What's happening? What's the problem?" The problem is him. His difficult personality, the people he hangs around with, his fragile nature, his wanderings. "He does nothing all day. He's not like you: whatever he tries to do, he fails. He gave up school at fourteen. He's never managed to stay in a job for longer than a week. He was offered a job at a market stall, but he couldn't get up in the mornings. He just hangs around, basically. He says he can't find anything. It's like he's doing it deliberately, or maybe he's just unlucky, I don't know . . ." "Mom, he's twenty-four. He's an adult. Just let him live his life." "But he's not that old in his head, believe me. I worry about him all the time." Furtively, Samir strokes his mother's shoulder. "It's terrible for a mother to have two children, one of them a success and the other one . . ." she says in a voice made hoarse by suffering. "If you had children, you'd understand . . ." Samir stiffens. How has he been able to keep silent for so long about the existence of his children? He thinks about them now. How he would love to be able to call them and say: "Here's your grandmother." Several times, his children have asked him about his parents, but his answers have all been lies, inventions. In the story he told them, his mother was a beautiful intellectual feminist and his father a tall and overly strict university professor.

She says she's not eating, not sleeping anymore. "I need you, Samir. Please, don't leave me on my own. He's my child. You could be a good influence on him. I'm worried he will do something bad. He's been hanging around the wrong kind of people recently. Ten men were arrested near here for an armed robbery, and I found weapons in his room. I didn't tell you on the phone because you didn't want me to. But why didn't you, Samir? You don't have any problems with the police, do you?" "Of course not, Mom. But I'm a lawyer, and some of my cases are sensitive. It's possible my telephone line is tapped, that's all. I'm careful." "Come with me—I'll show you what I found." He follows her through the hallway that leads to the bedrooms, glancing at the pictures of her and François hung on the wall. In the photographs, the first thing you notice is the incongruity of their family bond: her so dark-skinned and him milky white; her dressed in old-fashioned clothes, her body

hidden under baggy gandouras (only in the apartment, though:
outdoors, she never wears anything but dresses she makes herself
with fabric bought by the yard in Saint-Pierre Market), him in XXL
Nike sweatshirts. When he sees his brother's bedroom, he recoils
slightly. The bed is made, the windows have been cleaned, but there
are objects scattered all over the place: newspapers, documents,
empty boxes, clothes, scrunched-up cans of Red Bull and beer. "He
doesn't like me touching his things," she explains when she notices
the look of disgust on Samir's face. In the corner is a collection of
Nike sneakers, including several pairs of high-tops that must have
cost more than $100 each; a PlayStation console with ultraviolent
video games; dozens of horror DVDs; and a few porn movies that
François has not even attempted to conceal. Where has he gotten
the money to buy all this? And how does he dare leave it here
so brazenly when he knows his mother goes into his room every
day to clean it? *When he's not hanging around with his friends, he
locks himself in his room and spends the whole day playing video
games. But recently, I've realized that he's been doing something else
in there . . .* With these words, she kneels down and, pointing at the
floor, asks Samir to come closer. "Look," she says, revealing a large
hole hidden under the grayish, stained linoleum, sliced through
with a box cutter in places. "Come closer," she urges. And, with
a little flashlight that she takes from the pocket of her apron, she
illuminates the interior of the cache so that Samir can see the revolver, the knife, the grenade, the billy club, and the various other
sidearms whose names she doesn't know but which clearly scare
her. "See all that?" she asks, her eyes wide and filled with tears once
again. "If he doesn't have those things to threaten people, or rob
them, or kill them, then why does he have them?"

She is in a panic, convinced that François took part in the armed
robbery she mentioned. The police have been searching other

apartments in the building. "They were here, I saw them, all of them carrying guns like soldiers. I'm scared, Samir. I'm scared that he's done something bad, that he'll go to prison . . . oh, the *hchouma!*" "The word is *shame*, Mom." "No, for me it's a *hchouma!* Some words have more power in Arabic. 'Shame' sounds too smooth—it's not violent enough. It's a lying little word. '*Hchouma*' is a harsh word—it comes from the throat . . ." And she bursts into sobs again, screaming: "What a *maktoub* he's had!" Automatically, Samir translates in his head: "What a fate!" She's right: "fate" is such a small, quiet word; "*maktoub*," with its *k* clacking under the tongue, translates the weight of violence, the threat of inevitable doom, so he doesn't correct her this time. She cries out: "Oh, my son! I'm so glad you are here! Don't leave me alone with him, *yaouldi*, I beg you!" She's hysterical, he thinks, bored. He has never been able to stand these exuberant displays of feeling, these exhibitionistic shows of rage. He has lived his life secretly, with discretion as his watchword, and in moments like this he detaches himself from this woman with whom he seems to have nothing in common. His life is so different from hers now, with a set of behaviors and beliefs that is almost diametrically opposed; a lifestyle more in keeping, he thinks, with the man he has become: the respected/famous/role-model lawyer. In a quiet voice, he asks her to calm down. She sobs and hiccups, gasping that she's going to die, and he says nothing. She starts to tear at her clothes, to scratch at her skin until it bleeds—*You want to see me suffer?*—so, coldly this time, in a metallic voice, he tells her: "Enough, Mom. What do you expect me to do? He has his life, I have mine. I can't solve everyone's problems. And can you imagine the repercussions on my own life? Can you imagine how it would look if someone found out my brother had an arms cache in his bedroom? I have too much to lose. I understand that you're worried. I'll talk to him. I'll try to help him, as far as I can, but I can't do any more than that without the risk of compromising myself—and that is out of the question." "Please, Samir, I'm begging you—do something!" At what point did Samir realize that he has to keep his distance from this affair, to separate himself definitively from his mother and his brother? When the word "prison" was pronounced? When he discovered the weapons? Or even earlier than that, as he walked through the ghetto? He feels hot suddenly. He knows what the risks are if he is discovered here, in the proximity of those weapons. His whole body is clammy with sweat. He takes off his jacket and tie and tosses them on François's bed. "You must not mention this to anyone, you understand? No one must find them! I don't know what I can do, to be honest—reason with him? You know as well as I do that I've never had any influence on him. I barely even know him. We only lived together for about five years! We have nothing in common, and you know it. The only one who might have any influence on him is his father. Maybe you should talk to him about it?" At the mention of François's father, Nawel really does collapse, sliding to the floor like a puppet with its strings cut. Samir does not react. His face is impassive. But she continues to weep—nothing seems to calm her—so he speaks again: "I don't see any reason why you shouldn't call Brunet—it's his son, after all. You've spent your whole life protecting him, but what are you scared of? All he has to do is help his son, find him a job—he has the resources to do that, the contacts, the money. And it's his duty. Why should I be the one to take all this on? I'm not his father! You had this child with him, and you took it upon yourself to raise him single-handedly when that man should have helped you. It's his problem, not mine!" Just then, there is a thud in the hallway, the sound of a door banging, and footsteps on the linoleum. A voice calls out: "Mom?" "It's him," Nawel whispers, her face a mask of fear. Swallowing her tears, she closes the lid on the arms cache, stands up, and leads Samir to the hallway, where

François is waiting impatiently. "Mom! Where are you, for fuck's sake?" "I'm coming!"

Every time Samir sees his brother, he feels the same shock. Physically, they have nothing in common. François is wearing jeans with rips in the knees and the backside, a round-necked black T-shirt, and garishly colored high-top sneakers. Seeing Samir, he moves toward him, fist-bumping him like a teenager, and crowing sarcastically: "Ah, His Lordship is here!" Samir does not reply. He detests this familiarity, the fist-bumping. He follows his mother, who asks them to sit at the table. The tension. The aggression. The mistrust. All these forces he has to struggle against each time he finds himself in the same room as his brother, as if Samir were battling the darkest, most sordid part of his past: not of the shame of poverty, but of this brother whose existence he never wanted, and with whom he shares nothing. Intellectually, socially, they are in absolute opposition. François gave up school after failing his professional exams in mechanics; he writes and speaks poorly—a savage, thinks Samir, watching him rock backward on his chair, use his fingers to eat, make strange noises while he drinks.

"So? What're you doing here?"

"I came to see Mom."

"Come to visit the prisoners, have you? We're in here for a life sentence, but you come for twenty minutes, talk to us through the Plexiglas window, and *basta*! See you next time, bro!"

"You seem to know a lot about incarceration . . ."

"No, believe it or not, I've never gone down. Amazing, eh? I've messed around, but I've never been to prison."

"Don't speak too soon."

"What? Have you come here to threaten us?"

"Are you incapable of speaking without being aggressive?"

"You're the one who's aggressing me! You turn up, preach a sermon, and then you fuck off again . . ."

Samir does not reply. François continues chewing noisily.

"Could you try to eat more quietly?"

"Fuck you."

Samir looks at his brother. François is holding his knife in his fist, struggling to cut his meat. "Don't you know how to use a knife properly?" In a flash, François is on his feet, brandishing the knife at Samir with astonishing agility. "You wanna see?" he hisses, before throwing the knife across the room as his mother shouts and sobs. "This is my home! I live how I want! If you don't like it, you know where to stick it!" He takes a few steps toward the door, then returns: "And don't forget to leave us some money before you go!" Then he disappears down the hallway that leads to his room, abandoning Samir and their mother. "You see?" she says, in a tear-choked voice. "He's going crazy! I can't even talk to him anymore." Her words are drowned out by the deafening din of François's music. Samir listens to the words:

> We'll see how pretty you look with a broken leg!
>
> We'll see how well you suck when I've smashed your jaw.
>
> You're just a bitch in heat, a pig in shit, you should be in the abattoir!
>
> You're just a demon disguised as a woman. I want to see you smashed to pieces, I want to see you in tears!
>
> I want to see you lose your soul!
>
> I want to see you burn in Hell!

Samir stands up but his mother holds him back. "Please, don't go in yet. Let him calm down first." So he sits down, eats without appetite, indifferent to his mother's tears. Out of nowhere, he thinks of Nina, his desire to be with her. In the background, François's voice rises over the music, angrily chanting the chorus: *You're just a filthy whore! A filthy whore! A filthy whore! A filthy whore! A filthy whore! I'm gonna get you pregnant, you bitch! And abort it with a switchblade!*

"Can you hear that?" Samir shouts. "He's sick!"

"He's not well at the moment—don't be angry with him. He's unemployed. I hope it's just a phase. But what worries me is what I showed you earlier."

"Stop making excuses for him. He should just go out and find a job, instead of sponging off you. He's a man, not a kid."

"Don't talk about him like that. He's doing what he can. He doesn't have many friends, so he hangs around with two guys that I don't like. But he has a good heart. He's a nice boy, really, you just have to know how to deal with him. He's been unlucky . . ."

"How has he been unlucky? What are you talking about?"

Silence, suddenly. François has turned off the music.

"He doesn't have a girlfriend?"

"No. Go and talk to him now. He must have calmed down."

Samir gets up and heads toward his brother's room, thinking about what he might say to him. He knocks on the door and, without waiting for a response, enters. François is sitting at his computer, apparently lost in a video game. From where he stands, Samir can see the images on the screen showing a muscular man wielding a machete, his T-shirt soaked with blood; the goal of the game seems merely to kill as many people as possible. In a sudden movement, François turns around.

"Who said you could come in? What the hell are you even doing here?"

"Don't talk to me like that."

"I'll talk how I want. If you don't like it, you can fuck off. This is my home."

For a moment, Samir wants to hit him, but he controls himself. He does not want to find himself in the local police station accused of assault and battery; he doesn't want to have to listen to any more of his mother's sobs or his brother's threats.

"I'm not here to make trouble, I'm here to help you. If you have problems, I—"

"Since when did you give a shit about me?"

"I would do anything to make Mom happy. And I know she's worried about you. Why don't you have a job?"

"Can't find one."

"What kind of jobs have you looked at?"

"A bit of everything . . . security, mechanics . . . it's okay for a week or two, but no longer than that. And the pay is shit. I'm sick of busting my ass for peanuts."

"You won't achieve anything unless you put in some effort."

"Have you come here to preach? It's easy for you to talk. Look at you—you've been lucky!"

"I made my own luck! No one gave it to me."

"You've got all the cash you want . . ."

"That's not true. And I work damn hard for it."

"Oh, give me a break. Poor little rich guy . . ."

"If you have problems, I can help you. But you have to promise not to do anything stupid from now on and not to let Mom get mixed up in your business."

"You know what? Fuck you! You're not my father!"

"Obviously not, because he wouldn't deign to set foot in here!"

As soon as these words are out of his mouth, he regrets speaking them. François gives him a look of the purest hatred and screams: "Get out now! Get out, you jerk!"

Samir picks up his jacket and tie and leaves the room. François has put the same song back on, and the rapper's yells pierce the walls—*Filthy whore! Filthy whore!* In the hallway, he stands for a few seconds in front of a photograph of François in kindergarten: with his shock of strawberry-blond hair, his big blue eyes, and his gap-toothed smile, he looks like one of those models in magazines for children. His mother is in the kitchen: he can hear her clearing the table. When he reaches the front door, Samir opens his wallet and takes out a wad of bills. He places them on the chest of draw-ers, next to a framed photograph of his father. *Filthy whore!* "Mom, I'm leaving now," he says, embarrassed. And, seeing the crumpled bills, he feels ashamed. He has done this hundreds of times, and it always feels wrong: he shouldn't leave the cash like that, without a note or a card, not even in an envelope. It's twisted, perverted, and it infuriates his mother. She doesn't ask him for anything—*Filthy whore!*—she can manage on her retirement pension, she doesn't need much money, and she starts to protest: she doesn't want this money, it's too much, "Keep it!" He loses his temper: "Enough, Mom! Just stop. I have to go." He only realizes how brutally he has spoken those words as he hurtles down the stairs, running away like a criminal, like a man pursued by gunfire, the explosive rhythm echoing under his footfalls—*Filthy whore!*—hearing the words of the song played by his brother as if they were aimed at him.

14

Nina no longer feels any desire to talk to Samuel. She goes out of her way to avoid him. She can't stand the way he thinks anymore, the way he lives, his character, his personality. She's had enough. Enough of this resignation, this constitutional weakness that makes him take on the role of failure, this desire to be a victim that is fostered by writing. Enough of this apartment where nothing is ever achieved, where doubt and fear overshadow everything. Enough of this relationship based on coercion, this absence of love/desire/common interests. Enough of being incarcerated, circling their cage like lab rats with nothing to eat but each other.

She cannot go back to her old life, the way it was before Samir, enmeshed in this dreary, despairing routine, and she is seized with anguish at the thought that she might end her life here, in this commuter town where hundreds of people swallow handfuls of antidepressants, hoping they will let them cope better/bear the horror of daily existence/the economic and social nightmare. But such hopes are groundless, because nothing will ever change here. Nina surveys the future like a fortune-teller, but all she sees is a terrifying darkness, a vision of horror: everything is converging toward misery, toward the loss of her looks, her only possession, the only thing that has kept her going until now. And she blames Samuel then, hates him. If she feels this way, it's because of him, his lack of ambition, his neuroses. "You're a little man, that's what you are," she tells him. "You're too easily satisfied, you never aspired to anything, you have no dreams, and you will end up the way you began—a mediocrity. I look at you now and I feel no admiration, no respect. In fact, what I feel sometimes is disgust." Samuel listens to this and does not contradict her. He does not mention the previous day's argument—cowardly/weak/given up the fight. He acts as if nothing has occurred to trouble their peaceful existence. He plays dead, withdrawn into himself, shoulders hunched, a man trying to disappear, aspiring to nonexistence. If he speaks, if he provokes her, he will lose her—he can sense it—and the idea of losing her is unbearable. It sickens him to think that she is so corruptible, that all it would take is one word and she would leave. So he's decided to wait. Samir will return to New York, and he'll never call her again. He'll find someone better, younger, and they will forget him . . . eventually. Today, Samuel goes off to work, telling Nina he loves her. But what's the point? She doesn't react. She watches him move away and thinks: *I don't love him anymore.* Finally, she is alone. What choice does she have? She knows she can no longer bear this sparkless routine, this (so she convinces herself) loveless existence. She can no longer bear the thought of him touching her, talking to her. It's over. She's wearing shorts and a tank top and she glimpses her reflection in the long hallway mirror. Is that really her, that beautiful, firm-breasted, voluptuous woman? She undresses—she wants to see herself naked, in the dazzling sunlight that filters through the slats of the blinds. She lets down her hair, surprises herself. She has lost the habit of looking at herself in a mirror. Once, in a magazine, she read Brigitte Bardot's advice to a young actress: "When you enter a room, lift your head and act as if you want to sleep with every man there. You are the most beautiful woman in the world. Enjoy it—it won't last." This is what she does now—stands up tall and proud—and at that very second, the telephone rings. It's Samir: he wants to see her again; he needs her; come right away; he misses her so much. She laughs: "You called just as I was getting undressed. I'm naked." "Don't say things like that, seriously. You could kill me with those two words. Are you really naked?" "Yes." "All right, listen to me carefully. You're going to put on a dress, but nothing underneath—do you hear me? And you're going to take a cab over here to see me." "What if I refuse?" "You can't refuse me anything." Without warning, she hangs up. He calls her back, but she doesn't reply. He leaves her several messages—she's driving him crazy, he's so turned on, he wants her. He tries to calm down, but it's impossible. He calls her again, and again, and again. He feels like he's falling to pieces. He takes a shower, drinks a glass of whiskey. Where is she? And then, an hour later, there's a knock at the door. He rushes over, opens it, and there she is, her body sheathed inside a cotton dress with snaps running up the front. He pulls her to him—"I thought I was going to die"—then, pressing his body against hers: "I'm going to have to punish you for that." He kisses her, holds her tightly, breathing in the scent of her hair, and then he takes her to bed and lies down next to her. Her dress is undone in an instant, and his hand is touching her bare hip. He pulls her roughly toward him—he likes brutality, enjoys violence—pins her to the mattress, and fucks her in a way that will make her understand he's the one in control, that he is her savior.

She is lying on top of him. Her tongue teases his, then moves down his neck. Her fingertips caress his scar. "Are you ever going to tell me how you got this?" He pushes her back a little. "What is it? Tell me . . ." He holds her gently by the shoulders: "Do you really want to know?" Nina nods. "It's violent. You might be traumatized," he says sarcastically. Instantly she replies: "I like your scar. It makes you seem more manly, it—" "Stop!" He frees himself from her embrace and sits up, hands behind his head as if trying to encourage himself. "This is the first time I've ever told anyone about it. Usually I just say that I was defending a woman who was being attacked in the street and I got stabbed—the heroic version, you know. People are always impressed by that . . . It's not true, of course. It didn't happen like that at all. I was fifteen. My mother asks me to take a suitcase down to the basement. She doesn't want me to go alone—no one likes going down to the basement. It's filthy and there are always guys smoking down there, dealing drugs. So she asks the night watchman's son to go with me—she sees him as someone who can protect me. In fact, he's a gang leader, but my mother doesn't know that. Anyway, he tells my mother he'll take care of it . . . We go down the stairs and he asks me if I've ever slept with a girl. I say no. He tells me now's the time. But I don't think it is at all: I have math homework due the next day, I have work to do. I don't want to go with this sick jerk, but he won't take no for an answer and I can tell from the mad look in his eyes that it wouldn't be a good idea to press the issue. We enter a long corridor, a sort of dimly lit tunnel. At the end, there are a dozen guys the same age as me waiting outside a door. I can hear heartrending screams coming from the other side of that door. He grabs my arm and shoves me past all the others, through the door, and into the base-ment—and there, in the middle of a damp room, on top of a half-broken desk, I see a girl of thirteen being violently fucked by a guy of sixteen, and she's screaming, she's screaming like a wild animal, begging him to stop, telling him it hurts, shouting for help . . . it's horrible, horrible, you can't even imagine. The gang leader tells her to shut it. He pushes away the guy who was fucking her, points to me, and tells the girl: 'Suck him off.' The girl walks over to me. She's in tears. She kneels in front of me. The guy smacks her in the head and yells: 'Suck him off!' There's blood pouring from her eyebrow and she's sobbing. And I say I don't want her to. I say: 'Leave her alone.' One guy starts insulting me, saying I should lose my turn. The guys behind me are getting annoyed. One of them yells that I'll probably go to the cops. The leader says: 'What are you, a fucking pussy? She's just some slut!' But I don't move. I feel paralyzed by fear and horror. The others are egging him on now, encouraging him to punish me so I'll keep my mouth shut. So he takes out his penknife and he cuts my neck. He says if I ever breathe a word of this, he'll put his knife somewhere else and twist it till I'm dead. I leave. I forget about the suitcase and I run like crazy. I never told anyone about the girl. They were never charged." "I'm sorry," Nina whispers. "I had no idea . . ." "I've never been able to forget that girl. She's the reason I became a criminal lawyer—so I would never again find myself in a situation where the victims are unprotected and their abusers go unpunished."

Nina strokes his hair, almost like a mother. "I had no idea," she breathes. "You've never talked about it before." "There are so many things I've never told you." "I thought I knew everything about you." Hearing this, Samir turns away from her and says: "No one knows me. And if anyone ever claims they do, they're lying."

15

In all romantic relationships there comes a time when you have to find the best way to capture love, to safeguard it in an appropriate framework—an apartment, a marriage. This is an option that leads irretrievably to failure: the lovers know it, everyone knows it. And yet this knowledge does not dissuade anyone from doing it. After a certain amount of time, the lovers want to live together, in spite of the fact that it is precisely because they are not living together that they love each other. Samir and Nina are lying on the unmade bed in bathrobes. They feel good, happy that they are back together. Samir's cell phone rings: it's his wife. He doesn't answer it. He is too afraid of altering the intensity of this moment. Theirs, he knows, is a rare passion. Ruth might call four or five times, it won't make a difference—he's in love, he's crazy. It's dangerous. It's a risk. He feels recklessly free. He tells Nina: *I can't live without you anymore.* But she remains lucid, she calms him down: they have no choice; he will go home to his wife and they will each go back to their own life. She says this coolly while, of course, hoping that the opposite will be true. And it works: Samir becomes even more impassioned. *You don't understand—I love you, I really love you.*

"What I want, you can't offer me. I've just turned forty—I want a child. And you're married. You have a family."

"So what? I'll leave them."

"So you say now. But how can I believe you?"

Why does he say that to her? Why suggest something unthinkable when he has already chosen to lead a conventional, perfectly ordered life? His existence is privileged, the kind of life that everyone wants—though only in appearance, because the freedom from financial worries comes at a price: the loss of his true freedom. He is the husband of Ruth Berg. The son-in-law of Rahm Berg. No matter how he might try to forget this or to pretend otherwise, the fact remains: he owes his social position entirely to his wife and her family. Yes, he has forged a successful career on his own, but his entrée into the most exclusive clubs, his meetings with the most influential clients—those who can be approached only through private recommendation—he owes to the Bergs. He might promise Nina a better life where everything will be possible once again, but he's lying.

She stares at an invisible point on the wall, as if trying to escape his gaze, his control. "Let's go swimming," he says, turning toward her. "Now? The hotel pool is closed, isn't it?" Laughing, he kisses her: "They'll open it for me."

16

In the airport, outside the departures lounge, Samir asks Nina to come to New York. *You don't have any children. You don't have anything to keep you here. Come with me.* This is it, she thinks: *This is the moment—my chance has come.* She says, *Yes*, which is what he wants to hear. He will take care of everything: her ticket/her accommodation. She won't have to think about a thing (and instead of terrifying her, making her run away screaming, as it should, this idea reassures her). He'll meet her at the airport, he'll stay with her, he'll never leave her again. They will live together. *Yes.*

PART THREE

1

Since Nina had told him that she was going to leave him, Samuel no longer had any reason to live. She had made the announcement in a solemn tone, eyes lowered as if she, not he, were about to be sentenced. She told him it was a matter of hours, days at the most; she was going to leave him because she was in love with Samir—and he was in love with her too, she explained, as if their love counted double, as if the figures spoke for themselves, amplifying their feelings, the reciprocity validating the love, whereas by withdrawing from her relationship with Samuel, she was reducing it to a singularity, a one-way street, a dead end; she was dividing, subtracting . . . it was scientific, mechanical. She had hesitated for a long time before making this decision; she had talked about it with Samir—and she left it to Samuel to imagine the endless discussions, the arguments for and against; she left it to Samuel to assume the consequences of this betrayal. They loved each other, let it be known, and what did it matter to them that a third party had to be sacrificed? Their love legitimized the destruction, justified the suffering. Love was a tyrant, a totalitarian state that brooked no opposition. She was leaving him in spite of their years of closeness, the two decades they had spent together; she was leaving him in spite of the worthless promises she had made, mere words that bore no weight when faced with what the future held; she was leaving him out of love for another/weariness/boredom, with determination and a few other moods quickly swept away by the power of the nascent passion, the once-in-a-lifetime opportunity; she was leaving him out of indifference, as if their shared memories had been frozen, mummified, melted into lead, as if they no longer had any use or meaning. Their love was over, it was dead: a slag heap to be incinerated with the touch of a lit match to a trail of the strongest, purest, deadliest alcohol. She had tried to reason with him, using specious arguments to explain to him that it was better this way: her and Samir on one side, him on the other, a strict application of the principle of the separation of the species. You don't join one who loves with one who no longer loves. You don't mix the pure and the impure, the profane and the sacred. She had always tried to help him, to support him, to accompany him; she had listened when he was feeling bad, loved him when he was suffering, pretended to sympathize when he expressed his impotence. She didn't say this, but she thought it: she had been an exemplary partner; he had nothing to reproach her for. She had fallen in love with Samir without any premeditation or intent, because it was him—Samuel—who had wanted her to get back in touch with him, even at the risk of losing her. She had not betrayed anyone and it was pointless to blame anyone; these things just happen, there's nothing you can do about them. She minimized everything, reducing their breakup to a banal minor news item. People break up every day—it's nothing compared to a war, a disease. It's nothing compared to death.

But no, don't you understand, it's a disaster! The aftermath of love, the generalized infection, the amputation, the gangrene! Look at him, a medical incongruity, incapable of breathing, of calmly and objectively analyzing the announcement. Quick—an oxygen mask, a ventilator, a fan! Quick—turn up the A/C, open the windows, can't you see he's suffocating! He can't put things in perspective, can't calm down. The tear-making machine is going into overdrive! I love you (he loves her). He tells you that he loves you, and his opinion is of no importance. His feelings are irrelevant and should not be taken into account. He will get over this—it's fate—and he'll end up accepting it. He'll meet another girl in the street or he'll sign up for a dating site or he'll ask someone to set him up. He'll get rid of her things without emotion. He'll delete her from his address book . . . or will he continue to see her? What would he have to say to her? We can stay friends, she'd told him, we can remain on good terms. Or maybe it will be like "Helen's Song" in the movie *The Things of Life*: *I loved you so much . . . we had to break up . . . I don't know how to love you anymore . . . it's better this way, it was love without friendship* . . . He won't ask her out anymore. He won't be able to hold her hand or kiss her in public, to make love to her without prior agreement. He won't buy her perfume or books anymore—remember *The Book of Disquiet*, *The Book of Imaginary Beings*, *The Book of My Mother*, and *The Book of Sand*? He'll no longer turn up at home without warning—*à l'improviste*—he loved that expression, with its suggestions of natural spontaneity and sudden urges. He would no longer phone her at any hour of the day or night to say, I love you, to ask her: *Where are you? Who are you with? What are you doing?* To spy on her: *You're not answering! Why don't you answer? When are you going to answer?* He will no longer ask her for advice or arrange to meet her in a sleazy part of town so that she'll be scared and hold on tightly to him. He won't invite her to spend the weekend in Rome, or anywhere else, as long as she'll be with him. He'll no longer be able to seduce her with rare words. He won't perform any more magic tricks or take her on carousels. He will no longer provoke her enthusiastic remarks. He won't create any more portmanteau words—like *poustache*—to make her laugh. (She used to love that.) He won't get angry with her anymore for forgetting to put the lid back on the soda bottle so that the gases escape. (He is sure about this, irrespective of scientists' denials.) He will no longer make her read his manuscripts. He will no longer ask her advice about where to put a comma or the future of the apostrophe. He will no longer dress up as Groucho Marx to surprise her as she comes out of the Métro, wearing a T-shirt on which he has written in black marker, "Your bed or mine?" He will no longer read her the poems of Yehuda Amichai. They will no longer argue over ideology. He will no longer wait for her in front of her agent's building with two hot dogs (one without mustard). He will never again be able to hear the second movement of Mozart's Piano Concerto No. 23 interpreted by Horowitz without thinking of her, without crying. He will no longer look at dark-haired women, because all dark-haired women will remind him of Nina. He will no longer think about finishing his degree. He will no longer go running every morning so that he can hear her say, as he gets undressed, "Wow, look at that body!" He will no longer choose which DVD to rent, wondering whether she will like it. He will no longer book "a table for two." His dinner will be a pizza ordered from PizzaHut.com. He will double his consumption of cigarettes and alcohol. He will skim frantically through the pages of his dictionary, searching for the word that most precisely expresses that combination of melancholy and confusion that pierces him with the violence of an electric arc. But no word will articulate the feeling of failure and impotence, the pain, the rage of being left for another man; no word will translate the anger and the hatred, will express the fear of a future without her, of daily life without her, of love without her.

2

Moving into a large apartment on the top floor of an opulent-looking building in the heart of SoHo, chosen by Samir—a construction made in gray stone striped with green metal, with the fire escape attached to the façade in a perfect architectural shape. "If you ever want to leave me," Samir jokes, "all you have to do is take the stairs." She laughs, enters the building ("This place is unbelievable!"), and follows Samir to the elevator. In the spacious metallic car, he kisses her—they kiss—indifferent to the clamor of the outer world. "Close your eyes." He takes her hand and leads her toward the apartment. When he has opened the door and she is standing at the threshold, he asks her to slowly open her eyes again . . . slowly, so she won't be blinded by the rays of sunlight diffracted by the huge bay windows. He takes her on a tour of the apartment: Here's the kitchen, this is the bathroom, and here is *our* bedroom. He pushes her, a little roughly, onto the bed and rips her clothes off. With her head buried in the hollow of his collarbone, she repeats to herself: *Our bedroom.*

His double life—that exhilarating period when the intensity overwhelms him. The feeling that he is living twice as fast, twice as fiercely, coming, going, running, loving, lying, hiding, pretending, inventing, manipulating, acting, overacting, dodging traps, never sleeping . . . the agony and the ecstasy. The incredible freedom of being able to live in two parallel worlds, each world knowing nothing of the other, each world ruled (so it seems to him) by King Samir, but without the risk of treason usually inherent in such power. Who would betray him? Ruth? She suspects nothing and is not one of those fragile women prone to spying: she is too sure of herself for that. As for Nina . . . he is giving her a lifestyle she has never even dreamed of before. He can see this in the way she marvels over everything: a gift, a restaurant, even places that he would describe as banal were it not for the effect he can see they have on her. She is constantly dazzled, and this is exactly what he likes. She is not one of those blasé, spoiled rich kids who has never been insulted outside of a bedroom. She is the very opposite of his wife. He needs both of them now, moving from one to the other with disconcerting ease. He has always dreamed of such an arrangement—a sort of accepted, bourgeois bigamy—and for him it represents a relief, a private reconciliation after so many years being torn apart, confined, in the grip of rules that he himself enforced for his own survival. His wife is over here, Nina is over there. On one side he has the serenity offered by the family unit— the perfection of his children's education, the mental and material security provided by his marriage (and yes, he can admit it: every time he receives his bank statements and reports on the family's assets, he is impressed)—while on the other, he has the delights of transgression and sexuality: everything he felt the absence of in America, everything he kept on a tight leash before and which he has now set free: wonderfully, shockingly free. He wouldn't have believed himself capable of such liberty anymore, so incarcerated was he by duty, by the cage of his lie. Finally, at forty years old, he feels completely happy. When he is with Nina, in their apartment, he is Samir Tahar again. He allows himself to reintroduce elements from his childhood into his daily life: things as simple as a meal his mother used to make or some Arabic music that she listened to while she was pregnant. Little things, but perhaps identity is made up of such scattered, insignificant, inexplicable fragments.

This is undoubtedly the best he has ever felt: his life now is true to who he is, to what he wants, as if his childhood aspirations— all those daydreamed fantasies of a perfect future—have become real; as if he is now exactly the man he dreamed of being when, at eighteen years old, living with his mother and his brother in a run-down ghetto, he swore to leave that place and *never* to return. Is he aware that he has created an artificial world? A world where money is never a problem, never even a slight worry? No, probably not—this is the only world he knows now.

3

Samuel's sorrow filled up his whole life. It was a dull, throbbing ache that moved in waves over his heart, with sudden sharp pains whenever he thought of *her*. He convinced himself that it was the end, that his organs would simply give up, one after another; that what he had was irreversible, terminal. He could not imagine there could be anything after this. Something was broken inside him. One morning he went to a medical bookstore, hoping to find a rational explanation in a book—a description of his symptoms, an answer to the question that plagued him: Was it normal, this pain he felt? Was it the herald of a ruptured aneurysm, or cancer, or a slow death by suffocation? Had Nina been temporarily insane when she left him? They were together for twenty years, and it has been scientifically proven that love lasts three years: Were they being punished for having defied science? He spat on medicine and the Arbitrary Laws of Love. In the Psychiatry aisle (because he was going mad), he opened a book at random, searching for the words that might summarize his case: emotional withdrawal syndrome, he thought. A sort of blinkered autism: without Nina, he felt nothing, cared for nothing.

He had spent years of his life listening to people tell him about their sufferings; he had suggested solutions, some of which had profoundly changed their lives; and now here he was, seeking reasons for the Inexplicable, crying over a woman he loved, trying to understand why she had left him: Was she really in love with Samir? Why did she want to keep her distance from him? And to what extent? Didn't she feel the slightest desire for him anymore? He could open up the Book of Love whenever he wished, and for him it had become a sacred, mystical text. Nina had created his world and now she had withdrawn from it: Why? There were thousands of possible interpretations. But none of them soothed the pain he felt at having lost her. She left you—don't you get it? She doesn't love you anymore! Can you hear me? SHE IS NOT COMING BACK! He was talking to himself. *It's over*. He repeated this to himself, learning it slowly by stumbling over each syllable as if it were a phrase in a foreign language that his mind refused to grasp. He read and reread the words of Cesare Pavese in *The Burning Brand*: *She did that. She took me on an adventure during which I was judged and declared unworthy to continue.*

Barely had he gotten back home before he began throwing away all the things she had left behind, all the presents she had given him: the red leather diary, a silver pen, the statuette she bought in an antiques store with one of her modeling fees, and any little sign of love—words scrawled on a paper napkin, postcards, letters, charms—that he had, until this point, kept as if they were treasures. Then, one by one, he removed from his library every single book that reminded him of her: there were more than thirty of them. He began the mourning process that evening. He respected all the rites: He tore his shirt, slept on the floor. His evening meal was two hard-boiled eggs dipped in salty water. He covered all the mirrors with white sheets so he wouldn't have to see his reflection anymore. He stopped shaving. He stopped listening to music. He stopped washing. He recited the Kaddish for a dead love.

4

The realization of a happiness that, for Samir, had long seemed impossible. The possibility of a new beginning, of a rebirth. The possibility of being in love again. The ability to push back the deadline, refuse the inevitable, reject social conformism, to re-invent his existence by living in a different way, with a different woman, in different places: it was conceivable, it was "reasonable." ("Life is not a rehearsal," he told a friend once. "There are no sec-ond chances. This seems obvious, I know, but most people forget about it; they don't live that way.") At forty, he felt as if he had not only achieved his objectives—those determined by society and those he set himself during different stages of his life: adolescent hopes, adult dreams, modest or wild ambitions—but actually gone beyond them. He may have wanted to be a lawyer, but he hadn't imagined being one of the most influential members of that pro-fession in New York. He may have hoped to marry a charming, well-educated woman from a richer background than his own, but he hadn't imagined seducing the daughter of one of the most pow-erful men in America, a girl who was both beautiful and brilliant. He may often have dreamed of starting a family, but never had he dared to imagine one like this: two perfect children, good-looking, well mannered, extremely intelligent, and already—at only four or five years old—with a highly developed social sense. Thanks to a favorable conjunction of disparate elements—good luck, hard work, influential friends, and his own audacity—he had possessed and experienced everything. What do you give to the man who has more than he can consume? The one thing missing from his life. The essential thing. The love of the woman he loved most in the world. And now he had it—he had conquered her.

He has never been as happy as he is now, with Nina. Everything seems extremely simple to him, as if people and events are moving forward calmly, in the right direction, without any danger or risk. He loves her; he is mad about her—and this is new for Samir, who has never been able to feel anything for anyone. It's new, and that explains why he does not obey the will of Berman. It also explains why he lets his guard down. He's no longer as careful as he was. He knows this could be fatal, but he tries not to think about it. He risks losing his wife, his position at the firm, but that is the price he pays for living life so intensely. It's the price he pays for enjoying this sexual tension—naturally, without any effort, without any artificiality—this quasi-animalistic communion whose workings are mysterious to him. People can tell him that it's ephemeral, that it won't last, that he is taking crazy risks for a passion that will fade in the end, but it makes no difference—he dives in anyway. He is possessed by her, haunted by her body, and all he wants is to be with her, inside her. With Nina, there is no need for cunning or the contrived creation of exciting situations. He thinks about her and he is excited. He looks at her and he desires her. It's automatic. Sometimes he can hardly believe that she is with him, that she has given up everything for him, and that all he has to do in order to see her is cross a few streets or make a phone call. He has never had any difficulty recognizing that the one quality he values above all others in a woman is her sexual availability. And with Nina, he has exactly what he wants. Not that she is especially submissive— she is not one of those docile types, brought up to believe that a woman's role is to satisfy her man (her father was not that reactionary)—but she has no problem with sex. She has no problem with orgasm. Does she have a problem with seduction, predation, social relationships? Yes, absolutely. She can't stand being hit on/ hassled/wolf-whistled in the street or at work or wherever else she goes. But in a bed, with a man she loves and desires, she has no inhibitions. And this is what unites them: this sexual intimacy, this genuinely joyous complicity. When Samir is with her, he does not feel responsible for anything—she is every bit as willing as he is. Guilt? What guilt? All they are doing is beginning again after their love was broken by emotional blackmail, by forces beyond their control, a kind of fatalism to which he had grown used—perhaps the time simply wasn't right then. But now, he feels certain, there are no longer any obstacles to the course of their true love. What kind of life would they have now if Nina had stayed with him back then? He probably would never have gone to Montpellier, but he would have faced the same discrimination when he applied for work. Perhaps in the end he would have capitulated, would have settled for a lowly position in a two-bit law firm. By now they might well have divorced. But he no longer wants to think about those dark times. It's all in the *past*. Remaining anchored in reality, living the present moment with intensity—this is what has meaning for him, and he surprises her, takes her on trips, responds to her every desire. With him, he thinks, she is no longer afraid, submissive, deprived. With him, she is able to shine: people notice her, she is the center of attention. And at last, what had always been his greatest fear has come true—this man who made discretion his watchword, who lived life in the shadows, now, on the arm of such a beautiful woman, is himself the center of attention.

5

Alcohol. From the moment he wakes, there's a bottle close at hand. Nothing else can liquefy this concrete block, this dead body lying inside his head. In alcohol, it dissolves a little, becomes more bearable. Samuel feels the warm slide of its effects, lying on his bed or standing at a bar or, sometimes, underground, in a basement, lining up with all the other sheep to buy some hash or coke, just enough to keep him going for another five or six hours. He quickly moves on to harder drugs that explode in his head, finally giving him the energy, the power that he needs. It works on paper and in ink too, this explosion: for the first time, he feels as if he is writing something worthwhile. He's better, he thinks, than all those pen pushers who have never known violence, deprivation, that fear in the gut, that dread of going out, the possibility of murder, the taste of blood and iron, all those innocents who don't know what it is to be woken in the middle of the night by gunshots, a kid moaning, a siren screaming, by neighbors fighting/running/crying, while he has seen everything—poverty/shit/death—and nothing can scare him now. He's mired in it, and he feels good. He wouldn't change places with anyone now. He's at home in this hole, where one day he will die, a broken man. He sits at his desk, writing so fast it feels as if he's sitting on a rocket, speeding, driving drunk, close to crashing at every turn, seeing nothing, hearing nothing but the words unfolding inside his head, spending his days and nights writing, on the verge of collapse, his body tense, heart pounding, pupils dilated, mouth dry, no longer eating. He can't even look in a mirror anymore: his reflection horrifies him. He doesn't wash, scratches himself till he bleeds. All his clothes are too big for him. But he still has enough strength to take more coke, and that keeps him going. He's in danger—he might die, might never return from this edge—but he's not afraid. What he wants, now, is to write about reality, his reality: this solitude, this suffering, this misery, this isolation, this social leprosy imposed by the government, encouraged by the government. And those men and women in power, cut off from the rest of us. It would take him an hour on public transport to reach the capital and set fire to it. They've given up on us. And he thinks: It's all true. He's not inventing anything. This great social novel is his life. He writes with a line by Hemingway in mind: "A true writer . . . should always try for something that has never been done, or that others have tried and failed. Then sometimes, with great luck, he will succeed." All these years, there had been a terrible distortion between what he wanted to write and what he wrote, as if, when committed to paper, the most powerful thoughts became banal phrases and each word seemed badly formulated, each comma and period in the wrong place, and he would rewrite endlessly without ever finding that perfect match between his thought and its expression. And it was only now, at forty years old, after losing Nina, that he suddenly felt in full possession of his abilities, his intention meshing precisely with his ambition.

He works, and only ever leaves the apartment to get his fix. Maybe he should kill himself. His situation is drastic. As the door bangs shut behind him, he feels his strength leave him. His legs give way—this is happening more and more, it needs to stop—and his fingers tremble too as he holds on to the wall, pressing against it so he doesn't fall. On the landing across from his, a twelve-year-old kid smokes and watches him, not lifting a finger to help him. He's keeping watch, sitting on a shaky old chair like a curator in a museum—he'll be there all night. He supports his family by doing this. Fifty euros a night, in cash. Samuel walks downstairs—the elevator's out of order. And it will stay that way. Like this, the cops have to take the stairs, their boots scraping loudly against the enamel tiles of the steps—it's Us—their handcuffs clinking as they shake from their belts, so loud you can hear it upstairs—it's Us— their walkie-talkies crackling and hissing as they talk to the support on the ground—it's Us, we've got the situation covered—and by the time they arrive, there is nothing left: it's all been stashed, hidden, thrown away. The babysitter's looking after it. She's a young widow, three young kids to look after. Her husband was shot and killed in a parking lot nearby—three bullets in the chest—and now she's under the protection of a gang leader. What choice does she have? She hides the drugs in the baby's clothes, sometimes in the cloth diapers that she uses to save money—she couldn't give a shit about saving the planet. They say hello and goodbye to her; everyone does what they can. On the eighth floor, it's like a hurdle race, with iron barriers blocking access to the higher floors. It takes him a good fifteen minutes to force his way through, and when he finally reaches the ground floor, when he leaves the building and walks toward the median strip ablaze with light, he is hit in the head with a bag of shit. He should wear a diaper on his head. He walks on, stinking of excrement. He doesn't even yell or get mad—he's used to it. And he knows tomorrow will be just the same.

Chêne Pointu—"Pointed Oak"—is the name of a housing estate in Clichy-sous-Bois. It's a picturesque name, but the estate doesn't really live up to it. No one ever comes to visit him here anymore— it's "too dangerous." It is a no-man's-land that reeks of death/sex/ money, but it is swarming, it is alive. He takes the stairs down to the basement and walks past jeering kids, scurrying rats, deal- ers, and whores. He knows where he's going, but when he reaches his dealer, he collapses. He needs a fix but he has no cash. Please, please, he'll pay tomorrow, he promises, swears on his parents' graves, swears on his own life and his unborn children's, then goes home, the same way he came, takes an Ecstasy pill, and writes until the middle of the night, feeling like the king of the world.

Two days later, his door is smashed down. Armed men enter his apartment and tear it to pieces. They want to be paid. Samuel says he has nothing on him (in reality, he has nothing in the bank either; he has nothing left at all) but they see his laptop and help themselves. Samuel screams, holding on to their legs. The first chapters of his book are in that laptop, in a document entitled *novel 5*, his only copy . . . he'd rather die than let them take it. The two guys punch him in the face, take his laptop, and tell him he can have it back when he's brought them their money, plus interest payments—*You have twenty-four hours, you piece of shit.* They leave him in a pool of his own blood, like roadkill, his face swollen and one tooth missing. And here it is, at last—he's reached rock-bottom.

6

Samir knows exactly when it began—the moment when everything imploded and confusion reigned, a confusion so total, arbitrary, and definitive that he could no longer distinguish anything, his brain fogged, his vision blurred, anxiety choking him, absolute chaos. It happened about three weeks after Nina arrived in New York. He remembers precisely how his life began to disintegrate. All it took was one sentence, pronounced in a gloomy voice by his secretary, one Monday morning, about ten a.m., and his smooth world—a world made smooth by years of lies and sordid compromises, of social constructs created by his imagination and his vaulting ambition—started to creak and then collapse. One sentence—"Your brother is waiting for you in your office"—and he was suddenly outside Eden. His brother? What brother? He had no brother, had never had a brother. *I don't have any family— you know that.* Yes, she knows. She almost laughs as she explains that this man—who introduced himself as his brother but did not have the same surname ("François Yahyaoui—does that ring any bells?")—announced that he was looking for "Samir Tahar." *That's not me.* She knows it's not him, and asks if she should inform Berman. A man comes to his office, without an appointment, claiming to be his brother—he might be a madman or a pervert or something. Is he dangerous? Armed? "He wasn't very clear, if you see what I mean. The guys in the lobby downstairs let him right up when he said he was your brother. Should I call security?" A surge of dread. "No, don't call anyone, I'll deal with it myself." Anxiety grips him: he thinks of Nina, of his wife, and imagines the worst. François is not the kind of man who can be controlled, hushed up: he might kick up a fuss, cause a scene. His face creases into a smile that looks more like a grimace. He feels hot. He can hardly breathe. His brother in New York—this is a possibility he never even considered. He never gave him his address or invited him over. He has always been wary of social networks. And he hates him—*really* hates him—a repulsion that is almost physical and that goes back years. And yet he keeps on walking, moving toward the room at the end of a narrow corridor lit by a geometrically perfect sequence of warm yellow spotlights. Berman's office is only a few yards away: he might appear at any moment and ask, "What's going on?" Samir pushes down gently on the door handle—it's slippery in his sweat-gloved hands—then opens the door and sees him: François, his brother.

A physical description of him is necessary because, that day, there is something scary about him. Is it the denim jacket spotted with black stains (grease? ink? soot?) or his jeans with the ripped knees or his T-shirt emblazoned with the image of a hard-rock band or his flashy high-top sneakers with their frayed laces? Or is it something in his blue-eyed gaze—a spark of insanity? You look at him and you sense that he is capable of *anything*. He is sitting on a brown velvet chair, tense as a loaded pistol with its trigger being squeezed. But Samir doesn't even give him time to speak: having closed the door and checked that there is no one around, he bombards him with questions: *What are you doing here? How did you find me? Who gave you my address? What do you want from me? Is Mom with you?* There's no lack of ammo. *How long do you intend staying here? Who have you talked to about me? Who told you you could say you were my brother? What the hell do you want?* "Whoa! Take it easy, man . . . Is this how you welcome your brother?" He has just endured eight hours in a piece-of-shit plane with a layover, his legs crushed by the seat in front, curled up like a sick animal—and he puked several times during the flight too—he's exhausted, he hasn't slept all night . . . he's done all this to come see his brother, and all his brother can find to say is: "What are you doing here?"

"What the fuck kind of way is that to talk to your brother? You asshole!"

"Calm down, please."

"Oh, I should calm down? Well, how do you expect me to do that when you greet me like I took a shit on your carpet?"

"I just wasn't expecting you, that's all."

"I wanted to surprise you . . ."

He's cut his hair since the last time Samir saw him, and in places you can see his white skull scattered with freckles. He's also lost weight, and there's something eerily skeletal about the way you can see his bones protrude through his corpse-pale skin, about the flint-sharp edge of his Adam's apple. A large, torn, green sports bag is lying at his feet.

You must never come to my office without telling me in advance.

François stares at the carpet and plays nervously with a small metal chain that he's taken from his pocket.

I'm not moving my ass from this chair.

Samir cracks open the blinds and thinks through the problem, going through various hypotheses. He needs to react quickly, get him out of here by any means necessary. Turning around, he suggests in a quiet and suddenly friendly voice that they meet in a nearby café: "It'll be more relaxed there. I feel tense here, I feel stressed." He has no wish to be seen with this man, in his office, or to have a personal conversation here. He does not want anyone to knock at the door and say: "Hi, I'm X, Y, I work for the firm. And you?" Yes, he is probably a little paranoid—life has made him that way. He has two cell phones, never talks about his private life in his office. He fears revelation, fears transparency. François agrees and gets to his feet abruptly, his long legs surprisingly agile. Picking up his bag, he leaves the office first. *See you in a minute . . .*

Relief and fear. Nothing more than a temporary reprieve before the inevitable defeat.

I'm fucked.

The sweat that sticks to his skin is spumescent. It's the anxiety. His pulse speeds up, crackling and sputtering. Can a person die of fear? He is incapable of seeing past his confusion. When he walks toward the exit five minutes later, his secretary asks him who that man was, the one pretending to be his brother. And, smiling, without thinking, he replies: "A client who would do anything to make me represent him." What assurance he has in moments like that, erasing doubts, forestalling questions.

He has a panic attack in the elevator and almost suffocates; his lucidity makes everything seem unreal. What does his brother want? He feels trapped, and that terrifies him. He feels vulnerable, and for a man who prides himself on never being intimidated, this is something new. He tells himself to calm down, but he can't hold back the wildfire of fear inside him. He stands in front of the mirror and adjusts his tie, combs his hair. *Come on, come on, just chill out.* He knows he must show no weakness. He has to win the battle of wills, maintain the balance of power between him and his brother, and send him back to Paris clueless, unsuspecting, happily distracted by the wad of bills in his pocket. (He manages to convince himself of this, until he *truly* believes it.) But when he enters the café where he had arranged to meet François, his brother is not there. Samir walks all around the café, even asks the waiter if he's seen "a blond man with a green duffel bag." No, he's seen no one fitting that description. And yet, Samir wrote down the name and address of the café for him. For twenty minutes he sits and waits, incapable of concentrating on anything else. (He doesn't read the newspaper, doesn't touch the tea he ordered, doesn't answer his phone—it's his wife again.) He calls his secretary to ask whether anyone has left a message for him ("Yes, your wife called," she replies. "She said she tried to get hold of you on your cell phone and she couldn't understand why you didn't answer") and then finally gets up and leaves. End of round one—and he is losing on points.

Walking back to his office, he tries to think of a reason why his brother wouldn't turn up: he changed his mind, he couldn't find the café, he's dead . . . Oh, yes, how he would love to find out that François had died in an accident, never to hear his name again . . .

François did not return to the office, and at seven p.m. Samir went over to Nina's place to tell her what had happened. To lie down and talk. With her, he can be himself. Love and trust release the shackles on his words. He feels free to tell her whatever he thinks; he doesn't have to hold anything back or calculate or control what he says—all those defensive postures he adopts on a daily basis with his family and his colleagues, so that he always comes across the way they expect him to. He tells Nina that he doesn't know what to do: he feels paralyzed by this situation. All day long he has been in a daze, unable to concentrate, to answer his clients' questions. "You have to understand: I have no hold over him at all." He has never gotten a real understanding of his brother's personality, and—he can admit this to Nina—he has never loved him. Nina listens, and tries to reassure him: "He'll leave in the end, don't worry. He's probably just come to ask you for money." Yes, this is what he thinks too, and for a few minutes this belief is enough to calm him. Money, he can give him. But affection, friendship, any sort of brotherly love . . . no. He can't work out what his brother wants—François is a mystery to him—but he is sure of one thing: he needs to beware of him. "You think he's simple, but he's complex. You think he's harmless, but he's dangerous. He doesn't have the intellectual training, the language, the education to express the nuances of his personality, so his complexities sometimes express themselves only in violence. His father rejected him, and he'll never forgive that: he won't forgive his father, and he won't forgive us. And that's why he's here now: he wants to make me pay for it." Nina feels sure that he found out Samir's contact details on the Internet and came, spontaneously, for a few days. "He'll go back." If he does get back in touch, all Samir has to do is play along: hug him, kiss him. When he talks to Nina about all of this, everything seems simpler and clearer.

That evening, driving home, Samir calls his mother and asks about François. She is clearly upset, and it takes her ten seconds or so before she can speak clearly. That is when she tells him that François is gone—that he left their apartment with all his belongings, *and you know what he said to me?* No, Samir doesn't know, would rather not know—he should have broken off all relations with them, that's what he thinks—but his mother keeps on talking, her voice raw with hurt, the words coming fast: "He said he was never coming back." Samir feels a sudden pain in his chest. The telephone slips between his fingers and falls to the floor. From the speaker, his mother's voice crackles, calling out his name. He steps ever harder on the accelerator and the engine roars and he feels a sweet lightness, a kind of innocence, that he knows he will lose forever if he stops, so he floors the pedal, overtaking other cars, freight trucks, a sign on the back saying flammable materials, the word DANGER in big white letters on red, and he thinks, *I could hit that tank and explode here, now, in the middle of the road,* but he swerves around it—he's the king of evasion—and continues at full speed until suddenly the car skids out of control, squeals to a standstill. Samir hangs on to the steering wheel and manages not to be thrown through the windshield. Blood is pouring from his nose, staining the leather seats. Samir raises himself slightly to look in the rearview mirror, but all he can see is his own terrified face.

7

Samuel's downfall has been violent and painful, but there is also something—he is able to see this himself—almost funny about it. Tragicomic, that's it. So here he is, waiting for something to happen, for a solution to magically appear—or perhaps simply waiting to be put out of his misery. He dreamed about it the night that those guys threatened him, in fact. He might die . . . well, so what? He's alone now. Let them kill him. Let them finish him off. He's losing everything anyway. Look at him—gap-toothed before his time. What does it matter if they smash all the rest of his teeth, his ribs too—why not, just for the fun of it?—his bones are fragile, it'd be easy. He can no longer feel his body. Everything is numb except his hand and his head—the only things that let him know the difference between nothingness and suffering, absence and solitude. He's all out of drugs, his bank account is in the red, and his laptop is gone. He has no choice: he calls Nina and begs her to send him cash—a money order, a bank transfer—because he's dying here. He won't call her again, he promises, swears, and she ends up agreeing: the price of her mental and moral tranquility. It's humiliating—the fact of being paid by her, the fact of having called her simply to obtain money—but it's nothing compared to the desperation/fear/tension he feels, nothing compared to the certainty he has lost. The only certainty now is that he is damned, that he won't last long. And yet he doesn't give in: he clings to life, to what he might still make of it. And the next day, he makes the payment—hands over the cash and is given his laptop. Everything's fine—no threats, no violence. They're quits. But he'd better not come back expecting a fix from them, because they won't give him anything. The drugs will go to those who stick to the only system that still works: consume/pay, consume/pay. He'll die alone, as he no longer has the means to be an active participant in this system. He'll have to make do with alcohol.

So now he spends his days drinking, reading, and taking notes, as if what he were writing is a manual on romantic despair and solitude, and all the time he thinks: *I'm not alone.* Other writers have lived, loved, suffered, and have been able to turn their ordeal into literature. He has never been as disciplined as he is now, working for hours on his novel, waking up in the middle of the night to write passages of shocking violence in a sort of trance, as if they were being dictated to him by some kind of inherent rage, as if he were intoxicated and asphyxiated by anguish and anger even while he was in his mother's womb. But in fact, the rage is just him. He is this writer with the wounded language, the chaotic sentences, the words pouring out of him with a power that sweeps away everything, wrecking all that was built, revealing all that was hidden, befouling all that was pure, convulsing all that was calm.

It is urgency, after years of reflection and waiting. It is mastery, after years of passivity. The moment when finally, at forty years old, he feels at the zenith of his intellectual maturity, in full possession of his powers. And for a man like him, whose life has been an exercise in renunciation, this is orgasmic. Nothing excites him now but the arrangement of words, the composition of sentences in rhythms that stir him, the invention and inhabiting of characters in a world that he created for them—a world that has to be virtual in order to bear that other world, the real one. He feels good, alone and writing. He knows his place now: in his office, laptop on, his dictionaries close by, always open, his black hardback notebooks scattered all over the desk and floor, his thousands of notes accumulated over the past twenty years—press cuttings, essays, book extracts, hundreds of handwritten pages that he has to decipher. Never has he felt so intensely the need to extricate himself from the world, not to marginalize himself—he sometimes has the feeling that his life up to now has been a slow process of social eviction—but to find his true place, which only writing can give him. Only writing offers a direct view of the world, without any distortion. He loves this life; he loves the state of extreme tension into which he is plunged during these moments of withdrawal, and he thinks again of that concept, born from Jewish mysticism, that his father once recounted to him: having created the world, God withdrew from it, leaving man to make of it what he would. Intellectually, he had been very close to his father, who had initiated him at a very young age into literature, both profane and sacred, into philosophy and exegesis. Since Nina's departure, he has been rereading and annotating all the documents and books he inherited from his father—essays about Judaism, essentially. When he met Nina, having discovered the truth of his origins, he had severed all connections not only with his parents but with their religion. But now everything he had assimilated during those long years of learning comes back to him: the prayers and sacred texts, the commentaries and mystical interpretations, the commentaries on commentaries and the questions that are answered with other questions, the commentaries on commentaries on commentaries, the Hasidic stories and tales. His novel is full of this glorious mysticism, full of biblical characters with unpronounceable names. Everything he had buried for twenty years now resurfaces, and he welcomes those words back into his life without attempting to filter them. He feels as if his eyes had been opened at last. He feels a great peace. As if, by leaving him, Nina had allowed him to reconnect with his true self. For a long time, he had been incapable of mentioning his origins, his parents, and now the opposite is true: this is what his book is about. He is writing this dual story—his, and his parents'—in the novel on which he is working now, and which he has entitled *Consolation*, because the truth is that he has been searching for this all his life: to be consoled. And even now, alone, all he wants is to be with Nina. He misses her terribly. When he thinks about her, he feels the most awful pain, as if the jaws of a pair of pliers were digging into his heart. And yet he has managed to convince himself that he is finally able to write because she is no longer there. He has reread Kafka's diary—the pages about the relationship between creation and solitude. He is writing well because he is alone, and he knows now that he will never give up this solitude, will never agree to live with a woman, to commit himself, and certainly will never have children. Social life, in spite of the useful observations it offers, turned him away from writing, and all he wants now is to write. For a long time, he has wondered what made him persist as a writer in spite of his repeated, endless failure to be published. Sometimes he felt as if he were a puny, inexperienced swimmer thrown in an Olympic pool and able to do nothing more than tread water, keep his head above the surface, while he dreamed of cleaving through the chlorinated water with a kick of his legs, holding his breath, eyes wide open, conquering the blue space around him—because this was how he saw literature: as a vast territory to be invaded, a territory that cannot be breached without perfect breathing, masterful technique, total determination, without the drive to advance, to continue, to dive in every day even when you would rather stay in bed, to swim underwater even at the risk of never resurfacing. Most of the time, this ended in drowning.

He'd had this close, intimate relationship with writing ever since he was a child, sitting on his father's lap and deciphering passages from the Torah. A man found fulfillment in reading and interpreting texts. A life without books was inconceivable. And—he could admit this now that Nina was no longer there—this had been the principal subject of incomprehension between them. Not that she was resistant to literature—she was a curious-minded woman with an instinctive intelligence—but she never understood how he could sacrifice his time, his energy, his friends for it; she never understood what it was in books that so absorbed Samuel. His obstinacy disconcerted her. The drawers of his desk were filled with rejection letters, but still he worked—hoping for what? Publication and recognition could no longer be expected. "Try to think about this clearly," Nina exhorted him. To write—to choose to live alone most of each day without any contact with the outside world—you had to be crazy or willing to risk becoming so. And Samuel is—more and more. Crazy with solitude and sadness, crazy from missing her. And one day, when the pressure becomes too much, one day when he senses that he might be tempted by suicide again, he decides to call Nina. "I need to talk to you. I need to hear your voice." He tells her he's begun writing again, and says he would like her to read it. "No, Samuel. The answer is no. We must never talk again. You must never call me again. It's over."

I'm not asking you for anything

I don't want money

I just want to hear your voice

I miss our conversations

I miss you

It hurts

It hurts so much

At the other end of the line, she remains cold and impassive. He silently searches for the words that might touch her, like a man rummaging through his wife's things in the hope of uncovering a letter, a compromising object. Because that is what he wants: to compromise her. He wants to hurt her. He wants her to change her mind, wants to make her come home, so he can forgive her. He wants to coerce her through manipulation and lies: betray Samir.

The day before, as if unconsciously hoping to increase his own suffering, he had reread a short memoir by the poet Joseph Brodsky, "Flight from Byzantium," and he now surprises himself by saying to Nina the words the poet's mother, who remained in Russia, had repeated to her son, exiled in the United States: "The only thing I want in life is to see you again." But this makes no impression on her. For her, it's over: she doesn't want to see or talk to him again. She has *turned the page* and her life has changed for the better: it's *more intense, crazier, richer*—the kind of life she always wanted. She doesn't let up: she is not seeking merely to dissuade him, to distance him, but to destroy him. There is a sort of sadism in her determination, and this is a facet of her personality that they are discovering together. He is aghast, in pain; she is jubilant. She enjoys playing the role of the predator that catches/crushes/kills. She feels alive at last, fully aware of what she is doing: putting an end to twenty years of emotional alienation, avenging herself for all he made her lose, ridding herself of the humanity inside her, and winning. Armed with her new strength, she is supercharged by Samir's love for her, by money and confidence, the certainty that everything is possible now, the knowledge that she has arrived, that she is at the top of the ladder while he is down at the bottom— and is going to stay there. *Stay there and forget me!* You think she's cruel? So what? She owes him nothing, and in a cutting voice she says: "The last thing I want in life is to see you again." Why such contempt? Why such brutality? Is she testing his resistance? There is a long silence, undisturbed by even the quietest whisper, and then suddenly he is reborn. He gets to his feet like a boxer sprawled on the canvas hearing the macabre count—1-2-3—and there he is, dancing again, proud, armed with what remains of his dignity and strength, and he avenges himself for what she made him suffer. The balance of power tilts. *Now I'm the dominant one; now I'm in charge.* "So you're happy, are you? Happy, in your gilded prison, your artificial cocoon, your castle built on sand? Happier than you ever were with me, back when you were poor? Perhaps . . . but are you free? Do you really have the life you dreamed of? So your ambition was nothing greater than making yourself financially dependent on a rich man? All you ever wanted was a precarious romantic status that kept you from the clutches of poverty? It's a false security, and you know it. He could dump you tomorrow and there would be nothing you could do about it. He loves you, he desires you? Sure, for now. But how long will that last? You think he'll still be with you when you start to show signs of aging? How long do you think you have left? Three, four years of tranquil happiness . . . and then what? Shall I tell you what will happen after that? He'll begin by cheating on you, though you won't know about it. Then he'll cheat on you openly but he'll assure you that it doesn't mean anything—just a fling, nothing more. In the end, he'll leave you for someone else—a younger, more desirable woman—and all of this will happen without him ever divorcing his wife, because she gave him everything. It's just reality. Life is unfair, it's terrible . . . so what? What is he giving you? A life of luxury. You have a beautiful apartment, a cleaning lady, an expensive purse? Can't you see that he's treating you like a whore? That he doesn't respect you? Can't you see the machismo and the misogyny in the way he keeps you isolated in the name of his love for you? You've become exactly what you despised when you were twenty: one of those forty-something women who think they look ten years younger because they're wearing a miniskirt that shows off their legs, one of those women who simper in front of men like little girls in front of their fathers, dressed-up dolls, sex toys that obey the masculine order, that indulge the fantasies of the powerful men who chose them! You used to tell me you would always be independent, and look at you now! Do you tell him how handsome and intelligent he is when he comes to see you between two business meetings, or in the evening before he goes home to his wife? Do you relieve the tension he feels after a hard day at work? Do you thank him when he leaves you cash on the table before he leaves—a wad of nice, smooth bills that he withdrew from the nearest ATM before he came to see you? Or is it a sort of tacit agreement between the two of you: I give you everything you want and, in return, you give me what I have the right to expect?"

She is about to start crying—she can feel the tears welling behind her eyes—and suddenly she drops the phone. *Bastard.*

He somehow saw it all. That discreet/available mistress he described is her. He saw the cash that Samir leaves in her wallet, the underwear and sex toys he gives her or has delivered—surprise!— the clothes and shoes and handbags he buys her every day, money no object, so that she always looks her best and he will go on desiring her for a long time to come. (He takes care of her, and he does it well.) And he saw the day when Samir entered the apartment, grabbed Nina by the hair, and pressed her mouth down on his cock when she was feeling ill—No, I'm not forcing you, I would never do that, but please, just do it for me—and she was SICK, she told him that, she said, Not tonight, I'm tired, I have a cold, I'm NOT WELL, and him insisting: Look at the state I'm in, you can't leave me like this, DO SOMETHING—and she did, the docile woman. Yes, he saw all of this, and she feels as if the entire world is watching her naked on giant screens. Her crying and them laughing.

8

Samir is still reeling, in shock, when he finally gets home. It is nearly nine p.m. and he has just walked across the sodden grass of Central Park—a detour he took to recover a little. He felt like he was choking, strangled by the thought of his brother in this city: he is toxic, toxic and venomous. And there is no antidote to this poison. François is a gun aimed at his head, a gun that might go off at any moment. Samir is no longer at the center of the social conflict; he has gradually moved away from it as he has climbed the ladder of success. Struggle? What struggle? His only real battle is professional: he wants to win his cases, gain more clients, raise his fees, merit yearly bonuses, be the lawyer everyone says is the *best* in his field, and that's all. François is from the other side of town—the dark side, where life has less value and people disappear in the night. *Well, that's not my problem*, Samir thinks. *Let him disappear . . .*

Entering his apartment and seeing his children in their cotton pajamas, hair freshly combed and smelling sweetly of baby perfume, seeing their English nanny with her hair tied back, wearing a black-and-white apron, he thinks how much he loves his life and how he would do anything to protect it. He loves this effortless calm, this metronomic regularity, this natural discipline, everything that contributes to this perfect order, the little details that comfort him when he thinks of the choices he has made over the years. *This* is the life he was destined for. Pushing open the door of his apartment, he has often imagined what his life would be like if waiting inside was another woman, other children—a Muslim wife, for example, modern and secular like him, or religious and traditionalist, whatever, but a woman with whom he would share a common identity and certain values—and that woman, for some unknown reason, does not excite him but fills him with anxiety. His children shout happily and jump into his arms, covering his face with kisses. He asks them about their day, strokes their hair affectionately. Then the nanny takes them by the hand and tells them it's time to go to bed, and they follow obediently. This is what most fascinates him: this self-control, this discipline. He remembers his own father coming home from work, at one or two in the morning. He would already be in bed, on the foam mattress that his mother had picked up from a neighbor, his head covered by the blue blanket his grandmother had knitted (with poor-quality wool, rough and drab—he knows now that the quality of the fabric that touches your skin is a good measure of your social value). He wasn't afraid of the dark. In fact, he liked it: in the dark, anything seemed possible. He would hear the key turning in the lock and his father's heavy footsteps in the hallway. He would hear the toilet flush and then the drone of the TV that he always switched on, and that he would end up falling asleep in front of, as suddenly as if he'd been shot in the head. Sometimes Samir would get up and join his father on the couch, kissing his face, wriggling into his arms. But his father would always reject him. *Go to bed*. Hard. Cold.

Samir calls his wife and hears her voice coming from the living room. He puts down his briefcase, removes his jacket, and goes to see her. But when he enters the living room, he has a shock: his brother is there, sitting across from his wife, a glass of wine in his hand. Dressed in a black suit and a blue tie, he looks like some life insurance salesman from the 1950s. For an instant, Samir is paralyzed: he has no idea what he should do or say. His wife—after first expressing her surprise at the blood on his shirt (it's nothing, he assures her, I just had a nosebleed)—introduces him as François Duval and explains that he works at Pierre Lévy, is spending a few days in New York, and wanted to meet Samir. "Oh, yes, Pierre mentioned you might be coming," he replies with false enthusiasm. "Pleased to meet you." He offers François his hand, which is clammy, and sits close to him. "You must have forgotten to tell the night watchman," Ruth chides him. "I had to go down to the main entrance. I was a little doubtful, I must be honest," she says, laughing. "I called you but you didn't answer." "Luckily, I had my business card with me," François jokes. Samir is tense, nervous, somehow conducting the conversation in English. François's English is terrible, so Samir switches to French, asking him abruptly in hard-to-follow street slang what he's after, why he has come to his house and embarrassed him in front of his wife. Ruth watches them uncomprehendingly. François looks at her, then turns to Samir: Does he really want him to answer now, here? Yes—Ruth doesn't speak French well enough to follow. Go ahead! And suddenly, François panics. He is terrified by the thought of expressing himself in front of this woman, to Samir's face. He is frightened of measuring himself against his brother. Even when he first arrived here and found himself standing next to her, having to explain himself and the reasons for his visit, having to coax her into inviting him into their home, he had been seized with the most awful anxiety. Thankfully, she had not been suspicious. Probably she took pity on this poor young Frenchman who stammered and barely spoke English. He too, like everyone else, is impressed by the money, the furnishings, the decorum, the self-assurance that speak of power. He had thought he had the upper hand, but no: here in the United States, in this immense apartment, where every object had been chosen at the most prestigious antique dealers, where everything seemed in its place, surrounded by this silent staff that came and went, he is nothing. Ruth watches them. Samir turns toward her and explains that he is sorry, but François finds it difficult to speak

English, so they're going to continue the conversation in French if that doesn't pose a problem for her. No, she says, that's fine: she has work to do (and, she thinks, nothing to say to this man). Before leaving the room, she smiles and says goodbye to François with the usual polite formulas, not forgetting for a moment the codes of her rank. Finally, the two men are alone. Samir attacks first. He is trembling, his face red. He feels like punching his brother, but controls himself. "What the hell gives you the right to come to my home without warning me? What exactly is it that you want from me?" This is quickly followed up by a threat: he could file charges against him, prevent him physically from ever coming back—he has the right contacts and connections. He'd better not be trying to blackmail him: you can't play that kind of game, with him, Sam Tahar, here in New York. All it would take is one word and he'd be deported, imprisoned. Does he understand the risk he's taking? Does he understand the seriousness of what he's doing? No, François doesn't understand. He shrugs. All he wanted was to meet his family, his nephew and niece, to see where his brother lives. "Your brother?" Samir asks sarcastically. François is nothing to him: he is not and never will be part of his family. The only family he has is his mother. He starts to talk too loudly: "Go home!" "Take it easy . . . do you want your wife to find out your real identity? Do you want me to go into the kitchen and *tell her the truth* about the father of her children? I could . . ." Samir stands up, pours himself a drink and swallows it, then asks in a shaky voice how François found out where he lives. "Oh, you're not very careful, Samir." (And, at this, he takes a step back, as if his brother were talking about a stranger.) "Don't call me Samir here." François smiles contemptuously. "When you came to see Mom, you left your jacket in my room. I went through your pockets, found your passport, opened it, read it, and put it back. I also took a business card from a guy in your firm. That's it. But actually, how should I address you now—

Samir or Samuel?" "What do you want? You come to New York, you turn up at my office and now at my home. You want money, is that it? How much?" François leans toward the pedestal table to his left and, pointing at the large, seven-branch candelabrum that sits on top of it, asks: "That's nice. Where did you find it?" Samir does not reply. "This thing's Jewish, isn't it?" Clearly this is an attempt to provoke; Samir remains impassive. François starts wandering around the room. Pointing out an old photograph of rabbis studying a page of the Talmud, he says: "You have pictures of rabbis in your home? Have you turned Jewish?" He continues, pausing at every object that attests to someone's Judaism—a prayer book, a mezuzah—and suddenly Samir tells him to stop: *That's enough!* "Wait for me outside. I'm going to talk to my wife." Samir leaves the room, struggling to conceal his discomfiture. He tells Ruth that he has to accompany François to his hotel. "Can't he take a taxi?" "No, he's a new employee. I can't let him go back alone. Anyway, I need to talk to him." And he goes.

Outside, François is circling Samir's car. He admires it, covets it, imagines himself driving it, thinks of the women he "could have with a machine like that," and when Samir reappears, he asks him: "Will you let me drive it?" Samir does not respond. Inside the car, François switches on the radio and finds a rap station. He looks distractedly out of the window.

"Will you let me drive or not?"

"Maybe . . . Not now. Why didn't you go to the café, like I told you?"

"I was pissed off with you for the way you greeted me. When I left your office, I decided I didn't want to see you again."

"So why did you come to my home?"

"To see where you lived. I was intrigued . . ."

"It's up to me if I want to invite you to my home or not."

"Would you have asked me to come? Really? Give it a rest, Samir, you've never given a shit about me. You arranged to meet me in the café because you were scared, that's all . . ."

"Why would I be scared?"

"You're asking me? Your own mother doesn't know you have children! She spends her whole time hoping you'll marry one day and give her grandkids! If she knew . . . Why haven't you told her, by the way? Do you have something to hide?"

Samir does not reply. He keeps his eyes on the road, imperturbable.

"It must be your wife you're protecting. Because you couldn't care less about me and Mom, could you? You must have told her that your family was rich. You were ashamed to introduce her to your mother. In fact, I bet there's more to it than that. I bet she doesn't know that you're a—"

"Shut up! Now you're going to listen to me. I'm going to find you a hotel room and I'm going to give you some money so you can buy some clothes and stay here a few days. I'll pay for a guide to take you round the city. You can see the Statue of Liberty, Central Park, the Empire State Building, and so on. After that, you go home, you say nothing to mom, and you forget all about me. Do you understand?"

But François merely smiles insolently and says: "Okay, have you finished? Now, are you going to let me drive this thing?"

9

That evening, after dropping his things in the hotel room that Samir booked for him, François goes out. Dressed in leather jacket and jeans, his fingers aglitter with big flashy rings, he chats up a girl[1] near a club where Samir promised to meet him at midnight and asks her to go with him, but she says no. Outside the club, the bouncer[2] lets him pass. He doesn't even need to say the name Tahar—he's white, he's blond, he's a good guy, he's in. So François walks through into the darkness checkered with strobes, intermittently dazzled by multicolored spotlights, feeling . . . what? Desire? Something animal? The lights flash brightly, reflecting the rocks on girls' fingers, the purses hanging from their shoulders—bling bling! He's never seen anything like these girls, so beautiful, so easy, all whores/bitches/sluts, laughing loudly, *Check it out, they're almost naked, they bend over and you can see their pussies, their tits, man, this is hot*. They're like the women from the porno movies he watches all the time, he thinks: the kind of girls who fuck and suck on the first date, maybe even at first sight. None of them virgins, he's sure. None of them pure like the girls in his dreams: untouched child-women never soiled by another man's hands. No, here, there's nothing but shameless bodies, stinking of impurity (deodorant, semen, blood, sweat, shit). He hates everything about them: their alcohol breath, their brazenness, their corrupting smiles. A man

---

1 April Vincente, nineteen, of Hispanic origin. An average student, April's ambition is to "start a family."

2 John Dante, thirty-five, a former boxer. Having dreamed of being "champion of the world" from the age of eight, John had to settle for a career in nightclub security.

like him knows how he'd take them if he got the chance, knows what they want, deep down, the little whores—to be dominated, to be fucked—and, just like that, he's hard. *Shit, guy, control yourself.* They might not let him, after all, so shy, simpering, intimidated . . . Ha, yeah, right! *That* is all they're here for! And at this very moment, he notices a tall redhead[3] near the bar. Shit, she's hot: rose-colored skin and those huge tits that wobble as she dances. Man, he'd like to fuck her. He puts his hand on his rock-hard dick and imagines what he'd do to her if he had the money: tell her to suck him off . . . *Calm down* . . . he sees his reflection in one of the massive mirrors that make the club look like a whorehouse—do they like to watch themselves necking and groping? does that turn them on too?—but it's his father he sees now: the spitting image of his father, white, blond, his complexion creamy when he wants to be coffee-colored, curly-haired. He's sick of walking around with his cute little angel face, being allowed in everywhere. No one's scared of him—not like his friends, Arabs or Africans, who are never allowed in anywhere, who everyone's scared of. But no, not him, and yet all he wants to do is blow the place up, destroy, go crazy, sneak into his father's house and set fire to everything—the linen sheets (white), the porcelain plates (white), their hairless genitalia (white, very white, talcum-powdered) . . . God, he hates him! He hates it all, this white bourgeoisie, so respectable, polite, unfriendly, avaricious, their asses clean but their mouths bitter, filled with acid. He hates his father. He himself is unbending, stubborn, untamable—all his teachers told him so, and he knows it's true, but so what? He hates his father and he hates his brother—for his opportunism, for the way he looks down on everyone as if he belongs to some higher

---

3 Graziella Beluga, twenty-one, from Texas. Abused by her father at the age of ten, she lived with several foster families before moving to New York to work as an au pair for a French family in the hope of changing her life.

sphere to which you can never gain entry—and, yes, that is why he's come here, it hits him now, the truth of it: he's come to destroy him. And the day of his brother's fall, he'll be in the first row, the best seat in the house, clapping until his hands hurt . . . Oh, and talk of the devil: here he comes now. Samir, in a skintight black T-shirt, walking toward him. "Why are you standing? I've booked a table. Follow me." Why is he doing this? Why put so much effort into pretending to be friends with his hated brother? To snare him, lead him on, lull him into a false sense of security. He buys him drinks, and after a couple, François is relaxed, the music pounding in his head. He asks for another drink—a third, a fourth, a fifth—Samir gets up and heads toward the bathroom with a skeletal blonde. He seduced her effortlessly, while François doesn't even dare nod or wink at that redheaded slut. A sixth drink, a seventh, and ten minutes later François is staggering toward the club's exit because he thought he saw the redhead leaving. Reeling right and left, it takes him fifteen minutes to walk fifty yards, and then he sees her, behind a car—the redhead from the bar, leaning against the driver's door, her skirt riding up her thighs, blouse open, and he thinks: *That's all she wants*. He walks up to her, starts talking to her. She shouldn't smoke alone—why don't they share? But she doesn't want to share, or to talk, she just wants to smoke, and she tells him to leave her alone. She's speaking English, so he doesn't understand everything she says, but she's yelling now and he can sense the violence of her rejection, see the red veins in the whites of her eyes. She's upset, she's had too much to drink. He mutters, "Slut" (in French), and throws himself at her, ripping her blouse (*Filthy whore!*), pulling up her skirt and shoving his hand inside her panties. Roughly, aggressively he tries to get his fingers inside her, indifferent to her screams, her punches and kicks (*Filthy whore!*), and, holding her down firmly with his left hand, he drops his pants, whips out his dick (*Filthy whore!*), and, as she screams so loud it seems to fill the night sky, it happens—he comes over her bunched-up skirt as the bouncer arrives, carrying an iron bar. François makes out his heavy figure in the darkness, lets go of the woman, and bolts toward the road. He runs so fast, no one can follow him, no one could ever catch him: his strength is all in his legs, agile and supple, sprinter's legs that seem to glide over the asphalt. Like a vague murmur, he hears the squeal of a police siren, merging with the girl's screams. But they are far, far away now.

10

Francis Scott Fitzgerald revealed that he began to be a writer the day he discovered that his mother had lost two children before he was born, and Samuel too can date precisely the moment when he became a writer: the day his parents died. This provides the subject of his book—identity, bereavement, parents, and children. He has never gotten over the death of his mother and father. The tragedy that led to other tragedies: his suicide attempt, the breakup with Nina, his slow reconstruction (into what?). He never got over it, and so this is what he writes about. The unconscious state that precedes writing. The writing that resolves nothing and makes everything worse.

What weighs on him is the contrast between the intellectual demands of his parents (demands that also affected their religious choices, because they, like their son, studied sacred texts, without ever giving up their more literary and philosophical readings), their obsession with scholarly success, the absolute glorification of knowledge, and the outcome of this approach, of all those years of work. He could have been—should have been—a quantum physicist, a rabbi, a philosopher, a geneticist. Instead of which he took law because of a computer error during registration and ended up abandoning it and becoming a social worker in a place where he had to hide the fact that he was Jewish. What a failure, he wrote, that dissimulation should become the key to his survival! What a failure to think that he had fled his family, given up what he was out of simple opposition, out of rejection, perhaps, but also out of personal desire, by his own free will, and that now he had to lie about himself in order not to be insulted, rejected, in order to keep a place in life that was not the one he had chosen. He had thought he would be published, but everything he had written had been rejected, without any justification or reason, so much so that he had stopped even sending out his books. He kept all those rejection letters in a shoe box. He had never found the resolution to throw them away. Had Nina believed in him, in his literary potential? No, never. So, from now on, he wrote against her.

11

Samir does not understand why his brother fled. He does not understand why he isn't answering his phone. He is worried. He can't explain to his wife why he is so depressed, why for the last few days he has been taking anti-anxiety pills at bedtime, why he no longer feels like making love/getting up/washing/dressing/checking the kids' homework, and now he feels the full consequences, the full implications of his big lie—this pain: *I can never be myself*. He can't sit next to his wife or next to a friend and say: Listen, I'm Samir Tahar. And even with Nina, to whom he feels so close, Nina who knows almost everything, he often feels as if he is playing a role. It is a fleeting sensation, and he can't put his finger on where it is coming from. In the office, his colleagues observe that he is anxious, nervous. And they're right: he is. *He's hiding something.*

Hey, there, Sami, everything okay?

No, everything's not okay. He is hiding the shame he feels at what he has become: this parvenu who would rather die than admit the truth of his origins. He is hiding the brother he despises: that vulgar stranger, without manners or education; that coarse, disturbing man, driven by some inner violence. He is hiding his moods: the rage that rises within him and then vanishes; the helplessness he feels at being at the mercy of others, of chance, at no longer being the master of his own destiny. He's in such a terrible state that the only future he can see is a sort of desperate escape—eloping with Nina. He knows that he could never bear to be there when the truth is revealed, and François's presence in New York offers a constant threat of this. Because he did reappear suddenly a few days ago, without providing any explanation for his absence, and now he calls Samir every day, sometimes several times a day—conversations in which he sounds unhinged, menacing. Samir knows he must talk to someone about this—he'll go crazy if he doesn't—but who? He's still able to keep up appearances in wider society, but for how long? He needs a few lines of coke every day now to hold it together. Inside, he's a complete mess, and one day, when he senses that he can't take it anymore, that he's about to collapse, he decides to call Pierre Lévy and tell him everything. Lévy is in New York for a few days: the time is right, he thinks. And even if their last meeting in Paris ended in failure, Samir knows he can count on his friend. So he calls him, and Pierre notices instantly, just from the sound of his voice, that something is wrong: "What is it, Sam?" "I have problems, Pierre, serious problems. You have to help me." They agree to meet that evening in a restaurant on Madison Avenue. As soon as he hangs up, Samir feels better. Knowing that he will finally be able to confess the truth of his identity fills him with calm. Nina is glad: this desire for truthfulness, for transparency, is just the beginning of a bigger change, she says. One day, they will be together—Nina and Samir. She persuades him of this and he believes it.

Pierre, I asked you here because I have something important to tell you. You're the only one I can talk to about this.

And he tells him everything.

I'm an Arab, and I'm a Muslim. My real name is Samir, not Samuel.

It takes Pierre Lévy a few seconds to react. Although he is overwhelmed by Samir's lie (and he tells him: it's a "monstrous betrayal"), he does feel responsible for the nightmare in which his friend is now trapped: it was he, after all, who first mistook him for a Jew and presented him to others as such. In some way, he was the trigger for this hoax, but he would like to understand why Samir didn't tell him the truth earlier. *Impossible!* Doesn't he understand? The lie grew every day, nurtured and fed by his imagination, becoming a social construction, something solid and real to which he added new elements constantly as if to convince himself that his initial decision was the right one. His life was a complete fabrication! How on earth could he put an end to it?

"What choice did I have? If I'd told you the truth back then, you'd have fired me!"

"No . . . of course I wouldn't. What do you take me for? I think I would have tried to understand what had made you lie to me."

"Bullshit. I'd have been out on my ass! And, just like all the others, you would never have interviewed me in the first place if you'd known I was an Arab."

Pierre is silent for a few moments. He detests this sort of attitude: *I'm a victim.* He got to where he is today without any help, through hard work and determination, and he does not accept Samir's defense—and tells him so brusquely. He swallows a few mouthfuls of wine and puts down his glass extremely slowly. "You want to know what I really think?" Samir nods.

"You talk like a failure. Your mentality is defeatist. This way of thinking, of seeing the world . . . it's narrow-minded, small-minded. If you follow that logic, then we are perpetually doomed to being a victim of our origins, our background, our education. And that's not true. Succeeding in life is a question of determination and desire. It's a question of opportunities, meetings, seizing your chance. I am certain of this, and I will go further: I am the living proof of it. A door slams shut in your face? Knock on another one. And if worse comes to worst, you smash it down."

"I sent my CV to dozens of firms, and I never even got a single interview. You think that's normal? Do you seriously refuse to recognize that there is a real discrimination problem?"

"I recognize that there is real discrimination, but I think it's social, not racial. Maybe your address led to you not being interviewed, but not your name . . ."

"You only say that because you've never had to deal with it yourself!"

"Oh, I've had my share of humiliations as a Jew, believe me. Segregation, exclusion . . . I've experienced those things. You think I wasn't called a "filthy Jew" in school? You think I never got dumped by a girl because she discovered I was Jewish? You think I never heard the worst anti-Semitic clichés from people I considered my closest friends? Oh, and I think I've lost opportunities because of my name too. We've all been there . . ."

"You're just telling me anecdotes. I'm talking about integration, access to employment. I'm talking about organized humiliation across an entire society!"

"You want to know the brutal truth? The kind of thing no one ever says publicly because they don't want to disturb the peace? The truth is that Arabs feel humiliated and Jews feel persecuted. The truth is that Arabs still react as if they are being colonized, oppressed, and the Jews as if they are still at risk of being exterminated. Each group has to come to terms with that, and sometimes that leads to a kind of competitive victimism: Who has suffered the most? Who is suffering the most? Who's got the highest death toll? Who's the oppressor and who's the victim? We are! No, we are! It's pitiful, pathetic. It depresses me. It depresses me to exist only through this prism of martyrdom, this contest where the weakest are the winners. Did you really feel so discriminated against? You passed all your exams, didn't you? You were top of your class, in fact—you told me so yourself. Maybe, once or twice, you had a teacher who was harder on you in the oral exam because he had racial prejudices, but so what? Anyone can face that kind of situation. The son of a rich bourgeois family who turns up to the exam wearing thousand-euro shoes and a luxury watch might also receive a bad grade just because someone takes exception to his appearance. You see what I mean? It was paranoia that led you to lie about your identity . . ."

"You think *I'm* paranoid? What about the Jews? As soon as they're subjected to any kind of criticism, as soon as they feel unloved, wronged, slighted, they accuse you of anti-Semitism! You dare say a word against Israel, and you're labeled an anti-Semite. Fail an oral exam? The examiner must be anti-Semitic. Job interview goes badly? Anti-Semitism, what else? Come on, we all know the routine—even my own kids know it. Their mother taught it to them. It's obsessive with Jews, this fear of not being loved, not being accepted. Jews never think inwardly, never examine their own conscience, because they're too busy accusing everyone else! But if an Arab says he's suffered racism, that he's been targeted because of the color of his skin, discriminated against because of his name, then he's a whiner, he's exaggerating, he's playing the victim, he's failed to integrate, *it's all his fault*, he should go back where he came from, or where his parents came from, or he should change his name . . . which is what I ended up doing. I'm not paranoid, believe me. I know what I'm talking about. I sent my CV to more than fifty firms and didn't get a single interview, but as soon as I changed my name from Samir to Sam, I suddenly became interesting, intelligent, someone worth listening to, someone whose opinions were worthwhile . . . I became *visible*! Dropping the last two letters of my first name gave me a legitimacy that my skills and my qualifications somehow failed to give me. Can you believe it? In this day and age! In a democracy! Ha! The number of times I've been asked to show my ID, or I've been stopped while driving for a 'routine check' . . . it's become a joke among my friends. But my wife doesn't find it funny, not at all. It drives her crazy that people might think her husband is an Arab. Although admittedly I get stopped a lot less often when I'm driving my Aston Martin, that's for sure! Come on, Pierre, admit it—you hired me because you thought I was a Jew! Of course I was competent, I was very well qualified, but you also thought I was one of yours, and that reassured you. It reassured you to work with a Jew. Don't try to deny it. The first thing my partner's son notices when he starts a new class is whether he's the only Jew or not. And if there is another Jew in the class, you can bet your ass that's who he'll become friends with, even if they seem to have nothing else in common. It'll be the Jew he invites to his parents' summerhouse for the weekend, and it'll be the Jews' parents that Berman and his wife end up meeting so they can talk about political power and Jews, about Israel and Iran, about the rise of anti-Semitism and the price of real estate in Jerusalem and Tel Aviv! That's how it is!"

"All right, that's possible. We all seek out our own, but so what? I'm no better or worse than anyone else in that regard . . . But that doesn't alter the attitude I would have had toward you if you'd admitted the truth to me."

"So you'd have trained me exactly in the way you did? You'd have given me the keys to your office? You'd have paid for my studies in New York and given me control of the branch you wanted to start here? You'd still have been a friend to me, a mentor, if you'd known that I lied about my origins? You remember what you said? 'You're like a son to me . . .'"

"I might have felt betrayed, that's true, but I would have tried to understand. How exactly do you see me? You think I'm a sectarian, a racist? Let me remind you that I just hired someone of North African origin . . ."

"Am I supposed to congratulate you?"

"Don't be ridiculous. I chose him for his qualifications, his experience, and the fact that he made a good impression at the interview. Sofiane is a brilliant lawyer. If I hadn't taken him, another big firm would have, believe me! Your problem is that you divide humanity into monolithic groups. The reality is more complex. I'm sure there are lots of employers who wouldn't hire you because you were named Samir, because they had prejudices, in most cases passed on to them by their parents. It's called stupidity, ignorance, and no society, no matter how equitable and just, can ever eliminate those traits. But there are other employers, maybe not as numerous—and it would probably have taken you longer to convince them than it would someone else—but there are other firms who would have trusted you and given you a chance. Maybe it would have taken two or three interviews, maybe you'd have had a temporary contract to begin with, a trial period, but in the end they wouldn't just have hired you, they'd have made you a partner a few years later! How many CVs did you send out? Fifty? And you gave up, when you should have sent out a hundred!"

"I needed that job, so I took it. And I remain convinced that, had I told you the truth back then, you would have gotten rid of me."

"You're probably right. I wouldn't have kept you on. Not because of the revelation of your identity, but because I would no longer have felt able to trust you."

At that, Samir puts his forehead on the table and is silent for a few moments.

"I'm screwed, Pierre," he says finally. "Ruth never knew that I had a brother. She thinks I'm Jewish. If my brother tells her the truth, I will lose everything I've constructed: my family, my career, my social position. I'll be in the street. Do you understand?"

"You're thinking about yourself. But have you thought about her, about your children?"

"Don't rub my nose in it . . ."

"This is important! You knew all about the woman you married: her background, her genealogy. This is a woman whose entire existence is centered around Judaism! How could you marry her, knowing that you could never tell her the truth? You lied to her, you cheated her, and you shouldn't act as if it doesn't matter. It's serious."

"What bothers you is that an Arab seduced a Jew and had two children with her. Isn't it? Admit it!"

"Don't talk nonsense! What bothers me—what horrifies me—is that a man could not only lie to his wife, but raise his children in denial of their true identity. That is unforgivable."

"What denial? My children are Jewish. They were raised as Jews. They even took their mother's name. From that point of view, I lost out completely . . ."

"You denied them part of their identity."

"What does that matter?"

"It doesn't matter, as long as they don't find out. But what if your brother tells them everything? Imagine the shock, the trauma they will suffer . . ."

"So you acknowledge that they won't be able to bear it if they discover I'm a Muslim?"

"Sami, be realistic! You married Rahm Berg's daughter! A man whose father fought for Irgun! You told me that yourself. What do you think? You think they'll be happy when they find out the truth? You think they'll smile and give you a big hug and everything will be fine? You lied to them, Sami. And now you have to tell them everything. No matter how hard it is. No matter how much you have to lose . . ."

"Never."

"There's a Yiddish proverb about this," Pierre says. "You can go a long way with a lie, but you can never go back."

"What do you want me to do?"

"You must admit the truth! They'll find out sooner or later."

"Never. Do you hear me? Never!"

"What about your brother? You think he won't tell them?"

"That's why I came to see you—because I need your help! I need you to advise me, not judge me!"

"All right, listen to me. You don't say anything for the moment, but you try to distance your brother."

"How?"

"What do you think he wants from you?"

"Money. I was planning to ask him how much he wants to leave me alone."

"Fine. The problem with money is that he'll always come back wanting more. And what do you do then?"

"I don't know."

"Think strategically! What you want is for him to go away. Money is not enough to keep him at a distance. You have to give him something else that he wants. Your attention, your affection. Be a brother to him and he'll stop being a problem in your life."

"You think so?"

"Just trust me, for once."

12

The next day, Samir invites François to lunch, as an act of contrition. He tells him that he *sincerely* regrets the way he has behaved toward him since his arrival in New York. He regrets having been so offhand, regrets not having tried to understand his motivations, regrets the distance he has kept between them, this climate of tension and suspicion he has created. He acknowledges that François came with the laudable intention of making peace between them, and that he has responded only with a declaration of war. He regrets not having acted *like a brother.* "I should have welcomed you into my home, made you one of the family. Instead of which I have only tried to push you away, as if you were some sort of threat. And that's wrong, because I used to protect you when you were a child, I used to look after you when Mom went out to work." So yes, he's playing the "brotherly love" card this time. The aggressive, offensive approach doesn't work with a man raised by a fragile mother and no father. So yes, he is going to appeal to his feelings in the hope of persuading him to return to France, and the first thing he does in this cheap Indonesian restaurant—a quiet, out-of-the-way place where he is certain not to run into anyone of his acquaintance—is tell him that he's been thinking and he's decided he wants to help him, wants to take an interest in him: *I want to know EVERYTHING.* And he manages to coax him: François blinks nervously, somewhat embarrassed. Clearly he is not the armed robber his mother imagines. Sure, he might have dealt drugs a few times. Sure, he looked after the weapons as a favor to one of his friends, to earn a few euros, but he probably doesn't even know how to release the safety catch. He's a harmless kid, basically, a little hoodlum. A hothead, yeah, but he wouldn't really hurt anyone. The kind of guy who can be manipulative and aggressive when he feels threatened/under attack/confused, but nothing more than that. In any kind of duel with his big brother, he would lose every time, because he doesn't have the charisma, the perverse intelligence, the cerebral gifts conferred by a good education, by the assimilation of the most complex social codes. He's not bad, just simple and unsophisticated. At worst, he can be like a bull with a red rag—and, consequently, a little dangerous—but master him and he will submit. Tame him, and he'll be eating out of your hand. Nothing can hide his lack of depth. Hearing Samir's words, he becomes more trusting. And, soon afterward, as if making a police statement after being mugged in the street, he says: "All right, I'll tell you everything."

To begin with, there is his name, François Yahyaoui. He has never been able to stand his first name—he hates it. François is so French, and yes, he has no problem admitting that it pisses him off. He would rather be named Mohammed or Djamal or Kamel like everyone else he knows, and he would rather have the surname Tahar like his brother. He would rather be dark-skinned and dark-eyed and dark-haired like his mother, a Muslim like all his friends. In this mainly North African housing estate, he struggles to fit in. They call him the Blond, they call him Honky. What can he do about it? Sometimes they even mockingly nickname him King François—that's the worst one, as it brings to mind the father who rejected him. His mother, who has a love of storytelling, invented a story that she makes him repeat: My father was in the army, you tell them. My father was a pilot and he was killed in action, you tell them. He adds: He was a hero. Yes, and you tell them: My father was French. And that's all you say. That was a very difficult time for his mother: Samir had just left home, and Brunet had cut her off completely. A few months before this, after several aborted attempts at reconciliation, François had tried one last time to reestablish a relationship with his father. He had waited for him outside the National Assembly. Seeing him arrive from a distance, accompanied by a young executive in suit and tie who was carrying a stack of thick folders under his arm, François felt a sort of pride in his father's career. But when he approached him, the old man blanked him and kept walking. François watched him walk to the nearest restaurant—one of those noisy Parisian brasseries where the cheapest item on the menu cost €20; the kind of place where François could not even afford to buy a drink—and then went home. He didn't turn back. In the corridors of the RER station, he wept with rage.

That's when he starts going off the rails. He stops working in class and begins hanging around the housing estate. One of the guys in his building—the caretaker's son, mixed race, with dark hair and green eyes—offers him work as a lookout. For about €40, he has to walk around the building, checking all the exits, and warn the others if the cops turn up. He does this conscientiously, but it's not exactly difficult: in general, the police only enter the estate in convoys, the lights of their vehicles flashing, because they're afraid of going there without backup. So he is usually able to see them coming from miles away. But occasionally, when they suspect a major drug deal or are targeting a big fish, they come more stealthily, in plain clothes, and then suddenly they rush out of vans that you hadn't even noticed arrive, grab you, shove your face to the ground, hands behind your back, and handcuff you; they don't worry about the charges until later. They run up the stairs and bang on doors, yelling: "Police! Open up!" It's total panic. When that kind of thing happens, you have to react quickly, and as everyone there knows, François is the fastest thing on two legs. He can race up three flights of stairs without panting; he can run across town without ever slowing down. It is his one and only talent, and he puts it to good use.

So, having proved his worth as a lookout, he's offered the chance to sell hash—and he agrees. They are putting their trust in him: it's a sort of promotion. It's no big deal, though—just a few joints hidden under his coat. He has to hang around train stations and parking lots, spotting potential clients, and one night he walks over to two guys in a car who turn out to be plainclothes cops, and he's arrested. He is locked up in a detention center before his trial, but he tells the judge a sob story and is sentenced to a number of hours of community service. So he ends up scrubbing graffiti off the wall of an elementary school, shoveling dead leaves and trash in the playground: empty orange juice cartons, sticky candy wrappers, dog-eared trading cards. He spends hours doing this, supervised by a twenty-five-year-old social worker, a laid-back far-left idealist, and everyone is happy. When he gets back home, he wants to get back into dealing, and by hanging around the gang leaders, he is eventually given the job of hiding weapons imported from the Balkans. This is more serious shit, but he accepts right away, no questions asked. Officially, these weapons are to protect the housing estate, but in reality, as everyone knows, they will be used to train young jihadists or will be bought by gangs of armed robbers or drug dealers. But that isn't his problem, and selling guns is a potential gold mine for him: he would have been crazy to pass up this chance to make a success of his life, to get a piece of the action. He finds a nice, quiet spot in a nearby forest: no one ever goes there, and he sometimes even gets to shoot the guns himself. He loves that: feeling their weight in his hands, the smell of gunpowder, the deafening noise when he pulls the trigger. But most of all, what he loves is throwing grenades: pulling the pin like you'd pull the tab on a Coke can and tossing it as far as you can. It's dangerous, of course—it could go off in your hand—but what a fucking kick.

"It was around this time that I saw you at Mom's place. I thought to myself: *He's made it, so can I.*"

Deep down, though, even if he likes guns, even if this small-scale arms-dealing is exciting and sometimes makes him feel like he's living in an action movie, he knows that it is more likely to lead him to prison than to Australia, the place he has dreamed of going ever since a kid from the estate went there and made his fortune manufacturing tiger-stripe sweat suits. "So anyway, I found your address . . . and you know the rest."

François has tears in his eyes—he takes a long drink to hide his emotion—and Samir realizes that he's done it: coaxed the beast from its cage, tamed it merely by listening. He tells him that he is going to help him. "Go home, and I will pay for your studies. I won't let you fall. But you have to promise me that you won't go near drugs or guns anymore, that you'll be a good boy. And give it a rest with those ultraviolent video games too: that stuff messes with your head." François nods obediently. "Okay," says Samir. "You can stay another two or three weeks, then—I'll take care of everything and . . ."

But no, François wants to go back to France right away. He is pale; he looks like he's about to throw up. And it is now that he confesses to Samir that he is in trouble. He tells him what happened outside the club the other night—the woman he messed with. He regrets it now, and he's scared—scared that she will press charges or tell someone. He was drunk that night: *You got me drunk—I'm not used to drinking that much.* He has forgotten what really happened—did he hurt her? He doesn't see why he should be punished for something he doesn't even remember, and anyway, *She was asking for it,* he yells: *She was like a whore in her miniskirt, her blouse hanging open so you could see everything. They're all asking for it, those sluts, so you give 'em what they want and then they blubber about it! I don't get it—are you supposed to ask their permission, when their whole attitude says come and fuck me? Samir, I'm scared now—she might make up anything. She might say I raped her when I hardly even touched her. They're crazy, those bitches, they might do anything. I want to go home.* Samir is disgusted by this speech. Did he rape that girl? Did he try to touch her? He wants to shake his brother until he remembers, until he confesses. Let him spend the rest of his life in prison. But he doesn't say any of this. His single most pressing preoccupation is to get François as far away from New York as possible, to keep him at a distance from his family and himself. He persuades him that staying in the United States would be dangerous: "You're right to be scared. She might well press charges. You have no idea what kind of risk you'd be running if you stayed here. Cops specializing in sex crimes—and believe me, they're the worst—could turn up at your hotel tomorrow with DNA samples that would put you in jail. You'd get twenty years, and even the best lawyer in the world wouldn't be able to reduce that sentence. You'd have all the feminist groups on your back. You'd have public opinion against you. And you're French, on top of everything else. Listen, you're right—you need to go home." He is going against his deepest convictions, he is betraying himself—but fear is dictating his every word now. "Hang on," says François, "what am I supposed to do when I get home? I need money—I can't go on like this. I want to put my life straight. No more messing around." He came to America to ask for help, to try to escape his situation, "not to go back to being a small-time dealer."

"I'm going to help you."

"You'd do that for me?"

"Yes."

"But why? You told me yourself that I'm nothing to you."

"If you don't believe I'm doing it for you, then think about it this way: I'm doing it for Mom. So she won't have to worry about you constantly anymore. So she won't wake up in the middle of the night, panicking that you're not home or that you're drunk or high. So she won't call me to say she's not eating because all she can think about is you and what you're up to and how she's scared that the cops will arrest you and her reputation will be ruined—honor is important for her, you know. For all these reasons, I will provide you with money. But in exchange, you have to promise me that you'll stay there and find a job or even go to college. Promise me you won't use this money to buy drugs or blow it all in a casino."

"You'd find out from Mom, I guess?"

"I've got better things to do than spy on you, François. I have a job, a family. I prefer to trust you."

This word—"trust"—removes all the tension between them, and it is François who continues, in a calm, relieved voice:

"The best thing would be if you paid me a certain amount every month. That way, I couldn't blow it all."

"How much?"

"I don't know . . . what do you . . ."

"No, go ahead, I'm listening. Work out how much you really need . . ."

"Two thousand euros a month? That wouldn't kill you. You'd get to live in peace, and so would I—I'd have enough to pay all the bills, and to get something nice for Mom occasionally. So, I'll go back to France and leave you in peace . . ."

Samir feels so relieved, he laughs. Two thousand euros is nothing for him—he could have asked for eight thousand and he still would have said yes. He nods his agreement.

"But how will you do it? Get me the money, I mean?"

"I'll just open an account in France and put money into it every month. I can sort that in a couple of days."

"What if your wife finds out?"

"Oh, you're worrying about me now, are you?"

"I don't want you to lose everything because of me . . ."

"She won't find out. I'll do it discreetly. I have contacts in the banking world. It's not a problem."

"Samir," François asks, "why do you let Mom rot in that hell-hole when you have enough money to set her up in a nice apartment?"

"She refuses to move. It's her choice, not mine."

"I bet I could persuade her . . ."

"You want more? Isn't this enough?"

François does not reply to this. He grabs his sports bag and announces that he is going to take the subway to the airport: he wants to leave right away. But Samir refuses: he wants to accompany his brother (less out of affection than the desire to know for sure that he really has left). In the airport, they hug as his flight is called, and Samir pats his shoulder. *Forget what happened. Have a good trip!* Samir watches him walk toward security, waving and calling out, *See you soon!* when all he really wants is never to see him again.

13

It is a question writers are asked all the time: How long does it take you to write a book? As if writing had some sort of connection with architecture and construction, as if it were possible to forecast deadlines and delivery dates. But writing, because it has no rules, is not so easily constrained. There is something asocial in the act of writing: you write *against*. Given all this, how is it possible to establish the basis of any kind of social contract? Samuel has never managed it: that is why he chose to be a social worker—to stay in a place filled with people who are suffering just as much as he is, in different ways, perhaps, but all of them wounded, cracked. Since Nina left, his life has been structured around solitude. Writing enables him to keep depression at a distance. He writes in order to survive, to not fall sick. Working and working, he catches a glimpse of the building's shape, and is now able to answer: "One year."

Another question, asked less often, is nevertheless at the very center of the creative process: At what point do you know that a book is finished? Samuel has been trying to answer this question every day for the past month. He rereads, adds, cuts, corrects . . . His emotional stability now depends not on the love of a woman but on the position of a word or a semicolon, the rhythm of a sentence. The musicality of language. This need to be connected to writing as if you were mining your own soul (but mining it for what?): he has never found anything as intense that can make the chaos of existence bearable. When Samuel can read what he's written without annotating it, he knows the book is finished. There is nothing more to say. He can send it out. Here and there, he notices a dip in the tempo that might destabilize the reader; he senses the parts that people might not like. But he doesn't change anything.

Writing means accepting that some people won't like it. He hates perfectionism, that obsession with "good writing." Literature is disorder. The world is disorder. How else can writing describe its brutality? The words don't have to be in the *right place*. Literature exists in precisely this area of precariousness.

Samuel is not aiming for anything in particular; his only ambition is to write, feeding his story every day as if it were some insatiable predator. Crazy, isn't it, the way his mental and emotional equilibrium depends on putting his own fiction into words?

His greatest regret is never having been recognized as a writer. Several times, at different moments of his life, he attempted to get his work published, but he remembers that dreadful period as if he had contracted a serious illness, some terminal disease that twisted his entire being with violent pain. Yes, he remembers it as a time when he felt the constant desire to put a bullet through his brain. He collected rejection letters—his novel did not correspond to the editorial line; the publishers regretted to inform him that . . . etc.—and he read and reread a quotation by Singer: "I thought about killing myself almost every day. What tormented me most of all was my lack of success as a writer." He wasn't even a writer at all.

He never felt he had succeeded at anything in his life.

Samuel no longer fears his novel being rejected. Something inside him, some sort of ambition, has simply died away: not literary ambition—he still feels the same obsession with creating his own personal language, a language that is identifiably his, a strong voice that will carry far—but social ambition. He no longer seeks fame/recognition. He has given up on that furious, destructive fixation. The desire to elicit admiration, to be loved for his achievements, to have a clearly identifiable social position . . . he gave up on all of that as he neared forty. And he has to admit it's a relief no longer to be dependent on others' approval for his own happiness: the pressure has eased, and he feels as if he has passed to the other side. Yesterday, it was still possible; yesterday, it was an obligation, an imperative: SUCCEED! A social norm to which everyone had to submit (or be marginalized, excluded from the society of men). But today, it's over, and he can say that without anger, without the fear of being judged. His promise has been shattered, and it lies now in fragments . . . all that remains of his ambition, or the ambition that his parents had for him: the construction of an EXCEPTIONAL being, a member of the ELITE. What a joke! What a hoax.

And so, when he sends his manuscript to four publishers, he has no expectations at all. He is calm, lucid. He knows that no one can succeed in literature. To write is to be confronted on a daily basis with failure.

14

And so he returns to his calm and perfectly compartmentalized existence: two apartments, two women, two lives. Nina has shown signs of impatience, it's true—she is *weary* of this isolation, she's *not happy*—but Samir reassures her: she has an important place in his life. This place is off to the side, admittedly; it is a quiet and shadowy place, but no less important for all that. And, he explains in order to appease her: "The most intense feelings, the greatest love stories, are always played out in the shadows, in secret." "But I feel there's something missing, don't you understand?" No, he doesn't understand. "Look at it objectively: you have everything." Everything: money, material comfort, sexual closeness. That should be enough for her, he thinks. What he experiences with her every day belies all Berman's prophecies of doom: never has he felt so serene, so free of the anguish and confusion and guilt engendered by the mechanics of imposture. He has entered that phase of personal and social euphoria where everything he attempts is successful: he wins all his cases with a new authority, his mind ramps up in a frenzy of excitement. He plays, he wins.

This lasts for some time.

Samir and Nina live in a vacuum, disconnected from the outside world. She sees no one but him. Samuel is right: she lives like a geisha. That is what she tells herself—like a geisha, not like a whore—but deep down, she has her doubts. (What does she do apart from wait for him? Obey his desire? Does she have any independence at all? No. Sometimes she wants to rebel against him, but she always suppresses this urge.) For a long time, her sole ambition was to be loved by Samir, but her desires have evolved (a fact not unconnected with Samuel's harsh words): now she wants a child. She has been living like a recluse in this beautiful apartment for nearly a year now; she wants for nothing, of course, but her status as a kept mistress—which had suited her perfectly well at the beginning, in the first flush of romantic rapture—that status (which she can sense will be gradually downgraded and marginalized) is no longer something she can bear. She can no longer be at the mercy of Samir's desires and availability, in the shadows; she wants more than that. But there is something else: the fear of aging. The fear of aging and of being supplanted when he grows tired of her—that insidious threat that Samuel evoked, out of jealousy perhaps, in order to make her suffer, and yet that does not make it any less true. She knows it is true because she is aware of Samir's lust for young women. When they are out in the street together, he doesn't attempt to conceal his roving eyes; she even saw him give his card to a salesgirl barely out of her teens while she was trying on underwear that he had chosen for her. She knows it is true because she heard him tell a story about one of his clients, who said: "I'm leaving my wife now, because she's still young enough to be able to find someone else." He had laughed, but for her it was tragic. It is tragic to realize that, after a certain date, your ticket simply expires. No matter how fiercely women struggle against the passing of time, no matter how hard they try to appear younger and more desirable, it is a battle that, in a man's man's man's world, is lost before it begins. Nina might hope that this relationship lasts two, maybe three years, but what happens afterward? The truth—which she does not want to hear—is that Samir will ultimately leave her. He is too in thrall to the excitements of change, of new love, of easy sex. In all things, he is a consumer, a pleasure-seeker. He has always loved the company of beautiful women—the most beautiful women, those whom other men do not dare even approach. She is sure of all this, and she thinks that a child would save her—it's a form of insurance, isn't it, and hardly an original one. He should have anticipated this situation; it was entirely predictable. Sooner or later, the question of maternity always rears its head. And Nina planned it all. One evening, she is particularly delicious in bed—playing the imaginative, racy mistress: exactly what he loves best—then, after they have made love, she makes the announcement: she wants a child. She does not say that she is seeking some sort of legitimacy; no, that will come later—naturally, she thinks—once the child is born. Samir had dreaded this moment: he thought perhaps she'd gotten over her desire for children, hoped so anyway—she hadn't mentioned it for so long. But now here it is again. He reminds her that it's *impossible*. They are together: he loves her, they love each other; and they are free, no attachments; so why create a problem? A child would only complicate things. *A problem?* She insists: "You promised me before I left France." Maybe he did promise, but the words came out in a burst of trust and love. She has to be realistic:

he is married

he already has two children

he cannot run the risk of destroying everything he's built

he doesn't want to lose her

but she has to be reasonable about this, she has to calm down

She listens, and his words echo inside her. The fear rises, stimulating her resentment, and with a coldness that chills him, she says: "Give me a child or never come back." The demand is excessive, simplistic, childish; it betrays the fragility of her position. Nevertheless, she is issuing him a threat and he knows she is capable of following through on it. Panic seizes him. Insidious blackmail. And what if she had his child against his will? She has sworn to him that she's taking the pill, but she could be lying. "I don't understand you anymore." "You don't understand me? I'm in a foreign country, without friends, without any form of contact apart from you, living alone in an apartment—because you always advised me not to work. I just want something else, that's all! I want some other connection to you than this apartment." "I love you. That should be enough." "If you love me, you should give me the child I want so much." And so he turns to her and says with a detachment that petrifies her: "You're ruining everything, and I don't understand you anymore. You have everything a woman could possibly want." Then, without even glancing at her, he picks up his jacket and leaves.

For a while, it's fine, but after two or three days, Samir can't take it anymore. It's physical: he wants to see her, he misses her. Her absence does not weaken his desire, but feeds the flames. Alone at work, he is incapable of concentrating on his cases; his replies to his clients are evasive; he doesn't call people back; he cancels all his meetings. The lack of her is like a hole inside him, widening into a chasm that terrifies him. He feels as if he is standing on the edge of a precipice. Without her, he has vertigo; he might fall. Fear makes his body tremble. He had no idea he could miss her this much. The idea haunts him because it hints at a new feeling that, until now, he had managed to keep at a distance: dependence. He thinks about her incessantly, and the suffering quickly becomes unbearable. He wants to resist—he doesn't want to surrender to her, to lose this battle of wills—but he has to admit: he is impressed by her strength of mind. She hasn't called, hasn't shown the slightest remorse or concern. And yet, as he reminds himself, *Without me, she's nothing; she is dependent on me for the roof above her head, the food on her table. Here she is in New York, utterly isolated, with no money of her own: she must be afraid of losing me—I could dump her, never call her again. Yes, she's nothing without me.* In his mind, he belittles her—it's a way of saving face—but the truth is that he is the little one, the one who feels helpless and lost without her. He has not felt like this since the day she chose Samuel over him and he came to the conclusion that he should never see her again. He doesn't want to admit that he's nothing without her: this is something new for Samir, who has never wanted to be attached to anyone or to fall in love again. But the fact remains: *You love her. You love her and it hurts.* He had not envisaged this: he threw himself into love as if he were diving from a boat into the ocean. Now, far from her, he finds himself sinking, dragged down to the depths by the lead weights of those he loves most in the world: his wife and children. His material comfort, his family life: he abhors them now. And so he persuades himself that he can take the risk of conceiving this child. Ruth need never find out. And in the long term, maybe he'll divorce her. He feels strong enough now to face up to the wrath of the Bergs, to overthrow their hated, phony authority. He makes the decision at nine p.m., and is about to go to the apartment to break the good news to Nina when his wife calls: "Aren't you coming home? It's Shabbat. Don't forget to buy cheesecake for my father." *It's Shabbat*. These Jewish rituals that make him feel like a stranger in a strange land; these interminable meals where everything revolves around *them*; this cumbersome Jewishness that he has never quite gotten used to . . . how he would love to give it all up. Give it up for good! Deep down, he has never felt Jewish in a religious sense. What he loves—really loves—is the feeling of solidarity that exists between Jews, the connection that would make a French Jew happy to meet an Argentine Jew. That is something he has never known. He felt alienated when he lived in an attic room in the sixteenth arrondissement, surrounded by middle-class kids with huge allowances. And he felt just as alienated when he returned to Sevran to live with his mother and brother. What dreadful memories! Yes, he can say for certain that he has never felt at home anywhere. He's still in his office, practically alone, as most of his colleagues and partners have left—on Fridays, they sometimes leave work early in the afternoon. Only Berman is at his desk. A pale light filters through the blinds. He wants to call Nina, but forces himself not to. He writes her a text: "I love you. I want to have a child with you." But he deletes it immediately, unsent. Picking up his belongings, he leaves the office and runs to a bakery in the next street, where he buys ten slices of cheesecake for his father-in-law, thinking: *I hope he chokes on it*. Leaving the store, he feels an irrepressible desire to see Nina, to kiss her, to hold her. He needs to talk to her, touch her, but he reasons with himself: He'll wake her up tomorrow morning. He'll get to her apartment early and tell her that he wants to live with her. He can't keep this information to himself—it's too hot, too big. He needs to share it. He doesn't dare call Pierre—he doesn't want to give him the news by phone—so Berman will be the first to hear his secret. He heads back to the office and finds Berman about to leave. "Don't go yet—I need to talk to you!" "Can't it wait till Monday?" "No, it can't wait!" Berman is staggered by what Samir tells him. *I'm in love, and I have to tell someone . . . do you understand? What I'm going through is so intense. This woman I loved came back into my life at a moment when I least expected it, at a moment when I felt dead. And she has made me feel alive again. Nothing happens anymore with my wife. I feel like I've been transformed—I don't even recognize myself! Her name is Nina Roche*. Berman listens and says nothing, offers no judgment. What could he say, after all, this fine father, this scrupulous husband, this devoted son who has never crossed a line in his life; this model citizen who votes at every election, pays his taxes, always uses the crosswalk; this man who hates risk? Samir is a better, stronger man than he is, and he knows it. He became asthmatic after the birth of his fourth child; he feels like he's suffocating under the weight of his family, of his overprotected, security-mad building created according to the iniquitous laws of transmission; he has acted like his father and he is unhappy like him; he envies Samir his disregard of convention, his self-assurance; he's simply not like that, not capable of such things, and he admits the fact himself: he could never imagine changing the course of his life. Samir continues: "I have to tell you something, because my decision affects the firm: it's likely that a few clients, under pressure from my father-in-law, will decide to change their lawyer." Hearing this, Berman tries in vain to interrupt him. "Listen to me!" Samir shouts. Then, in a softer voice: "I'm going to leave my wife. I'm going to tell her tomorrow." "What? You can't do that!" "Why not?" "Why not? Because it's just not Jewish." It is a simple moral judgment, tied to the weight of history, tradition, education. In truth, Berman is shocked. Having a brief affair or a one-night stand, experienced as guilt and ended with relief (and with the certainty that he will NEVER do it again) . . . maybe he can imagine that. But this double life, this meticulous organization with a woman set up in a plush apartment, provided with everything she could possibly want, this betrayal . . . no. Samir becomes angry when he hears this. "And what would be Jewish, in your opinion? You think there's a moral position that is the sole privilege of Jews? A corollary to election?" He pronounces these words with savage sarcasm. "If there was a Jewish morality, we'd know about it!" Berman is horrified. Paralyzed by these words, he looks at Samir and feels that something is wrong, something that can never be put right: his partner is a stranger. In a cold voice, he concludes: "You've gone crazy . . . I don't recognize you anymore, Sam . . ." But Samir won't stop. "You want me to tell you the truth? You scare the shit out of me with your sickening moralism, your probity, your obsession with doing the right thing. It's unrealistic to think a person can live without betraying anyone. It's unrealistic to think a person can stay pure. Purity is not a concept that should be applied to human beings. A stone can be pure. So can that ritual bath you take once a year on the eve of Yom Kippur to purify yourself of all the dirty tricks you have to pull in order to win cases! You come out of the bath and you're holy, but believe me you become soiled again the moment you touch anything in this world." "But, as a Jew, it's my duty to—" "Oh, give it a rest! Jews are no more moral than anyone else, they're just more moralistic." Berman freezes: "You speak as though you're not part of the community."

Samir gives him a contemptuous look: "Have I ever been part of it?" Their friendship seems to have been wrecked in the space of a few seconds. This man is an ashamed Jew, Berman thinks. He is a traitor to the Jewish cause, indifferent to his people's sufferings. He is one of those Jews who regurgitate assimilationist speeches of the worst kind—an immoral, unscrupulous Jew with no love for his own kind. Suddenly, he feels disgusted by Tahar. But he doesn't say any of this to him. All he says, in a monotone voice, is: "I don't think we have anything else to say to each other."

PART FOUR

Consolation

A masterpiece!

ERIC DUMONTIER[1]

Shocking.

DAN SBERO[2]

A great book!

SOPHIE DE LATOUR[3]

A writer is born.

MARION LESAGE[4]

An amazing story.

LÉON BALLU[5]

---

1 Eric Dumontier wrote this review in order to please Samuel's book publicist, an attractive blonde with whom he was in love.

2 The renowned literary critic Dan Sbero declared: "My greatest success was, without any doubt, my interview with Saul Bellow, two days before he was awarded the Nobel Prize for Literature."

3 Sophie de Latour, thirty-four, aspires to edit the cultural section of the newspaper for which she works.

4 Marion Lesage was also the author of a forgotten novel that sold only four hundred copies: *The Inconvenience of Being Dead*. She was recently fired from the editorial board of her newspaper—officially for economic reasons, unofficially because she refused the advances of the newspaper's managing editor.

5 Although professionally successful, Léon Ballu, fifty-five, confided to his psychiatrist that his private life was a "complete failure."

1

Samir hadn't called Nina for two weeks. She spent those long days prostrate, her isolation seeming to accentuate the gravity of the event, giving it a particular character, as if, by withdrawing from him, she was giving Samir enough space—a vast emptiness, she hoped—to make him realize how much he needed her, how pointless his life felt without her. And then, when she understood that he was never going to call her again, either because he was disgusted by her ultimatum and had decided not to see her anymore, or because he didn't love her enough to risk losing his family, she decided not to let things drift but to get back in touch with the few people she had met in New York—women she had encountered at the hair salon or in the gymnasium of a luxury hotel, one of those places where everything is organized to satisfy your every whim and where Samir had signed her up on his own initiative. How many phone numbers did she have in her address book? Three or four at most. She saw practically no one apart from Samir: he had made it perfectly clear that he wanted her to be available for him whenever he was free. So she had to match her movements to his. Once and once only, she had arranged to meet a woman she had met in the gym—a Frenchwoman—in that little movie theater near Fifth Avenue that showed French films, and she'd had to cancel at the last minute because Samir had reminded her that she had to subjugate her timetable to his—it was *the least she could do*. Their meetings always followed the same unchanging routine: he called her to tell her he was on his way. She had to make sure she was ready for him (i.e., hair nicely styled, makeup on, dressed to his tastes). When he appeared, he kissed her. (She *had* to kiss him. Once, he came in and found her on the phone—he

had been furious and had stayed mad at her for hours afterward.)
They made love, then ate lunch or dinner together. After that, he
would leave, though always after checking that she didn't want for
anything. She had given up everything in her life for him: first,
her relationship with Samuel, which, while never perfect, nor very
passionate (had she ever felt any passion for Samuel?), had suited
her well enough that she had seriously considered having a child
with him; second, her career, because while it was nothing to write
home about and had never made her big money, it did give her a
sense of pride to see her photograph in major store catalogues or
on the posters that decorated the stores during promotion periods. She was a model—not a top model, admittedly; a model who
worked in the world of supermarkets and food, not the world of
catwalks and cocktail parties—but all the same, there was something cool about being regularly chosen to incarnate the French
ideal: the healthy, well-balanced mother; the model employee; the
smiling, devoted wife who would pose with the *sturdiest and most
affordable* satchel, the *tastiest* ham, or the *most absorbent* diapers.
Women looked at her and wished they looked like her; they saw
her and immediately wanted to use the same products she used.
While the job was not well paid considering the number of hours
she had to pose for those photographs, or for all the time she spent
making her face and body look desirable every day, it did have
quite a few advantages: no two days were ever the same, and she
could organize her time as she wished and was constantly meeting
people who told her that she was stunningly beautiful. (And she
was, of course, but her upbringing by a strict, paranoid father had
drained her of any objectivity toward herself.) So, yes, for Samir
she had given up this life that she had chosen for herself, and
now—after a year—he was leaving her, without having given her
the child she dreamed of having, without even having organized
their breakup, without telling her clearly what would happen if he

never came back. Her mother had abandoned her, and now Samir had abandoned her; her kindness, her beauty, and her other qualities had not been enough to keep their love; they had grown weary of her or had preferred other people to her—a man in her office, in her mother's case; his wife, in Samir's case, that rich heiress whose photograph Nina had seen on the Internet.

She calls her few acquaintances and tells them what has happened—and none of them deign to see her. In New York, she is a woman without friends or any personal prestige, a penniless woman. Samir used to give her money on a regular basis, but for two weeks she's received nothing; she is surviving on what she has left. She doesn't know how long she'll be able to stay in the apartment. He hasn't officially broken up with her. Should she leave? Keep waiting? Where could she go? She can't afford to pay rent. Soon she won't be able to afford to eat. Suddenly she is afraid of losing everything, and she wonders if this is what he wanted to prove by not calling her: You are dependent on me. Without me, you are nothing here. She wants to resist, but how can she? What resources does she have? She decides to call Samir to ask him for help. This will be difficult—she doesn't want to do it. If she calls him now, she will be capitulating, giving up on the idea of having a child, a life together. But her existence is becoming increasingly precarious. She feels as if she is digging her own grave. Too pessimistic? *No, I'm just being realistic*, she thinks. And she calls Samir's cell phone, which goes directly to voice mail. If it just rang and rang, she would have come to the conclusion he was screening his calls, avoiding her, but every time she dials his number, she gets the same message. She tries three or four times in forty-eight hours, and then she becomes panic-stricken. What if he's had an accident? A medical problem? No one would inform her, because who even knows about her? She calls the local hospitals to check that he has not been admitted: this takes her several hours, but she gets nowhere—no patient has been admitted under that name. After another week has passed, she decides to call Samir's firm, as that is the only place she is likely to be able to obtain information about him without compromising their secret. The secretary's unpleasant tone[1] immediately makes Nina uncomfortable and she is practically stuttering when she asks to speak to Mr. Tahar. "He's out of the office for a while," the secretary replies. "Is he on vacation? When will he be back?" Nina asks. "I can't tell you that." "Could anyone else tell me?" There is a long silence, then the secretary finally admits: "I don't know when Mr. Tahar will return. If this concerns an urgent professional situation, I can pass you to one of his partners." "Yes, it's urgent and confidential," Nina replies. "Hold the line please. Your name?" Nina hesitates, then says: "Nina Roche." For three or four minutes, Nina hears nothing but a Chopin sonata, and then a male voice comes on the line: "This is Berman." She introduces herself and Berman instantly realizes who she is. Samir has mentioned her to him; he absolutely does not want her asking questions on the phone. He could ask her to call him later, but he senses that she would be capable of contacting Ruth, so he agrees to meet her in a café close to the office: "I'll be there in fifteen minutes."

Berman spots her as soon as he enters the café. He knows it must be her: she's like a diamond in a coal mine. There are plenty of pretty girls in this packed café, but a woman like her—so beautiful and deliciously sensual—stands out instantly, without any effort, without any aggressive exhibitionism, without the artificial

---

1 It has to be said that Maria Electraz is something of a terror. Fifty-six years old, she is divorced, with three children, and has only one obsession: her job. Her rigorous screening of calls has led to Tahar nicknaming her Checkpoint.

paraphernalia of seductiveness (the usual battery of beauty care products—polished nails, styled hair, powdered face, black-lined eyes, skintight dress showing every curve of her body—and the usual sideways glances). She is simply there, without any affectations, with a beauty so pure that he envies Samir as soon as he lays eyes on her. He wonders if even he would have been capable of resisting her, then immediately answers his own question: *No, I would not be capable of resisting her.* He moves toward her, shakes her hand with excessive amiability, and sits down. He looks her over—he can't help it—but Nina is used to these moments of silence while men's eyes linger on her face, her body, and she waits patiently. Finally, he explains that he arranged to meet her because "there are things that can't be discussed on the phone." He tells her she doesn't need to explain the situation: he knows who she is and why she has come. Nina struggles to conceal her surprise. Samir never told her that he had mentioned their relationship to anyone, and this fact reassures her, makes her feel more valued. She almost relaxes. Does he know where Samir is? Is he okay? She hasn't heard from him and she is worried: that's why she felt compelled to call his office. Berman's mouth tenses and she understands that something serious must have happened—probably something irreparable—because why else would he suddenly look so stricken? Why else would he touch her hand in a gesture of friendship when she doesn't even know him, has never seen him before? The world tilts toward horror. One of those appalling twists that life takes sometimes. She can feel her heart quiver violently in her chest, as if a torrent of blood were rushing through her veins, destroying the fragile edifice of her rib cage and transforming the slow pulse of ordinary life into a succession of jerks and jolts that betray her fear and anguish. She wishes she could force him to say everything now, right away: get it over with, just stick the damn needle in her and be done with it. But she says nothing, remains outwardly impassive and immobile, like someone who knows her turn is coming and that she must remain calm and mute before the fatal moment. For a long time there is silence between them. They are inside a bubble, indifferent to the shouting of the waiters and waitresses, to the hubbub of voices from other tables, to the ceaseless flood of words all around them, and suddenly Nina surprises herself by praying, silently, that Samir is alive, just as Berman says in a whisper that sounds like a monk's chant: "I'm sorry, I'm so sorry, I don't know how to break this to you . . ."

2

What more could he have asked for, this man who had made his desire to write the driving force of his entire life? A man who had organized his professional, personal, and social existence around this vocation despite the fact that he had no training and no one had ever encouraged him—least of all Nina, who had never taken his writing seriously for a reason that remained obscure to him. Because, while she never read his work and never asked to read it, she would buy any and all novels that he recommended to her, reading them intently and commenting upon them with formidable seriousness—the kind of seriousness that only someone who considered literature the most important thing in their life would exhibit. (And how humiliated and jealous he felt, noting the contrast between her indifference to his own work and her fascination with that of other authors, some of them less talented than him!) So, yes, for a man like him, whose previous books had been rejected by so many publishers, as if every possible factor (human and situational) were opposed to the realization of his literary aspirations, what could be more exciting than to be accepted by one of France's biggest publishers and, upon publication, to be immediately consecrated as a great writer? All his life, he had thought of himself as a failure—because his parents, crushed by the tutelary intellectual figures that they kept choosing, had raised him to a position of inferiority and denigration, according to which a person is as nothing before his masters and before God. He had also thought about the day he discovered the truth of his origins, imagining himself the son of an alcoholic, a loser, a nutcase, because what other kind of father could have produced a being as spineless as him, a man who had experienced only one piece of good luck in his entire life: meeting a woman as beautiful as Nina and managing to keep her for twenty years, though even that he had accomplished only through blackmail and cunning. What a failure! This fact had been confirmed to him each time Nina had left him for Samir, each time he had read people's thoughts as they looked at him and Nina together: What the hell is she doing with *him*? Everything in his life brought him back to this contemptible self-image. He saw himself as a dull man, physically and intellectually incapable of wooing or keeping any desirable woman, incapable even of finishing the degree he'd begun. And what was he trying to prove by systematically and efficiently sabotaging any plan that fortune had enabled him to put in place, if not his own stupidity and incompetence? Yes, all his life he had felt mediocre, and yet now here he was being described as "brilliant," "dazzling," "talented." Who were they all talking about? He wanted to tell them that they had it all wrong. His continual self-deprecation and self-flagellation was his way of justifying his failures—of protecting himself, essentially—and he had ended up finding a certain comfort in that marginal zone where no one ever deigned to visit or hold him to account. He was used to it.

Nothing had prepared him for this reception. Only a few weeks after sending out his manuscript, he had been contacted by a publisher whose back-catalogue Samuel greatly admired, and this man had asked to meet him. He had phoned him around eleven a.m.—it was a Monday morning; he remembered it vividly—and had simply announced his identity, then asked: "Am I speaking to the author of *Consolation*?" "Yes." "Have you signed a contract for this book with another publisher yet?" "No." "Do you live in Paris?" "Near Paris." "Could you come to my office tomorrow? Let's say ... around three p.m.?" "Yes." And, just as he was about to hang up, he'd heard the publisher's last words: "Oh, I almost forgot ... your book . . . it's very good. I mean that sincerely—you have a great talent. And I am not the kind of man who uses that term lightly."

He didn't sleep that night. All he did was rehearse in his head what he would say to the publisher the next day. And yet, when the time for their meeting came, they barely exchanged a word. The publisher spoke very little, Samuel not at all. But he signed a publishing contract. Later, when a journalist asked him the question, *Where and when were you happiest?* he replied: "In my publisher's office." During the weeks that followed, the publisher called him several times to suggest a few changes. He remembers a phone call at dawn about a comma: Should it be kept or deleted? He wasn't sure. It was in this world and no other that he wished to live from now on—a world where the position of a comma was more important than one's position in society.

3

You are under arrest.

It is six in the morning when the heavily armed policemen (are they soldiers? how many of them are there?) surge into Samir's home. *Hands up! Turn around! Don't move!* Handcuffs click, boot soles clack . . . brutality, pain, authority. *But what are the charges? I haven't done anything! Tell me what the hell is going on!*

All it takes is a glance through the window, at the cloudy sky, and Samir can see it's early morning—not night anymore, but the sun is barely illuminating the misty, Klein-blue expanse. Follow us! One of the men presses a heavy, damp hand on Samir's head to hold him still while another handcuffs him in front of Ruth, who is screaming that she doesn't understand, screaming and threatening, invoking her influence, her power—*You can't do this, you'll regret it*—demanding the names and ranks of these men who act like the police, but who are they really? "Who are you?" Ruth yells. "Show me your badges. I'll file a complaint against you!"

Take it up with the authorities, ma'am.

Ruth stands in the doorway of her apartment, head bent forward as if she's about to fall over. She's wearing beige silk pajamas, hardly a hair out of place, but her face is distorted by tiredness/incomprehension/anger. That aura of the untouchable aristocrat, the perfectly controlled sovereign, is gone, her urbanity vanished in a few minutes. How could she ever have imagined she would one day experience anything this dreadful? A dawn arrest, carried out with brutal efficiency: it's the kind of thing you associate with movies or the Bronx or novels with embossed lettering on the covers, not with an opulent building on Fifth Avenue, not with this apartment complex where no one may enter without ID, a place of perfect social respectability filled with slick-haired yuppies and white-haired patricians—a place that has never been burgled, and you can see why. Take a look around: an armed guard outside, a crabby, paranoid caretaker inside, and surveillance cameras placed in every corner by the best security technicians, each one linked directly to the security firm's headquarters, where men and women work four-hour shifts, zealously watching the feed to ensure no one disturbs the serenity of the building's occupants. At the slightest sign of trouble, five men armed with assault rifles are poised to arrive within five minutes . . . but there are more than five here today (seven or eight, maybe?) and they are here not to defend the owners of these luxury apartments but to arrest one of them like a drug dealer or a gangster—the horror! Ruth looks up and notices her neighbor,[1] who has emerged from his apartment to observe the landing with a hard, judgmental stare. In these apartments, where a square meter is worth more than thirty-five thousand dollars, scandals are frowned upon, as is anything that might devalue the asset, and the neighbor retreats into his apartment as if he has seen nothing and has no desire to know what is going on in the apartment across the landing. Ruth looks at the neighbor's closed door—a door that he has double-locked (she heard the key turn in the latch, the metallic thud of the dead bolt)—and she feels as if she might faint with shame. Something has died here, on the landing outside her apartment, something that has dethroned her forever. She forces back her

---

1 Allan Dean, seventy-six, a person of independent means. His only ambition is to acquire the Tahars' apartment.

tears and watches the policemen, without yelling this time—her husband is struggling like a fish trapped in a net—then puts on an overcoat and follows them to the elevator. They go inside, Samir repeating that he has done nothing wrong and demanding: "Who are you? What do you want? Show me your badges!" Ruth takes the stairs, hurtling down them, breathing heavily, almost tripping more than once, and catching up with them as they walk past the dumbfounded caretaker and the cleaner who is mopping the floor and does not dare stop. The policemen move forward quickly, pulling Samir by the arms, and noisily exit the building, watched by a few joggers in Central Park. Some of them stop and take pictures or videos on their cell phones, which they will later put on YouTube, those bastards. A dark-colored van is parked out in front of the building. Ruth walks toward it, but Samir does not even have time to say a word to her before he is shoved inside, flanked by two heavyset policemen, and the door is banged shut. The van speeds away, immediately followed by two other police cars, sirens screaming.

The van is driven at breakneck speed, running red lights. It starts to rain, hammering on the windshield, and the wipers wave like two metronomes. Samir can hear the noise of the city beyond the van's walls. He can hear crackling voices on the cops' walkie-talkies: *Operation successful*. He finds himself remembering the opening words of Kafka's *The Trial*: "Someone must have been spreading lies about Josef K., for without having done anything wrong he was arrested one morning." That was exactly what had happened to him: he had done nothing wrong, and yet men had come to arrest him.

4

The good fortune—or misfortune—of finding success just at the moment when he had given up hope. The good fortune—or misfortune—of being famous, admired, and loved for a book, because he had written a book, while as a man he had felt isolated, profoundly alone, not through choice but because he had never been popular, never at the center of things: he had spent his life on the sidelines. What had he done that was so extraordinary? What had he done to deserve this renown? He had fictionalized his own life, he had lined up a bunch of words—that was all. Was his book really so exceptional? He had been lucky, that was what he thought: his book had been read at the right time by people who happened to be in the right mood; the critics who reviewed his novel had just fallen in love or they'd read it while they were drunk. All success is based on a misunderstanding, his more than most. There had been an error, a terrible mistake, and in a few days or weeks, everyone would discover this fact and he would return to his habitual anonymity. But this is not what happened. Every day brought him more encounters, more good news. The week before publication, there had been reviews in all the biggest newspapers and his book entered the best-seller list on the very day it first appeared in bookstores. Foreign publishers outbid each other for the rights in various languages. He imagined his picture on those WANTED posters you always see in old westerns, with a vast sum of money emblazoned beneath. Everyone wanted him and they were ready to pay.

His success was so overwhelming that he had to take time off work. His publisher put him up in a grand Parisian hotel, and his days

became a series of interviews with journalists, answering readers'
questions, posing for photographs in magazines, and traveling—
around France, around the world—to sign copies of his books.
Everywhere he went, he was treated like a king . . . or a foreign
secretary, at the very least. And every single time, he felt there
must surely have been a mix-up of some kind, a case of mistaken
identity. Surely it wasn't really *him* that all these people had come
to lionize!

To begin with, he had been flattered by all these panegyrics. People
kept telling him he was exceptional, and he ended up believing it.
He felt important. He felt untouchable. Now he had access to places
he had never dreamed of entering, he was able to meet people he
had long admired—intellectuals, politicians, even actors, including one particularly great actor whom he had hero-worshipped
since childhood, and who asked him to write a role for him.

What you wrote about filiation, about determinism, about the
pressure that parents/society put us under . . . I have lived through
that. This was what all his readers told him, in person or in writing.
And he listened to them, read their words, feeling helpless, having
no desire to be a spokesman for anyone or anything.

With women too, he discovered that he was suddenly endowed
with new qualities. Beautiful girls called him, asked him out. It
was in this way that he found himself in bed with a female novelist[1] (a fact which, far from being a minor detail, actually made the
situation more complex, with the writing intensifying the strife
between them, as if each lover were reliant on conflict and anger as

---

1 Léa Brenner became a novelist in order to "disappoint" her father.

the engines of their creativity). Léa Brenner was a fifty-two-year-old woman, the author of a challenging and much-feted oeuvre, who had contributed to his meteoric rise on the Parisian literary scene by writing a rave review of his book in a prestigious literary supplement—a review that was immediately reduced to a single word, printed on a red strip of paper that embellished the cover of this book by an unknown author ("though not for long," as she proclaimed everywhere she went): "Prodigious"—a word that might have been dictated by admiration or love, or quite possibly both, and which seemed to describe not only the book itself (a book Léa Brenner really did find interesting, and in which she detected some of the biting irony of Chekhov's best stories), but also the love that she instantly felt for the man who wrote it (even though he was quite cold and distant).

Four months before this, before the book was available in stores, Léa Brenner had sent a note to Samuel via his publisher, explaining that she'd read the proofs of his novel and thought it wonderful. She loved him before she ever met him; she loved him because she'd *read* him. She knew that meetings with authors whose books you love could sometimes be disheartening. She remembered an evening spent with an American writer, whose work she had studied at university, but who, when she met him, had seemed obscene, disappointing, completely lacking in subtlety, whereas his work was so powerful. It was as if the writer, obsessed by his oeuvre, had emptied himself of all substance, given the best of himself, leaving nothing but a dried-up husk.

She imagined making love with Samuel, the erotic attraction fed by the reading of his book. For her, words alone were enough to trigger desire. Which was why all her romantic relationships had been with writers. Before Samuel, there had been a long love affair with an Israeli writer, but she didn't want to talk about that, she said, because the mere mention of his name could make her cry.

Samuel had replied with a short, polite note, and—that same evening—she had written him another letter, a long one this time, in which she discussed not only his work (in great detail, mixing criticism with eulogy), but also—and this was what touched Samuel—the death of his parents. At the end of the letter, she suggested they meet for coffee at her place—a large apartment that she rented in the seventh arrondissement.

Three weeks later, he found himself in her living room, the walls covered with old books. He was impressed by this, having always borrowed books from libraries or bought them as cheap paperbacks or from the secondhand booksellers who offer their wares by the banks of the Seine.

Meeting him for the first time, she was paralyzed for a moment. This man awakened something in her. As soon as she shook his hand, she knew they would make love that very day.

They made love and it was a disaster. Samuel could not get hard. She told him it didn't matter, but it did to him: he picked up his things and left. She kept calling him until he gave in. They saw each other for a while. They could talk for hours about Russian poetry or South American/Italian literature or politics/philosophy, but in bed, their bodies had nothing to say to each other. Not that she was repellent. On the contrary, she was a beautiful woman, tall and slim, with very short blond hair and milk-white skin, but he was never able to feel any sexual intimacy with her. The injustice of sexual attraction. Why could he not fall for the curves of her body, the scent of her skin? Everything about her was perfect for him, so why did he feel only the most profound indifference? After two failures, she advised him to see a doctor and he refused. She didn't understand: he didn't desire her and never had. He had loved Nina so much, loved her body so much. All he'd ever had to do was look at her, brush her hand, and he would want her instantly. Now he missed her more than ever. This was the first time he'd slept with another woman since her departure, and he realized it would be the last time. He had thought he'd managed to forget her, but suddenly the memories were overflowing, spilling everywhere. So it was possible, he understood, to be cursed and blessed at the same time, to be a winner and yet a loser, to be happy and yet unhappy.

5

Samir's arrest lasted only a few minutes. In front of the building, all has returned to normal. Ruth walks back into the lobby, fists balled in the pockets of her overcoat. She has the impression that her husband has been swallowed up by some great beast—crushed in the powerful jaws of a shark, pulverized by the aftershock of a Tsar Bomba, wiped clean from the surface of the world. This is the first tragedy of her life: her parents have sheltered her from everything until now, sparing her pain, want, loss. No man has ever made her suffer, because no man has ever left her. No friend has ever hurt her, for who would dream of knowingly passing up the opportunity to be invited to her home, to spend their vacations at her summerhouse and to say: "I was staying with Ruth Berg"? No professor ever gave her bad grades—she was beautiful, intelligent, influential, so why would they penalize her? "Even God Himself never dared slight you!" one of her friends had joked once. But Ruth hadn't laughed: she felt certain that, sooner or later, good fortune would have a price. And she was paying that price now. She was paying for all those years of carefree happiness, those years when, displayed and kept safe like a priceless painting by her loving father—a father who was literally crazy about his daughter, who had no qualms about spending a fortune to satisfy her every whim, who had organized his life around the realization of her dreams—she had never once been the subject of the slightest criticism. What could anyone possibly say against her, after all? She wore the most fashionable clothes; she had good taste, sensible opinions. You couldn't even accuse her of lacking thoughtfulness or introspection: she was subtle—and spiritual with it. Her father liked to repeat the story over dinner of how Woody Allen had once said of her: "If I had to be reincarnated as a woman, I'd want to be Ruth Berg!" Had she ever suffered a setback? No. Not even the smallest failure. And no one had ever called her a "filthy Jew" in public. Oh, she knew her father regularly received anti-Semitic hate mail, but she had never been sent anything of the kind. She had been spared even that. Perhaps she had felt slightly disillusioned when her father told her that she must not look for love beyond the exclusive breeding tank of wellborn bourgeois American Jews (men who had gone to Harvard, Princeton, Columbia)—but even that minor ruling, she had defied. She had fallen in love with a Frenchman of uncertain origins and her father had finally accepted her choice. Why? Simply because he didn't want to lose her, was reluctant even to upset her. How could she ever have imagined she would one day have to witness a situation as horrific as the dawn arrest of her husband, in their own home? *Ruth, you have been spared unhappiness for three decades,* she thought to herself, *and now it is your turn. You are going to experience the trials of Job. Your life is stained now, and this stain will never wash out. Now matter how many times you rewrite the family history, your husband's arrest will always be part of it, a sordid little news item that will dishonor the Bergs unto the third generation!* This is what she thinks as she walks back to her apartment. Had there been any signs or omens heralding this fall? Had she really seen nothing, or simply looked away? She stands in the hallway of her apartment now, her face a mess of bitter tears, and looks up at the photograph of a famous rabbi, begging him for help. And she prays—prays that her husband is innocent and her family protected, prays for the return of a normal life, prays that this is just a nightmare, and prays for herself, that she might become again what she was before this morning's tragedy—that spoiled woman, carefree and light-hearted, who likes green tea ice cream, Visconti's films, vacations in Porto Cervo, and navy-blue cashmere sweaters. Her thoughts are interrupted by the sound of her children's footsteps—and suddenly there they are, their eyes still sleepy, asking what has happened, where is their father. She reassures them: it's all over now, they should go back to bed. And that is exactly what they do, with a docility that amazes her. When the apartment is silent again, she sits down, clears her throat until she is able to speak in a normal voice—a voice that does not betray her feelings—and calls the family attorney, Dan Stein. It is early, but she knows that when he sees her name on the screen of his cell phone, he will take the call instantly. She doesn't call her father, not yet, because he's abroad, and anyway, with him, everything takes on a political dimension. To inform him is to expose him, and for now, she sees no reason to do that. It is herself she's protecting, really, of course, for as soon as her father is aware of the situation, he will take over, and perhaps in a way that will make her uncomfortable. Ruth knows that her father has never really liked Sami and that he is waiting for an opportunity to exclude him from their lives. All it would take is a single wrong step and he would solemnly tell him: "Get out, Tahar. Go back where you came from." She tells Stein what happened. He listens calmly, and when, at last, she asks him what she should do, he replies: "Don't do anything. I'm on my way."

He's there twenty minutes later, attaché case in his right hand, cell phone in his left. Ruth is soon sick of his ringtone, which imitates the sound of a harp. He is a man of average height, with a round face, at the center of which is a wide, flat nose with abnormally large nostrils. The first thing everyone thinks when they see him is: What happened to his nose? For twenty years, he had a very big schnoz with a dent in it; finally, he decided to have a nose job, but the operation went wrong and he was left with this wide, flat, short proboscis that made people think he was the child of a mixed marriage. "Yep, I'm the son of Mordechai Stein and Tina Turner," he would joke. In a family environment, he often came across as the strong and silent type, but put him in a courtroom and he instantly became a great orator, with a sense of tragedy, theater, emotion, and humor. Before becoming one of the most renowned criminal lawyers in America, he was a stand-up comedian at Carolines on Broadway. His inspiration was the brilliant and outrageous Lenny Bruce, and he didn't need to be asked twice to perform those sketches for his friends. He got up onstage and everyone laughed, but then his father died of a heart attack and his mother told him: "Dan, either you pass your bar exam or I'll go the same way as your father. Do I really need a *bodh'en* in my family? No. A lawyer, however, can always be useful." He gave in to this emotional blackmail, quitting his comedy career and transforming himself into this famous attorney who treated the courtroom as his theater stage, the jury as his audience. His trials were the star attraction of the New York legal circuit because when Stein pleaded his case, you knew you were about to witness something unforgettable. This morning, however, in the Tahars' apartment, he was keeping a low profile. He had called the prosecutor's office on the way here and been met with a blank wall of silence. He wanted to find out if Ruth knew anything about this—if she was aware of any danger, anything that Samir might be involved in. "He's been kidnapped." She says this suddenly, in her usual cold, disdainful voice, and Stein wonders if she is being serious. He does not believe it for a second, not because it is out of the realms of possibility—people as rich and famous as the Bergs are always targets for extortion—but because he cannot imagine armed men would turn up at the most secure building on Fifth Avenue to kidnap someone. They would wait until he went out. This is what he believes. He does not say anything, though, because he does not want to risk offending his client: at an hourly rate of $800, he knows when to keep his mouth shut. Ruth explains what she means: she never felt that the men in her apartment were real policemen: "They didn't read him his rights or tell him he could contact a lawyer, and they were so brutal! I never even saw a badge. They stormed in, they took him, and they left." Stein asks her several times if her husband had enemies, if he ever felt threatened, and suddenly it comes out. Ruth says yes, he has often been absent recently—not only physically but mentally: "When he was with us, he would look worried, suspicious. Yes, he's been like that for a few weeks now. I did ask him about it, but he told me it was nothing." Stein suggests she wait an hour or two. If, after that time, she has not received any news, she should inform the police. Ruth nods, cool and dignified, and accompanies Dan Stein to the front door. Two hours later, she still hasn't heard anything.

6

Hooded like a man being led to the gallows, Samir yells that he wants to know where they are taking him and why. He's still inside the van, the tires squealing on the asphalt. They drive for a long time, and then finally the vehicle comes to a halt. He hears doors banging. He feels hands grip him violently, fingers like metal vises on his arms, and he is propelled outside to the sound of laughter and insults. He feels like a captured beast. He is suffocating under the black cloth. He tells them he wants to breathe fresh air and someone answers: "Shut your mouth." He walks, shakily, tentatively, for about a hundred feet, like a man who has been drinking, although the truth is that he has never felt as lucid in his life as he feels now in this instant of terror. He is taken inside somewhere, down some stairs, and he tries to guess what it is: A cellar? A cave? A basement? The air is cold and damp. A stale smell. The stink of sweat. He hears voices, sounds, distant shouting. "Where are we?" he asks. "Somewhere no one will ever look for you," a male voice replies. A heavy hand pulls the hood from his head, scratching his right eyelid. It takes his eyes a few seconds to adjust to the light, then he sees that he is inside a concrete space that looks like an interrogation room: a table, three chairs, a bare bulb hanging from a faulty electric wire. "State your name. Place your finger there. Hold this sign in both hands. Higher . . . yes, under your chin. Don't move." Click! *You evil bastard! You fucker!* Body search. Thorough. Invasive. "He's hiding something." *You piece of shit! You lying cunt!* Incomprehension, confusion, and, yes, terror—Samir is terrified. He tells himself over and over again that it is a nightmare: *Any second now, I'm going to wake up.* What are the charges? He's done nothing wrong—he can prove it. This is a mistake. "Let me go! Call my lawyer. Call my wife. I'm Rahm Berg's son-in-law!" And one of the men starts laughing. "Yeah, well, we'll see if your father-in-law still supports you after this." "I'm innocent! I haven't done anything!" The door bangs shut, and Samir Tahar is left alone in a tiny prison cell.

This must be about morality, Samir thinks. To them, it's a crime. It's a crime to have a sex life that is too aggressive, too free. In France, he's a libertine, but not in cold, corseted New York. For a long time, he had felt sure that one day his sexual adventures would cause him irreparable harm—that he would face charges of harassment or corrupting a minor. That premonition hadn't caused him to alter his habits, however: he believed himself invincible, untouchable. His pathological craving for sex, and the two or three flings he'd had with minors a year or two ago . . . that was enough to get him locked up for ten years. That was enough to make him a criminal. Had one of those girls brought charges against him? It's possible. *Anything* is possible. He's trapped like a rat, surrounded. There must be evidence—traces of saliva/semen, words that he wrote and forgot, texts he'd sent that were litigious/provocative/transgressive, compromising emails full of sexual allusions. He'd left all this evidence, without a doubt. And yet, each time, he'd moved on to the next thing. Each time, his craving for new flesh had blown away his reservations. He thinks suddenly of that secretary he refused to hire, officially because she wasn't qualified, but really because she had refused his advances, when he'd been sure that she wanted it, wanted it just as much as he did! He can sense things like that. He remembers the flight attendant whose rump he patted on a New York–Los Angeles flight, shouting out, "What a beautiful ass!" (she had looked a little offended, but had smiled after he apologized), and that young prosecutor with whom he'd had a brief affair purely in the hope of influencing her, softening the charges against his client. (He wasn't attracted to her—she was ugly—and that was the first time in his life he'd seduced a woman in order to secure a professional favor; he had immediately regretted it and sworn he would never do the same thing again.) For the past few months, fear had shrunk his desires. He knew that a story, real or invented, might come out. He'd said it to Berman over lunch: "One day, a woman will file charges against me. She'll say I raped her in a parking lot. She'll do it for the money. Because I would never do anything like that. Never—you hear? I would never rape a woman, and you'll know that she is lying."

So this is what runs through his mind as he sits in the cell. *I was weak. I was reckless. Berman warned me! Pierre warned me! But I didn't listen to them, I didn't take them seriously. And now I'm going to lose everything! I need to calm down/react/find a solution—and quickly*. He makes a mental list of all the lawyers who might represent him in such a case. There are three or four who spring to mind—big names, procedural obsessives capable of spotting a technicality at ten paces, zeroing in on the slightest chink in the prosecution's armor and exploiting it; single men, divorced men who live in apartments on the same landing as their offices. Then he thinks about Ruth, about Nina—about how they will react when they learn the truth. And the question that haunts him: How far would the investigators go to uncover that truth? Would they take everything he had? Would they reveal everything he hid? Fear runs through his veins.

7

On the advice of her lawyer, Ruth contacts the police. She is trembling as she enters the station; thinking about her husband, she is terrified. A small, surly blond woman[1] at reception asks her to fill out a form and then wait. But after waiting for forty-five minutes, Ruth can't take it any longer: her husband was arrested several hours ago and she still doesn't know why. "You can't treat people this way! You can't arrest a man in his own home and refuse to provide his family with an explanation! This is America! We have rights, don't we? All I'm asking you to do is obey them!" "I would advise you to calm down and sit down until you're called. Yelling at me won't change anything," the woman replies in an aggressive voice. "You're not the only one here, you know. We'll call you when it's your turn." Ruth's mind is a whirlwind of confusion. She imagines the worst: an abduction, a false accusation, a financial scandal. She tells herself now that anything is possible. The wheels of the great machine are in motion and she has no idea how to switch it off. And, for the first time in her life, she is alone—there is no one to accompany her or help her. Seventy-five minutes later, she is finally led to a policeman's[2] office—a small, white-walled room hung with missing persons posters. The man asks her to sit down and make her statement. She stares at him while he types her words into his keyboard; she recounts everything, not omitting a single detail, attempting to reconstruct the morning's events in their exact order. Suddenly, he looks up at her and says there's a problem. "What problem?"

---

1 Samantha de la Vega, forty-five, would have no hesitation in saying that she hates her husband and her job.

2 David Beer, twenty-six, felt "drawn" to enroll in law enforcement.

Ruth asks anxiously. "Wait here." She waits for what seems forever, imagining that Samir is dead—and this thought makes her feverish. She is on the verge of fainting when the policeman returns, now accompanied by a man who is clearly his superior officer.[3] The man sits next to Ruth and informs her in a toneless voice that they have no information for the moment.

"What do you mean, you have no information? Have you arrested him or not?"

"I can't tell you anything."

"So it could be the Mafia—is that what you're telling me?"

"No, this has nothing to do with the Mafia . . ."

"So you do acknowledge that my husband has been arrested?"

"He's been arrested, yeah, but not by us."

"I don't understand . . ."

"I can't tell you any more than that for now."

"They didn't even want to show me their badges! They arrested my husband and took him away like a common criminal."

"That is correct."

"Doesn't that shock you?"

"Not as much as the crimes for which your husband has been arrested."

Now she screams: "What are you insinuating? I don't even know what the charges are! They didn't tell us anything! Not me, not my lawyer. I have the right to know who pressed charges against my husband!"

"You'll be informed in due course."

"No, you are obligated to tell me! This is a democracy, isn't it? I have connections, you know . . ."

"Please, ma'am, don't threaten me. In a case like this, if I were you, I wouldn't dig any deeper . . ."

---

3 John Delano, sixty-two, has the career he always dreamed of.

"What are you implying? Just say it! I have the right to know. Who has pressed charges?"

And suddenly, hands on hips like a comic-book hero, the chief of police turns toward her and calmly replies: "The United States of America."

8

No one is made to cope with fame. It is not natural to be known/loved by thousands of people. Ten or twenty thousand is a lot, but hundreds of thousands? Samuel could never have imagined how violent this sudden shift from anonymity to celebrity would be: physically violent, morally violent; an intense human experience that electrifies and short-circuits the brain. He is flooded by incessant calls, ass-lickers and sycophants hoping for a helping hand up the social ladder; requests for meetings (people who want to see you, approach you, invite you places because you have become interesting; now they want to be seen with you because your presence brings a certain added value—you are *great, gifted, exceptional, call me back*). He used to dream of this kind of success, passionately desire it; he remembers the rage he used to feel at not being able to have it. And now he feels slightly ashamed to acknowledge that he cannot bear this false, superficial fame, the crowd of courtiers at his heels. He can no longer bear all the traveling, in France and abroad, when he would rather stay home and write. He can also no longer bear the media coverage and all the preparation it requires: the hours spent with makeup artists and hairstylists so that "the camera loves you," so that "you can steal the limelight," the confessions he must make to millions of unseen judges. He wishes he could say no, or love his celebrity, but instead he just keeps quiet. Michel Houellebecq is right: success makes you shy.

What does he miss? Silence. The silence that precedes, surrounds, and accompanies writing. Every morning, when he discovered the vast number of messages that had accumulated on his cell phone, he would feel paralyzed by anxiety. Unwittingly, unwillingly, he found himself at the controls of a noisy machine, this man who had chosen writing because he liked silence and solitude.

He can no longer bear human contact—interviews, book signings. He feels like a captured beast, being prodded and examined. When this happens, he despises himself. He despises himself for smiling at a potential reader who picks up his book and says: "Give me one good reason why I should buy it." He despises himself for brandishing a copy of his book and waving it above his head after a bookseller reproached him for not daring to sell it like a newspaper vendor: *You don't know how to do it.* He despises himself for not having punched the writer who said to him, on a train station platform: "You must have sucked a lot of cocks to get the kind of reviews you got for your first book." He despises himself for not quoting Jim Harrison to his publisher when the two of them had a violent row because he refused to take part in a prime-time TV show: "Being an author is a curse and a mission. I realized that at 21, when my father and my sister were killed in a car accident. After a loss like that, no compromise is possible, with publishers or with anyone else." He despises himself for having agreed to do a big interview in a national newspaper and for having told his life story to a stranger who betrayed him by writing that his father was a "crank" because he became an Orthodox Jew. He despises himself for not having had the courage to send an insulting letter to a journalist who wrote: "Samuel Baron uses the death of his parents to move his reader." And, most of all, he despises all those people who now only talk to him about the money he's earning, who alter the way they behave toward him because of his material success. Money affects everything. It affects your relationships with your friends and family, it affects the people you meet, and it affects you: it's like a strange soul that seeps into your body and makes itself at home, mutating you without you realizing, making you become what you hate.

9

"I want to speak to my lawyer! I'm innocent! I didn't do anything! Let me out of here!" But Samir's demands fall on deaf ears and he remains behind bars. One hour later, two men open the door of his cell and lead him out. "We're going to interrogate you now by putting your version of events against your brother's." Samir nearly faints when he hears these words. And then it comes to him: that dinner in the Indonesian restaurant, his brother's confessions about attacking a woman, his fear, his desire to go back to France as quickly as possible. Samir hadn't taken him seriously. "My brother did something bad?" One of the policemen starts laughing, repeating the words: "Something bad?"

"Listen, I know nothing about this. I haven't done anything wrong, I swear it."

"Sure . . ."

"I don't know anything about this!"

"That's what you both say! That's what they taught you to say! You're fucking liars! Liars and parasites!"

They lead him into an overheated interrogation room. Samir asks for a drink of water.

"Talk, and then you can drink."

"I don't have anything to say."

"All right, then . . ."

One of the men turns up the heat and taunts Samir by holding a bottle of cold water in front of his face.

"Want some? Then you'd better start cooperating."

"I don't understand! What am I charged with?"

"Like you don't know . . ."

"I *don't* know!"

"You're charged with involvement in a terrorist operation against American interests."

The dread that invades his body in a matter of seconds. What happens when a man is destroyed? At the instant when he feels the sharp metallic teeth of the crusher puncture his skin. What happens in the moment of his fall? Is he afraid? Does he feel suddenly light, relieved of the weight of his lies, his compromises, his fictions?

"Do the words 'Al Qaeda' mean anything to you?"

Hearing this, Samir begins to tremble. It takes him a few seconds to calm down and reply.

"What does that have to do with me? I haven't done anything!"

"You are suspected of being a member of Al Qaeda."

"This is insane! I don't understand! What am I charged with?"

The policeman plays with the bottle of water for a while, then finally responds: "I told you. You're a terrorist."

Samir passes out. When he comes to, he asks to see a doctor. One of the cops laughs. "This one obviously knows the drill!"

"What are you talking about? I feel sick. I'm having trouble breathing."

"I know what you think is going to happen: you ask to see a doctor, then you demand to speak to a lawyer. You say you need something to eat. You deny all the accusations against you. You claim they were fabricated by the intelligence services. It's classic . . . but let me tell you, buddy, that's not going to work this time."

Samir's hands are cuffed behind his back. This hurts his wrists, so he begs the policeman to remove them. "I'm-innocent-this-is-all-a-mistake-I-haven't-done-anything-I'm-a-lawyer."

A man with pale blond hair comes closer: "You are suspected of having participated in a terrorist operation on behalf of Al Qaeda."

"What are you talking about? I haven't done anything. I don't understand! You can't possibly have any kind of evidence against me because I haven't done anything wrong! Who made this accusation?"

"Shut the fuck up!"

"Someone's framing me. It's a lie! You have to set me free! You have no evidence!"

"In the war against terrorism, suspicion is enough for us to detain you."

"What is your connection with Djamal Yahyaoui?"

"Djamal?"

"François Djamal Yahyaoui claims to be your brother."

"His name is François, not Djamal, and yes, he's my half-brother. But what does that have to do with me? Is he mixed up in something?"

"Your brother is a jihadist. He was arrested in Afghanistan, where he was being trained to carry out an attack against American interests. The federal police have evidence that you financed his terrorist activities."

"What?"

"They discovered his bank account in France and saw that you have been putting money into it every month for the past year. That money was used to pay for your brother's trips abroad, his paramilitary training, and to distribute his incitements to murder."

It takes him some time to reply to this. He feels as if he's been plunged into black water, his head held down, his mouth full of mud, suffocating. He stammers over his words like a man learning to breathe again.

"This is a mistake! François came to New York because he needed money. He was going through a rough time. There's no law against giving money to your brother! I agreed to help him, but I didn't know anything about his activities. How could I know what he was doing with that money? I'm a lawyer, let me remind you! And anyway, why would I want to finance terrorist activities? What connection could I possibly have with Islamic terrorism?"

"That's exactly what concerns us."

"I'm an American citizen. I have a half-brother in France who I barely know, but who I felt obligated to help so that my mother wouldn't have to—that's all! My brother is not an Islamist. I don't understand! How could he have ended up like that?"

The man hesitates for a moment, then stands up and says: "We're going to tell you."

10

After his brief stay in New York, François returned to France in the middle of 2007. He became friends with an ex-con, Eric, now known as Mohammed. The circumstances of their meeting are not clear: some say they knew each other from the housing estate, others that it was François's mother Nawel who put them in touch, after encouraging François to donate a portion of the money he received from Samir to the mosque's social activities. Eric/Mohammed is a charismatic guy in his forties, dark-haired and black-eyed, whose mission in life is to spread the word of Islam to the greatest possible number of people; a proselyte who can be seen around the neighborhood preaching from the books he carries with him. One morning, when they are in Paris together, he suggests that François accompany him to a mosque where he often goes. Eric/Mohammed discovered Islam in prison through one of his fellow prisoners. He converted while he was there and, as he explains to François, "found peace." Hundreds of worshippers are crowded around the temple, which is hidden behind the porch of an abandoned-looking building. François walks in. The imam, Hamid Oussen, is a small man with a thick black beard dressed in the traditional garb of an immaculately white *qamis*. As soon as he begins to speak, François falls under his spell. Eric/Mohammed whispers to François: He admires this man; he knows how to reach the young people who regularly gather around him. He speaks to them and listens to them with great gentleness. Never forcing the issue. He understands their social distress, shows his anger at the injustices they suffer. He vibrates when he speaks, and soon the whole room is trembling. Truth is in prayer, he says. Let us pray together. And when they kneel together, pressed close to their neighbors,

François knows that the truth is indeed here, in this communal prayer recited in one voice. He knows he is one of them—one of God's children. One evening, on his way out of the mosque, François goes to speak to Hamid Oussen. He has been deeply moved by all he has heard and seen. He never imagined he would find such brotherhood—he dares use that word. This is the first time the imam has noticed this young blond man with blue eyes who says his name is François, and he asks him if he is a convert. François hesitates before replying—he is impressed by this man in his white gandoura—and in the end it is Hamid Oussen who, understanding the young man's embarrassment, takes him aside and asks him to tell his story. They sit on large purple velvet cushions and François talks about his father, whom he has never known but who is, he knows, "a famous politician"; about his mother, who tried to "integrate herself in French society so she could become a real French person"; his brother, whom he never sees anymore and who gives him money every month "to ease his conscience"—he talks about how alone he feels. Hamid listens, sympathizes, analyzes: "You don't know who you really are. You must choose your side." What most intrigues Hamid is François's claim to be the son of a politician. The young man may be a lunatic or a liar, of course, but if he is telling the truth, he should be careful about what he admits to him. He invites François to his home, a nice house in the center of town where he lives with his wife—a small, dark woman whose hair is hidden beneath a large headscarf—and their four children, all dressed in traditional clothes. There, during a meal consisting of chickpea soup and home-baked bread, he asks François many questions, seeking to discover what the young man is really looking for. François seems disturbed to him: he is a very inhibited young man, full of suppressed rage, whose only ambition appears to be to avenge his mother's stolen honor; his target is his father. But Hamid tells him this is not true: it is not only this man who is guilty, but the entire society he embodies, "this society whose values are not ours. They dare to tell us that we mistreat our wives because we protect their virtue, their modesty, but look what they do to their own women! Look how that man treated your mother! Like an object! He violated her honor and then he threw her away like garbage! Believe me, it is the infidels who are wrong—we have found the truth!" François is moved: feeling tears rise behind his eyes, he has to breathe heavily to hold them back. Hamid puts a hand on his shoulder and gives him a book about Islam: "You will find peace in this book." François takes the book and puts it on the table. He feels suddenly calm. Religion helps him orient himself, helps him find his place in the world. "What should I do?" François asks. "First, you should change your name." François is thrilled—this is something he has always dreamed of doing—and, with Hamid's help, he chooses the name Djamal. When he goes home that evening, he announces to his mother: *From now on, my name is Djamal.* She does not protest. Djamal means "beauty." Yes, *Djamal*—that's a good name. It holds the promise of a better life.

After that, Djamal stays close to Hamid. He feels good in his company, strong. The older man seems to fill the gaps inside him. He knows nothing of his mother's cultural and religious heritage. He neither reads nor understands Arabic. He doesn't eat pork, but he has never observed Ramadan. He would like to learn. Together, they study a few texts and the rudiments of Arabic. In these moments of complicity, Djamal feels reborn. He thinks of Hamid as a father, a brother, a spiritual guide. He goes to the mosque every Friday evening. Hamid has many worshippers and friends there, some of whom are militant Islamists linked to the Salafist Group for Preaching and Combat. There, surrounded by hundreds of fellow believers, François knows this is where he belongs. Never has he felt so intensely this spiritual communion, this conviction that he is included, loved, that he is part of the same family. They eat together, sitting on the floor. They sing together and his soul awakens. His blood family would never understand. His mother and his brother don't know what it is to find a true family, to belong to a community, a group, a clan, to have not one but a hundred brothers, a thousand brothers around you, sharing the same ideals, working toward the same goal.

His mother is not worried yet—her son is studying, praying. The fear will come later when she notices the physical changes in him, hears him give a radical speech that chills her, and she realizes he has been indoctrinated. A few months after his first meeting with Hamid, Djamal has a thick beard and wears a white *qamis* that the older man gave him. He likes to be seen in this garb out on the street or on public transport: it asserts his identity with pride; it makes him feel strong, tough, powerful. At home, he makes his mother cover her head. One evening, when he invites Hamid to their apartment, he even asks her to veil her face. Nawel's first reaction is to refuse, but she ends up yielding under pressure. Hamid advises his disciple to read certain books and shows him certain documentary films in order, he says, to "strengthen your political conscience." That adjective—"political"—is new for Djamal. He has never been interested in politics or society; his only thought has been his own survival, the pursuit of money. "You have never realized that, because of the way you look, people think you are a real French person, but France is a racist country. They deliberately serve pork in school cafeterias so our children will go hungry, because they want to provoke us . . . I am certain to be stopped almost every time I drive my car, and if I take the Métro, I am always one of the people whose papers they check. As an Arab, you have no chance of finding a good job—and as for a nice place to live, forget it. The French invited our parents here by promising them a Utopia, and instead they herded them like beasts into dormitory towns and exploited them, mistreated them. And now they want to get rid of them and they expect us, their children, to say thank you? The Jews are always weeping over their dead, but who cries for our victims? Shall I tell you what they think? Not all lives are of equal value! They want us to believe that we don't matter. Look what happened in Chechnya—they massacred the Muslims! It was ethnic cleansing! Look what is happening in Palestine! And here, have you seen how they treat us? We must rise up. *Allahu akbar!* Well, we are going to make France—the most Islamophobic country in the world—sit up and take notice of us!" Hamid pauses for a moment. Djamal says nothing; he merely watches his teacher as if hypnotized. "You know," Hamid goes on, "there is only one way to help our oppressed brothers around the world: we must fight alongside them! We must have the courage to take up arms!" Djamal is moved by this speech and he unhesitatingly agrees when Hamid suggests he take part in a hike he has organized in the Forest of Fontainebleau. They are not really going to discover the joys of nature, of course: Djamal knows that it is actually a network for recruiting French jihadists, who will then be trained prior to being sent to Pakistan and Afghanistan. Men preparing for jihad, just outside the gates of Paris. These men choose to leave for Chechnya or Afghanistan, in order to become terrorists; they leave democracies for dictatorships, the lives of free men for dangerous existences controlled by the Taliban in the mountains of Kashmir.

So it's a sort of country ramble with paramilitary overtones. About sixty volunteers in their early twenties turn up to the meeting place, all wearing walking boots and carrying backpacks. Hamid is there, smiling constantly. He counts them as they line up to board a bus. When everyone is inside, he gives a welcome speech. He is friendly, walking down the aisle and greeting each participant. He spends a few moments talking to Djamal—he admires his commitment—then returns to his place and, in a deep voice, reminds them of the aim of the operation. His face grows hard. He has something to show them. A small TV screen shows images of war; images, Hamid says, "of our Muslim brothers being murdered all over the world—being ruthlessly killed like dogs." There are pictures of bodies that have been dismembered, decapitated, burned, and exploded, images of disfigured faces. After this, they are filled with hatred. After this, they can aim a gun and fire without trembling, without hesitating. It is less certain that they will be able to kill, but that will come—when they are isolated far from home, in Chechnya or Afghanistan. Only then will they be able to prove that they are real soldiers. An hour and a half later, they reach their destination. The forest is thick, and they walk for hours without eating or drinking. It's a physical test, a moral test; they're being broken. To keep up their morale, they chant war songs about the struggle and the deliverance to come, the death of the Western enemy that dominates and humiliates them, smashes and colonizes them. Their yelling is drowned out by furious noises coming from a boom box: the rumble of helicopters, the sound of gunshots, Kalashnikov fire, bomb explosions . . . this sound track provides an atmosphere, a taste of what they have to look forward to. It is brutal. It is violent. The weakest among them trip or slip, fall or pretend to fall, whine and curse; they are picked up and pushed onward. Some collapse. It is better that they give up now. If they're not capable of doing a five-hour hike through a Parisian forest, how would they possibly survive several weeks in the mountains of Afghanistan? Let those weak ones stay in France. Let them help their mothers, look after their sisters, smoke their dope. But the others—those who are strong enough to take the exertion, the tension, the pressure, those who keep going even when they're on their last legs, those who fall down and get back up again, who suffer without complaint, watch the most cruel images without looking away or crying—those strong ones will go away, take up arms, and fight. François-Djamal is one of those. Already, he knows where he's going, what he wants. He tells his mother that he's doing sport, that he's in training. She watches his body change, become more muscular, his face become harder and thinner. Djamal takes part in several "hikes" in Haute-Savoie; in those mountainous areas, the physical test is even tougher: you have to climb up the rock face with your bare hands. Each time, he stands out for his tenacity, his sangfroid, his courage and determination. His friends remember him. They call him Djamal the Blond. He doesn't want to tell them that he is the fruit of an adulterous affair between a Muslim woman and a Christian man, an employee and her boss, a Frenchwoman of Tunisian origin and a pure white Frenchman; they would reject him, he feels sure. And what he wants is to belong to the group. So he tells them his father is a Frenchman who converted to Islam after having a revelation, that his father died and left him a small sum of money. They like the idea of converts here. He does not feel he is betraying anything or anyone. He also says that he uses his mother's surname—an Arab-sounding name—because that is what he is, what he wants to be: an Arab. They repeat to him: "Christianity is the religion of slave owners." These hikes radicalize him. His mother, he thinks, practices a slack, halfhearted version of Islam, an Islam without conviction, a spineless Islam, while he dreams of a strong, hard, pure Islam. Not a religion that can be diluted by Frenchness. His mother is terrified by this desire for purity, this moral intransigence, this warlike rigor, but she says nothing and bows down to the new rules issued by her son: you will wear a veil at home and outside . . . you will not speak to men . . . you will not contradict me. And that's how it is, how it should be: the docile woman, executing his orders, and him, the omnipotent monarch who rules/controls/forbids.

Finally, the time comes for him to leave . . . Djamal marries a young Muslim woman from the neighborhood. Her name is Nora and she works on the markets. He meets her by chance, during a dinner organized by one of her aunts. He notices her as soon as he enters the room: a dark-skinned girl with long, curly hair hidden beneath a bandanna. Nora is not an overt, flashy beauty, but that is precisely why Djamal is attracted to her. She is from a traditionalist background, but she falls in love with him at first sight—the clash of his blond hair and white skin in that room— and persuades herself that he will not force anything on her. They marry in a very private ceremony at the mayor's office in Sevran. Djamal chooses Hamid as his witness. The couple move to an efficiency. The apartment is owned by a slumlord, a former cop who buys places at rock-bottom prices and rents them out by the room at exorbitant prices. Sometimes there are up to fifteen people in a three-room apartment, one family in each room. It's a precarious existence, but for the first time in his life, Djamal is happy. Islam has brought him peace, and he loves his wife. But something is missing. One evening, he asks Hamid why he has not been sent to Afghanistan to fight: "I can't stay here doing nothing! Have you seen how they treat our people? Have you heard the lies they tell us? They act like we're rats, Hamid! I want to serve Allah with all my strength." For the first time, Hamid feels uneasy. Djamal has proven himself loyal and determined on the hikes; he has passed every test he's been set. And yet Hamid has not been able to move past his initial distrust. What if Djamal is an informer, a double agent? In spite of their friendship, he does not feel ready to send him to the East, to give him his list of contacts. So he has the idea of giving Djamal one final test: only two months after his wedding, he suggests to Djamal that he be sent to Yemen to undertake religious and linguistic training. Djamal likes this idea. His dream is exactly that: to move to a Muslim country, a country where he can finally live the life he has chosen without feeling judged or op-pressed. He tells his wife that he is going there to prove his faith. Nora says nothing; she lets him go. Deep down, she knows she will never follow him there, and she hopes and believes he will give up on his plans when he returns. And when she reads his first letter, she realizes she was right: life there is difficult. Even the flight there is an ordeal, the seats on the plane all broken, and squeezed so close together that he can't even open his legs more than an inch apart. He is in pain but says nothing. During the flight, he prays, reads passages from the Koran, and eventually falls asleep. After the plane lands, he vomits on the asphalt. The heat is suffocating, and his clothing sticks to his skin like a bandage on a burn wound. He is thirsty, he is hungry, and by the time he reclaims his luggage, he doesn't believe he'll be able to last more than a few days in this country. But he is wrong: not only is he able to stand it, but he likes it there. Once he has moved his things into the apartment he will share with a Yemeni couple, once he has splashed water on his face and shared a dish of meatballs with the couple, using his fingers, he feels better. That day, he enrolls in a Yemeni university to study the Koran and improve his Arabic. This, at least, is what he will tell people later. The real reason is probably murkier: it is said that the dean of that university is in charge of recruiting vol-unteers for Osama bin Laden. He picks out the most active, most zealous foreign students, then approaches them, talks to them, trains them. He does this very carefully, choosing only the tough-est and most reliable among them. The more fragile types—the docile, submissive ones—he leaves to their books. Djamal is not easy to categorize in this way: while he is undoubtedly a follower of a very strict brand of Islam, he is not as yet truly politicized. He enjoys those days of study, meditation, and prayer, he enjoys eating meals as part of a community—he appreciates the feeling of brotherhood in such moments. In the evenings, he eats hot soup or couscous which he shares with the other men, all of them eating from the same large earthenware plate while the women, sitting on the floor, grind almonds in a cooking pot to extract their oil. After dinner, Djamal likes to sit by a big campfire and spend the rest of the evening listening to the cantilena chanted by the insomniacs. Then, late at night, he returns to his little room and writes his wife letters in which he explains that he is learning, and that he will serve Allah until the day he dies: *I left to discover how to win my ticket to paradise, and I have found what I was looking for*.

One morning, he is arrested on his way out of the university. Soldiers pin him to a wall and handcuff him. They lock him in a tiny cell and interrogate him all night long: Does he have links with the university dean? With Osama bin Laden? Why did he come to Yemen? Where does he live? What does he do during the day? What are his intentions? His political opinions? Djamal is frightened. As this is happening, his mind is a blur of incomprehension. He prays and studies, he tells them. It's true he has met a few preachers, but he never called them back; he stayed away from them. This is his version. The armed men who question him have their own: Terrorist acts have been perpetrated in this country by an Islamist army. What does he know about that? Nothing, he swears. One of the soldiers stares at him with hatred: "I repeat: the Yemeni government is hunting down troublemakers and we have reason to believe that you are one of them." Djamal repeats that he has nothing to do with all this, that he is here to learn and improve his Arabic, that all his intentions are peaceful, but he doesn't have time to finish his sentence because the man rams a fist into his left eye and he is bleeding, screaming, he can't see. "Remember anything now? Is it coming back to you? I'll ask you again: Why did you come to Yemen? You're an Islamist, aren't you?" *No, no.* Djamal trembles and pisses himself: he feels the warm liquid run down his legs and feels ashamed. He is too hot and he can barely understand the language. He starts crying and they call him a woman, lock him up in a tiny, dark cell with three other bearded men, all dull-eyed and shaggy-haired. The air is thick with the stench of urine, sweat, and shit, the odor permeating the men's hair, clothes, skin. He wants to throw up, wants to smash his head against the wall until it explodes. He curls up into a corner, knees folded against his chest, and starts to pray for his future deliverance, although he no longer believes. On the wall, there are words written in Arabic that he doesn't understand. He sobs himself to sleep.

He is woken in the middle of the night by a warden who prods him with a stick as if he were a venomous snake, yelling: "Get up! Slowly!" Djamal is led to a room lit only by a dim bulb, a sort of damp basement room without windows. The interrogation begins again: Who are you? Why did you come here? What are your links with the dean of the university? Etc. Djamal demands a lawyer and his questioner laughs: "Where the hell do you think you are? This isn't France!" He is beaten and threatened, but does not give in. Finally, after asking repeatedly, he is put in touch with the French Consulate. This is his get-out-of-jail-free card. Never has he felt such desire before to assert the fact that he is French. To the man from the consulate he tirelessly repeats what he has already told his jailers: "I came here to study Islam and learn Arabic, and that's all."

He does not ask his mother or Hamid for help: he wants to get out of this situation himself. And he succeeds, because after three weeks he is released. The man he's been staying with is waiting for him outside the prison gates. Together they walk back to the apartment and eat dinner, lit by candle flames that flicker in the breaths from raised voices and bursts of laughter: they are celebrating Djamal's return. At the evening's end, two men dressed in black enter the apartment through the back door. They greet Djamal warmly and hand him a return flight ticket to France. Who are these men?

When did he ask for their help? The reply is vague. When he gets home, he tells his wife that he still had some money left, but she doesn't believe him—and for the first time she suspects that he has been aided financially by the men he calls "my brothers."

Upon his return, Nora no longer recognizes him. He has become radicalized, mistrustful, paranoiac, suspicious, obsessive. And, most of all, he has become anti-Semitic. He sees Jews everywhere and squanders the money that Samir continues to send him on the publication and distribution of anti-Semitic tracts. He and his wife have terrible rows. Djamal gets back in touch with Hamid, who no longer doubts him. In the housing estate, he goes regularly to a small mosque located in a former gymnasium and becomes friendly with other "brothers." He does not talk about his experience in Yemen: for him, it represents a failure. One morning, one of the worshippers at the mosque advises him to train as a halal butcher. "Halal is the future," he says, backing up his case with figures that show the size of the market and the importance of this activity for the rebirth of a pure Islam: if Muslims have the choice, they will eat halal meat—*You'd even be able to open your own butcher's shop one day, Insha'Allah*. With Samir's money, that will actually be possible, Djamal thinks; he enrolls in a training program, enjoys it, and receives his diploma. Two months later, he gets a job in a slaughterhouse. He has to caress the animals to calm them down, then lead them to a rotating trap where they are killed while facing Mecca. The bovine's head is held still, the neck lengthened. Djamal triggers the rotation of the trap along a horizontal axis—a sort of aerial rail—so that the beast is suspended upside down with its hooves in the air. The bovine starts bellowing now, so Djamal has to act quickly: he places the knife under the glottis and cuts its throat. He does this without fear, without emotion, and in one rapid motion, so that the animal doesn't suffer. Blood spurts out, splashing into the trough, but Djamal continues undaunted: this is a sacred act and he is proud to have been chosen to perform it. When the animal has stopped breathing, he skins it, eviscerates it, splits open the carcass, then trims and weighs the meat before refrigerating it. After that, he only has to perform his ablutions, and everything is ready. Not only does Djamal like his work, but he takes it very seriously. He is the one who slits the sheep's throat for Eid; he does it cleanly, in the abattoir. He takes the orders, organizes the deliveries. He hates finding sheep's heads, their disemboweled carcasses, their stinking entrails, tossed into his building's garbage chute, as often happens. In fact, it disgusts him, and soon he is also taking charge of the slaughter of his neighbors' animals. One evening, coming home from prayer, he sees, out in the wasteland near his apartment block, a sheep hanging from a rope tied between two trees. Facing the sheep are two children, age ten or eleven, armed with a huge knife. The first one skewers the animal, while the second prepares to cut it up. Djamal runs up to them and starts yelling at them so angrily that they are dumbfounded, too frightened to say a word. Their hands are covered in blood and the sheep's head is hanging. But the animal is still alive, making pitiful moaning noises. Djamal grabs the knife from the boy's hands, raises it above his head, and, with a single stroke, puts the beast out of its misery. Only then does he look the children in the eyes and threaten them: if he ever finds them doing this again, they'll be the ones to feel the sharpness of his knife's blade. The words come out without him thinking, and afterward he feels slightly ashamed of what he's said, but he loves animals. In Yemen, where dogs and cats roam freely in search of leftovers, he had found a skinny, starving kitten in a garbage can and fallen in love with it. He took it home, looked after it until it was no longer skinny or starving, and then set it free again—nobody wanted it.

———

From now on, his life is the abattoir and the friends he has made there. He spends his evenings in the mosque with his work colleagues. They discuss a passage from the Koran or talk politics; he still dreams of going off to fight. He enjoys their company, but when he goes home, late at night, still smelling of dead animals— viscera, skin, blood—his wife pushes him away. He disgusts her. He scares her. She no longer wants to make love with him, and one evening when he kisses her, she says: "I don't feel anything for you." She sees his face tense up and becomes frightened. In spite of this, though, she stands up to him and she is the first to utter the word "divorce." When does he become violent? When she pronounces that word or, a little later, when she begins hitting him as hard as she can because he tried to kiss her, holding her face securely in his blood-stinking hands? He launches himself at her, pins her to the wall, removes his belt, pulls down his pants, and rapes her brutally, yelling insults at her—*Filthy whore*—and repeating that, if she ever leaves him, he will kill her. Finally, after a few minutes of this, he lets go of her and gets dressed. Nora is in tears, one hand covering her breasts. She shouts at him that she will call the police. *Go ahead, call them. And I'll throw you out the fucking window!* He can't stand being dominated by women anymore—first it was his mother, now it's his wife. He dreams of a society where everyone will know their place: men out in town, women at home. While he's thinking about this, not paying attention, Nora escapes, holding her torn blouse, leaving behind all her belongings, and takes refuge with her parents. He will never see her again. But she doesn't press charges, terrified by the threats he makes to her the next day.

Djamal no longer wants to live in this apartment, which reminds him of the shame his wife brought down on him by asking for a divorce. He divides his time between his mother's apartment and the home of two brothers—activists he met during a dinner at Hamid's house. That summer, he decides to go to Morocco to find a wife: one of the brothers has told him about a sixteen-year-old girl from a good family whose parents want to marry her off. Three weeks before his departure, he burns his passport and declares it lost so he can obtain a new one, without any foreign stamps in it.

In Morocco, he meets his future wife,[1] a young girl who is rather plump but has very pure, innocent eyes. He has a discussion with the father, where they negotiate the dowry sum, then marries the girl a few days later. On their wedding night, he makes love to her on a small mattress that his parents-in-law have put on the floor in one of the rooms in their house. When it's over, he gives the family the bloodstained sheet. He hears ululations through the dividing wall. He feels happy.

On returning to France, he moves with his new wife to a one-bedroom apartment that he sublets and starts back to work at the slaughterhouse. He still sees Hamid, but his friend seems worried, and Djamal wonders why. Then, one day, Hamid takes him into his confidence: he is going to fight alongside his oppressed brothers. He can't bear staying here and doing nothing in this country where "nobody likes us."

In the nights that follow Hamid's revelation, Djamal sleeps badly. He dreams that he too is going away, carrying a gun, a hero. With Hamid acting as an intermediary, he gets in touch with the men whose job it is to recruit Westerners. Djamal has references and a spotless résumé. Best of all, he looks completely European: the enemy is less likely to suspect him. The men ask him to shave his beard and to swap his traditional clothes for a shirt and jeans: "You must blend in with the crowd." He goes to see them again, transformed by these changes, and they laugh: "You'd get in the Ku Klux Klan looking like that!" That very day, they give him a

---

1 Latifa Oualil, sixteen. Has no idea what she wants to do with her life.

false passport and a telephone number that he must call when he arrives at the train station in London. He must recite a sentence in code, then take the Tube to Finsbury Park Station. At the exit, a bearded man in a blue scarf will be waiting for him. The problem, it turns out, is that most of the men there are bearded and wear dark-colored scarfs. He waits for forty-five minutes before a man matching the description he's been given approaches him and mutters a few words. He follows the man. They walk for a long time—maybe an hour—before arriving at a small white-brick building. The man motions him to enter. Inside, men are coming and going in all directions. The place looks like the headquarters of some sort of research firm. Djamal feels lost and unsure, so he asks the man where they are and who brought him here. But the man responds only with a frown and a finger pressed to his lips. Djamal realizes that he must not ask questions. He does not feel very reassured by this. The man barely speaks a word, but takes him to a room and tells him he should wait there until he returns. He waits for maybe four or five hours in that cramped room, the air smelling of urine and sweat, without seeing anyone. Then the man returns with an aluminum box, a bottle of water, and a plastic spoon. He tells Djamal that he will stay here this evening, then leave in the night to catch a 6:50 a.m. airplane to Islamabad. The meal inside the box is cold, probably because it has just been thawed. It's a lamb stew with potatoes, but the meat is fatty and gelatinous and gives off a sickening odor, as if the animal were cooked in its own viscera. Djamal decides not to eat and takes a copy of Sun Tzu's *The Art of War* from his bag. At two in the morning, he is woken by the sound of a man's voice and the harsh brightness of a flashlight aimed at his face. Still sleepy, he struggles to his feet, listens to his final instructions, and then—holding his flight ticket and the bus ticket to the airport—he exits the building and disappears into the night.

He passes through customs without difficulty and falls asleep as soon as he is seated in the airplane. When he wakes up, the flight attendant informs him that the plane will be landing in Islamabad in a few minutes.

When he emerges from the plane, what first hits him is the suffocating heaviness of the air, even more unbearable than it had been in Yemen. The second thing is the bright clusters of dust that seem to swarm from all directions, forming a yellowish paste that sticks to his eyelids, gets everywhere. Djamal takes off his jacket and holds it tight to him. He is startled by the throngs of men in turbans, all with jet-black eyes, who swarm through the neighborhood around the airport. Half-starved animals wander between abandoned cars, pursued by hordes of fat flies and mosquitoes whose buzzing seems to echo the agitation of the men. Street hawkers run around, carrying their shabby merchandise, attempting to escape the eyes of the uniformed police who prowl, weapons at the ready, faces shining with sweat. After an hour of searching, he finally finds a public phone from which he can call his contact. He is told to stay where he is, with nothing to eat or drink, his face exposed to the burning sunlight. For the first time, Djamal wishes he were François again, wishes he could go home. This killing heat, this foreign speech, this poverty—it all serves to distance him from his strongest desire. He says nothing, however, and when, two hours later, a man arrives and asks him to follow, Djamal obeys without question. The man is huge, with a boxer's face and hands, and his body smells of engine oil. He gets into the man's rickety white van. Inside, the heat is unbreathable, the air like an oven. Through the window, Djamal watches the landscape speed past: cerulean with green dots and slashes. The mountains vanish into the distance. Women imprisoned in chadors carry children with sun-weathered faces. Herds of goats walk through clouds of dust, haloed with buzzing flies. The trip lasts forever:

the road is full of rocks and holes, and the van jumps up and down
as if its wheels were on springs. Djamal throws up several times.
Finally, they arrive in front of a large jihadist mosque, a "center of
preaching and good conduct." A few yards away, a scrawny man,
holding a comb and a pair of scissors, cuts the hair of a younger
man who kneels before him in the middle of the street. Locks of
black hair fall to the ground. Farther on, a man leans over a huge
cast-iron dish, searing pieces of bloody meat. Djamal follows his
guides, who disappear inside the mosque. He is greeted by a man
in white who gives him a new name and tells him a room has
been reserved for him in a neighboring hotel. He will stay there
for two weeks, while his background is investigated. Is he a spy?
A journalist? With his European appearance, Djamal is an obvious target for suspicion. In his hotel room, he begins to wonder
what he's doing here. The peacock-blue carpet is covered with
blackish stains. The paint on the walls is peeling in places and he
can see roaches through the cracks. But he spends most of his
time in the mosque, where a succession of prayers, discussions,
and meals follow an unchanging rhythm, and finally—at the end
of the two weeks—he is told that all is well and he can now go
to Afghanistan. They explain what will happen there. Djamal is
calm. The man responsible for conveying foreign volunteers to
the training camps—a man in his early thirties, dressed like a
soldier—will accompany him, helping him to pass through the
Pakistani police's checkpoints without any problems. Djamal
reaches the training camps belonging to Lashkar-e-Taiba—
a movement created in the late 1980s to take part in the jihad
against Soviet soldiers in Afghanistan, and which, following this,
joined the Islamic Front carrying out a broader war against "the
Jews and the Crusaders."

Djamal arrives at a remote camp divided into several sec-
tors, where Lashkar's leaders live. He is given a military uniform:

combat pants, a khaki shirt, and a sort of beret. Here, he meets two men: Abdel, known as Abdel of Mecca, and Mohammed, a member of the mobile Pakistani army who liaises between this camp and Afghanistan and reports on the situation there. He is in charge of recruiting foreigners, irrespective of their nationality.

Djamal stays in this camp for a few weeks, then is sent to another camp, concealed in the mountains of the Punjab. The units are mobile in order to avoid discovery. A day in the camp follows an unchanging ritual: the trainees are woken at three in the morning; they pray together and listen to speeches about the importance of the jihad and the holy war. As in Fontainebleau, they are shown images of war, mutilations and acts of violence committed against Muslims. Along with other men from all over the world, Djamal undergoes a military training that takes the form of long walks during the day and, at night, in the mountains; shooting practice; and the assembly and disassembly of firearms. He is taught techniques for ambushes, camouflage, the use of weapons (grenades, Kalashnikovs, sniper rifles, mortars), and the manufacture and installation of explosives and detonators. The trainees follow orders, they run and crawl, climb, roll through sand, jump into trenches, carry weights, attack a military convoy. It is cold and Djamal is hungry. Exhaustion begins to overcome him. Here too, the weakest are removed, sent back to wherever they came from. Djamal lives here, surrounded by two or three thousand Mujahideen. He swaggers around, defying the enemy, his brain afire. They are guided by a military sheikh, who reports to Abdel, picking out the best men for him: those steel-hard recruits who will have the glory of dying as martyrs. Here, with them, Djamal has a goal—he exists, he is important—whereas back home in Sevran, in peacetime, he is nothing.

Sometimes, in the middle of the night, the men are rudely awoken, mobilized into groups, and evacuated from the camp,

their weapons well hidden. They disappear into the mountains.
The Pakistani army and some American officers are about to arrive,
so it's said. They flee without fear, informed in advance of every
move by members of the Pakistani army itself. It's a well-oiled machine. In a secluded area, Djamal devotes himself to cleaning the
camp. He does it quickly and efficiently, picking up the spent shells
and collecting them in a large metal box. This process takes a few
hours, sometimes a few days, and after that it's fine. They return
as soon as the Pakistanis and Americans have left, *empty-handed,
those pathetic losers—we will destroy them all, the Western dogs!*
In the evening, around the campfire, they recite verses from the
Koran predicting the coming victory, *and our enemies shall perish
beneath our sword, we shall invade their lands, we shall kill them
all unto the last!*

They sleep on the ground, rolled up in blankets that smell of
sweat and dust, defying the cold and the heat, the wind and the
fear, and dream of women whose marble-like bodies they uncover
from beneath the thickest chadors, pure virgins who do not cry
out during lovemaking, who offer themselves without resistance,
open and close their thighs upon command, oh, it's so good, they
think, like the celestial paradise, those hairless, unblemished bodies waiting to be deflowered. They dream so intensely that they
do not hear the American soldiers who have them in their rifle
sights, ready to blow their heads off. They are woken roughly, with
iron bars, meekly releasing the grenades from their hands, which
they hold during sleep in case of a surprise attack, and as Djamal
opens his eyes he screams that he is French—I'm French!—that
he hasn't done anything—I'm French! I haven't done anything! I'm
innocent!—but one of the soldiers smashes him in the face with
the butt of his rifle, almost gouging out his right eye, and Djamal
collapses in a cloud of ash and dust.

But . . . I' . . . Fren . . .

11

"So Sami is in jail because of this brother, who he never even mentioned to me," Berman tells Nina. "After being arrested on the Afghan border by American soldiers, his brother was taken to the United States and then incarcerated in Guantánamo. But apparently no one understands what role Sam played in this exactly, or how deeply he was involved in it. It's still a mystery." Nina has listened to Berman without interrupting, feeling as if he were talking about a stranger. Could Samir have deceived her so thoroughly about this? Is it possible for a man to have not two but five or six faces? Who *was* Samir, really? A cruel hoaxer? A lovable schizophrenic? A perverted polymorph? Was he the victim of some dreadful conspiracy or was he part of that conspiracy? An activist of some sort? Surely not a terrorist. Not an Islamist or a fundamentalist either. He loved alcohol and sex, loved provocation and transgression. And he loved her. *Didn't he?* In her mind, everything had become vague and murky: she was no longer capable of separating reality from fantasy, fact from gossip, truth from falsehood. She felt nauseous—felt the bile rise like some deadly lava inside her—and if Berman hadn't ended his monologue there, she would have fainted in this café where the voices of other people buzzed and roared like an engine . . . she would have fainted and perhaps even died. Because, for her, what other way out was there from this? She possessed absolutely *nothing*. During all these months in New York, she had let herself be carried on his shoulders, like a child, and how light she had felt! Cleaning the house, paying her bills, working for a living— all those shackles imposed by society, she had been free of them all.

"You can't stay in New York," Berman tells her. "They'll interrogate you. And your presence here might damage him even more. They're going to freeze his bank accounts. Believe me, the best thing you can do is return to France as quickly as possible." Nina does not reply. She feels sure that Berman does not know the truth about Samir's identity because he keeps repeating that he doesn't believe this story: "Why would a Jew be on the side of radical Islamists?" She decides it is better to remain silent. "What do you think?" She says she would like to see Sami, speak to him, but Berman dissuades her:

"I'm afraid that's impossible. He's kept in total isolation. They regard him as a danger to society, you see? No one is allowed to go near him. Even for his lawyers, there's a whole routine they have to go through each time. What they're trying to do, by keeping him away from people in this way, is to make him weak, make him crack, make him believe that everyone on the outside has abandoned him; it's a fairly standard torture technique."

"In that case, I'll write to him."

"I don't think that would be a good idea. Do you really think they'll just let your letter through to him unopened? Every letter he receives will be censored. Each one will be read very carefully, and if by any chance it is handed on to him, most of your sentences will be blacked out anyway. Don't look so shocked—when it comes to anti-terrorism, there are no rules anymore. They can do anything they want. So imagine what they would find out from your letters . . . The judges would learn that he was leading a double life. You'd risk damning him even more. It would help them build up a picture of a man who was two-faced, secretive, and in many ways manipulative. That's all it would take for them to keep him in prison for months to come . . ."

"Whatever, I have to see him and—"

"What do you mean, whatever? What kind of world are you living in? This isn't a romantic comedy, Nina."

She is revolted by the machismo of his speech. But she says

nothing and, as he lectures her, listens to him obediently like a six-year-old girl.

"Listen, Nina, what do you expect from him? He'll probably be in prison for a long time. For now, you can't help him at all. All you can do is make things more difficult for him. The only people he needs in his life right now are his lawyers."

"I'll wait."

"Wait? Where? His bank accounts will be blocked. The owner of the apartment he rents for you will kick you out . . . And anyway, why would you do that for him? He put you in danger, didn't he?"

"I'm going to stay. He'll need me eventually. Because we're together."

In an infuriated voice, Berman finally tells her: "You are not together! Sami is married. He has a wife, a family, and the only person he will need by his side is Ruth Berg. With her money, with her influence, she's in a position to help him. You can't even imagine the lawyers' fees for a case like this. Without his wife, I'm not sure he'd even be able to afford it."

"You don't understand. I love him. I can't just let him . . ."

Hearing this gorgeous woman, for whom he feels a powerful erotic desire, say that she loves Tahar is a severe blow to Berman's convictions, to his strict code of ethics, to his certainties about life, to everything that has enabled him to lead this calm, moral existence—an existence he would be ready to give up at the slightest sign of any reciprocal feeling. How he would love to be loved by her. He tells her: "Sam is lucky to have you." Nina gives a faint smile—a sad, disillusioned smile.

"Nina, I can help you stay here. You won't be able to see Sami for quite some time, but I'll be here for you."

He moves closer to her, places a hand on her arm. Nina pulls away brusquely.

"I'm sorry."

Nina looks away.

"Don't look so scared. I'm telling you, I could help you."

"Oh . . . and what would you do?"

"Well, to begin with, I could find you somewhere else to live because it's not a good idea to stay in that apartment. The investigators will check all his outgoings and there's a good chance they'll pay you a visit there. Or his wife will find out and you'll find yourself face-to-face with her. That's the worst-case scenario."

"And afterward what will happen?"

Berman's hand creeps toward Nina's. He catches one of her fingers.

"That would depend on you."

He wants her, now, here, in this packed restaurant. He feels bad about it, terribly guilty. And he's baking-hot, the sweat running inside his cotton shirt. All the same, he doesn't give up:

"What do you think? It'd give you time to get things organized, to think about your future here."

"I don't want your help."

He lets go of her finger suddenly and shifts back in his seat slightly, as if she were a source of toxic heat.

"Nina, there's something you should know which might affect your decision . . ."

She freezes.

"I'm just going to come out with it. Are you ready to hear this?"

"Go on."

"The day before his arrest, I had a very long discussion with Sami . . . about your relationship. It was late at night. We were the only ones in the office. We'd had a drink together, and . . . he told me that you'd threatened him that he would never see you again if he didn't leave his wife . . . He told me you wanted a child . . ."

Nina's mouth tenses. Her eyes fill with salt water.

"I thought he wanted my advice, but it wasn't that. He'd already made his decision . . ."

Nina looks away.

"He was going to tell you that it was over between you."

12

The shock of it. He's having a nightmare—trapped inside a concrete block—but, each time, Samir wakes up thinking it's over, that he's free, unscathed . . . and then he feels the handcuffs cutting into his wrists. Under the white light of the bare bulb swinging above his head in a hypnotic movement, he tries to understand what's happening/what's at stake/where this is heading. He demands/threatens/yells: "Call my lawyer! Where is my wife?" "Shut the fuck up!" How long has he been locked up? He has no notion of time. He feels as if there's a plastic bag over his head: he can't breathe, his limbs twitch, his entire metabolism seems to have slowed down, as if his blood has been mixed with some poisonous substance that is atrophying his muscles, a slow and horrible death creeping over him inch by inch. The nights are the worst: the shouts and screams of his fellow detainees—some of them sounding like the wailing of wild beasts or of a child getting its throat cut—keep him in a state of terror that lasts until the early morning, when, worn out and thirsty, he is called for another round of interrogation. He is exhausted by the lack of sleep and by the despair he feels at having to go through it all again: the psychological harassment, the threats, the humiliation, the bullying.

You knew what your brother was up to.

No, he didn't know. He knew *nothing*!

What was your connection with Djamal Yahyaoui? Did you know what he was doing with the money you sent him every month? Why did you send him so much money? Why did you come to the

United States? What is your connection to the Islamist movement? Are you Jewish? Did you convert to Islam? Where did you get that scar? Who do you work for? Did you know your brother was preparing to carry out a terrorist attack? Did you know he lived in Afghanistan? Did you know he'd become a radical Islamist? Why are you a member of a shooting club? What were your relations with the organized Muslim community in New York? What do you think of Bin Laden? Did you know your brother was being trained to kill Americans? Did you plan to take part in a terrorist attack against the United States of America? How do you feel about America? What was your brother doing on American soil? When did he tell you he was planning to convert? Did you know he was married and that his wife wore a chador? Did you know your brother had published anti-Semitic tracts in France?

I didn't do anything! This is all a big mistake! It's just a terrible misunderstanding!

A legal error, an accusation based on a tip-off, a rumor—Tahar's obsessive fear—and here he is, now, in this cell, head in hands, face lined with the effects of fatigue and shock. He calms down—he knows he has done nothing wrong—and finally falls asleep, exhausted. Every five minutes, a warden shines a flashlight at him to check that he hasn't attempted suicide. (How could he?) He decides to go on a hunger strike, hoping this will draw attention to his case, prove his innocence. Systematically he pushes back every meal he's given, ignoring the pleas and threats of the wardens, who are under orders to make sure he doesn't die. After two weeks, Samir—dull-eyed and hollow-cheeked—is urgently transferred to a military hospital, where he undergoes tests. They begin force-feeding him.

We want terrorists alive.

He is alone in this white-sheeted bed, on a drip, as if he's been in a serious accident. For the first time since his arrest, he starts to cry. He wishes he could roll over into the fetal position and rock himself back and forth, slowly at first, and then faster and faster. Once he realizes that they are not going to let him die, that they will not alert anyone to his situation because they have the means to keep him alive anyway, he gives up his hunger strike.

A few days later, he is sent back to his cell, where he slips into a vegetative state. He makes himself do a few gymnastic exercises every day, but this resolution does not last long. He thinks: *I'm disappearing, day by day. I am going to die without ever finding out what really happened.*

One morning, Samir is rudely awakened. Sleepy-eyed, ashen-faced, hair and beard grown wild, he cuts a scary figure. "Your lawyer is here," the warden tells him. His lawyer? He sighs. Is the nightmare ending? The warden takes him to the visiting room, where Dan Stein is waiting for him. The two sit across from each other.

"Dan, I'm going crazy!" Samir shouts, pressing his hands to the window. "Get me out of here, Dan!"

"Ruth called me as soon as you were arrested. I know you've made demands but they've only been passed on to me very recently. We've been doing everything we can while you've been in here, but so far they've refused all our requests."

"Can they do that?"

"They can do whatever they like, Sami! You're lucky they even let me in today. They sometimes keep guys for weeks on end like this, without any legal representation. The security of the United States overrides everything. You're nothing compared to that . . ."

"Dan, I don't understand what's happened to me. Why am I here? I haven't done anything. You have to get me out of here!"

Stein opens his briefcase and takes out a notepad and pen. He asks Samir if he has been told why he was arrested. Yes, yes, they told him but he doesn't understand—it's all a big mistake, or a conspiracy, they're framing him . . .

Stein interrupts: "Let's cut to the chase. We don't have much time. Anti-terrorism laws have become much harsher since 9/11—you must be aware of that. They can do whatever they want to you. Since Congress voted in the Patriot Act, individuals have no real rights at all if they are suspected of being involved in Islamist terror activities. They think you're a sleeper agent, Sami. They think you came to the U.S. a long time ago to make a career here, to blend into American society, to become the kind of person no one would suspect, purely so you could commit a major attack years later. But what they don't understand—this is what they're struggling with—is why a Jew would be working for radical Islamists. They've got the CIA and the FBI on the case. I wouldn't be surprised to learn that they've been in touch with Mossad."

"And what conclusions did they come to?" he asks, with an undertone of animosity in his voice.

"That either you're not a Jew—which is a possibility . . ."

Stein looks at him as he says this, and Samir struggles to conceal his embarrassment.

". . . or you've converted to radical Islam. Or, the last possibility, you really are a victim. But if that's the case, then they want to understand: Why you? What is their true target? You, your wife, your firm, your father-in-law?"

"I am not guilty of the crime I'm accused of."

Dan Stein suddenly flashes him a hostile look. "I'm not yet sure I can accept that."

"What? Why? You can't just let me rot in here! I'm telling you, I'm innocent! What do you want from me? Do you want me to get down on my knees and beg you? All right, then, I'm begging you. I need you!"

"I'll have to think about it."

"I'm your colleague. I'm the husband of one of your best clients! You came to my birthday party last year—don't you remember?"

"First of all, I would like to understand how your brother can be a radical Islamist when you're a Jew. And, above all, your wife and I would like to know why you hid your brother's existence from us."

"That's very simple: François is not my brother—he's my half brother. We don't have the same father. He converted and I knew nothing about it. I barely even know him! I only lived with him for a couple of years. Listen to me, I'm begging you—I have nothing to do with any of this!"

"Prove it."

Consolation

A fake!

SOPHIE MAUROIS[1]

A minor writer.

DAVID KASSOVITZ[2]

After reading this book, the reader is the one who needs to be consoled.

TRISTAN LANOUX[3]

The worst novel of the year.

JEAN DE LA COTTE[4]

---

1 A literary critic renowned for her integrity and discriminating taste, Sophie Maurois wants to give up everything to move to Ireland with a writer forty years her senior.

2 David Kassovitz justified his acerbic review with the words: "When a Sephardic Jew complains, no one believes him."

3 A writer and columnist famous for his cutting wit and brutal attacks, Tristan Lanoux likes to tell people that he has everything a man could possibly want: the best books and the most beautiful women.

4 An extreme right-winger and failed writer, Jean de la Cotte told a colleague, with reference to Baron: "I'm going to get him."

13

The sound of gunfire and the thunder of hoofbeats. Well, Samuel had been warned: *Critics hunt in packs*. He doesn't want to read the virulent reviews. He has stopped buying newspapers, never listens to the radio or watches TV, and avoids social networks. But he always receives a phone call or a text from someone telling him how sorry they are, as if a family member has died.

It hurts—he doesn't deny it. He never imagined this kind of reception. He can't read a negative review without feeling devastated. He remembers the day when, after being panned in the press, he thought about throwing himself under the wheels of a truck on the Paris–Honfleur freeway. Some people might consider such an act disproportionate: Why should artistic criticism provoke someone to end their life, and especially in such a brutal, showy way? But Samuel doesn't see it that way. The hardest thing is certainly not success—success and the recognition that accompanies it, all those invitations from bookstores, all those journalists wanting to interview you, all those readers writing to you to tell you how much your book moved/thrilled/transported them and/or how it changed their life; all that money, transforming what had for so long been a *problem* into something that provides you with a freedom you had never experienced before: the freedom to write when you want, where you want . . . So, all of these symptoms of success had been wonderful. The most difficult thing, the most painful ordeal he'd had to face as a famous writer, was unpopularity. Being hated, criticized, publicly reviled . . . this is something completely new, and puts him in a dreadful state. He opens a newspaper and reads that his book is "awful." He switches on the TV and watches himself appear on a literary program during which, in front of hundreds of thousands of viewers, a journalist points at him accusingly and says: "I don't like you one bit." And no matter how courageous and dignified Samuel's response to this—he told the man that he had the right to dislike his book but not him as a person, because he didn't know him, had never even met him before—the truth is that it destroyed him. Morally and physically, being hated to that degree makes him collapse internally, leaves him paranoid. He wonders what it is—in his book, in his behavior, in the way he expresses himself in interviews—that could engender such a flood of insults. He feels as if, at any moment, someone might come up behind him and fire a rifle shot through the back of his head. For years, as a social worker, he had been perceived as a person of value, a "good" man, esteemed, well liked, and yet now here were all these people—people he had never even seen—stating publicly that they hated him. He feels like he has been the victim of a terrible injustice. And, rereading the words of Thomas Bernhard after the publication of his novel *Frost*, Samuel appropriates them: "I felt sure that the mistake of putting all my hopes in literature was going to suffocate me. I no longer wanted to hear about literature. It had not made me happy."

He had never been as unhappy as he was now, and his only comfort was alcohol. He started drinking again, went out every night to parties, kissed everyone *mwah mwah*, and one morning, on a high-profile TV show, signed his own death warrant when he answered a journalist who asked how it felt to suddenly become so unpopular, with the words: "Success is the worst thing that ever happened to me."

14

Locked up in his cell, only a small amount of news filters through to Samir—and it's always the worst news. His firm's clients are withdrawing their business, changing lawyers. The story even made the front page of one of America's biggest newspapers:

French lawyer suspected of role in
planned terrorist attack on U.S.

Berman calls Pierre Lévy and tells him everything in a litany of reproaches, his voice thick with bitterness. Everything he built up is crumbling, and someone is going to pay for it: "You're the one who recommended this guy to me! You brought him over here. You trained him. You paid his way through law school! You have a moral responsibility for what's happened. Who *is* Sami Tahar? Do you know? Shall I tell you what I think? You put your trust in a man who charmed and duped you. You recommended a lawyer who is causing my ruin!" Pierre Lévy is distraught. He has heard Berman's version of events, he has read the papers, but he is in such a state of confusion that he can't reply. He is the only one who knows that Samir is a Muslim Arab, and now he too is plunged in doubt. What if he had been manipulated? What if Samir deliberately orchestrated his confession so that one day (and that day has arrived) he would be able to claim his protection, even expect Pierre to pay his bail if it came to trial? Objectively, the facts are stacking up against Samir. Everything seems to suggest that he invented an irreproachable life story for himself in order to deflect attention from his real purpose. Everything seems to suggest that he is guilty. "Now he's asking for you!" Berman continues. "He says he will tell the truth to you and you only." Pierre replies immediately that he will fly to New York in order to try to prove Sam's innocence, to prove that this is a miscarriage of justice. "I certainly hope you're right," Berman says. "Because if it turns out that he was a spy, a terrorist, a traitor, we'll have to close the firm! And you know what that means for me? I have a family to look after, I'm deep in debt. What the hell is going to happen to me?" "Everything will work out, believe me," Lévy reassures him, without believing it himself. "That's pretty optimistic. It must be the Sephardic Jew in you, because my guess is exactly the opposite: Things will only get worse. No client will go near us. Shelley and Associates have already taken over about a third of our business. If we don't come up with a strategy pretty damn soon, we're headed for disaster." "Have you called Tim Vans? He handled publicity for the boss of Vertigo after their financial scandal and they ended up steadying the ship." "I can't afford to spend two hundred thousand on a guy who writes press releases!" "All right, I'm on my way!" As soon as he has hung up, Pierre Lévy begins organizing his departure. That evening, he takes a flight to New York and, after struggling through a mass of red tape, finally receives approval for a meeting with Samir. He *has* to talk to him.

When Pierre Lévy enters the visiting room, he has difficulty concealing his shock. *Sami?* Samir has a slightly wild-eyed look, his lips tensed. There are bald patches in his hair—a new geography marking out the borders of his pain. His skinny arms hang down by the sides of his gaunt body like artificial limbs, moving only when the handcuffs dig into his wrists. Which they often do, clearly, because his wrists are ridged with swollen red marks. His face is emaciated, the complexion waxy, almost yellowish. His eyes, deep in their hollowed-out sockets, betray a new fear. His cheeks are overgrown with a thick black beard that gives him a neglected appearance. He looks weak and sick—so different from the Tahar that Lévy last saw in Paris. This is what a fall from grace can do to a man. This is what mental confusion can do. A complete metamorphosis, as if the pains that racked his body had contracted his muscles, shrunk his stature as a man. Samir can't hide his surprise at seeing Pierre. Never would he have imagined them approving this meeting. His former boss must have pulled some serious strings to make this happen, using his political connections, making promises. And here he was. "You came," Samir whispers. "Thank you." Samir sits down and collapses, burying his head in his hands. This lasts three or four minutes. Finally, he controls himself and sits up.

"Pierre, I'm begging you—you have to get me out of here!"

"Don't worry. I'm here to help you."

"I know what you must think . . ."

"You're going to explain it to me, I hope?"

"All I did was give money to my brother. I had no idea it was funding terrorist activities. How could I have guessed? I swear it's the truth! I was completely in the dark over this!"

Pierre moves closer to Samir and whispers into his ear: "First, does anyone other than me know that you're a Muslim?"

"No. Well . . . a few people."

"Have you told your lawyers?"

"No."

"You withheld something as important as that from the people who are representing you? How do you expect Stein to defend you? Can you imagine what would happen if the prosecution revealed that information in court and your own lawyer didn't know?"

"It seemed better to keep it to myself . . ."

"Are you aware of the implications of that?"

"What do you want me to do?"

"You have to tell them. They'll find out anyway, sooner or later . . ."

Samir nods and lowers his eyes. Without looking at Pierre Lévy, he asks: "Do you doubt me?"

"You want me to be honest? I don't know. You have to acknowledge it's disturbing."

"You think I would have revealed my real identity to you if I'd been intending to take part in a terrorist attack?"

"No."

"I had no idea what my brother was doing with the money . . ."

"Weren't you curious?"

"My mother told me he did some traveling and that he was training to be a butcher. She said he was thinking of opening a shop and that she was going to work with him . . . and I believed that. I never doubted it for a moment!"

"So your defense is gullibility, thoughtlessness, good faith . . . I'm not sure a judge will believe you. Didn't your mother tell you he'd converted to Islam?"

"No, she didn't tell me anything! If she had, I would have stopped sending him money! I would have been suspicious, obviously. Did she keep it from me because she was afraid I'd cut him off financially? I don't know! How could I have known what he was plotting? He was in France and I was here! Do you believe me, Pierre?"

"You have to tell the truth—the whole truth—to Ruth and to Dan Stein."

"How can I? Ruth will divorce me if I do that! And Dan will refuse to defend me . . ."

"You don't have a choice, Sami. If you say nothing, they'll find it out for themselves, and that will be worse. You can't hide this—Berg is going to investigate your personal life, and believe me, he'll find plenty of people to testify to your amorality! Berman will be first in line. He's after your blood! And he's blaming me for everything. I vouched for you. It was my idea to create this branch in New York and to put you in charge of it. And what about Berg? Have you any idea what a man like him will be prepared to do if he feels offended? And if your wife discovers the truth from the police, she'll think you really did fund terrorism! Is that what you want? If your wife stops believing in you, you'll lose everything. You'll spend the rest of your life in prison and you'll never see your children again!"

"But all I did was help my brother! I didn't know what he was doing with that money! I'm innocent!"

"Have you heard from him since this whole thing blew up?"

"No. All I know is that he's incarcerated in Guantánamo."

"Don't try to find out anything else. That's not your problem now."

"I'm innocent . . ."

"You'll have to explain that to Stein, the police, and the judge. But first, you have to tell your wife everything."

15

Ruth didn't bat an eyelid when she discovered the reason for the arrest. The first thing that went through her head was that it must be some terrible misunderstanding, a miscarriage of justice, a plot against her husband/the firm/her father's interests/her. As a couple and as a family, they inspired so much admiration/envy/jealousy that a multitude of people might seek to cause their downfall. She wasn't frightened. Her husband was innocent. How could a Jewish-American lawyer possibly fund Islamist groups that were anti-Semitic and anti-American? There must be some logic behind the accusation, so let's establish that. Let's be serious. Let's be objective. Yes, the federal agent agreed calmly, it would be surprising. But so what? He'd seen plenty of other cases; he knew what men were capable of: betrayal, manipulation, crimes of hubris, indoctrination, and madness . . . yes, the madness of men was all he saw in his job, every day. Nothing surprised him. The ability to assimilate, to transform into Evil, it fascinated him. *Anything is possible.* Did she know about double lives, about secret agents? He had evidence and he would verify it; he would carry out his investigation. The facts were there. Objectively, they were flagrant. "You can't deny the facts. A Frenchman who had converted to radical Islam was arrested in Afghanistan while preparing to commit an attack on American interests. This Frenchman, Djamal Yahyaoui, is known to the security services for his extremist views: anti-Semitism, Holocaust denial, incitement to racial hatred." Ruth looked away; these words shocked her. Mechanically, she tapped with her fingertips on the edge of the desk as her emotions came surging back—her existential crises, deeply anchored in her personal history: a family history of loss. "Now, this man, who was arrested while in possession of a weapon, had a bank account in France into which *your* husband made a monthly payment." "That's impossible." "We have proof! It was this money that enabled Djamal Yahyaoui to pay for his trips to Yemen and Pakistan, enabled him to pay for sophisticated weaponry and for the dissemination of his anti-Semitic tracts. And believe me, those tracts were bad: he was inciting murder. Come here, I'll show you something." The man led her to an adjacent room in which stood a huge desk covered with monitors. "Sit down," he said, gesturing to a broken-backed chair. Then he played her a video in which she could see a very pale man with a light auburn beard, wearing a long cream-colored gandoura, yelling at the camera: "Have you seen how they treat us? The land of the free? Don't make me laugh! That country is controlled by the Zionists! But we will take our revenge! *Allahu akbar!* We'll kill them all!" As Ruth listened, she felt the terror mount inside her. She recognized this man on the screen: he was the same man who had come to her home one evening and introduced himself as a colleague of her husband's. She had forgotten his name. He had been dressed differently then and he had been clean-shaven, but there could be no doubt: it was the same man. She felt a sudden wave of anguish, but did not let it show. In a cool, composed voice, she said: "Someone is framing him." Now it was up to him to prove her right.

A conspiracy. An anti-Semitic plot. Someone wants to bring him down because he's a Jew. But why in this way? What are they aiming to destroy? Stein—to whom Samir has still revealed nothing—has a theory. "It's manipulation. Sowing the seeds of doubt. Letting people believe that a French Jew might be an enemy to Americans. And not just any Jew: the son-in-law of Rahm Berg. Your father is the target here. It's his company that they want to damage. The accusation is grotesque and outrageous, of course, but that only intensifies the rumors, the debates, the sterile concatenations. Remember what happened after 9/11: some people started whispering that there were no Jews among the victims, that the Jews had been informed beforehand that a terrorist attack was imminent. It's misinformation, provocation. What they want is to bring you down and, in doing so, sully your father's reputation. They want to destabilize you. It's fairly standard practice in big business." Ruth is convinced by this theory. Her husband is innocent, and nothing—not the federal agents' words nor the devious and deceitful remarks of Berman, who is railing against Sami again—can shake this conviction. *They* manipulated him.

The man who said the Friday evening prayer with a glass of blessed wine in his hand and a yarmulke on his head; who attended auctions of Judaic objects and always returned, on his own initiative, with illuminated Hebrew Bibles, with portraits of rabbis, their faces lined by nights of studying, with books in Hebrew that once belonged to Rashi, Buber, Steinsaltz; this man who never missed a Kippur service, who ate lunch at least three times a week in a kosher restaurant where he would *at least be sure not to end up with pork* on his plate . . . this man could not possibly have any connection with Islamist movements. And when Ruth saw him through the glass of the visiting room—his face gaunt, his hair disheveled as if a bird had nested there, his hands crossed in a defensive gesture as if he were anticipating an attack (*And perhaps they have beaten him*, Ruth thought, and the vision of her husband being assaulted by torturers brought tears to her eyes)—she reassured him: she was going to get him out of there. She loved him. She would support him. I trust you. She repeated it to him: how she loved him, how she would always be there for him, how he could count on her, her love and support, she had hired the best lawyers to defend him, he'd be free within a few days. She knew perfectly well that he hadn't paid that money; the bank transfers must have been made without his authorization—he'd never been very careful when it came to things like that—it must be a hacker or—But Samir interrupted her. He relaxed his hands and said in a solemn voice: "I put that money into François Yahyaoui's bank account." (The confession—the horror of the confession.) "What?" He saw the panic in his wife's eyes, the frenzied blinking of her eyelids; he saw the tension in her body, which began to twitch. Something had been lost, he knew, something that could never be found again. "What? What did you say? Say it again!" "Calm down, please. Let me explain." "Explain what?" "Listen to me." And she went silent. She edged back a little, moving away from the window as if she wished to keep a safe distance between the two of them, as if she had suddenly become aware that she was in the vicinity of a wild beast and she was frightened. "You remember the man who came to the apartment—the guy who said his name was François Duval and who claimed he was a colleague of mine from France?" Yes, she remembered. (She said this coldly as if already seeking to detach herself from him.) "That man is François Yahyaoui. He's my half brother. I never told you about him because I barely knew him—he was very young when I moved here. He came to the U.S. purely because he wanted to squeeze some money out of me. He told me he was broke and he wanted to go to college, so that's why I made that monthly transfer. To help him. I felt sorry for him—you understand? I did it out of pity!" "You have a brother and you never told me?" "I hardly even know him. I have absolutely nothing in common with him—I'd expelled him from my life. If I'd talked about him, that would have brought him back into it. He's a dropout, a failure. What else could I have done?" "And you made a monthly payment to a man you hardly even know? Why? You could have refused. He would have gone home and—" "No, it's more complicated than that! I was forced to give in, otherwise he would have blackmailed me." "Blackmail? For what? Were you hiding something?"

Yes.

The moment had come to tell her everything, he decided. She would end up finding out anyway, from the newspapers or the police. The moment had come to break the vicious circle of lies and hypocrisy. The thought made him nervous, it terrified him, but he did it anyway—he confessed everything, from the very beginning. He spoke quickly—they didn't have much time. How can you tell the story of your life in only a few minutes? Finally, he admitted: "My real name is Samir. My mother's name is Nawel. She's alive. I'm not Jewish, Ruth. I'm a Muslim."

And then, something completely unexpected happened—an option that Samir had never envisaged, pure tragedy unrelieved by any comedy, not even preceded by the kind of lull that sometimes intervenes in moments of high emotion. He had imagined her walking out—getting up without a word and leaving the room—or forgiving him out of love (a less likely option, admittedly) or rejecting him for a period of time (days? weeks? months?), during which he would of course fight to regain her trust, fight to keep her, to obtain her forgiveness and to have, once again, the position he had before this revelation: that envied/enviable position that had provided him with access to everything he had always wanted—respectability, esteem—notions that might strike others as old-fashioned but which, for a man like him, who had come from nothing, who had been raised by parents with no money, no power, no illusions, just poor simple folk, were hugely important because they gave him so much confidence, so much pride. Yes, he had envisaged each of these possibilities quite vividly, but never, not once, had he thought that his wife would go stark, raving mad. But, as soon as he had ended his confession, she threw herself against the visiting-room window, slapping and punching it with all her strength, driven by rage, her eyes unseeing, screaming abuse at him. He had never seen her like this before: this woman was a perfect stranger. She looked capable of smashing the Plexiglas divider and killing him on the spot. Finally—after a long, nightmarish period that lasted no more than a few seconds—the police appeared and subdued her. That's enough, lady! But when she lifted her face and their eyes met through the blood-streaked window, he understood the truth: they were at war now.

16

Ruth spends the hours that follow in a state of shock and mute fury, curled up like a snail in its shell. Inside her husband's office, the door double-locked, she sits in an emergency meeting with Pierre Lévy and Dan Stein, who has learned the truth from Lévy. Ruth is clear: she never wants to see *him* again, she can no longer trust *him*, she wants to divorce *him*. As for his defense, *sort it out between yourselves*. Stein is persuaded by Lévy not to withdraw his services. The meeting becomes a discussion of strategy, a war council. This is a serious, sensitive case. They must be strong, solid, *together*, and it is Pierre who convinces Ruth to go back on her decision, who persuades her not only of Samir's innocence but even of the need to forgive him. "He lied because he had to. He had no other choice if he wanted to work as a lawyer in France. You can't imagine how much discrimination there is over there. It's different in America. There are safeguards, due processes. Discrimination is a political issue here—a social and electoral issue. In France, the subject is still taboo. I'm not saying that no one ever mentions it, but the debate is poorly handled. Why do you think would-be lawyers in the U.S. don't have to pass oral exams in order to get into law school, like they do in France? Quite simply because, here, you have raised the issue of religious discrimination, facial discrimination, racial inequality! In France, a black or North African student, a student with a name that sounds Jewish or foreign, can fail their oral exam and think that their failure is due to their origins. It's poisonous, this suspicion of inequality. And the worst thing is that, sometimes, they are right to suspect that. When I received Samir's CV, I noted his skills and qualifications, and I also noted the fact that he was Jewish. Did that influence my choice? Maybe. Would

I have chosen him if he'd told me he was of North African origin? Probably, because I have often hired people from many different places and origins. I can't be sure about that, though, and he felt sure that he *wouldn't* be hired if he told the truth. He believed that his best chance of success lay in skirting around the ethnic issue, and he failed because the only way he could do this was to lie about his identity. It was deceitful, treacherous, yes, but can we really blame him? How would I have acted if I'd found myself in the same situation as him, with the same doubts, with the same obstacles put up by society in violation of the most elementary requirements for equality? To be honest, I think I might have acted like he did! And I'll admit something else—I have actually lied sometimes, by omission; there have been times when I've not mentioned the fact that I'm Jewish because I thought it would damage my chances . . ." "With a name like yours," Stein jokes, "that must be rather difficult . . ." "Yes, but there were times when I didn't make it clear, when I let the subject remain unclear. You can have a Jewish-sounding name without actually being Jewish." "It's pretty rare." "Yes, but not impossible."

Ruth remains impassive, as cold and immobile as an ice sculpture; this frosty attitude preserves her, keeps her alive at some level of consciousness. If she starts to cry, she will collapse. She is in shock. Pierre understands this: he would feel the same way in her situation, discovering that the face of the person she loved most in the world was merely a mask. She is mad at Sami—and who wouldn't be? It's a normal, human reaction. She has discovered that the man she has been living with is a stranger to her, that their closeness was a fiction. She is bound to feel disillusioned, despondent; he had felt the same way when he found out the truth. When Sami told him, he had felt betrayed. "I believed in him. I gave him everything he needed to succeed. I was like a father to him—probably more than his own father had been—and for what? I could simply assume that he had never trusted me, that he had manipulated me, but I think it's more complicated than that. You have to put yourself in the other person's place. You have to understand the defense mechanisms that are triggered when your career, your integrity, your very being are put in danger." Stein listens to Lévy for a long time without interrupting, then suddenly cuts in, because there is a moral problem here that he wants to articulate in front of Ruth: he needs to be sure that Samir is innocent before officially agreeing to represent him. As a Jew, he cannot possibly defend an Islamic terrorist. Lévy waves away his fears with a sweep of his hand: "On that point, I think we're all in agreement." "But how can we be sure at this stage?" "Their suspicion was enough for him to be locked up and accused of a terrible crime. Our intuition, our years of friendship and trust, should be enough to convince us of his innocence and for us to do all we can to free him." Lévy stands up and takes from his pocket a letter that Samir wrote to his wife and children in which he asks them for forgiveness—a long, moving epistle, tough to read and tough to write: he was in tears as he wrote it. Pierre hands it to Ruth, asking her to give the matter some thought and to change her mind: "Sam needs us. We can't abandon him. He was manipulated by his brother. He is innocent, and we will prove it."

17

It is Ruth who will break the news to Rahm Berg. The official announcement comes in his private office with a vertiginous view of Manhattan—a huge room with diplomas and photographs on the walls, the pictures showing the Berg family or Rahm Berg with famous people from all over the world: presidents, actors, *everyone who's anyone*. Berg's power, influence, and prestige can be read on the walls of his office and in the wide, sunny expanse of New York seen through his window. On the desk, in his sight line, is a large photograph of Ruth and her children taken at sea, on the family yacht. She looks smiling and relaxed in this picture, hair blowing in the wind, her nose slightly sunburned, wearing a linen blouse. There is no picture of Tahar in the room, a fact that has always bothered Ruth, who attempted many times to make her father display a *real* family portrait, with everyone present: "I'm not a widow or a divorcée." His only response had been a cold, unsmiling look. On this point, he was not willing to negotiate.

Ruth enters slowly, perched on sharp metal heels like steel rods that scratch the Hungarian herringbone parquet flooring. In spite of the tranquilizers she took before coming, crossing the threshold of his office makes her chest swirl with dread and anxiety. She walks like a zombie, her expression blank with fatigue, her eyes already wet with tears. She has never quite been sure what most impressed her about her father: his presence, his charisma, that corrupting eloquence which leaves no one indifferent, or—on the contrary—that shyness, real or faked, with which he blanks people sometimes in private, as if he is terrified of intimacy, as if it makes him feel like a prosecution witness summoned to the bench to explain himself, to account for his crimes. They are face-to-face, both tense. Rahm Berg realizes that something serious must have happened—but what? That morning, his daughter called him and in a sepulchral voice told him that she had to talk to him "right away. No, not by phone. This is very serious. I'm on my way." Her father has just returned from a long business trip in India, so he's completely in the dark. As soon as she enters his office, he assails her with questions: Is she sick? Is one of the children sick? "No, no . . ." He sighs with relief. Nothing else can really hurt him, he thinks, but when Ruth begins to speak, when he understands what she has come to tell him, he understands the intensity of this moral earthquake and the devastating effect it could have on their lives. His reputation could be ruined, and that idea alone is enough to put him in a rage. He is on his feet, facing the window, which reflects his shadow. "Not only will I do nothing to help that piece of shit, but there is no way I will ever forgive him or give you my absolution! Do you realize that you married a guy close to the Islamist movements? The father of your children is suspected of terrorism! What kind of a nightmare have you got us mixed up in, Ruthie?" Ruth lowers her eyes and waits for his pardon. Because what else, other than her father's assent, could have brought her here today to tell him that her husband has been "wrongly" imprisoned? She could have left it to the police to inform him, refused to explain anything, but no—she knows what she owes him and she knows what, without him, she would no longer be able to do. She knows what, without him, she would certainly lose: The power of the Berg name. His influence. Everything about him that is so fascinating and repulsive. Everything that seduced Samir. There is something tyrannical about this man who was raised in the poorest part of Brooklyn's Jewish quarter by an asthmatic mother and a spineless father, who grew up with a sort of split personality: friendly/gentle/charming, but also arrogant/contemptuous/loathsome. A man who could send you flowers and cancel your date six times. Could call you a pathetic loser and, at the same time, name you CEO of one of his numerous companies. He was disturbed but lovable, perverted but sweet, and Ruth had learned how to come to terms with this overbearing person. She knows she is taking a risk by talking to him, but she leaves out nothing.

"He lied about his identity, and maybe he betrayed me . . . but he's a good father and a good husband. And he's innocent!"

Rahm Berg turns to face his daughter and laughs loudly. This is what he does when he's angry or upset.

Ruth almost shouts: "He's not guilty of anything! He was manipulated! His lawyer even thinks that you were the real target!"

"Me? Well, maybe . . . but that doesn't alter the fact that you married a Muslim! My daughter married an Arab! My father must be turning in his grave!"

"He hasn't done anything!"

"How can you say that? Your husband is implicated in a case of international terrorism! And suddenly he admits to you that he's a Muslim, that he's been lying to you all these years. What was he trying to hide, do you think? Because for that, he could hardly have found a safer hiding place than our family! Who could suspect the son-in-law of Rahm Berg?"

"Are you suggesting he married me just to have a cover?"

"It's possible! Those types are capable of anything if it helps them achieve their criminal aims! You married a manipulator! A liar! That's the real tragedy! That marriage was a terrible mistake—and, believe me, it's a mistake you'll never be able to repair. That should be enough for you never to see him again, for you to divorce him like that!" He snaps his fingers. "On what evidence do you say he is innocent? He's suspected of having participated in a terrorist operation—you know what that means? You think the FBI would have taken the risk of arresting him in his own home if they didn't possess tangible, irrefutable proof? And if that were the case, if he really did—for whatever reason, out of conviction or for money, I have no idea—help terrorists, do you think you could continue to support him? Are you going to stay married to a terrorist? Why would you do that? Out of love? Blindness? A sense of justice? You're completely crazy, Ruth! People like that spit on justice and democracy and human rights. They use the tools provided by democracies and hijack them for their own ends! To kill *us*!"

"He hasn't done anything of the kind! It's impossible. He's the victim of a conspiracy, that's all, having first been the victim of discrimination . . ."

"This pervert has got you dancing on a string! He's not the victim of anything. I couldn't give a shit if he's innocent! He betrayed you. He lied to you. He pretended to be a Jew. That's enough to make him guilty. You're defending a monster who would kill Jews given half a chance. At point-blank range. Without batting an eyelid."

"That's not true!"

"It is true—you just don't want to hear the truth. Shall I tell you what I really think? I'm sure he's guilty. You've been taken in— and so have I—by a piece of shit."

"You're talking about my husband . . ."

"So? Are you claiming you know him? Let me tell you: You don't know anything about him! That's the whole problem! You sleep with him, he's the father of your children, and you don't know a thing about him."

"He was trapped!"

"Trapped? The only one who's trapped right now is you—and you've been trapped by a guy who deserves only one thing: to spend the rest of his life in prison! And believe me, I won't be the one to get him out of there."

———

She says nothing. Fleeing her father's gaze, she goes to a corner of the room, opens the window, and smokes a cigarette. "Ruth, what you're going through is very hard—it's terrible. I've always supported your choices in life, but you know I've never approved of this marriage. This guy who comes from France, who claims he's an orphan, who can't prove his Jewishness . . . personally, I always found that bizarre. I hated the thought of giving that man my only daughter, but I did it—I agreed to it. For you. But this . . . it's too much. Think about it! He's a Muslim. Even if he is innocent, even if they set him free, he'll still be a Muslim, and he'll start acting like one too! You really think he feels Jewish and that he'll go on with his life the way it was before, as if nothing happened? No, he'll become vindictive, aggressive, full of rage, because he'll feel humiliated. Is that the kind of father you want for your children? You have no choice, Ruth—guilty or innocent, you have to leave him. If you don't do that, you will never see me again. You won't see me, and you won't see any other member of our family."

18

It took the investigators only a few days to discover that Samir's life was based on a false identity.

> He's an Arab—and a Muslim.
>
> The lawyer who represented the families of two young American soldiers killed near Kabul is the same man whose brother has been arrested by the Americans in the mountains of Afghanistan!

After this, his isolation is intensified; visits are limited. This discovery increases the weight of evidence against him, makes him unforgivably guilty. He lied about his identity, his life story, his origins—and to what end? "No Muslim would pretend to be a Jew unless he had reason to—a reason he considered important," said the chief investigator. And it doesn't stop there: They keep digging. You should see them in the law firm's office, with their dogs, their questions, their insinuations, approximations, assertions, leafing through case files, picking people's brains . . . We have a few theories about this guy, why don't you tell us about him? And so it comes out. The enemies—Sami's, his father-in-law's—the "friends," the jealous colleagues, the angry clients, the abandoned women, the humiliated employees, the envious neighbors . . . they all turn up for interviews, a swarm of informers, their heads full of damning anecdotes. Tongues wag—for money or for nothing at all but the pleasure of bad-mouthing the fallen star. The gossip flies, and Berman himself testifies against Samir, telling the cops everything: graphic details about women and girls, underage and underdressed, prostitutes and call girls, on the street and in his office. The FBI branch office is buried under letters denouncing Tahar's debauched double life. "He had a *mistress*, for God's sake— brought her over from France and kept her in a luxury apartment. The man was practically a *bigamist*! He betrayed everyone, and he expected our approval! He wanted people to say: Bravo! You, at least, are a truly free man! The reality is that Tahar is a ma- nipulator, duplicitous to his very core." Samir knows what it's like here: the truth is sacred; family is sacred. Stray from those two principles and you're a dead man. The sky falls in. Ruth reads the revelations in the press and finally understands what humiliation means. *Have you seen this?* Yes, she's seen it. She is the betrayed wife, the blind wife who saw nothing, or pretended to see nothing. Everyone watches for her reaction. Will she support him or leave him? Whenever she enters a room now, silence falls. She no lon- ger receives the best table in the restaurant. At the hairdresser's, she must wait in line like everyone else. Her friends no longer call to invite her to parties. She's a pariah. Dark thoughts breed and spread in her perfect little head. How can she avoid losing face in public? For a brief period, she decides to go out less often. She stays at home, hoping the tension will fade. But nothing fades. Her father refuses to talk to her. Her friends turn their backs on her. Her neighbors demand that she leave. What does she really know about this man with whom she fell in love at first sight, this French lawyer with no family, no past, this elusive man whose mysteries she has never been able to solve, whom she has never felt truly close to, even in their most intimate moments? What does she know about him, other than the stories he told her, the lies he invented in order to seduce her, manipulate her? What does it say about a man that he has two telephones, one of which his wife has never touched? A man who refuses to give any reason for being late, who sometimes disappears for a day or two without even a phone call and who justifies his behavior by invoking *his liberty, his individuality, his refusal to conform to a conventional lifestyle that curbs natural human instincts and desires*? What future could she have with someone who is not the man he claimed to be? What future with someone who's been in prison? Would she ever really get to know a man like that, ever truly possess him? "A dangerous man," her father had said. "A ticking time bomb." What did she see in him? What did he have that the others lacked? She turned down Rudy Hoffman. She turned down Ben Lewinsky. She turned down Aaron Epstein, Nathan Mandelstam—all these Jews who had grown up in the same world as her, who had gone to the best universities, who laughed at the same jokes as her . . . and look at them now. They are all married with three or four children. They have all made a success of their personal lives. *But not me*, she thinks. *Not me*. One week later, she files for divorce and demands exclusive custody of the children.

19

When Samir finds out that his wife refuses to speak to him anymore, he falls to pieces. Nina? Yes, he thinks about her too—a lot. What has become of her? She was probably sent back to France because he couldn't pay her rent anymore. As for his brother, he has heard nothing. He doesn't even know if his mother is aware that he's been arrested and incarcerated in Guantánamo. He has no idea what is going to happen to him. He spends most of the morning writing a long letter to his children in which he tells the true story of his origins. He is convinced he will never have any kind of a relationship with them unless he tells them the whole truth. He'll ask Stein to hand it to them, along with another note for Ruth.

I am the son of Nawel Yahyaoui and Abdelkader
Tahar _____. I was
born on _____ in _____
_____. I lived
in London for a while, then in a housing estate near
Paris named _____. I studied Law in
_____.

I couldn't find a job. There was so much discrimination
_____. He
thought I was a Jew _____ maybe
it was cowardly of me, but _____
_____. I regret the
fact that you have never known my mother _____
_____ one day, perhaps _____ the
most terrible suffering _____ I only ever felt
completely happy when I was with you _____

_____
_____.

I am afraid that, by telling the truth, I will lose
everything _____.
I was the one who wanted to be _____. *For a*
long time, I was a man with no identity _____.
I want to see you both again _____. *I love*
you _____. *Please don't judge me.*

Then he falls asleep. At his bedside is a copy of the Koran, a
bilingual English-Arabic version. His interrogators gave it to him;
he never asked for it. When the warden wakes him to say that one
of his lawyers is in the visiting room, he has no idea what time it
is or for how long he has slept. It is Pierre Lévy who is waiting for
him. Samir sits down, shoulders hunched inward, as if trying to
disappear inside himself.

"I know what you're going to tell me," Pierre whispers.

"So why did you come? I listened to you. I told Ruth everything, and this is the result: I'm alone; her father has turned her
against me; she's divorcing me; she doesn't want me to have any
kind of contact with my own children . . . I've lost everything . . ."

"She would have found out anyway . . ."

"How do you know? Maybe they would have dropped the
charges before all this came out!"

"Dropped the charges? Are you dreaming? You do know
they're allowed to keep you locked up here as long as they like.
They don't even have to bring the case to trial!"

Hearing this, Samir grips his head tightly in his hands as if he
were about to smash it against the window.

"I'm sorry. That's not what I wanted to say. I just want you
to understand that they are mounting an investigation and that
they're not going to free you until they've cleared up every aspect

of your past. Now they know you're a Muslim, they're convinced of your guilt . . ."

"Let them investigate! I've done nothing wrong!"

"Stein and I are going to get you out of here, Sami. We have good reason to believe that you will be freed."

"What are you talking about? The only way I'll ever get out of here is if they send me to Guantánamo, where I'll spend the rest of my life in a fucking rabbit cage—and for what?"

"Calm down. I'm telling you, it's going to be fine. They have no proof of anything. It's just a question of time . . ."

"But I can't take it anymore, Pierre! I'm innocent—all I ever did was send some money to my brother! Ruth doesn't believe me. She doesn't want to see me anymore . . . She won't even tell me how the children are. She won't give them the letters I write to them!"

"I know . . ."

"But I'm not guilty!"

"It's not that simple . . ."

"What do you mean?"

"In a way, as far as America is concerned, you are guilty. And doubly so: because you are an Arab and a Muslim, and because you sought to hide the fact."

"I'm guilty because I'm a Muslim?"

"In this particular context, in this particular country, with all the traumas America has suffered in recent years, yes, you are guilty. That will be the prosecution's argument."

"But that's racist."

"It's political. The whole racial issue is political. Listen, the evidence that the prosecution has against your brother includes not only guidebooks on how to be the perfect terrorist, Bin Laden's preachings and bomb-making manuals, but a copy of the Koran! Incredible, isn't it?"

"The terrorists are perverting the values of Islam. The Islam

I grew up with has nothing to do with them. What do we have in common with people like that? How could my brother have become a fundamentalist? What could have happened to him to make a simple, stupid guy like him, obsessed with girls and consumer objects—this kid who said he 'adored New York' and spent an hour on public transport to get to the hippest shoe store in SoHo, where he spent two hours staring at a $1,500 pair of sneakers—seriously!—what the hell could have happened in his life that would make him decide to become a jihadist who hated America and was ready to die for the glory of Allah?"

"They indoctrinated him. It's as simple as that."

"The real problem here isn't that you gave all that money to François—because I honestly don't see how they could prove that you knew what the money was being used for—but that you lied about your identity. You're a Muslim and you pretended to be a Jew. To the judges, that has to look like aggravating circumstances."

"Yes, but only because people thought I was a Jew! Because society obligated me to hide my true identity. Believe me, I was ashamed of what I did—denying my origins, my history, my parents' history . . ."

"You married Rahm Berg's daughter! Rahm Berg—the great defender of Jewish memory! That's why you lied!"

"All right, so I'm guilty. So what do I do now?"

"Now, you do what I tell you."

20

Within seconds of learning that her two sons were incarcerated on U.S. territory, accused of involvement with international terrorism, and that they risked spending the rest of their lives in jail, she fainted—as if the news were a wrecking ball that smashed into her body. On the floor, she seemed to deflate, all the air leaving her lungs in a single gasp, and none returning.

I'm not breathing.

Later, she told the emergency team who came to her apartment and resuscitated her (called there by her neighbors, who had been worried by the prolonged silence) that, if she'd had the courage, she would have thrown herself off her balcony: *I wanted to put an end to this terrible pain.* In the ambulance that speeds across town, sirens wailing, toward the nearest hospital, she feels as if she is floating, her body lifted above the ground by some invisible force.

I want to die.

She wakes up in a bed, her arms lying flat beside her body, in a room with pink walls. She is alone, completely alone, as alone as she would be in the face of death. Yes, that's it—she is one of the living dead: physically she's still here, but in every other way she's absent, broken. And it is only in the moment when she feels herself falling (her blood pressure plunges, her heartbeat decelerates, her movements become abnormally slow) that she decides to pick up the phone and call François Brunet. She hasn't seen him for years, but she knows what he has become. She reads all the articles about him in political magazines and even, sometimes, in the newspapers; she sees the pictures of him posing with his wife, children, and dogs in the garden of his wife's family mansion, where a thousand varieties of flowers grow. In one article, the journalist recounts how this brilliant man points out the different species and names them, savoring the most poetic ones: *That's an eleven-o'clock lady. That's a love-lies-bleeding. Those are wild teasel, and at the back, over there, you can see some black-eyed Susans.* Susan is his wife's name, and he says it with a certain tenderness, in spite of the fact that he has never been able to stand his wife. The thoughts of all those flowers makes Nawel dreamy. She envies his bourgeois life, the smooth-haired spouse he holds by the shoulders for the cameras like an artist exhibiting his work. How she would love to stand where that other woman stands now—in his arms, in the photograph. She cuts out every article she finds about him and rereads them occasionally. She knows his answers to journalists' questions by heart. She sees him on television on Wednesday afternoons, when the parliamentary debates are reshown. Whenever she catches a glimpse of his face, whenever she hears his voice, she is moved. She tells herself silently: *I made love with that man.* All she remembers is the wild sexual passion of their affair. He never held back, and she loved being under his authority. What she liked best was his apparent indifference, his cold anger—that distance he set between them quite naturally as if warning her that she would never belong to his world, that she would never have any real connection with him. But when they made love, they were closer, more intimate, than either of them had ever been—or would ever be—with anyone else. So that was what she thought about when she heard him on TV, talking about France's taxation policy.

After the doctor's visit, she calls him, but it is his secretary who answers: What is this regarding? Who are you? Etc. The usual screening process. She is insistent, almost threatening, and he calls her back on the number she left. He says: "Hello? What do you want?" He is cold. *It's not a good time*—he has work, files to prepare—and he dispatches her in a single sentence: "I have nothing to say to you." She replies that she is in a hospital. He says he is sorry and, out of politeness, asks her why she is there. She admits: "François is in prison. Everything is going wrong." Hearing the word "prison," Brunet goes into a cold sweat. He knows all he has to lose if this affair were to become public; he knows what damage, however collateral, this kind of story can do to a political career. That son of his is a liability. He has no wish to know anything about him, and he says this to Nawel. Suddenly she is angry: "You don't understand! This is serious . . . François became a radical Islamist . . . he was arrested in Afghanistan by the Americans. He's incarcerated in Guantánamo." And with those words, Brunet's world caves in—that protected bourgeois world where everyone speaks in whispers, where no one complains. "I don't believe it." "I'm telling you the truth." Too late, Brunet becomes cold and decisive: It's not his problem. He didn't raise the child. There's nothing he can do for him. "Really?" For the first time, Nawel goes on the offensive: "If he's gone crazy, it's your fault! Because you rejected him! Because he grew up without a father! You have to help me!" Brunet does not reply. But Nawel hasn't finished: "Do you want your wife and kids to find out about this from me? If the newspapers get hold of this story, your reputation will be ruined. So help me, or I'll tell them everything."

I'm on my way.

He goes to see her. He has no choice. He has to talk to her—to convince her to keep quiet, to disappear. Two hours later, he is in her hospital room. Nawel has found the strength to put on makeup and get dressed: a pink nightgown, some lipstick. In spite of everything, she wants him to be attracted to her. When he enters the room, he has a sudden flashback to the birth of his son: seeing Nawel with her hair in a bun and the little one in his crib beside her—his spitting image. Twenty-five years later, this scene is replayed: the protagonists are older, and the child is no longer in his crib, but in prison. François Brunet moves toward Nawel. He sees her beautiful face distorted by pain, her eyes so intense and unforgettable, and suddenly he feels his heart contract. He is deeply moved by the sight of this woman whom he once loved. The reunion affects him much more profoundly than he could ever have imagined. He wants to sit on her bed and take her in his arms, to hold her tight against him and console her. But all he does is offer her his limp hand and tell her that he will give her the telephone number of a good lawyer, that he will cover the lawyer's fees, her travel and accommodation costs, and that this is all he can do for her. She starts to cry, begs him to help her, and he accuses her: this is her fault—she made a mess of raising François, he is badly educated, a wild beast without morals. At this, she stares at him, her gaze harder than he has ever seen before, and in a firm voice orders him to leave. Head lowered, he obeys.

Nawel looks at herself in the bathroom mirror of her hospital room. She is still a beautiful woman—*more beautiful than François's wife*, she tells herself—and she thinks how different her life might have been, how much more exciting, had she not been enslaved by her sons, by these men. She gave them everything—but what did they ever give her? She went from being a servant to her father and then to her husband, only to end up the slave of François Brunet and her sons. She will not go to the United States. She will not call Brunet again. For the first time in her life, she wants to be a free woman.

21

Suspicion, racism, discrimination—again. And for Tahar, a man who is respected, admired, and feared, a lawyer whose reputation goes far beyond the borders of the state of New York, this is not only unjust but unbearable. Which is why he loses his temper in front of his legal representatives, who come to the visiting room and act like military strategists (considering the best tactical approach to his case), like psychologists (trained to soothe the tensions provoked by this arbitrary incarceration in a suffocatingly small, high-security cell—and Samir needs to hear them, talk to them, so isolated and oppressed and stifled does he feel, as if his head were locked in a pillory), like war leaders (because that is what this is, they explain to Samir: a war against all those who seek to damage American interests, who wish to destroy the values of democracy and the West. And you have to understand that they see you as a threat—a *real* threat. Him, a threat? The most harmless, least aggressive guy on the planet? Someone whose personal mantra was, *Never talk about religion or politics at the table*? Sure, that never stopped him from speaking his mind to his closest friends, to people who knew him well and wouldn't be offended by his more provocative statements, who would understand his sense of humor. Sure, he sometimes let loose like that, but now they are asking him to justify his opinions in the light of recent events: they are asking him to explain why, during one dinner party, he criticized Salman Rushdie by saying that he owed his fame to the fatwa that had been declared upon him by the Ayatollah Khomeini rather than to the literary qualities of his book, and that he should have stayed home instead of constantly fleeing in search of safety "from a danger that he himself solicited." Wasn't it true that he had offered a violent critique of Israeli politics in front of one of his father-in-law's closest associates, provoking a rift within the family that took a great deal of time and effort to heal? Wasn't it true he had sometimes fasted during Ramadan? Wasn't it true he had made an "anti-American diatribe" in front of two French colleagues? Wasn't it true he was a member of a shooting club? And if so, to what end? Wasn't it true he had revealed to someone at his firm that he intended to take flying lessons? Wasn't it true he had been seen near a mosque? Wasn't it true he had once said, to his wife, a few months after the attack on the World Trade Center, "People here are racist against Arabs, don't you think?" and "Bin Laden was created by the CIA"? Wasn't it true he had been seen standing next to the president of the American-Arab Anti-Discrimination Committee in a Manhattan restaurant? And wasn't it true he had once worn a badge emblazoned with the words "Islam is not our enemy" during a rally in support of two Muslims who had been the victims of a street mugging?).

"Every detail, every word, every act will be used against you," Dan Stein explains, in a professorial tone, "so try to remember anything you might have done or said so we can anticipate the prosecution's arguments."

"I ate a kebab in Steinway Street once. Does that make me guilty of terrorism?"

"You can't imagine the things they'll find out and use against you. They are going to dig up your past, search your apartment, interrogate everyone you've had contact with, even the women you've tried to seduce. They are going to try to find anything that might compromise you. By any means necessary. Have they mistreated you?"

"You mean: Have they tortured me into making confessions? Well, that depends. Is bullying and psychological pressure considered torture? What about harassment, insults, blackmail, threats, intimidation? Are those things torture? Can being slapped in the face and placed in the most uncomfortable and humiliating situations—and I insist upon the term 'humiliating'—can those things be construed as torture? No, they didn't hang me upside down from the ceiling and beat me half to death, if that's what you're asking. I'm sure they wanted to, but I must have told them a dozen times that I was a criminal lawyer, that I knew my rights, and that I was ready to do anything to prove my innocence. I imagine they probably didn't want me to file a complaint to the International Court of Human Rights."

"All right. Try to stay calm at the hearing."

Early in the morning, Samir is taken in an armored van, cuffed at the hands and feet. He feels like a predator, a wild beast being transferred from one zoo to another, warily surveyed by men with guns because they know him capable of inflicting a mortal wound. Some of the guards are very young, and when he asks one of them (the oldest) to loosen his cuffs because the metal is digging into his skin, he is told simply: "No. You are considered a dangerous individual." After a drive of about an hour, he is ordered to leave the vehicle, keeping his head down. Does he want a scarf to hide his face? "No, I'm not ashamed," he says. "I haven't done anything wrong." A crowd of photographers is waiting for him, cameras and telephoto lenses aimed at him, stealing his image so they can sell it to the tabloids. Journalists prowl, holding their microphones like weapons, pointed at his mouth. He says nothing, moves forward, eyes down, faithfully following his lawyers' advice: don't talk to the press, keep a low profile. *Even if someone asks you a question or insults you, just keep your mouth shut.*

He enters the courtroom, frightened/distraught/exhausted. A thousand eyes track him as he sits in the dock. His foot taps nervously, in time with the throb of his anxiety. He is drowning in fear. How to stay calm, how not to tremble when all around him is disintegrating? He feels as if a fragmentation bomb keeps exploding inside him, sending shards of pain all over his body. He is a walking wound. Mouth ulcers burn his tongue and his gums; psoriatic plaques have appeared on his forearms, making him itch furiously; his lower lip is covered with blisters; shoots of bile inflame his esophagus—and no one, in prison, has done anything to relieve these symptoms.

His lawyers—Stein and one of his partners (Pierre Lévy having decided not to plead because, although he is a member of the New York bar, he has not worked in the U.S. for years)—sit beside him. Wearing dark suits, they greet him with a friendly squeeze of the shoulders. "The only thing I don't have is leprosy," he whispers to Stein, showing him his mouth and the reddish patches on his arms. The words are whispered in his lawyer's ear, barely audible, but Stein motions for him to stop talking. The judge has entered the room through a back door, like an actor taking the stage. The buzz of conversation fades to silence. The judge is a very thin man, in his fifties, with gray, almost purplish hair. Renowned for his professionalism, he has a reputation for being rigid and conservative. He sits on the thronelike chair in the front of the courtroom and, in a very quiet voice, summarizes the facts of the case and pronounces the charges. Listening to this, Samir feels as though he must be talking about someone else. He remembers having taken part, years before, in a meeting with law students, and the speech given by the famous law professor who had brought them together in praise of Sami Tahar: a speech that highlighted his rhetorical powers, his diplomacy and courage, reminding his listeners, who laughed appreciatively, that this was no mean feat for a Frenchman who had had to overcome the complexities of both the English language and the American penal system. Not so long ago, hundreds of future lawyers had applauded him as he ended an improvised, unprepared one-hour speech, hailing him as a "great lawyer," but now, sitting in front of the judge, he feels like an impostor. The prosecution lawyer stands up—a woman with diaphanous skin, pure features, dressed in a blue cotton suit. Simple, classic. The kind of woman Samir might have fallen in love with, the kind he would undoubtedly have desired.

She goes in for the kill.

He is guilty of having financed terrorist activities.

He is guilty of having supported a radical Islamist who intended to commit an attack against American interests.

She speaks for a long time, but Samir tunes out. What is the point of listening to every detail of his own execution? They can organize his death without him. For the first time, he gives up. He thinks about his children. He thinks about Nina. Will he ever see them again? Here he is, he thinks, in the dock of a courtroom, the accused, in a place where he once reigned as a defense lawyer.

When her speech is over, she sits down, taking care not to bare her legs. Samir hardly listens as his lawyers present his defense. The judge clears his throat. His gaze sweeps the courtroom. Samir trembles—he *really* trembles: he can see his fingers quivering—and this suddenly fills him with revulsion. He is filled with revulsion at being treated like a war criminal, a pariah, a terrorist, and he starts to yell: "I'm innocent!"

Stein grabs him by the arm and tells him to shut up. The judge gives him a hard stare and, in a scathing voice, orders him to remain silent or he will be held in contempt of court. Samir says nothing, but he doesn't look away. The judge stands up and retires for a few moments in an adjacent room before passing judgment. It lasts forever. Then he returns. Samir closes his eyes and, when he opens them, he sees the judge's impassive face, his angry, contemptuous gaze aimed at the accused.

I order the continued detention of Mr. Samuel Tahar.

22

The next day, a photograph of Samir in handcuffs appears in the French newspapers: right in the middle of the page, the picture shows his distress all too clearly, in spite of the slightly blurred image. Samir looks away, his hands behind his back, flanked by two huge, aggressive-looking armed men. To the sides, you can see a crowd gathered behind metal barriers; they look like they are yelling something. One of them, a woman with a lined face, holds up a sign saying "THE ENEMY IS AMONG US." Samir's face is lined, his back hunched. He's a hunted man, a broken man, seeming to rush toward the entrance of the courtroom in order to escape the crowd's rage; he is no longer that arrogant golden boy, that affected and condescending womanizer; Samuel can no longer see in him the student he once knew, the mocking charmer with the machine-gun delivery, open shirt revealing a bronzed chest, boastful and uncomplicated—an incarnation of virility. In the picture, he looks shrunken, a man weighed down by some vast invisible force, perhaps even sick. There are purplish circles around his eyes, which have obviously seen things he would rather forget but cannot. *It's over*. There is no way he can bounce back from this. After this, how could he ever again enjoy the same position he held before his arrest? After this, how could he ever again become the respected, influential, powerful, important man he was before? After this, how could he even dream of experiencing again the simple joys of family life, the pleasure of playing tennis with a friend, of reading a book, a newspaper, of going to see a movie: all those insignificant acts that make up daily existence and that he will never again be able to accomplish without feeling a great weariness, without sensing that he will never be happy again? After this, something has broken forever, something has fallen to pieces inside him. Physically, he is still there, but in reality he is elsewhere—in that prison of the mind that he will never again leave without his chemical straitjacket.

Samuel is sitting at the bar of the Hotel Bristol when he discovers the news, on one of those velvet sofas, away from the madding crowd, that he is now able to reserve for his meetings. He likes to come here every day—to the place where Nina and he met Samir, at his request; this opulent, luxurious place, the lighting subdued to accentuate the feeling of intimacy. Sometimes he books a room here for a night or two. He always arrives early, to order a beer and enjoy seeing from a distance his own empty table, reserved just for him, several other diners turned away because he is such a valued customer. The critical backlash had only increased his book's commercial success. There is a certain pleasure in finding himself in the place of the person who once dominated him, in now being the one who gives the orders, and Samuel, dressed in an elegant suit, savoring his newfound power, feels at ease in the role that Samir once (over)played, back in his glory days—that of the loyal and very important customer.

Samuel sits down and instantly a waiter comes to ask him what he'd like to order. He always takes alcohol. He doesn't drink as much as before—he knows how to control his thirst now—but he can never resist a good wine, and he always insists on tasting it first, with almost pathological stringency. This evening, he is waiting for a Swiss journalist who will interview him for a major literary magazine. He motions to a waitress that he'd like her to bring him his newspapers—two dailies that he always flicks through, starting with the back page and working his way to the front (a habit accrued from reading, right to left, the Hebrew texts his father gave him)—and suddenly, on the second or third page, he recognizes Samir. His initial reaction is to place his hand on his forehead, as if trying to wake from a nightmare, repeating to himself: *It's not possible, it's not possible.* And yet it really is him—Samir Tahar—with the headline above the photograph reading: *Downfall of a French-American lawyer*, and, below this, the words: *He is suspected of involvement in a terrorist operation*.

For a long time, Samuel studies the photograph, studies the look in Samir's eyes, then he speed-reads the article. He wants to know, as quickly as possible. He reads between the lines, puts the newspaper down on the table. In shock. The violent shock of suddenly entering turbulent air. Immediately he thinks of Nina, of what must have happened to her in these tragic circumstances. Has she stayed by Samir's side? Does she have an official place in his life now? Or is she completely independent? He has no idea if she is still in a relationship with Samir, and after reading the article, this soon becomes his sole obsession: to speak to Nina—he hasn't heard her voice in such a long time, in deference to her determination not to see him again, and he feels emotional as he types the letters of her first name into his phone's contact list. He trembles as he waits for the ringing—which always sounds strange when you are calling overseas, as if affected by the distance—but not for long, because a robotic voice informs him that this line is no longer in service. Nina must have changed her number, he thinks: he did the same thing, in fact, weary of all the calls he was receiving from people he knew when he was a social worker, asking him for help, money, a signed copy of his book. He hangs up and grabs the newspaper again, rereads the article, certain that it must have something to do with a settling of scores—some sort of business deal, maybe an illegal one, that had gone wrong. He does not believe for a moment that Samir was involved in terrorism. If that were the case, he would never have invited Nina to New York when he could have simply paid her regular visits in Paris, where he was so much freer in his movements—Paris, where he had no attachments and could easily lead a double life without anyone being suspicious. A man with a mission as dangerous as that of a terrorist secret agent would never have brought a former lover to live in his home city, to make her part of his life, knowing that if the scandal came out he would risk his own destitution and forced contrition. He asked Nina to be with him in New York because he felt untouchable, invulnerable, beyond reproach. A life without smoke or fire; a life like a calm sea, with nothing more compromising than a naked woman in a luxury apartment. But what was the connection with Islamist terrorism? What did that have to do with Samir, a moderate Muslim, someone who had always seemed slightly ashamed of his North African origins, just like all those Jews who Frenchify their names to unburden themselves of an oppressive identity? Not for a moment could he imagine Samir transformed into an Islamic leader, a wannabe martyr aiming to destroy a world whose values (even the most corrupt) he so obviously shared. He drank, he loved women, and he loved America! How could it have come to this? It saddened Samuel, but at the same time, he found it hard not to feel serene. He imagined Nina's reaction: Did she realize she had made the wrong choice? Did she regret it? He often wondered if she'd heard about the publication and success of his book. He hadn't dared send a copy to Samir's office. He did think about it, but decided he had too much to lose.

Samuel rereads the article, and then the full-page profile that runs alongside it—an accusatory profile for which numerous people were interviewed. *Strange that the journalist didn't think of asking me*, he thinks. Because everyone else was quoted—former friends, colleagues, neighbors, all describing, in considerable detail (and sometimes in incongruous detail, perhaps purely imagined or invented), the man they had known: "a brilliant opportunist who would do anything to succeed"; "a Muslim who always had a problem with his identity"; "a pathological womanizer"; "a brilliant, calculating student who could spend an hour chatting with his professors after a class in order to win from them what no one else was able to win: their trust and esteem." The article's punch line was a remark from a law professor at the University of Montpellier, who claimed to have known Samir well and who paraphrased Maurice Barrès in order to sum up his former student: "Young, infinitely sensitive, humiliated, he was ripe for ambition."

23

Nina wanders alone through the labyrinthine corridors of Paris's Charles de Gaulle Airport, carrying her small suitcase, a few bills stuffed in her pockets (enough to cover the bare necessities), her forehead pearled with nervous sweat. Passing the customs desk, she collapses: she is going to lose everything, she feels certain. How she envies those smiling passengers with friends waiting for them behind the fingerprint-stained glass wall, as excited as children looking forward to seeing their parents again—an emotional outpouring that electrifies the others and leaves her a pillar of salt. *Don't turn around*. Forget New York. Forget Samir and the life she had shared with him. Forget the tragedy. For the first time, she has the unpleasant feeling that people are watching her not because she's beautiful but because she's strangely alone. She thinks about something one of the women at her gym in New York said: "Once you get to a certain age, the only ones who whistle at you are construction workers high up on scaffolding." The obligation to seduce—it transformed her from an upright and rather shy girl into a doll ogled by men for pleasure, submitting to masculine order. Will she be able to find a job in France, where she has no friends or family? Is there any chance she'll get through this? And how can she justify the way she quit work and has now suddenly returned? She left her agency; the big stores must already have replaced her—other, younger women must now be incarnating the ideal mother designed to serve as a role model to thousands of perfectionist housewives. She had left Paris in a rush, without informing her employer, without honoring her contract for the next Carrefour advertising campaign. She had emptied her bank account—the few hundred euros of savings she had—without informing her bank, so her account has probably been blocked in her absence, perhaps even reported to the Bank of France. She had neglected to tell her few acquaintances that she was leaving, abandoning them without any explanation—how can she possibly call them now? And then there were all those meetings she never bothered to cancel, the people she never called back, the obligations she backed out of without providing any justification. She had run away like a thief in the night, certain she would never return to France, and now here she was, back in her homeland, without any ties at all.

Walking through the automatic glass doors, she relives the moment when Samir came to fetch her from the airport in New York: she had put on fresh makeup, a squirt of perfume, had changed her clothes in the public restrooms, and had entered American territory like a conquering goddess—proud and beautiful, hips swaying and hair shining. Now she is just this dull-eyed woman uncertain whether to take the suburban train or a taxi. Public transport is better, she thinks—cheaper, and she'll be at Samuel's apartment in under an hour. And then she will see, in the moment when they come face-to-face, how he reacts. She attempts to tame the dark thoughts in her head, but they are too strong, too wild. She's a bundle of raw nerves. Making her way through the long corridors, she looks at the billboard ads on the walls for "Paris–New York return flights at knockdown prices"—*bastards!*—and the emotions cluster inside her, constricting her chest. And then, as she's in the RER train, sitting on a ripped-up bench, the feeling rises and disgorges, her pain spreading, overflowing, destroying all before it like a river in flood, submerging her world. *Is everything all right, madame?* asks a street musician with a strong Eastern European accent. No, everything is not all right—everything is bad, very bad, and suddenly she rushes out of the train onto the platform, running at full speed, her feet seeming to glide over the ground as if she's wearing roller skates. *Get out. Breathe. Quick.*

HELL

Outside, the wind is molding the clouds into one solid mass of dark thoughts, herald to a storm, and Nina manages to reach the bus stop, finally hopping on board just as a streak of lightning splits the charcoal sky, followed by a crack of thunder. But it's okay, she's under shelter now. Sheltered from what, though? Because now it is time for the confrontation. Mentally, she prepares for the test of her contrition. She knows Samuel is not going to welcome her with open arms, *Let's forget the whole thing.* He will want to make her yield, confront her with her crimes: the selfish, reckless behavior, the insanity, because that is how you behaved toward me, like a beast wrecking/crushing/smashing my life, and she will submit. Why did she go to New York? What has she become? A good wife. A wife who submits to her husband's desires, who exists only through his eyes. She thinks about this, and for the first time she blames Samir, in spite of the tragedy that has enveloped his life; she blames him for not helping her to lead an autonomous existence in New York, for having thought of dumping her after she had sacrificed everything to be with him. What an utter defeat.

She's there in ten minutes, standing outside the tower block that rises up above her. She had forgotten these concrete towers, covered with dust, embedded in a dismal landscape where no light filters through anymore, the rays of sunlight ricocheting from the façades of glass-walled buildings in the business district a few miles away. Nina prefers not to analyze what she's feeling in the moment when she enters the building; she hides it from herself, thinks, *I'm coming home after a long trip*, and it is natural for her to slide her key into the lock in the door of the apartment that she once shared with Samuel. The door opens. The hallway is deep in darkness. Nina enters, switching on the light, and hears a cry of fright, sees the figure of a woman at the end of the corridor, then that of a thin man, staring at her darkly, moving toward her with his hand raised, ready to attack. She asks: *Who are you?* The man replies coldly in a foreign language. The apartment is now occupied by a Chinese couple and their children, who start to scream and laugh as if they are at the theater. She cannot understand a word any of them says. *This is my home! You're living in my apartment! Where is Samuel? Where is he?* (And, unknown to her, the Chinese family say: *What does she want, this madwoman? Do you know her? What is she talking about? Throw her outside!*) *Who gave you the right to move here? Did Samuel leave a phone number? I don't understand anything you're saying!* (*I don't understand anything she's saying! Call the caretaker—let her tell us what this crazy bitch wants. Go on—she seems dangerous to me.*) Five minutes later, the caretaker arrives—a woman of Asian origin, in her sixties, who grumbles at being torn away from her TV show, then explains in French/Chinese that Samuel Baron left this apartment a month ago, and no, she doesn't know how to get ahold of him. *He's gone, I'm sorry . . . Your things? I have no idea. He left without a word, didn't even say goodbye.* And then it's over, everyone goes back to their business, and Nina is left alone in the wasteland outside at nearly eight p.m., night about to fall, with nowhere to sleep and only a few hundred euros in her pocket, enough to last her a week at most. The horror!

24

What happens in the mind of a writer when he thinks he has found/defined a *subject*? The excitement of revelation, then the self-questioning: How should I treat it? In what form? With what ambition? What can I use and what result am I aiming for? Following his unexpected success, Samuel asks himself these questions with a new intensity. Already the pressure is on: What are you writing *now*? What project are you working on? Have you started writing again? When will it be finished? Can you tell us a few words about the subject of your next book? He was convinced that a book could be lost by talking about it during the act of creation; that by exposing any part of it, he would be dispossessed of it; that something would crack that could never be repaired. The power of a piece of writing was its marginality, its secret existence. Revealed by publication, by announcements, by its transformation into a commercial object, it became something social that, sooner or later, you would end up hating. Samuel had not yet thought about a second novel—he'd been too busy promoting the first one—and suddenly here he was, presented with a story that was rich and new, a story he could exploit for his own ends without any qualms, a subject that had fallen from the sky before he had even begun his search for it. At that moment, he felt no hesitation about the prospect of writing a novel about a friend, a living person. To write is to betray. He had always believed that the object of literature was not to be legitimate or useful or moral, that it died as soon as it became pure or clean or unstained.

The next day, Samuel called Samir's lawyers and told them that he could help them. He had been one of Samir's closest friends; he knew him better than anyone. He was the best possible character witness. This phone call—just when Samir was in direst need—was a stroke of luck for Stein and Lévy, and they immediately asked Samuel when he could come to New York, at their expense. Stein had no idea who this man was—he had introduced himself simply as a "French writer and close friend of Samir Tahar"—but Lévy knew very well, and was fulsome in his praise: "I read his book, and loved it. He's very well known in France. He could write an article about Sami for one of the national newspapers there—I'm sure it would have a big impact." But Samuel imposed a condition: he wanted to meet Samir in prison, ask him a few questions, hear his version of the facts. They said they could not promise him this, as their client was in almost total isolation: "Since the authorities discovered he was a Muslim, it's become almost impossible to get to see him." And yet, two days later, they managed to secure him this interview. Up to this point, no one—apart from Ruth and themselves—had been allowed to speak to Samir, and most of those talks had been granted before the federal authorities found out Samir's true identity. The prosecutors, Stein and Lévy explained, had been aware of Samuel's status as a writer. They were probably fearful that he would write articles in newspapers all over the world, denouncing the suppression of individual liberty by the American judicial system. They also knew that Samuel might be able to join a French delegation of the Red Cross and enter the prison under the guise of humanitarianism. Others had done it before. So that was why he was allowed to see Samir. Samuel's flight was organized that very day. To what extent was he guilty of manipulation, of opportunism? Massively, of course. The exploitation of a true story. The obsession with realism. He hadn't even thought about what he would say or not say; Samir's innocence or guilt mattered less to him than what the case represented in terms of material—a mass of information, a succession of facts. There was a book to be written about this story, which encompassed major themes, and he felt in full possession of the means to do it justice. Was he aware that he might worsen things by making the case public? Aggravation of harm? Not his problem. A writer is not a *bonus pater familias*. He does not have to act with due care and diligence. He doesn't have to worry about the damage he might cause. Morality? What morality? And so, during a very brief chat with his publisher, he recounted Samir's rise and fall. He recounted it because it was so amazing and he could hardly believe his luck in being presented with such a story, and maybe also because he felt pity, and when he had finished, he asked the publisher what he thought. The publisher smiled and replied in a monotone voice: "You know what F. Scott Fitzgerald said? *A writer lets nothing go to waste.*"

Samuel let nothing go to waste. He gathered every article he could find on the "Tahar case" and went through them, making notes and thinking of questions he might ask Samir. He kept all his notes in a large gray folder.

In the airplane, he thought again about Nina, testing out every possible theory and dreaming of seeing her in New York, bringing her back with him to France. And no matter how much he told himself that it was the book that obsessed him, he knew, deep down, that he was lying to himself: he was going to America for her—to find her and win her back.

It was early afternoon when he arrived in New York. He'd reserved a room at the Carlyle. The interview was set for two days later, so he had twenty-four hours to meet Samir's lawyers and obtain as much information as possible. They had agreed to answer all his questions. They felt certain that, if the case became a media sensation in Europe, there would be positive repercussions in the U.S., and they were also well aware of the impact a writer—particularly such a famous and acclaimed writer—could have on French public opinion and even the French government. They knew that Samir was innocent. But he was subject to the goodwill of anti-terrorist prosecutors. And against that, they were powerless.

"If you tell people in France what's happening, maybe things will shift in our favor," said Stein.

"A French-American lawyer held against his will for a crime he didn't commit," Lévy added.

"I will do all I can to help him."

Samuel took notes and, just as he was about to leave, finally worked up the nerve to ask if they knew whether Tahar might have another woman in his life—someone who knew him well and perhaps possessed valuable information. Stein shrugged. Lévy said:

"Yes, there was another woman in his life, but she didn't know anything about this case. Samir's law partner told me that she went back to France. Her presence here could have seriously compromised our defense."

"But she might have been able to tell you things . . ."

"We thought of that and decided that anything she might say would do more harm than good. It's not in our interests to bring her back here."

"Do you have any way of getting ahold of her?" Samuel asked, his tone of voice betraying a certain anxiety.

"No, none at all."

That afternoon, Samuel was supposed to meet Samir. He wore a very handsome gray wool suit and a chalk-white fitted shirt in ul-trafine cotton with mother-of-pearl buttons. He hesitated to wear a tie, but in the end chose a black one. He went to a hairdresser recommended by the hotel's concierge. There was something obscene in the care he devoted to these preparations. It was as if he were readying himself for a theatrical scene, the unspoken aim of which was the death of a man he had loved/envied/despised. Even at an age—at a moment in their lives—when the pressure ought naturally to have been released, the rivalry still held strong, as if this eternal power struggle was the only thing that could ever connect them. A confrontation, with one of them already on his knees. But then, what better moment could there be to mount an attack?

25

Samir had never believed in equality when it came to social relations: the world functioned through the complex interaction of
spheres of influence, through privileged admission, through services
exchanged, forced takeovers—various procedures often supported
by additional connections: the same sexual or religious orientation,
the same social or ethnic group, the complicity of friends or sexual
partners. (This last, according to Samir, being the most powerful of
all, the one that enabled the most concessions to be wrung from a
situation, the one that gave you a literal hold over the other person:
he had experienced its benefits on many occasions, and some of his
conquests had even been to see his lawyers in order to help him.)
Was that unfair? Probably, but he had long understood that injustices are *never* put right. Sure, you could condemn them, but that
was as far as it went. And it was because he hadn't wanted to be on
the wrong side of this balance of power that he had become a lawyer,
had lied, and that was why he had no expectations of today's sudden
and unexpected arrival of Samuel—the superhero who had flown in
from France to rescue him and his reputation. Yeah, right! All he had
ever done to Samuel before was hurt him, steal from him what he
most loved in the world. What could he possibly expect from Samuel
now but a precisely targeted personal attack? Samuel, who was now
"the great French writer," and who had expressed his wish to meet
him and write an article about him to make the French public aware
of his incarceration: that was the official version. "But honestly," he
had explained to his lawyers, "what help do you think I'm going to
get from a man whose life I deliberately destroyed, simply in order
to satisfy my desires? You've told me that he's written a successful
novel—good for him!—and you've said he intends to act as a witness

in my defense . . . But come on! I exploited his life to invent my own biography, and he knows it! I even stole his first name! I tried to seduce the woman he loves on two separate occasions, and succeeded both times! Why on earth would he want to help me, after all that? I don't believe a word of it. I refuse to be taken hostage!"

"But why else would he be doing this, if not to get you out of here?" Stein asked. "As a form of vengeance?"

"No, too childish."

"To humiliate you?"

"Maybe."

"Seriously? You think he's going to fly thousands of miles just to see you on your knees? All he has to do is switch on his computer. No, I honestly think he's sincere. You were friends before, weren't you?"

"In the past? Sure. We were like brothers. But that was twenty years ago."

Samir had asked his lawyers to get him a copy of Samuel's book. He wanted to read it before giving his response. He wanted to understand what it was, in this story, that had earned Samuel such repute—this man who, up to that point, had never even been published, and who had never been a charismatic man. Pierre lent him his copy, and from the moment he opened the book, Samir never put it down, forgetting to eat, giving up the right to leave his cell, even refusing to take a shower. The book was dedicated to Nina, and that was probably the only sincere thing in the entire novel, which seemed to him less an attempt to faithfully retell his story than a gigantic and staggeringly perverse hoax, a manipulation that even he—in the mendacious construction of his success—could not have achieved. Because there was nothing true in this book, this book that had crowned Samuel with glory. Not a word on his suicide attempt. Not a word on the tension between himself and his parents. In this version of events, their relationship had been idyllic, whereas the truth was that he had stopped speaking to them, had run away from home. He had told the story of a man who'd been abandoned: by his biological mother, by his adoptive parents, by the woman he loved, by his best friend, by society itself . . . An expiatory victim. A tale to bring tears to the most hardened cynic's eyes. Whole sections of the book were completely invented—the worst lie being his assertion that his parents had not died in a car accident, but had committed suicide. Nothing about his real mother, who really had killed herself. Nothing about his cowardice, his emotional blackmail, his threats. All he had wanted to do with this book, thought Samir, was to move his readers with his cardboard-cutout words—his camouflage sentences—and he had succeeded! Manipulation through fiction. Perversion by language. Now he understood why Samuel had come to New York.

"You should at least agree to meet him," Stein said, after listening to his client's reservations.

"He'll come, he'll look at me, he'll listen to me, then he'll go back to France and write a book about it all so he can go on being a great success. I know all too well what a man is capable of doing in order to keep what he has acquired through hard work, cunning, the compromising of all his principles. Maybe it's a false kind of happiness, but once you've tasted it, you can't let it go. You want me to be part of that?"

"Just consider your own interests. He's committed to defending you in France, and he'll do that."

Mechanically, Samir nodded.

"And anyway," Stein went on, "there's something pretty cool about being the subject of a book, don't you think? You could be immortalized. You've read *In Cold Blood*, right?"

Yes, he'd read it. He'd even liked it. But this was different.

"This is about *my* life."

26

Nina is staying in a room in a small Parisian hotel near the Place de la Bastille. What is she supposed to do now? Samuel has vanished and she has no way of getting ahold of him, as his phone number has changed; Samir is in prison; she has no family (her father died three years ago, and she has never seen her mother since she abandoned them), no friends (all marginalized by her beauty) . . . she has nothing left at all—her love for Samir has destroyed everything—and now, all at once, she understands that she will not survive very long in these conditions. She will not survive without a job, a place to live, an income. Not once, even in her worst imaginings, did she think her life would end up like this. She had envisaged the possibility of a breakup, but not of a total abandonment.

She struggles. She tries to find hints to Samuel's whereabouts in the phone directory, through his former neighbors. Never does it cross her mind to use the Internet: How could she have guessed that he had become a famous writer? And besides, she is afraid of typing Samir's name into a search engine and discovering further news of his fall. In search of work, she answers private ads she finds on supermarket message boards, she makes phone calls, but all she gets are a meeting that ends up being canceled and an interview for a job as a babysitter, which she fails due to a lack of references. In a real estate agent's, she asks about renting an efficiency, but hits a brick wall: *Sorry, we can't do anything for you right now—come back when you've found a job and you have a few pay slips, some money to act as security, etc.* She contacts her former agent, hoping to do some modeling for a catalogue. She calls a dozen times but never gets through to him: he is away from his desk/in a meeting/busy with another call/abroad/on a flight, and finally, one morning, he replies: "You didn't honor your last contract! You just ran away without considering the consequences. Now suddenly you reappear and you think you can just get your old job back? Get real, Nina!" Silence on the line. Then he starts again: "Anyway, I have nothing left to offer someone in your age range." This is the final blow. She has no money left: she can't even pay for a hotel room. In the space of a few weeks—it all goes so fast—she finds herself on the street.

27

Don't get sentimental, Samuel thinks, *I'm here to write, to do the dirty work*. So why does he feel so oppressed when he arrives in the prison where Samir is being held? It's a terrifying place: a concrete block topped with barbed wire, stuck in the middle of nowhere, and filled, so it's said, with the most dangerous prisoners in the United States. Why do memories keep flashing unsummoned into his head, he wonders, as he walks down the long metallic-gray corridors, struggling against the dread that grips him like a noose? Melancholy. Nostalgia. Poor Samir, shit out of luck. And when he finally reaches the room where Samir is waiting for him, he forgets why he has even come here: instead of taking out his notebooks, he spends a long time looking at his friend, one hand on the Plexiglas window, shocked by the horrific vision of this desperately thin man, citrine-colored skin, his hair balding in patches, vainly searching for his words as if he's just suffered a concussion and is trying to recover the power of speech. The tragedy of life. This is what misfortune, what the hazards of existence, can do to a man. In the second when his eyes meet Samir's, Samuel knows he will not write this book. Samir is seated, his fingers writhing nervously. Coming through the window that separates them, his voice sounds muffled.

"What are you doing here? Did you come just to see me in this state?"

As he says this, Samir feels a pain in his legs and grimaces. He bends over to massage his ankles, which are shackled by metal chains, and emits a feeble moan.

"How do you feel?" Samuel asks.

"Great! Never felt better!" Samir shouts, reviving. "Look at me—I'm the happiest man in the world! Everything's just peachy! And how are you?"

"I'm sorry . . ."

"You're sorry? What for? You're not responsible for what's happened to me. It's my fault I'm stuck in this shithole, not yours. A guy like you wouldn't last twenty-four hours in a place like this! Why have you come here?"

"To testify for you."

Samir sighs. "Oh, really? You're going to tell the judges that I'm a model of virtue? A man of great moral integrity? A good father and a loyal friend? Come off it—I'm a libertine. Morality means nothing to me except in a professional sense. Ethically, I'm irreproachable. But in every other way . . . I'm an adulterous husband, a lying father, a man who betrays his friends without a second thought. And a bad Muslim, as my mother would add . . . And the worst thing is, I don't even feel guilty! Not in the slightest! So tell me what you could say to the judges that might convince them. I'm exactly the kind of guy they want to find guilty! And anyway . . . I don't believe that you're sorry. In general terms, I don't think anyone is really affected by anyone else's sufferings. Maybe they feel a pang of compassion, but it doesn't alter their own happiness . . ."

"I came because I wanted to understand, and to see what I could do to help you."

"You came to clear your conscience. That's what all men want—to be able to fall asleep at night, thinking: *I'm a good man.* But in that respect, we always fail, no matter what we do . . ."

"I could never claim that."

"Yes, you could—just like everyone else! You've come all this way to prove to me that you bear me no ill will. You're the one who has the upper hand now—you should hate me for what I did to you! You should hate me and enjoy my downfall. Come on, admit it—in your heart of hearts, that's what you're hoping for. This situation excites you. You look at me and you think: *Could he have fallen any lower?* Maybe you even think: *This is karma. Nina has gone back to France and he'll never see her again. She's free . . .* that's what you wanted, isn't it?"

"I haven't heard from her at all . . ."

"Well, don't just sit there waiting! Go out and find her! She must be alone in Paris, with no money . . . It drives me crazy! I wasn't able to protect her . . ."

"I have no worries about Nina. She's tough."

"Tough? But she must be completely alone now. Find her!"

"And why would I want to do that?"

"Do it because I'm begging you to. Because I've lost everything and you pity me. You do pity me, don't you?"

"No one could ever pity you."

And for the first time in this meeting, Samir smiles.

"How am I supposed to know where she is?"

"You'll find her. I don't know how exactly . . . Use your connections. I'm sure you're at the center of things now. I know what that's like . . ."

Embarrassed, Samuel looks away. For a long time, neither of them speaks.

"Your lawyers told me you have a good chance of getting out of here."

"Considering how much I'm paying them, my lawyers have a duty to be optimistic."

"They say there's no evidence against you, and that's why you haven't been sent to Guantánamo."

"So? You think it's any better here? This place is hell! And I have special privileges too—they've put me in an isolation cell. Thank God—I'd never have survived amid the gangs otherwise. If you could see what it's like . . . They team up along ethnic lines and spend all their time beating the shit out of each other . . ."

"You'll be out of here soon . . ."

"So why don't they let me go now? If I'm innocent, if they have no evidence against me, why are they treating me like a dangerous psychopath? The only dangerous one in this case is my brother. He's rotting in Guantánamo, and deservedly so, the dumb little fascist! But me—what have I done?"

"I'm going to help you."

"Why would you do that? So I can get Nina back again? Because you like me and care about me? Shall I tell you why I think you're here? You came here purely and simply because you want to write a book and make money out of my misfortune."

"I could write a book without coming all the way here."

"Bullshit! You came here to observe me, that's all."

"You're losing your mind . . ."

Suddenly Samir gets to his feet. Standing up, he looks even scrawnier. His legs are barely strong enough to hold him.

"Yes, I'm going crazy! I'm turning into a fucking lunatic, locked up like this all the time! Sometimes they leave me in total isolation for four or five days in a row. I never see anyone, so I start talking to myself. I've created a double, and it's him I talk to! You're right—I am going crazy. Do you have any idea what I've gone through here? The interrogations in the middle of the night, in overheated rooms where they let me die of thirst so I'll confess to a crime that I didn't commit, so I'll say I believe in things I don't believe in at all? Or being left alone, naked and shivering, in a damp, freezing cell. Or having to stand up inside a cage so small it's impossible to sit down! Have you ever tried standing up for more than twelve hours, without even being able to bend your knees? Yes, I'm going crazy, of course I am, but I'm still lucid enough to understand that you are here to write a book about my downfall! My God, how that would sell! So go on, tell me, what are you going to write?"

Samir begins to pace in a circle.

"That's enough. Stop it!"

"You're going to write that I've lost my mind. No, you'll write that I'm like a Giacometti sculpture because that's more poetic. This is literature, after all—it has to have meaning, style, an appropriate form!"

"Stop it, you're insane! I'm not going to do anything."

"You remember the ultimatum you made to Nina: *Stay with me or I'll kill myself*? You remember your moment of glory when you found her sitting next to your hospital bed after you'd slit your wrists? Well, this is exactly the same: If you write about my life, if you misrepresent an element of my existence, if you distort every compromise I've had to make in order to survive, I will put a bullet through my head! You hear me? That's what I will do if you soil my reputation, if—because of you—my children never want to see me again! I won't survive that! And you won't survive it either, because your conscience won't leave you in peace! Your conscience will bother you night and day, just like mine bothered me when I slept with Nina while you were burying your parents, just like it forced me to take antidepressants for years so I could bear the shame of having denied my own identity, my origins, of having kept my own mother a secret in order to protect myself but also because I was embarrassed of her! But you'll do it—you'll write the book, I'm certain you will. The trouble with writers is that they're egocentric, narcissistic, and manipulative! I've known a few. There's nothing honest or true about them, because the only thing that matters to them is writing their book. Everything they do, they do for themselves. And yet how many books are there that make us think: *That book changed my life,* or *that book is dangerous*, or *I couldn't live without that book*? Very few! So they have to justify their madness, their lies, their abuses with literature that is sanitized, boring, unexceptional. Shall I tell you the truth? I didn't like your book. It's teary-eyed, sentimental crap. And you know me—I hate pathos.

People are always telling me I'm rude when the truth is I'm just direct. You're living outside social reality now, Samuel. So your ambition is to write a successful book? To find the mot juste? The perfect form? I'm sure you go around telling everyone that there is nothing in life harder than writing . . . Bullshit! Writing is just another way of getting ahead in the world, of keeping your place in society. *My* only ambition now is to be free again."

28

Locked in his cell, lying on his mattress with his arms by his sides, his body as stiff as if he were imprisoned inside an iron lung, Samir can no longer move his limbs—only his mind still functions—and this is, he thinks, how he'll be until the end of his life, condemned as a pariah for a crime he did not commit. I didn't do anything, he protests. He didn't do anything, confirms his brother. He had no idea what was going on. I spent the money he gave me without ever telling him what I was using it for. He is innocent, he is pure as the driven snow, agrees Nawel, hospitalized in Paris. Samir knew nothing about any of this. He is a good son, who always sent me money, checked that I was okay. And he is a good Muslim, an upright, exemplary, loyal man—a model of virtue. *Free him.*

Upon his return to Paris, Samuel had written a long article denouncing the treatment of Samir. Demonstrations in support of Samir were organized in many places. An American novelist even offered to write his story. (He refused.) He received abusive letters and letters of support, marriage proposals and death threats, an anonymous postcard saying that his wife was suffering and his children missed him—he reread that card every day. In Paris, voices were raised, denouncing his arbitrary arrest; other voices condemned him. But in his head, he heard always the same threat: *They can keep you here for as long as they like.*

29

Lying on the velvet sofa in the large apartment he now rents in Paris, on the respectable/chic/bourgeois Boulevard Raspail, Samuel fast-forwards through memories of his love affair with Nina. In which precise moment did he lose her? Where is she now? Where should he look for her? Where Nina is concerned, he no longer knows anything; *Nothing remains of our love*, he thinks.

So he grabs a book,[1] lies down, gets up, takes a bath, feels restless, and finally goes to bed. All he wants is to see Nina again, and one morning—after a sleepless night when every thought held him in a state of tension and wakefulness, when everything he saw brought him back to this woman—he decides to call a detective, a man he knew when he was a social worker, and who might be able to help him find her again: Lin Cheng.[2] He arranges to meet the detective that day in a tourist café on the Avenue des Champs-Élysées. Cheng, a tall man in his forties, gets there early. Samuel sits down next to him and quickly, without even taking the time to order a drink, in a toneless voice, a voice that betrays his urgency, his panic, his longing, the words rushing out in a jumble, unpunctuated, like people jostling to exit a building, he explains the context, then hands Cheng a photograph of Nina—Nina in her glory, at the peak of her electrifying beauty, her gaudy sensuality—and the detective, of course, is blown away. "My God, she's incredible!" he says, then asks if she has any friends in Paris, if she has

---

1 *Life and Fate* by Vasily Grossman. After being banned for a long time, this great novel was finally released to huge acclaim.

2 Lin Cheng has only one ambition in life: "To get out of here."

enough money to be able to stay in a hotel. Samuel replies that, as far as he knows, she has nothing. Cheng hesitates, then asks whether he thinks she might be living on the streets. The question sends Samuel into a panic. He has wondered it himself, of course, and not wanted to think about the answer. He can't imagine her sleeping on the ground, on a piece of cardboard salvaged from a dumpster, exposed to the eyes of other men, perhaps even to the desires of those few men who—due to inadequate schooling, low intelligence, a lack of care—have become like savages, beings without souls or consciences, with long criminal records, who would rape her in the middle of the night, and no one would hear a thing, because no one ever wants to hear a cry for help in a society like ours. He doesn't want to think about her lying on the ground, hand outstretched; he believes she must have gotten by somehow, because the contrary is impossible, unthinkable. He will do anything to find her, and he says this to Cheng, who listens while sipping his coffee. "I will give you whatever you want, but find her for me, please—I'm begging you."

"I have to be honest: the chances of finding her are pretty slim. She might have left the country again . . ."

"I'm not paying you for you to tell me that you're not going to succeed."

"I'm just saying: It won't be easy. It could take a long time and . . ."

"You have to find her. However long it takes."

"All right. Be patient."

30

A few days later, Samir discovers that the prosecutors have dropped the charges against him. As if from afar, he hears Stein's voice repeating: *The nightmare is over, the nightmare is over.* And yet he remains motionless, as if encased in ice, insensitive to pain. His right eyelid flickers slightly. He has been in prison for sixty-six days. He kept count. Each day, he chalked a line on the wall, each line representing a day of confinement.

I'm free.

Stein explains that his liberation will take a few days, but that he should prepare himself. Samir can't hide his emotion. He thanks Stein over and over again, and as his lawyer is about to leave, Samir swears that he will pay his fee, one way or another, even if it takes him ten years: he will honor his debt. "You don't owe me anything," Stein replies laconically. "Don't say that! I will never accept that! I will pay every cent of your fee—it's a question of principle . . . of dignity, even." "You don't understand," Stein says. "The fees for every employee who's worked in the shadows to prove your innocence have already been paid." "It's Ruth, isn't it?" Samir asks, suddenly moved by the idea that his wife has secretly been supporting him. "No, Ruth stopped paying us as soon as she left you. But that was never a problem, you know. I continued to—" "But who was it, then?" Samir interrupts. "Pierre Lévy."

In the last days before his release, he can't sleep. Will he be able to cope with a return to normal life? The confrontation with his former colleagues? With his family? What will become of him, once he's out of here? How will he be able to reconstruct himself? Will he be allowed to see his children on the day he's released? Will he go back to France to talk to his mother? He has been told he will be freed within a week, but has been given no further details, and this uncertainty has put him in a state of extreme nervousness: he exercises like crazy, writes down everything that comes into his head, desperate not to forget these last moments. The waiting.

31

"Turns out she wasn't very far from you," says Cheng, a few days later, handing Samuel a sheet of paper containing an address. "I didn't have much difficulty finding her." Samuel immediately grabs the paper, thanks the detective, and takes an envelope from his pocket. "It's as you feared," Cheng continues. "Prepare yourself. You showed me a photograph of her, the last time I saw you . . ." Samuel freezes, incapable of moving a muscle. "Well . . . let's just say you may not recognize her. She's living in a women's shelter an hour from here."

Back at home, Samuel had gone online and found the following information: *Shelter for women in distress. Can offer temporary housing for seven women aged 18 and over, alone or with their children, in cases of psychological, social or material distress.* The photographs on the website showed an extremely simple, no-frills place: bunk beds, a wooden table, a few chairs, a couch, a TV room. He had difficulty imagining Nina in this stark environment with its reek of desperation and poverty. As he looked at the photographs, he felt sad—sad and bitter. That day, he called the manager of the center and asked to meet with "one of your lodgers, Nina Roche." He introduced himself as a writer—that always impressed people. And yes, she was impressed, but still a little hesitant. She wanted to talk to Nina first: "She may not want to be seen here. Some of our lodgers prefer not to have any contact with their past life. They want to rebuild themselves first." So he lied—"She was the one who gave me your number"—and, after a few minutes (during which he made a few jokes, made reassuring remarks, attempted to make the woman laugh as a way of breaking down her resistance), she agreed to let him see Nina on the condition that he give a talk to the women in the shelter about his book. The manager argued her points with the relentlessness of an attorney: she knew him; she had read his book, had quoted lines from it, admiringly; literature was her life—she loved reading, and writing (she had written a novel, actually, that had not yet been published: "If there's any chance you could read it and let me know what you think . . ."), and encouraged the women in her shelter to do the same, recommending books to them. She had planned a literacy program for the most destitute among them, those who found reading difficult or made mistakes, and foreigners, and dyslexics, and those who'd had no access to education, culture, instruction. "Hard to believe, isn't it, here in France, in the twenty-first century?" She had even put together a library in the center (he had smiled scornfully at this remark, unable to stop himself from imagining that this library consisted almost entirely of schmaltzy, best-selling trash—what he thought of as *women's novels*): it had taken her several years to collect the three-hundred-odd books that lined its shelves. "I know that's not many, but the most important ones are there: the books that marked my life, the ones that made me think and made me the person I am today" (and only then did he start to change his opinion of her). She talked and talked, and finally, to end this conversation, Samuel agreed to do as she asked—*All right, I'll do the talk*—while thinking: *I won't go*. This whole discussion had irritated him; all he wanted to do was rescue Nina from the hell to which her relationship with Samir had condemned her. After hanging up, he felt relieved: he was now allowed to go see her. So he had gone to a department store and chosen a bottle of perfume and a scarf, and on the street on the way there he had bought flowers—giant fuchsia-pink peonies—as if this were a first date, as if he were in love, or wanted to seduce her. And what about her—did she love him? How could he rebuild the tower of their love after it had been partly destroyed? A series of betrayals had shrunk their love, and he was going there to reconquer Nina, to take her back in the tried and trusted way, and even the most appalling mental images he'd had of her had not been enough to alter this determination, his simple desire to be the best, the first, the only one to love/protect her. Had she been merely a pawn in a power struggle between himself and Samir? Maybe. What he wanted now was to bring her home, rebuild her, transform her back into exactly the woman she had been when she had left him: that blazing, carnal, solar flare of a woman who had been desired by every man who saw her, and who had been his; that ideal, sublimely erotic woman—he wanted to reinvent her now, and assign her a new position in their relationship. From now on, he would be the dominant partner, the one people noticed; he liked the idea of this inversion of roles. What he wanted was to make her part of his life's success—she was the missing piece in his jigsaw puzzle—and for that to happen, he had to see her. And talk to her.

He had chosen a black suit, handmade in the finest fabric, with a satin lining that was just a little too shiny, a white shirt with a narrow collar that revealed the vein in his neck, and a black knit tie. He had chosen his clothes slowly and carefully; he wanted her to like the way he looked. He was no longer the moaning, spineless man he had been before, no longer pessimistic and envious and angry. Before, his arrogance had been all front, his pride the false pride of a failure, a jealous man. His marginality, his unsociability, his rudeness: all that had been a posture. Success had calmed him, given him confidence, an internal peace; he had his place in society now, and—surrounded by all these people acclaiming/approving/admiring him—he at last felt visible, recognized by the world.

It is early afternoon when he arrives at the center, stepping out of a black, leather-lined taxi. The center is a dump with red brick walls, located in a large Parisian suburb, near a residential area. It is a sad, ugly place. What chance would anyone have to rebuild themselves here? Samuel wonders. It's the sort of place that would finish you off, not save you. The building is located in a backyard overgrown by weeds and brambles, with, at its center, a large gray-brown worm-eaten bench and, in one corner, a little hut containing some multicolored sun loungers that are brought out occasionally, when the weather's good, as the short, stout, plain, middle-aged redhead explains when she welcomes him. Nothing special physically, but what a personality she has! There is an authority about her, a strong and magnetic presence that suggests courage, combativeness. She introduces herself: she is the manager of the shelter where Nina now lives.

The manager guides him—*Watch out for the step, wipe your feet on the welcome mat*—explaining that the women have just eaten lunch and gone through to the salon. He smiles as he repeats this expression: "They have gone through to the salon." It sounds like the kind of thing you'd find in an old bourgeois novel, whereas what he sees here is grinding poverty. *They watch TV, read, work, chat. Go ahead . . . at the end of the hallway, on your right. You'll find Nina there.* In the hallway, he covers his mouth and nose with his hand: the air is thick with a strong, stale odor of food and frying oil.

There are six of them there today, in the large living room decorated with peeling greenish paint. They struggle to hide their embarrassment at seeing a man here, the question hovering on their lips: *What is he doing here?* He moves forward cautiously, greets them, blushing slightly, and oh, there she is, in the middle of these women of various nationalities, this little Babel—what a shock. He is tense, visibly uncomfortable, looking into her eyes— to see what? Desire? Emotion? A hint of tenderness that might make him happy? At this point, her mere presence is enough. Yes,

there she is, wearing jeans and an overlarge white T-shirt, a weak
smile lighting up her face. She doesn't move, doesn't stand up to
greet him, and yet she has recognized him, she has noticed his
metamorphosis: the fitted suit, the polished shoes, the bouquet
of flowers in his hand, the paper bag branded with a famous perfumery (*Hey, it's Prince Charming!* one of the women[1] shouts, and
the others start laughing: *Can we try on the glass slipper?*)—the
perfect replica of Samir the day they saw him on television. From
this distance, however, he has trouble recognizing her. She has
cut her hair very short (and she's done it herself, he thinks, maybe
in a fit of anger, or at least in the absence of a mirror, because
the cut is uneven and unattractive) and the roots are white. She
has put on weight. She is not wearing any makeup at all. He has
never seen her like this before. He walks up to her and, when he's
standing next to her, thinks about kissing her and decides against
it, despite their close proximity. He hands her the flowers and the
gifts. She takes them, but does not open or even look at them,
her face unmoved, while he asks her if they can speak in private.
Yes, of course. Back into the hallway, trying not to breathe in the
putrid stink. He leads her into the backyard and she sits on the
bench and there, amid brambles and thistles, he gives her the big
spiel: declaration-gifts-promises, his hands and pockets full, he
plays the self-assured success—he can, *now*. She listens without
any particular emotion. She radiates a certain hardness, something sharp-edged and incisive. "Why have you come?" "First of
all, for this," he says, giving her a copy of his book that he has
signed for her. She takes it, opens it, and reads the words: *For
Nina, the only one who knew how to console me.* "Did you know
I'd had a book published? Have you read it? Did you see the re-

---

1 Lila Rodier, thirty-eight, a former prostitute. Keeps a private journal in which
she invents "an exciting life with an upper-class guy."

views? Yeah, it's incredible. I'm so happy. I travel a lot these days, I never have a minute to myself, I try to stay calm, try to keep a cool head." A little later in the conversation, he will even speak these words: "I'm still the same, simple person, despite my success." She smiles, closes the book. "But I also came to bring you these," he adds, pointing to the gifts. "I'll open them later, after you've gone," she replies a little coldly, before asking, in a neutral voice: "Have you heard anything about Samir?" He never imagined she would mention Samir to him; instinctively, he bridles: "Hasn't he put you through enough already?" Then, in a gentler voice: "Sorry. But you know what's happened to him, don't you?" "Yes. One of his partners told me." "You haven't tried to see him again?" "No." "I think there's a good chance he'll be freed." She does not cry when she hears these words, she only turns away, and shards of gold sparkle in her pupil. Reflected sunlight? Time to change the subject: yes, she found out he'd been published, by chance, when she arrived at the shelter. She read and liked his book, that tension between the real and the imagined, that disillusioned humor undercutting the tragedy. She was not upset at reading her own life turned into literature; on the contrary, there had been something cool about seeing herself represented as the heroine of a novel. He listens to her for a long time, then interrupts, moving closer to her, noticing the lines that traverse her forehead, the sagging upper eyelid of her right eye. "I came here to get you. I'll take care of you. I'll give you everything you want." He says this with a certain pride in his voice: *I'm here to save her*, he thinks. *I'm here to save her from poverty, save her from the street, from idleness; it's a beautiful/great/powerful thing, it's heroic. I am saving her life because, twenty years ago, she saved mine.* "Come on, let's go. Pack your bags." And, with these words, he gently takes her hand in his. But she shakes him off unhesitatingly. *No.* Did he mishear her? He doesn't understand. *No, I'm not coming with you.* She will stay here, in this women's shelter, for another three months. And then? *I'll decide when the time comes.* This is ridiculous—she can't stay here—*it's ugly, sad, horrible.* No. She likes this place. She feels comfortable among these woman brutalized by life, by men, these women with bloated/wasted bodies, with callused hands, toothless mouths, these tough, combative, tenacious women who have lost everything and won everything back, these women who were manipulated and docile for so long, who were sexualized and desexualized, beasts frightened of their masters' wrath, reduced to the ranks of slavery, abused, shrunk to nothing, unaware of their own bodies, incapable of saying *No*, from fear of no longer being loved, invisible in society, in male society, nonexistent. Yes, she feels comfortable here; among these women, she has found her place. She loves those moments of untroubled complicity, listening to the tales of their thwarted lives; she loves the warmth of their meals, eaten together in the large refectory that they decorated themselves. She loves her body, now freed from her obsession with perfection; it's a new feeling for Nina, who has always sought men's approval and protection. Ha, what protection? They have exposed her to the worst of the world. She accepts herself the way she is now: a poor woman. *Poor but free.*

Samuel says nothing. He suffers in silence. A narcissistic wound—the deepest kind. Finally, he gets up—*If that's what you want*—and leaves. He walks away, does not turn back. He does not want to think about her, remember her. In the hallway, he sees the manager—*No, not now.* She wants to show him the library; she insists—he said he would—holds him back, and eventually he yields. *Well, why not?* And he follows her. He is gripped by nausea, almost staggers, holds on to a chair and keeps his eyes on the manager as she talks and talks like someone giving a speech to a packed room, when the truth is they are alone—*I'm alone, from now on*—no one can hear them, so why is she speaking so loud? Showing him the shelves filled with books, she explains that she has always considered literature as a tool for the liberation of women. "When you read Tolstoy, Duras, Stendhal, you learn more about men and women than you do from your own life. And then, you write about your own life." He does not reply. He looks at the books, most of them written by women: Simone de Beauvoir, Marguerite Yourcenar,[2] Marguerite Duras, Joyce Carol Oates, Sylvia Plath, Virginia Woolf, Cynthia Ozick, Anna Akhmatova, Marina Tsvetaeva . . . "Where are the men?" he jokes.

Everywhere.

---

2 Nina had been moved by this line from Marguerite Yourcenar's book *Alexis*: "There is a release in knowing that you are poor, that you are alone, and that no one cares about you. It makes life simpler."

32

The next day, while he is still devastated by the loss of Nina, Samuel discovers he has been awarded a major literary prize for his novel *Consolation*. His name had been mentioned in connection with the prize for a few weeks, rumors circling that he had a good chance of winning it; his editor called him every day to talk about it, checking his actions and movements, even going so far as to test his moral strength, "because not everyone is tough enough to deal with that kind of acclaim. Some writers are too fragile, and they never recover from it. But you're strong, you're ambitious. You had to wait until you were in your forties to get published, so you have enough perspective to cope." Samuel is not so sure. He does not feel strong—his life story demonstrates his inability to deal with social violence, the trials of competition—and he has never been ambitious. He thinks constantly about a line that Witold Gombrowicz wrote in his *Diaries*, in 1967: "I have known for a long time—I was forewarned, in some sense—that art cannot and must not bring any personal benefit . . . that it is a tragic undertaking."

Now he was seized with a panicked fear at the thought of being surrounded again by photographers, journalists, booksellers, admirers, publishers, of being the center of attention, the center of a world from which he had for so long felt excluded. "It will be a great honor," his editor told him, "for you, for both of us." But what use is a great honor? Does it make you any more likely to be loved? Does it make you immortal? Invincible? A superhero? Is it a guarantee against a broken heart? Against melancholy and self-hatred? Against aging and sickness? Do you sleep better after you have received it? Do you become a better writer? A better lover? Does it increase your chances of people taking your calls? Of getting a doctor's appointment at short notice? Of being given a better table in a restaurant? And what if those dizzy heights give him vertigo? When you reach a peak, the only way forward is down, and it's often a steep and fatal ride. He feels more comfortable in the foothills, with those who have retreated, or even down in the plains, with those who have failed. From there, it is easier to see the social circus: all you have to do is look up and you'll see men falling. Not that he loved himself when he was a failure, but at least then he seemed to possess a critical lucidity, a distance from beings and events, that success would deprive him of. When it comes down to it, you have to be just as arrogant and narcissistic to refuse honors and awards. Scorning glory implies wanting to prove that you are above it. Detached, incorruptible. The obsession with moral integrity, the desire for purity, are just other masks for ambition. It's true: he wanted to be a famous loser: Julien Gracq refusing the Prix Goncourt ("I persist in thinking that there is no longer any sense in playing along, directly or indirectly, with any kind of competition, and that a writer has nothing to gain from allowing himself to be caught in that avalanche"); Jean-Paul Sartre, the Nobel Prize ("No artist, no writer, no man deserves to be consecrated in his lifetime"); Samuel Beckett refusing to go to Stockholm to receive his Nobel Prize for Literature, because he believed it was a "catastrophe"—the term that Tennessee Williams used to describe success.

(And his greatest fear: what success would do to him.)

He remembers what his editor told him soon after he had signed his first contract: "You have talent, but you live apart from the literary world. You're an outsider, basically. Which is fine—that has a charm of its own, and personally I like it—but you will have to make an effort when your book comes out." An effort? Writing already demanded so much of him . . .

He has dreamed of this brief moment of glory. But he is too frightened of the possible consequences. Those tragic mornings-after when, having given everything, the words still resist your advances.

I refuse.

He had thought that recognition—however late, however sudden—that success, the achievement of the ambitions imposed by a competitive, consumerist society, would satisfy him. He had even hoped to profit from this sudden celebrity and the comforts it offered when events had taken such a favorable turn, but a part of himself, obscure and intangible, had resisted, had remained at the margins and had grown inside him like a stinging nettle. It is there, in that part of oneself overgrown with brambles and thorns—where every movement exposes you to pain and injury, to irritations and infections, where every advance sets off an opposing reaction, where every attempt at change ends in failure, falling to the ground, into the mire, over and over again—it was there, and not elsewhere, that the writing mechanism was engaged, with its risks of explosion, fragmentation, and destruction, a bomb that can never be defused. Away from this place, in the perfectly demarcated and manicured expanses beyond, life was good—but you couldn't get your hands dirty. And a writer must have dirty hands.

33

The day of his liberation, Samir is released through a secret exit in order to avoid the crowd of journalists and photographers who are waiting for him. He is alone: no one—no family, no friends—has come to welcome him, and that is a relief. It is a relief to him not to have to fake contrition, redemption, the big apology—that whole social circus, leading to what? Absolution? Reintegration? So when he sees his family, his friends, he's supposed to say sorry? Fuck that! He owes no debt (he thinks) to society, but society owes him big-time. He did something wrong—something morally wrong— in excluding his mother from his life and in depriving his children of part of their history and identity, and yes, he regrets this—he has difficulty forgiving himself for this—but that's all. Everything else—the lies, the broken principles, those little compromises he made with himself—he was forced into those, he is certain of this, led there like a beast in a slaughterhouse, crushed by the machine of discrimination, isolated by society itself, equal opportunity my ass—he'd had no other choice but to sever himself from his origins, to bleed away his identity, to rip out his guts, boiling, spurting, staining, overflowing, hard lumps of bitterness and hatred swept along, infecting everything . . . and then being reborn, getting back on his feet, however weakened, however dismembered, moving forward in order to survive, free at last, do or die, as his father used to say; well, the dying's been done, so it's time to do now, to walk the walk, straight ahead, not thinking, blinkered vision, corrupting again, and under the weight of his footsteps, New York unfolds beneath him, vibrant, aswarm, and he's running, trusting his internal compass, his emotional geometry; his body, stripped down, defused, finally discharged of its tensions, of the oh-so-heavy burden of guilt/lies/shame/childhood, speeds up for a few yards and then slows down again, a way of testing the mechanism—it works—the cogs of his body's machinery not yet completely jammed—*I'm alive, I'm free*—skimming the ground, then suddenly he stops and gazes up defiantly at the skyscrapers stretching up above him in the diffracted light: an outrageous, arrogant aesthetic, the lurid beauty of the city awakening, a dusty landscape pierced with shards of iridescence. He had forgotten all this, his eyes for so long embedded in the gray walls of the prison, nothing ahead of him, nothing behind, fading to black. And at last, he sinks into the insalubrious world of basements, wastelands, ghettos, places that speak to his compromised duality, his profound ambiguity, his taste for the secret, the shadowy, and in these subterranean streets, surrounded by musicians (saxophonists, clarinetists), by illegal immigrants, by the poor and the passionately adulterous, by squealing minors, bodies electrified with desire, he walks past walls with thistles growing through holes in the bricks, then stands still so he can embrace the horizon in a single gaze, the beauty of slack water perfused by rain, and he stays there, sitting on a slab of broken concrete, until the sky turns to a ball of soot, indifferent to the damp air, to the ripples of spume that roll and vanish like the gray clouds that rise from the cigarette he smokes. Free. Free and happy. The death of ambition—at last. The obligation to succeed, the menace that weighs on you from birth, the blade that society puts to your throat and holds there until you choke, removing it only in the hour of banishment, the moment when it exiles you, purges you, strips you away like a dead branch . . . and what release there is in this banishment, which you never know is temporary or definitive, that moment when you are admitted to the brotherhood of the washed-up/the desperate/the has-beens, those people marginalized by age or failure, the homeless and the nameless, the small and the simple, the drab anonymous masses, who line up for their welfare checks, who wake at dawn, whose names mean nothing to you, whom no one ever calls back, to whom everyone says "no" or "later," for whom no one is ever available or friendly, the ugly, the fat, the weak, the disposable women, the ridiculous friends, finally free of the fear of disappointing, the pressure created by the need to be liked, those imperatives that we force on ourselves, out of individualism/lust for glory/desire for recognition/thirst for power/mimicry/herd instinct—all those devastating effects of dreams aborted by parental authority/determinism/illusory utopias, the brutal injunction that governs the social order, rules even the most intimate relationships—Be SUCCESSFUL! Be STRONG!—he had submitted to that just like everyone else . . . But it doesn't matter as much now, when no one expects anything from him, when even he aspires only to make the most of his rediscovered identity. The blade has slipped. The next step is his.